THE STRANGER BESIDE ME

BY MABEL SEELEY

DOUBLEDAY & COMPANY, INC., GARDEN CITY, N.Y.

To Isabelle Taylor
of the green thumbs
and the warm heart

To how many people am I indebted on this book?
I don't even know. Certainly, for my basic
conception of the major character, I owe
something to Karen Horney, particularly
her *The Neurotic Personality of Our Time*.
Isabelle Taylor, as usual, has nursed
each step. Dr. Frederick Hinman briefed me
on asthma. The Minneapolis Public
Library and the Minnesota Historical Society
were again generous with their stored
periodicals and newspapers. Franklin Hodnefield,
Josephine Lush, Ann Jolly, Eugenie Heger
and Sigrid Okerlund read, criticized,
suggested, accepted, rejected, looked
things up. Son Gregory managed a remarkable
forbearance. To these, and to the many others
who have encouraged and helped me,
my most lively thanks.

THE STRANGER BESIDE ME

1 Why was it Christine who attracted him?

Once they were married, the question was usually lost in acceptance, but often before that it nettled and angered him. His first sight of her came on a Monday in June 1919; he was, at the time that he saw her, having lunch at the store where he worked, in its one major eating place, the Lake Room, with Barbara Ohman and Harriet Mains. Very much, he'd have said on that Monday, he was his own man by then—Carl Reiss, known all over the store as a comer, young, well-routed, expansive, at home. Few women anywhere—certainly none at the tables about him—bloomed as darkly and lushly as Barbara; few were as urbane as Harriet. The Lake Room's attractions were both fine and profligate—gaiety a contagion in its chattering patrons, deference implicit in its quiet, quick service, magnificence spread in the view from its bays. He'd seen a few cities by that time, but only Chapaqua had its main downtown street on a lake front, only Trurog's, of all stores, had a Lake Room, arched and chandeliered overhead, offering through its windows an eye-stretching vista of water.

As always on Monday, however, his companions, the amenities of the room, were but by-interests; what mainly engaged him was the core of his purpose: the five top men of his store and their Policy Luncheon. As Harriet said of it, the show just as a show was a good one and not to be missed. At twelve-thirty precisely the flutter, the break in the hum, and then, while the many heads lifted, the many forks paused halfway, first Barbara's father, Chet Ohman, sauntering in, thick-fleshed, slightly ponderous, and after him Newton Leverett, silver-topped, spare and tall, both men smilingly genial, their faces—those faces to which so many looked in fear inseparable from anguish—surrendered to nothing but an affable enjoyment of the hour at hand. Right hands up frequently in jovial salute, heads as frequently nodding, they moved through the maze of tables, pausing, here and again, for longer exchanges with friends.

While they were so en route, Vic Bodali, too, entered, striding more swiftly forward to catch the earlier comers at a midway table, Chet Ohman, when they met, turning to slap the younger man genially against the breast with a greeting which, even across eight or ten tables, could be seen as bringing forth the white discomfited Bodali smile, the furious Bodali blush. On then, Ohman's hand now on the shorter man's shoulder, to the big central lake-view bay, where the special table was set up with its special Lake Room crested crystal, its special Lake Room crested silver, its satiny and heavy damask. Carelessly and slowly, here, they settled, Ohman's hand dropping on the first chair to the left before, again with some quip, passing it to take the last chair in, Leverett following, Bodali, after a wry disclaimer and another blush, accepting the place Ohman ceded.

One brief second, then, before the stronger stir, the raising of significant brows, and Harrison Salloway appeared within the entrance-way, his square chunky body thrusting itself forward as if air about him were resistant, but he too yielding up the quick salute, the ready nod; at the important table he too pausing to clap Bodali's shoulder—"He rode again, boys," was what Carl thought he read on the familiar but now smiling lips. Scarcely had Salloway taken place when the one more man walked in through the wide doors alone—an older man, thin, dark, tall, hunched, one shoulder higher than the other as he hastened forward in a sidewise rush, his head, like those of his predecessors, rapidly nodding from side to side, but less in recognition than in what might have been intense appeal. "That's right, look at me, look at me," the strained eyes might have begged. "Surely you can see my humility, surely you can see you might like me, surely you can see I haven't nearly as much money as it's said I have, and even if I do you must like me anyway, pity me, buy from me, buy more, buy more——" In his wake as he passed spread the hush of his being John Trurog; ahead, as he came into view, the four waiting men rose, Harrison Salloway stepping sideward to pull out the head chair between his own and Bodali's. Only after the older man slid over this chair did the others, released to a new spate of bantering, sit.

"Men of such substance"—Harriet's lips curled from her purring affection—"that they can even comradely accept the presence of that sovereign fifth."

"What else can they do?" Carl more sharply asked, smiling and meeting her. "The Lake Room's no place to eat kneeling."

"You. Both of you." Barbara brought in a languorous purr of her own. "Don't be too quotable; things get around."

Carl laughed, but easily, lightly. Fond disdain, fond derision, these of course compassed the only attitudes possible. Over the room now all the heads that had turned and the eyes that had watched were returning to nearer activities, the hum was renewing its vibrance. Barbara went back to the dream of her creamy perfections, Harriet took up her running dry commentary, he recentered at least some attention on his sweetbreads and salad. As he did so, however, what he felt through his body was his own deep cause for relaxing. John Trurog hadn't noticed him, coming in, that would have been expecting too much. But Salloway had, and that was what counted, more than anything that could come from the others. Not Elmwood, certainly not his father's house, but this was what he had been stung to get back to during those seventeen thrown-away months of his war service. The insufferable insults of training, the disgust of sleeping in holds and in barracks where other men's breaths stank so closely above and beneath and beside him that no escape opened anywhere, the trench mud that was half blood and flesh slime, the weeks in the hospital, Estelle in Paris—he was away from that, free from it, back where he belonged, body clean, clothes clean, no odors around him except those of perfume and deliciously cooked food; he had been a quarter year back at his job.

Back at more than his job. Harrison Salloway, greeting his return, had been moved from his icicle coldness; Harrison Salloway had been almost exuberant. "Welcome home, Reiss, welcome home. Boy, you're welcome. Pull on your jeans, now, and grab up a shovel—where was it you'd got to? Oh, selling's no job for a warrior—how'd you like section managing, fourth-floor Housewares and China?" That next big step was there ready and waiting; all he'd had to do was get back. And from here on in——

Trurog, Salloway, Leverett, Bodali, Ohman. The vantage point he had so expertly chosen and captured was unexceptionable; his view of the table before him was quite unobscured. Ohman, Bodali, Leverett, Trurog, Salloway. Solid, corporeal, leaning forward, playing with silverware, resting back, jesting, ordering, greeting their food when it came with a robust enthusiasm, hungrily eating as other men ate. Men who controlled not only Trurog's, but, through directorates, at least one Chapaqua bank and a half dozen other Chapaqua enterprises beside. As long ago as 1910, 1911, when he'd still been no more than a stock boy, he'd already begun seeing that table as the node of his desperate longing. "He'll never work with his hands, not my boy, but you'll see what he'll be." His mother said that of him when he was no more than six, said it the day his father took him out to the barn forge to help set a steel rim on a wagon wheel. "That's right, son, now that's right," his father's instruction was careful, exhorting. "You hold that band tight, now, while I heat the ends red-hot; don't let go, now——" Only the steel was too strong for him, hot iron ran through his hands. He was screaming, his head in among his mother's skirts, his hands still untended while, folding him into her body, his mother cried over him, "Never, he's never to do your kind of work, ever; he'll be so much more than you——"

Mixed with pain and the need to find surcease by burrowing was another pull, as if he wanted to be one with his father, too—stalwart, belligerent, obstinate, even if at that moment the obstinacy was stammering and abject—"Making a man of him, that's all; he's got to start sometime at man's work." So often, since then, when he was stirred in some ways, his palms burned; under cover of the tablecloth he stretched his fingers out widely, then tightly reclosed them.

Never work with his hands, his mother said, and she of course was the one who was right. He hadn't worked with his hands, but he'd learned things and done things, he was well on his way. Give him fifteen years more, give him twenty at the most, and he too would sit at that table, he'd be one with the men there, he too would be making an entrance for the Lake Room to watch—admiringly or sardonically, he wouldn't care which. Inevitably obstacles before him peaked sky-high; he knew about obstacles; he'd already met obstacles. A harassing slowness in rates of promotion, illness, hatreds which fogged the whole store—sometimes, as recently during the war, the whole thing seemed too much, too impossible; he had moments of seeing himself with no talents such as Bodali's for finance, moments when against Salloway he felt lacks there too. But if he as yet had no special abilities those were what at a moment like this, with his hands burning, he must resolve to develop; if he hadn't Salloway's grounding, that must be acquired too. Determination was what counted, and of that he had enough and to spare. At first perhaps it might be Chester Ohman's place he'd hold—personnel would be a natural route for his advance. But eventually, finally, Harrison Salloway's——

"Just guess what our godlings are up to today," Harriet put in at that point, and willfully he switched off inner currents to pay more attention to what was at hand. It wasn't alone because he found her amusing that he kept up acquaintance with Harriet; she was Salloway's secretary. "Their bit to mow down the buyers' strike, that's what they're machiavelling right now. Look, aren't they wonderful? Poor customers, they should know they can't win. That newspaper going around, that's last Friday's, with McAdoo's picture on the front page, in the turned suit with patches. They let Father John sweat—that's where half the fun lies, letting Father John sweat. Watch Salloway, up to the rescue. He worked with Fidelman on that ad all day Saturday. It's got McAdoo's picture too, fuzzed enough around the edges so the name could better be McAtramp. Nobody needs go around looking like that, the ad says, not with Trurog suits. Now look at 'em chortle. Look at Father John shine. That, I think, ends their stint. Let's not hurry out, though; there's something I heard about——"

Exposé by which to be amused, exposé in which to interpolate his own mordant comments, but, just the same, with sagacities to be saved. As Harriet was saying, the meeting today promised brevity, Bodali and Leverett, at no more than one-twenty, were shoving aside dessert plates and coffee cups, hauling out watches—directors' meetings outside, Harriet supplied—and rather hastily leaving. The other three were more leisurely but they too, soon, stood up.

It was then the small incident started.

For a second, at the table, an impasse of courtesy, Ohman and Salloway waiting for Trurog to precede them, he refusing the deference. "No, no, after you, after you," he was seen as urging, gesturing outward. Good-naturedly accepting, Ohman and Salloway went on, John

Trurog trailing. Or at least, after what looked like a fumbling recovery of a notebook beside his plate, he might have trailed if he hadn't been halted by a waitress who burst at him from her station at the corner of the bay—the waitress, apparently, who recently had served him, a waitress, at any rate, in the wide hair ribbon, white middy and accordion-pleated skirt of all Lake Room waitresses, a waitress in a fury.

She spat, "Maybe you think I'm not seeing that. Maybe you think I don't know what goes on every week." For all its venom, or maybe because of it, her voice still was low, so low that most people weren't noticing, but a voice threatening to rise. At the first syllable, though, in fact at the first flurry of the girl's skirt as she flew forward, Carl's knees shoved him upward, while Harriet and Barbara sat transfixed. This was what never must happen. Very well that they, keeping it tight in the family, indulge in a filial scoffing, but that outsiders be given a good cause for disrespect——

"Maybe," the girl was continuing, "you think I don't know you're the rattiest——"

Her tip, naturally. For Carl, perception came instantly. That's why the old buzzard wants Bodali next to him. Bodali's a spender, and anyone would know a quarter was too much to leave for a waitress——

How was Salloway missing this? By now Salloway and Ohman were halfway down the room. Give him a second, though——

Only he had no need to hurry; other intervention preceded his. Beside the two appeared a third person, a young woman who, quietly, spoke a single word. "Frances." Not in outrage or warning, but in simple reminder.

The girl's mouth was still angrily working. "If you think I'll let——"

In exactly the same tone as before, the young woman repeated her "Frances." But even that was unnecessary; fury, on the girl's face, was already receding; it respurted, but instead of gaining new verbal expression it shook through her body until, in mute unspeakable protest, she turned on her heel and fled off to the right toward the kitchens.

"That girl." Only when retreat was in order did John Trurog get out a first gasp. "She's dangerous. Attacked me." Around the half-whispered words his lips writhed, above them his eyes sped to right and left, trapped, beseeching. "She must lose her place. No reference. No one should listen to her. She——"

"Everything will be perfectly all right, Mr. Trurog. Everything will be well taken care of." The young woman's tranquillity was undisturbed.

With one more darting glance at her, the old man, too, swung on his heel, scurrying, more hunched than ever, his gait more crabwise than ever, toward the Lake Room doors. At the table he left, as if that were her only purpose there, the young woman began picking up the menus the five men had tossed in toward the center of the table.

"Whew," Carl said. "That might have been almost—riot." From his first leap he had more slowly moved forward, until, as old Trurog sped doorward, he stood at the young woman's elbow. People in the farther reaches of the room, as he caught with relief, were unobservant enough, but at tables adjacent necks had begun craning, eyes showed a malicious intentness. If it hadn't been too dramatic a gesture he would have mopped at his forehead.

The young woman, he now saw, carried other menus under her arm, which meant she was one of the hostesses. Her job, taking care of an incident such as this. So her attitude said, but whoever she was, she had handled it well. When he waited she moved slightly, letting her glance no more than glide across his.

She replied, "Riot's not part of the routine." The voice was well inflected but as low as before, the instant of visual contact so slight it was almost non-existent, yet inexplicably he felt—what? Not shock, certainly; no, it was too minor for that. But still something. And why? For many years now, women, even strange women, had usually shown at least some response when they looked at him; good looks for the most part were birth accident on which he couldn't pride himself, but that didn't mean he was unaware of his ordinary impact. This girl showed no response whatever. Under a wide but low forehead rimmed by brown hair, her eyes carried little but a self-contained appreciation of the incident just past. When she had spoken she turned slightly more toward him, and with what seemed repetition of the faint earlier tremor he caught sight of a birthmark on one side of her neck—raised, rose-colored, lizard-shaped, rising from the high collar of her dress, extending to the ear, fingering even beyond. Composedly, once she had so turned herself, she again turned away, stretching far inward over the table for a menu she hadn't yet reached.

He stammered, "N-no one could have quelled it more neatly."

She answered, still within her own responses, not in any way touching his, "Thank you," and with that she too moved away, a slight, rather short figure in navy-blue taffeta, in the direction taken by the waitress.

Dismissing him as she dismissed the episode. And for him too, as he well realized, the occurrence should end there. Enough that for this latest example of an incredible avarice, Harriet, back at his table, should be reduced to fondling whisper, "I heard it, but it just seemed too good to be true," Barbara should be even more unbelieving, and he suffer return of old chilling contempt. The rest was to be shrugged away. It was none of his business, actually, if old Trurog stole tips; it would have been his business to cover for his employer if that had been necessary, but it wasn't; neither Harriet nor Barbara so much as knew the girl's name. There was no reason whatever why, simply because when she looked at him he had felt that small jar, the young woman with the birthmark should in any way stay in his mind.

But she stayed there.

Every so often, in his life, he met experiences which lived on with him unfading, so that at any time, anywhere, he had only to step momently sideward to be in them again.

Of these experiences, the most potent, the most thrusting—more potent and more thrusting, even, than the one of the wagon wheel— was his hiring at Trurog's, his meeting with Harrison Salloway. On that day of first meeting he was not yet sixteen, only three weeks out of high school, come up to Chapaqua from Elmwood for a try at a job. Apprehensive, determined and hopeful, in among a mob of other hopefuls drawn by news of an impending sale, he had stood in the long corridor outside Trurog's hiring offices on Trurog's eighth floor.

On his arrival at eight in the morning it was a mob on the whole good-humored, expressing itself mainly by pushing and shoving. As morning wore on, though, and no forward movement occurred, as nothing whatever went on except an accretion of numbers, some tempers worsened, trouble-groups of young men coagulated, there were catcalls and cries of "Hey, what you doing in there, sleeping it off?" By ten the crowd was moving forward and back in long surges, calls carried increasing ill humor—"What you think we are, anyway, beeves in a stockyard?" The trouble-knots erupted in fighting.

Distastefully, disdaining to join in this turbulence, he stood well away. That was where he was, aloof and alone, back to a wall, when the crowd was cut by motion like that of an in-streaking rocket.

"There'll be no more of that." Command came icy and hard. At all centers but one fighting died raggedly, the participants pulling shamefacedly apart to fade into the group. The battle remaining was one engaging seven or eight burly young roughs, but into this tangle, too, the incomer waded, grabbing one head by its hair to knock it resoundingly against another, sending a chin back from an uppercut; within seconds these combatants also were fallen apart, dazedly or sullenly looking about for what had hit them, while in the space he had cleared stood the clearer, a man of no more than average height, stocky, possessed, icily chill.

He said, "There'll be no hiring today. The next time you feel like a brawl, don't pick Trurog's. You, you and you—" a right forefinger stabbed. "You can stay. All the rest of you go."

One more surge in the mob, but not one of cohesive defiance. For the most part hangdog and defeated, as if they all, even the prim older women in shirtwaists, and the girls in merry-widow plumes and dusters, had taken part in the fighting, or as if their very being there in some way made them guilty, they filed away.

Against the wall Carl stayed until the dismissed had ebbed. By what principle of choice the man operated no one could have said; the stab of the forefinger was apparently not preceded by so much as a glance. Yet he was sure, and with each succeeding thick thud of his heart he was more sure, that one stab was for him. Later, but not very much later, heart even more wildly knocking, knees weak, he stood alone with the man in the office behind the blackly lettered door that read: "Harrison Salloway, Employment."

"Name?" Harrison Salloway shot at him then, not suggesting Carl sit, though there were chairs as well as a desk in the room, not himself sitting. "Age? Finished high school? Ever work before? Why have you picked Trurog's?" Questions fell with a Gatling precision. Harrison Salloway in this smaller room loomed bigger than in the corridor, and also, in stronger light, younger, a man who had gotten bald early, the pink crown of his head slightly ridged, the semicircle of closely cropped hair reddish brown, the face with its large features also highly colored, the square-set body moving forcefully, with an effect of controlled power, within the well-cut gray suit.

From this brief questioning Carl walked away with the temporary job which was his entering wedge; at the sale's end, instead of dismissal, his pay envelope tendered curt notice, "Report to Employment." It was in this ensuing interview that Harrison Salloway sliced Trurog's open for him as if it were a dripping ripe watermelon.

"I began at Trurog's myself as a stock boy; today I'm handling employment; in five years I'll manage the store. That's Trurog policy— we develop executives. Pick our men, start them at the bottom, give them working experience of every phase of the store. It's up to you, naturally; you make good or you don't. You reach your level. You look to me, though, like a young man who——"

Experience that came in two sections, but that was really one. Since then he had seen Harrison Salloway kindlier, seen him jovial, seen him boisterously exuberant, but the basic impression was one of cold steel-strong inflexible hardness; with whatever emotions the gray eyes and the blunt mouth might be overlaid, the hardness and coldness were still there beneath; Salloway could always within any moment be the Salloway of the clearing, pronouncing a final dismissal, "There'll be no hiring today." The Salloway of this episode was the one by which he had guided himself, the Salloway who for him had some meaning he didn't penetrate. Any time, when he was asking a customer, "Could we help you, madame?" when he was arranging lunch hours, when on Sunday he visited the Art Institute—this episode, all of it: the mob, the fighting, his hope, his selection, relived itself in and around him.

Now, annoyingly, in among the other experiences which so relived themselves—the suffocating moments, among the earliest, when as a child of three he had fallen headfirst into the rain barrel at the corner of the Elmwood back porch, almost drowning there, the last time—he was eight, then—when his mother called "Carl" and he ran to her, wrenching from his father, but she was no longer able to know he was answering, all the others, there now was added this new one. One less harsh and less clear, in some ways, but cutting across his most important concentrations: whether he should, or shouldn't, take another extension course this summer, what he might do about the unrest in the Housewares Repair Shop. He found himself reseeing the lake view from the bay, the disordered table, the cringing old man, the young woman who spoke merely a name. Having dinner that evening with Bob Gokey at Eihler's, he looked up once, startled and alerted simply because a slight girl in navy-blue taffeta was passing his table. Next morning, lying in the undisciplined drowsiness between sleep and waking, his fingers seemed to be reaching, and what they reached for, experimentally, was that birthmark. Within his body, again, was the muted small shock, and the sensation beneath his fingers was velvety.

As soon as he recognized this tactile imagining he woke the rest of the way, angered; nothing was more infuriating than unregulated action on his part. If he were to start dreaming of women, why not Barbara? He could re-create Barbara too—Barbara's silky dark hair, the lazy low lift of a glance fit to stir the pulses of St. Simeon Stylites, and certainly stirring his, the undulant softness of a body willowy but full in the important areas. If Barbara hadn't been at loose ends after college and insisted on coming into the store, he'd never have had a chance to know anyone like her. Any young man, certainly any young man at Trurog's, had more than one reason for night thoughts of Barbara.

Irritatingly, however, the other girl stayed with him. What, he found himself wondering, lay behind her control? What, in a young woman, produced so much restraint? One Lake Room visit in three or four weeks was all he allowed himself—it didn't do to hug the ringside too obviously—but as noon neared on that day, and the next, and the next, he resisted a pull to return there. One more sight of the birthmark—some perverse, perhaps even unhealthy curiosity must be what was prodding him—would let him forget it. Let him once more be intent on his own affairs. Behind those self-contained eyes might so easily lie just an emotional flatness.

Left to himself, he might have handled it, if Harriet, in the next week, hadn't produced her spur.

"Guess who I'm cultivating," she offered ingenuously. "Our heroine. Our girl from the Lake Room. Looked her up, Friday, and took her to dinner. You know, friend, I think maybe we flushed something there. Anyway, I intend finding out."

He supplied, "You do?" For the moment—it was at her desk, on his way from Salloway's office, that he spoke to her, and seeing Salloway meant decks stripped for action—he had been almost free from the unallowed nagging, and having it recalled made it doubly annoying. He managed continued indifference: "What's she like privately? Cannon ball all the way?"

Harriet's smile, over her typewriter, carried faint hints of malice. Harriet was a tall girl, too tall, her brown hair pulled forward at the sides and banded in place by a green ribbon passed across her forehead; not handsome, exactly, but invincibly smart. No one could tell what Harriet's purposes might be; she knew, naturally she knew, of his past dates with Barbara; she was Barbara's cousin. Harriet liked him, he was sure of it, but she also could flick with the thinnest of lashes. "You may be twenty-six," she'd said to him one day, "but you're still as finicky as an adolescent." And, at another time, "You and I might suspect, I suppose, that being supercilious is simply an older form of thumb-sucking."

"She doesn't give out all she is all at once, I'll say that," she replied to him now. "Landa, her name is. Christine Landa. Well brought up, very proper, unwed, twenty-three. Do I gather you're slavering? I might get up a foursome."

He grimaced. "Me slaver? Oh, Lord, let's not start things." Out in the hall and away from her, though, he met the push to go back. "Of course, if you're trying to fill in an evening," he could say with an acridity to match her own, "it's scarcely gallant of me not to offer myself as a sacrifice."

No, not that. Not to Harriet. Instead——

Rather abruptly, there in the hall, what he had been feeling about the matter reversed itself. Why was he putting up this ridiculous resistance on a matter so minuscule? Pique—he might as well face it—injured vanity, this was what was needling him. No man enjoyed being glossed over so thoroughly. Some faint curiosity about the girl too, of course, but mainly pique. Why shouldn't he see her? Get her out of his system. She'd notice him, next time. All he needed——

Crisply, that afternoon, he commanded his floor. Little by little—it came up from nowhere—he knew what his plan would be, and as it ramified a beginning elation came with it. Ideas such as this served more than one purpose. At ten minutes to closing time he was making his way to the Lake Room.

"Miss Landa? Third office. Back there." By a cashier who didn't so much as look up from her tallying, he was pointed off to the right. The Lake Room, shades pulled, tables stripped, chairs stacked, was a muted dim ghost of itself, but his agreement with what he was doing could now be neither shadowed nor muted; his footsteps fell firmly and evenly on the thick carpets, his body moved firmly and evenly in a diagonal across the huge room. At the designated cubbyhole he again said, "Miss Landa——"

In a space as bare as her own outward personality, holding little beyond a desk, a chair, a telephone and herself, the girl lifted her head from a small sheaf of papers. She was short, shorter even than he remembered; in the relative positions they now held, he standing, she sitting, his view of her was almost entirely one from above. As before, briefly, her glance crossed his, waiting and matter-of-fact—no glance, he might once more repeat, to rouse him, yet in spite of his firm hold on his causes for being there, he felt the bewildering tremor. Her eyes, he was able to see, were gray, quite a dark gray, lined by dark lashes, though her hair, simply pulled back to a figure eight low in her neck, was a very pale brown. Nothing in the eyes, nothing in the face surrounding them, the brow as he remembered wide but rather low, the cheekbones high, the mouth wide in a narrow jaw, explained the tremor; she was neither good-looking nor not good-looking; her eyes might have been pretty and so might her mouth, her skin was a light shade of amber, but she was too expressionless. Perhaps there was recognition in her glance; this time at least she didn't deliberately— one of the things that had teased at him was his certainty that the first time he saw her the turning of her head was deliberate—expose her disfigurement.

Forcing his other purpose, his idea and enthusiasm for it, to the surface, he proceeded quickly, letting himself be consciously boyish, "I'm here on a project—I'm a section manager, fourth-floor Housewares and China. You know Bodali's just done us a new batch of statistics, working out the returns for each separate department each month, balancing them against the average for the store as a whole. I've thought I might add to that—nothing very ambitious, but if I could get the number of employees in each department, then I could work out the average monthly return for each employee, or maybe the return per employee working hour in each department. It might give us ideas on staffing."

As he explained it he moved inward until he could lay the sheets he had with him on the corner of her desk. "I've begun here on China and Housewares——"

Apparently she had no idea he was there for any but a given reason; her head bent politely.

She said, "That's quite original." Once more he was caught by her voice, so well modulated, so colorless. He was now so closely above her that when he looked downward he saw the upward finger of the mark on the other side of her neck; again he couldn't have identified the reaction which swept him, whether it was distaste or quite the opposite.

"Of course you're welcome to the information from this department," she was going on pleasantly. "You may incur some dislike, you know, but I suppose Mr. Bodali has drawn most of that dislike already."

For the first time she was smiling, but her smile, too, while it lighted her face, had none of the in-striking quality women's smiles usually had, none of the expectation of rousing. She handed him two sheets of paper from a drawer. "Here's my current list of Lake Room employees and their hours."

He said, "I hope you're a good omen; I've not yet asked anyone else."

She answered, "Let me see what you get from it; it may be informative."

Nothing to prolong; he could only add thanks and depart. What held him as he left, though, was a mixed and dubious defiance, once more admitting retreat. All right, suppose he was more than piqued, suppose in some indefinable way and for indefinable reasons the girl did interest him. Suppose he had falsified his purposes a little—if he hadn't, he never would have lowered his barriers enough to look her out. Now that he had looked her out, though, he experienced no regrets whatsoever, only an increase of elation. Second and nearer sight of the birthmark was in some way stirring—even closely before him, actual and not the illusion of a dream, he could have borne to touch it. He had learned little of her, but she'd said, "Let me see what you get from it——"

2 That night, in his rented room at Morrison's, he still waked in the small hours, figuring. An inch-thick stack of data sheets—Miss Landa was quick, but not quick enough to see the economical way of getting his material, which was all at once, through Ohman's stenographer. His own two departments—secondary, but contenting—came out very well in comparisons, even if not as well as the Lake Room, which paid, as everyone knew, some of the highest profits in the store.

He could be in the girl's office first thing in the morning. Not that such a course tempted; store business went first to Salloway. In a way it was more tempting, really, to hold off, postponing, now he so surely would have it, the moment he'd see her. He couldn't, though, postpone taking his results to Salloway; Bodali, with his statistical curiosity, might be having the same inspiration this very night, and there was no reason, as he'd already seen, why his idea shouldn't pay twice.

Salloway, in the morning, was testily ill-humored. "Why the hell everyone in this store has to see me," he shot from his desk toward Carl coming in, toward Milo Geggenheim going out. "Why the hell no one makes any decisions for himself——"

Over Carl passed a damp consciousness of the many past problems manufactured simply to get him to Salloway's office. "What've you got now?" Salloway continued his barking, and with confidence and pleasure alike ebbing, Carl without speaking laid his sheets on the desk. Anything to do with any girl, anything to do with any matter outside his store life, as he was reminded then, had for him no real power; this and this only was paramount, his standing with Salloway. Of his idea then was left only its puerility; Bodali had probably done the same thing long ago. The Salloway who scowled at the figures painstakingly pecked out on the deceased Mr. Morrison's typewriter was the Salloway of the clearing.

As Salloway read on, though, his scowl eased. He growled once more, "—things that go on in this business," but it had little of the earlier ferocity; it might have been absent-minded.

He asked, "This an idea of your own, Reiss?" And, when Carl answered, swung in his swivel chair to face him, features clear and good-humored under the pink dome.

He said, "You know, you're a good employee, Reiss; that's accepted. Nobody here is apt to forget the time you traced down those thieves in the receiving room—how old were you then? Eighteen? You still can do things I don't expect. It may surprise you, but there's nothing I appreciate more than having a man do a nice piece of work without prompting. You can leave this with me."

That was Salloway. Hard, but when you pleased him he told you so, prodigally. Over Carl floodingly came the force of his original dedications, the wash of his closest desires; he lifted his hands to run thumbs over palms that stung warmly. Alight and uplifted, when he turned to go, he once again saw the matter of the girl in its truer perspective; whatever she was, whatever she might turn out to be in herself or for him—and he was willing, right then, to agree she might turn out to be more than he had glimpsed—she wouldn't be a big issue, she wouldn't deflect him. He'd better see about that extension course immediately—probably accounting again. Or business law. He'd get hold of Dubinsky, who certainly was causing the trouble in the Housewares Repair Shop——

For Christine Landa, then, such time as he casually had for her. Enough probing, perhaps, to find out what manner of person she was. This time he preceded the closing bell by no more than five minutes when he walked in through the Lake Room; Christine, back to him, stood pulling on a hat when he knocked at her door to lay the carbons of his figures on the desk edge.

"Not world-shaking, I'll admit," he told her, this also boyishly, "but Salloway took to it kindly. And you at any rate haven't much cause to scowl at me—the only departments topping yours are Wash Goods and Linens."

"Mm." A murmur as her finger ran down the list, caught at the figures for the Lake Room, and then moved on. Turned as she now was, the side she had toward him was the marked side, and what seemed like a flow of warm liquid moved through his breast as he saw it. Almost he had forgotten, in his devising of what he might want from her, that she had it. To keep his mind on what he was saying he averted his eyes.

"In fact, Salloway was so kind—you were so pleasant—last night I put in quite a night. Tonight I'd like exercise." Not dancing, he'd thought through the afternoon, dancing—pressed too hard. She might not, besides, be good at it. No, the other—"Maybe roller skating. I don't suppose you'd go with me, just to help celebrate?" He'd tried phrasing it several ways; this way might seem negative, but nothing else had the right negligence.

While he was in mid-utterance, while in fact he was saying, "You were so pleasant," she was speaking too, appreciatively. "You did a great deal of work very fast." After he completed his invitation there was a small wait in which her head lifted slowly, as if she heard what he said not directly but by recall.

She repeated, "You—wanted me to—go out with you?" And for once there was expression on her face, even if it was blank astonishment. She said, "I don't know you at all. Except, of course, that you work here. You——"

Her eyes rose to him, really looking at him, seeing him—yes, this time certainly seeing him, his eyes, his mouth, his shoulders, his hands. Whatever the result of this scrutiny, it didn't affect the returning quiet of her face. She continued, "You don't know much about me."

He smiled. "This might be my chance."

She said as slowly as before, "There's not much beyond what you see."

This time it was certainly deliberate; she stood so he must see the mark. Stood waiting, as if he might be expected to take an easy and hasty out—"Of course, if it's inconvenient, some other time——"

When, instead, he said, "I realize there'd be people you'd have to let know; I'd like it if you'd eat with me—Eihler's, maybe, or some other place I could afford. We'd have to take streetcars; I haven't a car," she once more looked at him.

"Oh, I wouldn't mind that. I——" Again an expression began forming on her face, the lines of her mouth almost hardening. She said, "If you'd wait——" and picked up the phone from her desk; as she drew it toward her the cord caught at the pages of his figuring, brushing them to the floor; he bent in retrieval but she didn't notice. Into the phone she said, "Mother? I believe I'll stay down for dinner tonight. No, nothing special, more or less as before." Her voice on the words was quite brisk; she dropped the receiver into its hanging arm with a swift plop, as if with it she dropped something else. To him she added, "I seem to be ready."

He was prepared for refusal; on his tongue was a rueful, "I know I'm asking too much on the spur of the moment; I'll look forward to better luck later," which would allow him a graceful exit and a chance at a later try if he kept on being needled. Acceptance put him almost at a loss. What was it—the query must push up again as it had pushed up before—that he seemed to want from her? Knowledge of who she was, what she was, why she so affected him?

He was also unprepared for the resurgent, zooming pleasure which, awkward or not, almost immediately hit him. Not even his Trurog promotions had brought him more sense of accomplishment. He said, "Then let's go! We're next door to treason, staying around here after closing time!" Gaily he drew her into the now entirely vacated and darkened Lake Room. She knew the paths through the tables much better than he, but the impulse to keep his hand on her arm was unconquerable; at the first contact with warm flesh under the taffeta, his own flesh moved as warmly.

"One thing about me," he told her, bantering, "you can trust me; I'm a Trurog landmark by this time; even with my war service I've put in more than nine years. You're rather new, aren't you? This Lake Room's the one place I've not worked; I've not carried dishes. No, no, don't——"

Reply came demurely. She wasn't too new, almost a year. Probably she'd come while he was across. If Mr. Salloway had forgotten the Lake Room——

From his two inches over six feet he bent to her; she was even more slight than he remembered. Yet the arm which she so immediately drew away from him everywhere but at street crossings had a firm roundness, her body when his brushed it had an equally firm and resistant solidity; for all her smallness there seemed more of her than there was of bigger girls, more, for instance, than there was of Barbara. She yielded so much less.

At Eihler's while they ate he began eliciting a few of the facts which, commonplace as they were when drawn forth, he was more and more compelled to know. Yes, she was a Chapaqua girl, her father taught history at Midwestern, she'd gone there herself, taking Home

Ec, of course, she had a mother and also an older brother, Douglas, who was married and living in Baltimore.

In one way she talked readily enough; at least after she had begun saying a thing it was ready; it was before she answered that, sometimes, small hesitances occurred. He kept probing for more. Perhaps her most informative reply came in response to his "Why Home Ec?" to which she returned, after one of the pauses, her glance toward her plate, "I decided quite early I'd be earning my living; that seemed as good a way as any."

He took that up, "Today? Girls can do anything today"; but while he talked on and she brought out the rebuttals he had his first flash of insight, and, at the same time, a spurt of something like understanding, protest and tenderness—she had sometime decided, because of the birthmark, that she wasn't marriageable.

This alone, if it came to that, might explain much that had pulled at him—her restrained and closed-in aloofness. But even if so soon and so clearly he gained this insight, it in no way was completing; more restlessly than before he felt the need to be near to her.

She, for her part, began an uncertain questioning of her own to which he must reply—no, not from Chapaqua, from a small town forty miles south. Elmwood. No mother, she'd died when he was eight, but an aunt, Aunt Stell, kept house; still kept house for his father. His father sold farm implements. No, not college—his father hadn't felt able (keep bitterness from it) to send him. But he'd taken some work——

Not knowing how he got into it, he poured out much more than that.

"I know what I want, what I need to do; I'm going to work up at Trurog's. It's easy, saying it, but I know it won't be; unless I can do it I won't care about anything else. Ohman's or Salloway's—for those two jobs there must be twenty men, wanting and pushing up; I've got to show I'm so good they can't pass me for anyone else. That's why I was so pleased with my idea about the statistics; I've got to have more like that——"

In a way, saying it, it sounded thin, when it couldn't be; the thinness, the flatness, came because he was unpracticed at phrasing ambition. While the words broke, while he felt through his body the release of saying them, while his palms stung, he at the same time heard himself saying the same things to Barbara or Harriet, and the very possibility was stifling; with Barbara or Harriet it was impossible to reveal you took yourself any way but lightly. This girl, though, this Christine—was this what he had seen in her, divined of her?—seemed to be drawing it from him; she sat entirely quiet, but her eyes and her mouth now were warm, as if she identified, understood, and consequently was softened toward him, in the same way that a few moments ago he also had identified, understood and been softened.

When she spoke it was drolly. "Ohman and Salloway both look to me like very good targets, targets you well might improve on. At least you might improve on John Trurog." Over the removal of Bodali's tips they laughed together, now, breaking his seriousness; but after this, too, understanding remained, emolliently, so that when dinner was long eaten and a waitress accosted him, "Could we clear this table?" he was impatient because they were interrupted.

Yet he was to find the rest of the evening as revealing. On the streetcar she told him, "I haven't roller-skated since I was little," but when in the entrance hall of the rink he brought skates and sat beside her to put on his own, she laced herself into the boots with no more apology and no more expressed misgiving; when she stood up and her feet slid she reached not for him but the side-wall bar. Experimentally, seeming almost to forget him, she moved back and forth along it, testing the skates and her balance.

Only at protest, "Teaching you is part of my fun," did she relinquish the bar for his hands. Very slowly at first, brows bent in concentration, holding his hands in a clasp hard and not the least coquettish, she moved with him, her body carrying some of the hesitation her speech had shown. The east-side rink to which he had taken her was a large one, and crowded; at one end of the floor under the raftered raw wood ceiling a band played "Beautiful Ohio" from a flag-draped platform; the place was a barn, but with the hundreds of skating couples, the girls darting streaks of bright color, it also had vivacity and movement and rhythm, everyone circling in an even and swaying progression.

Fumbling in anything he did was always intolerable to him, and after the first groping rounds Christine too began to catch the common contagion, sweeping along then in fairly relaxed swooping strokes, meeting him, keeping pace with him, never dragging or leaning; except for his grasp of her hands, and the occasional light brush of their hips, he scarcely knew he had her. Color stained her cheeks and her eyes once more lit; with a flush almost of pride he was thinking her charming when he was given his second flash of insight.

At an intermission a girl near him cried, "Eddie, you know what we should do? We should trade. You, how about you?" She swung to Carl, black eyes laughing upward, daring and promising; Eddie, beside her, was carelessly willing. But as Eddie began his own light invitation to Christine, "How about it? Would you——" the barest of momentary flickers crossed his face. He went heartily on, "—be willing to try me out?" but Carl knew what that flicker meant; he pulled Christine roughly away.

"Sorry, we're sticking together."

Christine, after a moment, said quietly, "Don't mind. He didn't mean anything—unpleasant; I'm entirely used to it." Inside Carl, though, a jet rose as high as his throat. "You, what do you think you know?" Against Eddie he could have used words like bayonets.

After that, while they skated, it seemed to him that every once in a while some pair of eyes rested on him, moved to Christine, produced that momentary flicker, and then returned, as if questioning, to him. Barbara—comparison was inescapable. If it were Barbara with him, she'd be gone from him often, snatched by one boy, then another. No one snatched Christine. Yet he felt no single impulse to cut away from her or even keep her inconspicuous. During the "Missouri Waltz," in a corner, he taught her to respond when he swung her outward and then drew her in under his arm; when nearby couples slowed to watch he forced her to repeat the simple elaboration around the room, and the emotion he did it with, as he well realized, was one of furious challenge.

Pink died from her cheeks; his affront couldn't be anything but noticeable. That too was insufferable but not to be avoided. In the anteroom before removing his own skates he knelt to replace hers with her shoes.

She lived, he found out, in a two-story gray frame house of perhaps seven rooms, a few blocks from the Midwestern campus. A good house but undistinguished, bearing no relation whatever, for instance, to a house such as Ohman's. When they walked up to it a single light showed upstairs; Christine said musically and colorlessly, "I see Mother's waiting," and then, as she fitted into the lock a key she had taken from her handbag halfway down the block, "It was a pleasant evening, Mr. Reiss. Thank you for asking me."

He lifted his hand toward her but she was already beyond the door.

He had anticipated this brief dismissal; in the streetcar on the way home he'd said, "That was fun, wasn't it? Let's go again," but he himself was drained, then, of emotion. She answered duly, "Yes, it was; I enjoy something new," but her speech and her attitude suggested that she didn't—except perhaps casually in the store—expect to see him again.

The house where he roomed, west and north, was a good twenty blocks distant; if he wanted a clear head for the morning he should take the first streetcar at the corner and go directly home. As he turned back down the steps of Christine's porch, though, he knew himself too unsettled for sleep. Setting his legs to a pace they could keep automatically, he started walking, freeing his thoughts to take on the harsh clarity toward which they sometimes verged.

This girl he had just left attracted him, no doubt of that. Even just now, on the porch, in his present mood of reaction, it was his left hand that lifted toward her left shoulder. If he let himself think of her in some ways—her slightness, her resilience, that mark—he began tensing and hardening. Last fall, in Paris with Estelle, he had found how treacherous his body could be; neither he nor Estelle had intended what happened; at the hospital she was nothing but an officer's wife come visiting out of kindness or boredom. They'd found something to talk of simply because, before she married, she too had worked in a store. He hadn't even liked her, especially; she was too much like himself, tall, nervous, fastidious. That afternoon when he was first getting around and dropped in to see her—he still broke into cold sweats, remembering. Nothing but mercy got him so shortly shipped home.

Suppose he began going about with Christine. No use not facing a possible issue: he might want to marry her. And marriage might not be his success at Trurog's, but it still was something. With his mind he didn't want to marry, never had wanted to marry, but if marriage was necessary, then why not with Barbara? Barbara might not take him, he hadn't yet asked her, he was far, yet, from asking her, the last few times he'd taken her out he'd been moved away from her rather than toward her, but, compared to this other girl, didn't he owe it to himself to make the try? "You landed Chet Ohman's daughter? Reiss, that's enterprise!" No use saying considerations such as this shouldn't enter, they entered. "For that new job we're setting up—I suppose we should consider that new son-in-law of yours, Chet." Marriage to Barbara couldn't make his way; only he, himself, could make that way, but it might be easing and smoothing. Impressed respect, whispers throughout the store, subdued surprise when he showed her to his father and Aunt Stell. Barbara would be one woman, anyway, who would keep his father to size. Never any repetition of such discomforts as the one with Eddie, not from Barbara.

Against this chance, what was some obscure and undisciplined agent within himself placing? A girl so schooled to being inconspicuous that until she drifted up and spoke you didn't know she was there. Against the backdrop of a Lake Room table and the bay she said, "Frances," and a waitress scuttled away, leaving John Trurog decently unrevealed, but if he married her he would get, at the most, shrugging indifference, "What do you ever think he sees in her?"

Moving his shoulders intolerantly as he walked, he tried to shake free of it. He'd made no promises, spoken no definite word about seeing her again. The evening had given him, hadn't it, what he wanted to know? Every fact of it ordinary—a well-disciplined, middle-class girl who'd grown up with a birthmark. Intelligent, responsive, warming quickly to understanding—hundreds, thousands of girls had as much, had more. Tomorrow he'd stop in to see Barbara.

Emerging from a dressing room with a froufrou of henna georgette over an arm—it was in second-floor Dresses that Barbara held down her sinecure—Barbara in the morning raised for him the heavy-lidded, sleepily smoldering smile, Barbara shed from herself that softly blooming, entangling aura which she so lightly turned on or turned off.

"You." As much provocation in tone as in glance. "You mean you dare show me your face? You've been neglecting me terribly. I might almost believe you've taken up with some other woman."

"Me? Never." Equal challenge, since that was what she asked, even if challenge took effort to produce against that enveloping aura. "I've been busy. But you could forgive me—say this Saturday night, at the Piatt."

"This Saturday? You mean dinner and dancing? Well, I——" Barbara, within her aura, approved of him, but Barbara also, like Harriet, had reservations; any girl as popular as Barbara had reservations about any man. Lightly swaying on her small feet, she considered, pulled obviously in several directions. "I should never do it—imagine your not asking me until this late! But——"

She'd go. And with this acceptance, too, came satisfaction; impossible to look at Barbara in a tunic dress of rippled ciel-blue satin, without being moved by what one saw. And if he needed other reminders of what Chester Ohman's daughter was in herself, what she might mean to him, those reminders were spread for him profligately when, on the Saturday, he walked up to the Ohman front door. In one way he was familiar with the wide white expanse of the pillared exterior; he'd approached it before. He knew by recognition the long entrance hall with its shining bare floor and its curving white-balustered stairway; he had previously seen the book-stocked library to the left and the big living room to the right, with its deep leather davenports, its many chairs, its orientals, its red velvet draperies, its tiled fireplace, its fringed roseate table covers, its mahogany Gramophone and cases of records. To comfort he in no way was alien; his own father's house in Elmwood was comfortable, so was the place where he roomed. This house, though, told of a way of living, exemplified by the uniformed maid who admitted him, by the extensiveness of its sixteen rooms, by the cool pleasant scent pervading them, by a general silky richness, which still was strange to him, belonging not to the possessed but to what he intended possessing.

Barbara herself, in the hall, came to meet him. "You can say hello, anyway." In chairs beside Mrs. Ohman, idly fanning and chatting in the warm evening, sat two other women; beside Chester Ohman in another group of three who idled with tall glasses in hand near the opened front windows were a Mr. Keating and Judge Mains. "You know my uncle. Harriet's father." These people, too—Chester Ohman with his thick iron-gray hair and firm flesh, Mrs. Ohman, as dusky as Barbara and indolently, pleasantly plump, the others—reflected a total absence of parsimony. "Hear you've a nice evening planned. Drink for you, Reiss?" Behind their indulgence was the sustenant comfort of being well able to afford that indulgence and others. Anything Barbara wants, so their attitudes said, she can most likely have. Including, if her taste runs that way, this young man. And he, if he joins our charmed circle, can probably be given what he wants too, or at least we can see he more easily gets it.

At the Piatt, as well, was that sense of doors readily opening. The headwaiter, bowing, knew Barbara; another waiter whisked a "Reserved" sign from a table. The Piatt wasn't Chapaqua's newest or its biggest hotel, but its Moonlight Room currently was the Saturday night rendezvous of the younger set, and while he was there with Barbara, while he danced well, was reasonably personable and paid his bill, he was tentatively part of the younger set too. Within a few minutes of their arrival couples and foursomes drifted up in the navy-blue half-light, the boys affable if indifferent—"Sure, sure, I remember—Reiss, isn't it?" The girls were questingly acceptive, "You're never as fierce as your eyes look. Don't tell me——"

On the way home, in the Model T borrowed from Bob Gokey, Barbara sat so her shoulder just barely brushed his, and the bloom, the aura, came out from her, cloud-clinging.

"Must we go straight home?" she lazily offered. "With a lake in the middle of town it's a shame not to know what the stars look like over it." And then, as they approached the parking area on the west side, "Let's drive in. You've no chance to take in this moonshine at all while you're driving."

He answered, "What I see if I look is your father in the front hall with a shotgun"; but he headed into the area.

Barbara, as soon as the car stopped, leaned back, not against him but the seat, murmuring, "Oh, bother all parents. Look at those before-mentioned stars. Look at that lake. You could walk on it."

He said, "And there's something about June." When his arms went around her she didn't draw toward him, but her body within the embrace was as plaintly yielding as a pillow; when he bent to her small mouth her lips didn't move to meet his, but they too yielded.

He drew away to look down at her, feeling the pull, bemused by the aura, but fighting to keep his head over the surf. No girl, anywhere, was more delectable than this girl he now held. The dress she was wearing was of tiered blond lace over georgette; around her shoulders lay a cape of blond chiffon banded in squirrel. Everything his hands touched was scented, fragile and exquisite; the cheek his cheek brushed was as scented and satiny, the dark eyes under the lazy lids met his with a tremendous knowledge, a tremendous waiting awareness both of herself and of him.

What he felt—yes, what was it he most felt? The need to let go, to bend farther, to drown, but also the need to resist. This, the ride, the lake, the parking, were the cost of this evening; they were always the cost of an evening with Barbara, and with each evening that cost didn't lessen. At the Piatt there had been a young man named Lucas, who, glowering, several times danced with her; she might very well have broken a previous date to go out with him. Any consideration of Barbara meant not only what he might want of Barbara but what Barbara wanted of him. And what Barbara wanted of him was his physical waking. He had begun to be uncomfortably aware of this the last times he'd had her out; he was more sure of it now. This was what the wise dark eyes dreamed, smoldered and waited for; she wanted to excite, to see and savor excitement in him, she wanted to be in turn excited. This, this readiness to abandonment, the desire to rouse abandonment in him—this was what held him apart from her, no matter what she might offer him. Though there were other things too. He didn't want to be offered what he didn't ask. He didn't want to be given things—not Barbara, not anything else the Ohmans might hand him on a silver platter. What he got must be his by a personal achievement.

Coolly, after that moment of measuring, he once more bent to her, insulated now from the aura, enjoying, this time, only the more lightly sensual responses that came with drawing his lips across hers, her scent, his realization of her desirability. While he was doing so she pulled away, sensing the change in his attitude; her hand stung his cheek. In the remote corner of the front seat she said, "Take me home; I could wish Father would be in that hall with a shotgun."

Amiably in control of himself, he answered, starting the car, "That's your choice." As they drove fury faded from her cheeks; she began collecting herself, straightening, smoothing her cape and her dress, sending out, now, no aura, no fog of enticement, keeping herself chilly. At her house, sulkily but no more than that, she told him, shrugging, "Well, tit for tat, I suppose. I'm sure it was as nice an evening as you wanted to give me." Then, beside her front door, suddenly as amiable and casual as he, in fact sleepily provocative again, she murmured, "I still wish I might be there when you cut loose," and shut the door on him.

Barbara's reply to the evening—that whatever it was, it left her unaltered. And for him too, he blackly reminded himself while he drove the car back toward Bob Gokey, it should change nothing. His criticisms of Barbara, the qualities in her he found discommoding, weren't entirely important; he could handle Barbara, giving her as much as he wanted to give and no more; he could control what might be given him by the Ohmans, as well. Restlessly, however, he was also aware of how ineffective Barbara was as a counterbane. All week, looking forward to this night's engagement, what he had really seen was Christine in the bay, Christine across from him as she'd been at Eihler's, listening, with that complete comprehension which was in her eyes when he told her what he wanted from living. Her arm under his hand, the self-governance with which she'd moved along the side bar, the free and yet disciplined way she'd responded as a skating partner. Walking into the Ohman front hall, he'd seen Christine awaiting him there. At the Piatt, dancing with Barbara, and just now, in the car—was it Christine who made resistance so simple?

Toward himself, toward his errant impulses, there was only one thing to be, deliberate and cruel. He wanted to be cruel and deliberate, to inflict damage on himself and on Christine as well. To Bob, over the beer which was the only repayment Bob ever took for the use of his car, he said, "Some night we should double-date. Maybe skating."

"Sure." Bob as usual was obtusely good-natured. "Sure. Why not? I can always get Lillian. You an eye on some especial mouse?"

"No." Not even to Bob, and with what he intended, could he refer to Christine as a mouse. "There's a girl, though, I owe a good deed to——"

Approaching Christine must be hard, again, not because of interior resistance but because of his purpose. When she turned from her desk to look up at him she had apparently stepped back to the untouched remoteness she maintained for most people.

She said, "Oh, Mr. Reiss," and no more.

Now he was seeing her, now he was close to her, his plan seemed impossible.

"I still—remember that skating as fun. Would you go again this week end? I know a fellow—third-floor Boys' and Men's—who's rather a good egg and who has a car. We could——"

Stiff, the words falling as if they had little meaning. And she, like Barbara, sensed difference; refusal began forming on her lips, in her eyes. But again, when he finished, the small hardening around her mouth preceded the opposite.

"That sounds very interesting; I'm sure I can go."

As soon as she'd said the words, as soon as, facing him with a shoulder lift that was somehow one of courage, she had committed herself for an evening to his keeping—yes, that was the way, to his keeping— he experienced another of the reversals which marked his approach to her, only this reversal was more shaking, more abrupt, than those preceding it. He could have blurted, reaching out for her humbly, "I can't wait until Saturday. Come with me tonight. Not skating. And not with anyone else. I don't mean what I'm doing to you. I just want to be out. The two of us. We'll walk by the lake. I'll hold your hands. I'll hold you——"

The need to say it was so overpowering that for a moment he thought she knew. In the triangular small face below him, the brow so wide, the chin so narrow, the eyes so deep a gray, there was an answering spasm, as if she did. But quiet in his ears was unbroken, and after the first instant his own self-possession was strong enough so he knew he wouldn't. But as he mumbled something—"We'll call for you at eight, then"—and quickly fled, he knew that if cure weren't soon this was what would underlie meetings ahead.

When he rang her bell on the Saturday evening he still was the two things at once: rebellious against what he was doing, determined on it. Christine herself answered the door, drawing him more primly but perhaps with the same intentions as Barbara into a hall—"Will you wait while I pick up my wrap? And my family's somewhere——"

The likelihood of meeting her parents hadn't escaped him; he in a way was prepared for it. Not prepared, though, for the youth, the good looks, the social smoothness of the woman who, at Christine's "Mother——" emerged from the living room. Somehow he'd thought her mother must be dowdy; this woman was taller than Christine, still reasonably slender, crowned by blond braids. She extended her hand.

"Carl Reiss, you say? I believe Christine's mentioned you before— aren't you a fellow worker? A place as big as Trurog's, I don't see how you manage these acquaintances. When I go there I get lost entirely——"

While he was murmuring, Christine came in with her father, too; the parent, he at once saw, that she more resembled—a man in the much later fifties, slight, stooped, with thinning hair brushed across the wide but low forehead, and behind the eyes a retreat so entire it was almost withdrawal.

He too, though, made social effort. "Reiss. Reiss? Do I know the name? Harry Reiss—no, no, I see not. No relation. No familial similarities."

"You must drop in again when you're not bound somewhere; Christine should have people here often, more often; we're often quite lonesome, now her brother's gone, we see so few men. But if you've people waiting——"

Graceful, sending them off well. Yet, for Carl, a new discomfort to add to his store. In Mr. Landa was only the bowing formal abashment of a recluse and a scholar dragged from his studies to meet a daughter's male friend. In Mrs. Landa, though, under the surface friendliness, were both sharpness and antagonism, as if she disliked and distrusted him. *Rightly enough*, he must hotly think——

No time, then, for self-condemnation; Christine, at the car, must meet Bob. For the evening—his heart twisted on seeing it—she had put on a dress of warm rose color, against which the birthmark blended even if it didn't fade. On the way out he had considered warning Bob, but that would have destroyed his intention; Bob would have to rise to his own occasion.

Bob did, clowning. "You sure you're big enough to be a person, Miss Landa? You sure you don't more often go riding in pumpkins or hollyhocks?" The silver slide of Bob's eyes when he saw the mark was the first infliction on which Carl had planned.

He and Christine sat in back. Lillian, Bob's girl, sat in front when they picked her up; it wasn't until their arrival at the rink that she produced her covert start, her quick cover-up. It was Bob who soon said, "My turn for a chance with Christine; come on, Carl, we trade."

From then on Bob took up a third of her time, he too deftly teaching her a figure and with pride displaying it—"Quick, is that girl quick? Lil, you sit in back going home." Yet neither Carl nor Lillian, nor, he was sure, Christine, was in any way misled. Christine's skating grew surer, her cheeks once more pinked, her eyes lighted with exercise, but her shell was untouched.

On the way home they dropped Lillian first; Bob kept up his verbal pyrotechnics as long as Christine was in the car, but when Carl returned from taking her to her door he sat largely silent, in the silence on which Carl meant the evening should converge.

And which he must break. "Say it."

Bob's shoulders rose in their elephantine shrug. "Nice girl. I could like her myself. For a sister."

He had known Bob almost since the day Salloway had jerked him too—a burly young tough with red hair and a slapped face—out of the fight on the day he himself was hired. For other young men at Trurog's he had sometimes felt strong animosities, but not for Bob; from the first he saw what Bob's level would be. Bob was the ideal men's floorman—easygoing, ungainly, but with a good humor which never diminished. The uncomplicated male frankness Bob had just produced carried all the implications he had expected Bob's response to carry; this was the slap toward which he had maneuvered the evening, his cure. No man wanted a so-so girl; every man wanted a girl other men envied him.

But instead of cure he felt merely incited. "Naturally we stick to the physical."

The large shoulders once more rose. "Can't say she meets you more than halfway, either."

"If you mean she doesn't carry a mattress, like some other women I know—no, she doesn't."

Slashing, and intended to slash; Bob, he suspected, would be driving back to Lillian's apartment.

Bob replied shortly, "We better shut up and forget it."

They shut up. But not because it was forgotten. In front of Morrison's Carl said only good night.

Stalking upstairs toward his room through the dark, he told himself he should be satisfied. He had what he wanted. That reaction, stripped. But what he knew in the backwash was that even this made no difference. For all of a week, almost, at Trurog's, he'd done nothing but go through his routine, he was letting the registration period for summer school slide by without signing up, the men of the Housewares Repair Shop were surlier than ever, but even that made no difference. Barbara, everything tied up with Barbara, no difference. Miserably and helplessly he had one, only one, preoccupation—how soon he might see Christine again.

3 And Christine. How came she to marry him?

In her mirror, on a Sunday morning that August, there was only the stranger one evening had made of her face, the eyes widened and tremulous, the mouth crushed and too soft, so soft it would scarcely obey her and move. Anyone looking at her, she thought, must know she was different; anyone must guess something had happened.

Her mother called up the stairway, "We're waiting breakfast, dear," and that meant she must hurry. She called back, "One minute," seeing the unnatural laxness with which her lips formed the words, hearing the quick beat beneath the forced naturalness of her voice.

Turning part way from the mirror, she raised both hands to her face, stretching her forehead sideward and upward, pulling the skin tight at her temples, pulling her mouth taut, pushing it in, trying with her fingers to remold her usual appearance, letting her hands slide away, the right falling to the dresser top, the left remaining to cover the mark on her neck. Long ago that had been habit, that covering of the mark with one hand; it had been habit until one of her teachers drew her aside. "It really looks better, dear, if you don't do that; you're just calling attention."

The words carried kindness, covered pity, when pity was something for which, all her life, she had only rebellion, formless and hard to hold in. At almost the same time she was struggling to break off the habit, her father called her one day to his study, his manner embarrassed and lost as it was when he tried meeting a problem away from his books.

"Christine," he said jerkily, "I think you must evolve more—

perspective. There are people who—knowingly or unknowingly—like to remind others that they bear—stigmata. Children especially—young people—are cruel; they hunt for ways of making themselves feel superior. But you aren't singled out; you must know other children, many of them, who bear petty disfigurements; you must know some more seriously injured or crippled. By the time we are grown, Christine, we all carry marks, many of them. With some, as with you, these are outside marks, with others the marks are inside—I hope you grow up to see. What I would want of you, Christine, is not to set yourself in any way apart, but to think of yourself and of others with a common comprehension, knowing you bear the lot of a common humanity."

His voice was dry and emotionless, as if he were lecturing, his gaze directed not at her but at the brown hangings around the one window; after a pause in which she whispered, "Yes, Father," he said much more normally, "Well, I guess you can go now," and that was all. She slipped from his study with little understanding of what he said because she was too young for it, but at least she realized he was trying to help in a way really helpful and without pity; later she understood better, and she hadn't forgotten.

Only she wasn't able to accept what he offered, either. Others might bear inside marks, others be more seriously handicapped; that day in the Lake Room, a month or so back, she had seen in John Trurog the terrible interior crippling. But that didn't mean she accepted her own marking comfortably; it didn't mean she enjoyed people's eyes when they snagged and surreptitiously clung; she'd still wanted to keep herself covered. Now though, now——

"Dear, are you——" began her mother's voice from the bottom of the stairway, on a rising inflection, and she had no more time for preparing.

"Right there," she called from her door, and made herself run lightly down, catching her mother's elbow, when she reached the hall below, in an affectionate squeeze.

"Sunday breakfast," her mother half deprecated, half scolded. "Our one leisurely breakfast, our family—Christine, if you hadn't let that man keep you out so late—it must have been two and after, last night, before you were in."

She answered, "I'm fine; just a trifle sleepy." "Two and after—" no other reminder was needed to reopen the wonder, though even running downstairs it hadn't seemed it was she, running; under her shoes was the stair runner, under her hand the banister, but she seemed to float. Everything this morning was different—her mother, the square small hall, the walnut upright piano, the photographs on it; the oak desk beneath the window looked like a stranger's desk, the living room, too, was a stranger's—the red Persian rug, the red velveteen draperies, the stiffly undisturbed fumed oak davenport and rockers—all alien. The dining room she entered was alien.

"I can't see how roller skating can be so fascinating," her mother still fretted. "I've seen people skating; it all looks so dull. Merely circling and circling, that terrible racket——"

A chair at the table, her father. He alone wasn't alien, sitting so familiarly with gaze not on the egg he was breaking but on the open book beside his plate. For her father there was only one thing to feel, smiling love.

"Morning, Father."

"Morning, Christine."

"And I didn't know"—behind the coffee service, her mother was emerging more clearly into her resentments of Carl—"that rinks can keep open so late. Hasn't that young man even carfare?"

Always, toward any friend of hers, her mother developed these— what were they, exactly? These severities, these disapprovals. One of the things most like rain in the desert, when Carl said he was coming, was thinking, "Mother can't say he's second-rate; he isn't." Her mother hadn't said he was second-rate; instead, brows humorously lifted, she asked, "Do you think he has the idea we may not bathe thoroughly? He looks so faintly doubtful." Woundingly, as ever, picking out a quality that made you, yourself, uneasy. Every word Carl spoke, every expression of his face, betrayed his fastidiousness. He would never keep his interest in her. Never. Any day now, any week, it would be like Howie Degnan in college. A date after other dates, a good night like any good night; Howie kissed her too. Twice. And then nothing. Just an embarrassed "Hello, Christine," when they passed on the campus. Howard's fraternity brothers had probably worked on him. "Sure, Howie, sure. She's all right. She's all right. But you take for this prom, now——"

Her mother, continuing, "You can't think you're doing your looks or your health much good——"

Not yet reimmersed in his book, after taking his coffee, her father twinkled mildly and absently outward. "Not raining last night," he observed. "Always a chance young people out walking late may add to our astronomical data."

Again her heart moved with the rush of her love for him. Not often her father stayed out of his books, but when he did he was on her side, immovably.

She shaped answers carefully, smilingly. "We didn't skate last night; we went to see As You Like It in the University Grove. We met friends of Carl's, stopped for sodas and came home. I know it was lengthy, but it all was quite proper."

She didn't need rescue; she might never need rescue again. No matter how lightly the words fell, no matter how she fended off memory, she was dreamily back in last night once more, sitting with Carl on the long backless bench with starshine overhead and the soft summer dark all around, watching the fairylike people wink in and wink out of the stage-lit space under thick trees.

"Too nice to ride home, let's walk," Carl said. They didn't meet people, they didn't have sodas, they just walked, drifting upward like the many others who drifted, out of the small grassy bowl of the theater, finding a street that led homeward, approaching the lake.

"Late, but not too late," Carl said then. "Let's go down near the water." That was where it happened, on the steps to the promenade. "Look down from here——" Who said that, she or Carl? Leaning against the stone balustrade with more trees over them, looking down at the gray pale cement of the lake drive and the walk, at water reflecting in ragged small ripples the tracks made by lights in the sky. Carl moved close to her, kissing her; he had kissed her before, saying good night. "This tonight," she thought as a guard, "and then maybe no more." But he grasped at her roughly, his cheek pressing hers.

"I can't seem to help myself, Christine." His voice was as small and as torn as the ripples of the lake. "You'll have to marry me."

He was trembling, awaking a trembling in her. She whispered, "You can't want to marry me." She thought, "Not this, ever before; he can't ask to marry me, and then leave me; he can't." Fright, like falling-fright, filled her; perhaps fright like that of falling filled him; they clung as if shipwrecked, and each were a rock for the other; they murmured.

"Since that first day, Christine, that first day in the Lake Room——"

"But I couldn't believe it, I haven't believed it——"

"I've tried not remembering you——"

"One of the times you came up to see me, I thought then——"

"I've decided for me, Christine. You and nobody else."

"You could have anyone——" She couldn't say, "Look at me, you know how I'm marked," but that was what she felt dishonorable in not saying. His mouth again covered hers; all along her own body she felt the rigid control of his. "He could be pretending," she thought wildly then, "but why should he be? He can't do this to make fun of me——"

In the great hollowed-out spaces of her person existed a delirious wonder, but she was torn, too. Belief and disbelief, these were what tore at her; it must be real, it couldn't be anything but real, not with Carl's arms crushing her and her own hands on his shoulders. Yet it was unreal too. Unreal then, unreal when she finally said, "We can't stay. My mother——" unreal as they walked home in the wonder, unreal on the porch, unreal through the rest of the night, unreal now. She sat at this small breakfast table, Sunday sunshine streaming in over the plants of the window, her father's head bent again above his book, her mother behind the coffee urn, saying, "You can scarcely have hurried."

"No," she admitted, "not hurry——" No break; her recollections of last night took no time; belief and disbelief took no time at all. Nor the wonder.

Yet they also filled all time there was. The rest of that morning at church, dinner, the afternoon when her mother sent her upstairs for a nap. At four she roused from light dozing to a voice in the hall—"I don't blame her for sleeping; I'll be back after supper."

It couldn't be Carl; they'd made no plans for today. Disbelief once more uppermost, wonder receding, she paused only to snatch on shoes before running downstairs. Carl, facing her mother with his hat in his hands, was as strange as the hall, no more known to her than the day he said, "That might have been riot." A meticulously fine-looking young man, flat and so tall, high clean temples forking his sandy curls, blue eyes humbled a little in meeting hers but still fiercely self-proud, thin cheeks deeply cut. If he'd come for anything, she numbly thought, it was to tell her he'd made a mistake.

He said stiltedly, "It turned out to be quite—fine. I thought we might—walk again, if you like."

She heard protest—"Oh, not again. We'd rather you stayed here for supper. Christine——"

But what was necessary was getting away. She moved through the doorway, Carl following. Weightlessly but dully, because in this no emotion was possible, she walked on beside him; because no other action was possible she offered release.

"Last night—if you're sorry—all those stars and that moonlight—I know you were—carried away. You mustn't think I took it too—seriously; you mustn't think I'll be—hurt."

"Let's not talk until we're there." He walked so swiftly she could scarcely keep pace with him; except for an uncomfortably tight grasp of her elbow he was drawn entirely apart from her, pulled away into what looked like suffering. It was toward the Midwestern campus and then the way down to the lake that he led her; not until they reached the exact spot on the steps under the trees did he stop, abruptly, holding her now by both arms just under the shoulder.

"Christine—last night—don't think I'm not tormented. You've been with me all last night and today; I must love you, Christine; you haunt me."

He bent forward to kiss her, but quickly, at once drawing away once more to press her harshly against the balustrade. His breath, too, came quickly, as did hers; the tightness of his hands communicated itself to her as a renewed trembling. His words brought an ebbing of numbness, an inrush of weakness. Belief, then. She could believe him.

He repeated more quietly, "I must love you, Christine," but he kept himself apart. "I don't ask you to say that you love me; you're— maybe you'll think you do. You're the one who must decide if we marry or not; that's what I've come back to say. I don't want you to decide on a—on a physical basis; I've told you what's important for me; I've got to get on at the store. Even now, here with you, when I'm so—badly in love I'm on a—torture rack, I still know what will be first with me. If we marry you'll have to accept that and agree to it; you'll have to work with me; I won't want to change."

Last night, here on these steps, she had been caught by fright, now again, as his phrases struck at her, an uneasiness returned, replacing the weakness. He loved her, he asked her to marry him—wonder had been too overwhelming to leave space for much else. Now she must once more be aware of what made him intrinsically: his ambitions, his intensity. Ambition had her understanding, her sympathy, it was the intensity that disturbed.

Trying now for a different balance, she answered, subdued, "Isn't that the same for most marriages? Men—work for things. If we marry"—the word was still too much a marvel and must be breathlessly spoken—"I'd expect to—help where I could."

He asked, "Have you thought, though, what that means? I'm not profligate; I'm making twenty-two dollars a week; with what I saved in the army I've better than sixteen hundred in the bank. That should take care of us, it should cover emergencies. But I can't use it up for emergencies. Someday, perhaps not too far ahead, I may get my chance to buy Trurog stock. Bodali bought last; shares then were three hundred. Merchandise men are allowed five shares—that may be as much as they'll let me get, too, at first. I can't be given my chance at those shares and be unable to take it."

This time as he spoke some uneasiness, too, departed, to be replaced by chill. The day was so warm and so easy, earth smelled warm, they stood in warm mottled sunshine and shadow, warm wind lifted and rustled the leaves, on the lake a line of boats slid past with sails flapping. It seemed wrong, out of tune, to be plumped into this talk of money; the world this afternoon didn't look like a world where money was important. She knew she was being ridiculous; no one could be wrapped in wonder forever. "One thing I can count on with Christine," her mother said of her: "she's always sensible." She looked up at Carl, held so stiffly away from her, eyes constricted, mouth taut; compassion for him washed up; she managed a shaky laugh.

"I suppose we can't very well buy cake and keep cash," she agreed. "But must we be so—anxious? Let's sit down, here on the step. I could keep working. I've rather planned on working."

He obeyed, dropping to the step, but his head stayed back. "I wouldn't like that. I'd prefer you didn't."

"One thing I know already," she told him, whispering. "If we do—

marry, my husband will have the stiffest neck in Chapaqua." Raillery, begun in effort to lessen his tension. But the words "If we marry —my husband" automatically brought back the filling shy wonder.

He too was affected; he repeated, "If we marry—my wife," and more gently, after that, took her hands. "Suppose we did use eighteen a week from my salary," he said, "that would still leave us four. For our savings. If we found an apartment for twenty-five a month, and we certainly should be able to turn up something at that figure—say two hundred for furniture—within a year we should replace that——"

"I've money saved too," she put in, antiphonally. "You might allow me to supply some household things. Brides usually do."

Tentative. In a way more tentative than the night before, but with a recurring solidity. Wonder, this time, engulfed him too; his emotions wrapped her as securely as her own. Perhaps—he was the one to whom this intrusion came—even if they weren't entirely decided, they should tell someone. Her mother. Her father. She in the dream was unwilling. Not yet. Oh, not awhile yet.

She was the one, though, who found how hard such a secret can be to keep. Early, barely ten, when Carl brought her home; they must—this was one of their sober decisions—be sensible. From the kiss at her door and the whisper, "Only until tomorrow," she entered the front hall to know at once, from the rustle abovestairs, that her mother was both up and waiting. A second, no more, in which to shake off some of the bemused daze around her, before her mother called.

"Christine, that's you?"

"Of course, Mother." Moving at all, mounting the stairs, was like walking against heavy wind. The hall abovestairs was dusky, the only light that of the small orange night bulb in the side wall over the dresser base in which they kept linens, but even that was enough to reveal how her mother's sharpness, her antagonism, had evaporated, leaving what lay beneath, real anxiety.

"Christine——" In anxiety the sureness was less. Over the face between the thick hanging braids, over the figure in the lilac brocaded kimono, hung a troubled uncertainty. "Christine, aren't you seeing too much of that man? Last night—so late last night. And now, five hours. Five hours since you left here this afternoon. I trust you, you know I trust you. But five hours——"

"We did nothing but walk, Mother. We talked. Can't we—have this discussion another time? I'm tired. We——"

"No, Christine. I must talk to you now." At the stairhead her mother stepped aside, leaving a path, but in the bedroom it was she who pulled on the light. In the flooding illumination, against which Christine felt the need to shrink, her mother's agitation, the effort of her mouth, the indecision with which her fingers found, raveled and replaited one of the long braids, were once more clearly etched.

Always, in the family, it was her mother who labored hardest at keeping the family cohesive; her mother possessed a hunger for closeness, as if she needed to live not only her own life, which was full, but that of her husband, her children, as well. When Douglas married and moved so far, the injury, for her mother, was one that perpetually hemorrhaged. Such a pretty woman; even now she was pretty, her hair shining and thick in its loosened braids, her large blue eyes more striking for being harassed, cheeks flushed, bosom high. "Just no one like Louise Landa," her friends said of her, and she had so many friends, legion. In prohibition work, in Red Cross, in women's suffrage, at St. Augustine's. And Christine hadn't envied her these, even if sometimes as a schoolgirl she had resented a little the outside encroachments; for the most part with her mother she lived amicably, content to be maternally guarded. Over this now, though, she couldn't be content.

"Christine," her mother said, begging. "There can't be—don't tell me there's beginning to be anything serious between you and this—Reiss."

Anything serious. Why, in that plea, was there something she must fight against and deny, even if, in so doing, she told less than the truth? She moved back until the beveled edge of her chest of drawers came against her shoulders as indenting support, and helplessly, there, she was aware of how often—this morning, too, at the breakfast table—she falsified truth for her mother, with no other purpose than to keep herself covered.

"We're friends, Mother," she managed with difficulty. "Isn't that all right? You've friends too. So many more than I'll ever have. I—haven't your talent for friendship. I——"

"I don't stay out with my friends until two in the morning."

"Friends can have a great deal to talk about." In spite of her discomfort in what she was doing, a smile came with this, and after a moment some of her mother's disturbance ebbed. Her shoulders relaxed, her hands fell away from the braid, though one went sideward to the white iron rail of the bed.

"Christine." The next was still halting but stronger, "Christine, you can't have missed how I've tried to advise you, protect you—when you were born you were such a rosebud of a baby, perfect except for the—the one thing. I made up my mind then you weren't to be hurt; you know I've done everything I could for you. We'd have paid anything—anything—if your one flaw could have been—taken away. You've had the best we could give you, the best clothes, the best schooling, the best—love. I've hoped that you'd see—about boys and about men—you can't depend on them, Christine, can't trust them. There may be men who—are attracted to a girl because she is—different, but that's not a good quality in a man, Christine; it's not a good quality in this—Reiss."

No question but that her mother meant what she was saying, no question but that it came from an anguished desire to protect; the eyes meeting hers were harassed. "She believes, just as I've believed, that no man could really love me," Christine thought, and through all of her body felt the nerve ends by which that belief had come home to her—the earliest playmates who stood owl-eyed and fascinated, whispering, "Christine, can I touch it?" The older playmates who shouted, "Christine, Christine saw a snake, swallowed it whole and now it's jake," the succeeding apparent obliviousness as good manners took hold during high school, the boys who never forgot their audacity in taking her out, Howie Degnan. Even Miss Yetstein, lifting her queenly white-winged head from a course schedule, "My child, have you seen specialists about that birthmark?" And then, at Christine's stricken accounting, "Still, you shouldn't stop trying; perhaps with new advances in medical science—it's every girl's duty to be as attractive as possible, to marry if she can." Not likely as you are, Miss Yetstein too had thought. Not likely to marry as you are.

She had held that belief for so long and so well, bulwarked herself against it so thoroughly. Impossible—again incredulity swept up—that Carl should love her. Yet even as she thought so, even as her mother said loving her couldn't be a good quality in Carl, his mouth pressed hers, his arms held her, his voice whispered, "I must love you——" And Carl was good, he was fine.

Against silence her mother labored on. "Even if he is all right, I don't see how you can throw away what you've planned on, what you've done in college and since. Any marriage, even a good marriage, can be far from the dream it may seem to you now, Christine; it can be very cruel."

When Christine still didn't answer she turned away.

"That's all I'll say, Christine. Good night."

Pulling her knees to her chin, rounding her head down over them, she lay in bed curled to a ball.

Easy to shove aside what had happened since she came back to the house, easy to resubmerge in that other, the wonder, the sweet loving wonder. Before she did that, though, it might be well to think through what her mother had said. She might mutinously—this Carl was doing for her—refuse the validity of the first of this, but in the last there was something which wasn't so simply dismissed.

"What you've planned on, what you've done in college and since." What she'd planned was so safe, so defended. It was socially, it was in the lists of possible selection as a mate, that disfigurements such as hers meant most; it was among adolescents, where any stigmata bore a blown-up importance. Among adults, where qualities other than the physical began taking on stature, she would fare better—she wasn't too overborne by her handicap to have seen this long ago. In a Lake Room hostess, seldom really looked at, it meant something but not too much; she was accepted because she worked well. Carl wasn't the only one who looked forward to enterprise; someday, she'd thought, she might have a small tearoom. There, working mostly behind scenes and with employees, a birthmark would bear little weight. One of the first things she'd had to do, going out with Carl, was harden herself in a different way against the notice, resenting it not for herself but for him. Married to him, there might be new injuries from which to shrink. As she grew older, after his first love was over, he might be repelled by her.

"Any marriage, even a good marriage, can be far from the dream it may seem to you now. It can be very cruel." In this her mother spoke from an increase of quiet and dignity. Many of the activities her mother went in for, women's suffrage, especially, had often seemed to her somehow ridiculous. All that belligerence against men, all that insistence on one's rights, all that talk about women's place in the world. Just the same she had reason to be grateful women now had chances; no more than a few years ago, marked as she was, she might have had no life except a dull one at home. Perhaps in the past many women had married because it was that or nothing; perhaps, as her mother's friends a little too stridently insisted, women from now on would be choosier, perhaps more of them find satisfactions through themselves rather than through husbands or children.

Carl too. Impossible to avoid knowing that, even as he spoke of marrying, he shrank from marrying. Perhaps he was right in reluctance, had been right tonight. They might owe it to themselves to get outside opinion. Not from her mother; her mother was too distraught by emotion. Not from her father—he was too unworldly. Some one of the girls she had known in college, it might be, girls who by this time were mostly themselves married. Esther Leslie. "Christine, you too?" Esther would at once cry, ecstatic, sitting on her bedraggled couch, surrounded by undarned socks, folded dry diapers and milk-smelling teething rings, hugging on her lap the squalling five-month-old boy who would be tearing at what remained of the side wisps of her hair, "Christine, that's marvelous. You know there's nobody on this earth I'd rather see get engaged than you——"

No, not Esther; Esther lived too much by illusion and precedent. Most people lived by illusion and precedent. No use, really, in talking to anyone outside. Instead, talk further with Carl. Let Carl, again, pour out doubt; pour out more fully the doubts he tonight had only half produced; poor Carl, she'd shunted aside what he might have said. While she on her side——

Just rehearsing what she might say, how he would answer, took her back to the dream. His hand covered hers——

But she did talk it over with someone else, and before she talked it over with Carl. In the morning, with Carl, there was only a stolen half moment in her office——

"Carl!"

"Christine, you're real, then, you're real!"

The kiss of their hands, the slide against her hair of his cheek, were all they could have before he said, "I must get to my floor." They couldn't have even a lunch hour together; lunch hours were her busiest time. It was midafternoon when her phone rang.

"Christine?" The voice over the wire was very light. "Carl's here by my desk; we're agreed—you can speak to him yourself—it's my day to take you to dinner. Man or no man, I'm seeing you sometime too. Now, don't tell me——"

Against Harriet's teasing she was as helpless, apparently, as Carl, who came on to say stiffly, "Do go ahead, Christine; I could use extra sleep tonight." Impossible to tell, from his tone before Harriet, what he really wanted; she found herself pinned. To the dinner, to not seeing Carl that night—illuminating how that loss loomed up as irreparable. Not that she considered any confidences with Harriet, not then; Harriet was still too much a stranger. It wasn't until the ensuing dinner was nearly over, dessert eaten, only coffee over which to linger, that she began divining any particular purpose in Harriet; Harriet, up to then, had been no more than her previous self.

"That Hubert Hobart," Harriet said of Christine's immediate superior in the Lake Room, "why doesn't he buy his clothes tailor-made? He should know, a paunch like his—he looks like a corseted back-side-to camel."

But then, as Christine obediently laughed and they waited, she at once knew Harriet had more to say. Harriet seldom fidgeted, at least the Harriet she'd seen seldom fidgeted, but the Harriet now sitting across from her in the restaurant booth was suffering an obvious failure of ease, lifting a left wrist to turn its bracelets, resettling the green sailor that tilted at so audacious an angle over one eye, resettling the green georgette fichu on her shoulders, smoothing up the hair at the back of her neck, avoiding Christine's eyes.

"Christine." The act of plunging, while still uncertain, was also forthright and obvious. "You've been seeing a lot—haven't you?—of Carl Reiss. I can't help noticing—I've known him so long, so much longer than you have. Since before he went into the army. He's a nice person, Christine, I like him. You know what Salloway says of him, don't you? Salloway says he wishes stores had figureheads the way sailing boats once had; he'd have Carl right out there on the prow.

He looks so exactly what the store's supposed to be, scrupulous and high-principled. You can't have missed——"

Frontal, if chattering, approach, against which Christine sat taken aback, feeling almost attacked, and yet curiously receptive. It wasn't for Harriet to enter this domain, but just the same, since she was entering—no one could say Harriet lived by illusion and precedent.

She said fendingly, "I don't think I should discuss Carl, not this way. I——"

Instead of being shunted aside, Harriet pounced. "As serious as that? You laughed without many compunctions when it was Hobart I talked about. You must really be thinking of marrying Carl."

In greater discomfort, more thoroughly caught, Christine struggled again both with protest and wanting to hear, now, what Harriet might come to. Up from her bosom, over her throat and face passed waves of flushing heat. She managed to stammer, "I can't say I'm thinking of marrying him——" but then another struggle, another honesty broke through; she said, "There's no question of my choosing him; if any-thing it's a question of whether he should choose me. He might do so much better than me——"

Harriet relaxed and laughed. "You know, I suspect that's like you. Carl *might* do so much better than you, mightn't he? He might, for instance, make a play for me. Salloway's secretary. Chester Ohman's niece. I can't exactly travel in Chapaqua's best social circles, but I'm a judge's daughter; I could if I wanted to hang on the fringes. And there's Barbara. Barbara almost *is* in. You can't help knowing he's paid some attention to Barbara. And he fascinates Barbara; Barbara says he has exciting depths, a fact I don't doubt in the least."

Christine half rose. "If you please, I don't——" Her handbag and her gloves were in a corner of the booth; she fumbled. But then Harriet laughed again, stretching a hand across to her wrist, contrite and cajoling.

"No, I'm sorry; I won't be insufferable. I probably don't mean that as it sounds." Then as Christine, still resentful, sank back, "To be frank, I may not know what I do mean. You know, if it were Barbara thinking of marrying Carl, I'd probably just think, 'Good for Barbara.' For you, though, I don't know."

Her glance came up, for an instant holding something that might have been both embarrassed and embarrassing if it weren't so quickly cut off. "It certainly isn't that I resent Carl as an intrusion; that would be too funny. It must be—one thing you can't miss about Carl, Christine, he's a man who intends to get on. I don't say that's a bad characteristic; he hasn't talked to me of it, but anyone can see——"

Nearing, at last, Christine's own uncertainties, or at least nearing some of them. Again she felt a finger tip of guilt, but also the urging of a need——

"But I admire that! If I marry Carl, I'd want him to get on; a man isn't anything if he hasn't a goal. He——"

Harriet's gaze had gone to her two hands, linked on the table top. "What I'm getting at, I suppose—I know it's again insupportable, my saying this—is my feeling that Carl's ambition, some of his other characteristics, may make him hard to live with. All giving in, I'd guess, would be on your side."

The thing said, out at last, or so Harriet's manner indicated; her hands now flattened on the table edge, her gaze was steady if averted, her voice come to full stop. Once more, and so hotly, Christine felt the geysering of guilt. Criticism—wasn't this criticism of Carl she was listening to? But above guilt the other need still was stronger.

She denied, "But that's nothing against Carl, either. Shouldn't that be the way with all marriages too? Is it so hard to be the one who gives way? Isn't that the least any woman can——"

Harriet leaned back, all intensity, all focus, now gone. She said much more equably, passing over to an abstract philosophy, "Do we come to that? That what you'd get, in Carl, is the way of all men and all marriages? I shan't argue. You'll be giving up something, you know, if you marry. Your job in the Lake Room. 'We hire married women at Trurog's, yes, but girls who marry automatically resign—' you know the regulation; good old Trurog's, it isn't going to waste money on female help during any adjustment period. You've had plans of your own, haven't you? This job, a better one, sometime perhaps Hobart's——"

Arrival, here, at what her mother had said.

"I—of course. But not intensively, not anything I——" Admission, but one which, now she was this far, she might as well make straightforwardly, "Not anything I'd have trouble giving up. At least I don't think so."

"Sure of that?" Harriet's eyes once more were direct. "We're fairly new in the world, you know, both of us. Twentieth century and a war product. Before us women have worked, yes, but only because they had to. If we're working it's for emotional reasons. Our fathers would keep us. No, wait," when Christine would once more have broken in, "this is something I've had to beat out. I know why I'm working; I I want a place in the world made by myself. I don't expect to marry, I'm not sure I want to, and I know that's heresy, as close to treason as a woman can get."

The lids fluttered downward, and the next came with renewed loss of ease. "I've looked around me at living; I see it as—conflict. If you don't marry, then no matter how many friends you have you're in a way solitary, you do your battling alone. If you do marry, then you're not solitary; you may think you do your battling jointly and for joint goals. But you can't look at marriage, not really look, without seeing struggle there too, battle crisis and armistice. Maybe what you do when you marry is choose your life's major antagonist. Then again I think otherwise—maybe it's just life that's the adversary, for everyone. We used to think it took human villains to be a ruin of hopes; now that's not necessary. Just the way things are is enough."

Roughened, this last, almost harsh, and when it was said Harriet sat silently, gaze not on Christine nor on anything else immediate, mouth hard. And Christine too sat caught, hands unclenched but rigid against the table. All this that Harriet said, was this what her mother last night had fumbled toward? What she herself had fumbled toward, as she lay later in bed? Was this what life really was, inevitable defeat, so that no matter what you did, marry or not marry, it made no real difference?

No, not acceptable. Not for her, Christine Landa. Not, young as she was, without trying, not with push in her bones and her muscles, not with pulse in her blood stream, not with will and desire in her mind and her heart. Denial didn't have to be a matter of thought.

She said flatly, "I'm not buying that; not taking it, either. Whatever I do, I'll manage. You'll see." But then that left her too; she sat limply, humbly, fallen to openness, "—if I'm doubtful, it's not about the way life is—or marriage—or Carl. It's about me. You can see what I'm——" The hand came to her neck. "No one knows——"

"Who doesn't know?" The Harriet whose brows now so amusedly shot upward might never have brooded; this Harriet was entirely brittle. "You're speaking, I might inform you, to a female who at eleven could rest her chin on the heads of any partners her teacher managed for her at dancing school. A female whose mother was on the small side, like you. 'I declare I don't know what to do for you, Harriet——' Mother's been dead three years, but I still hear her saying it, 'I declare I don't know what to do for you, you're such a behemoth.' She loved me, too. Sometimes I think the people who love you most want to hurt you most."

"That's different." Christine's trouble was too old for an easy giving away. "You——"

"Really different? Or just in your eyes?"

"There are people, though——"

"Are there? Oh, maybe a few. The right little, tight little boys and girls, up to college age. Seldom beyond that. The ones who are born in, and have money enough and looks enough and even spirit enough, and who don't seem to be flawed. Like my dear cousin Barbara. 'We're the ones,' they say, 'we're the only ones, no one else can get in.' Sometimes I think that's the worst birth-hurt of all, the cruelest to get over."

"Harriet, you're——" Christine sat back from it, blinking.

"All right, my friend, let's say it does pay to put up a struggle, or some part of a struggle. Any reason why you shouldn't struggle with the best? 'So I'm marked,' you say to yourself, 'and what of it? I'll show 'em. I'll get everything anyone else gets, including, if I find my little heart sets that way, this Carl Reiss.' "

Echo, such flippant echo, of what her father once said, and nothing to do for it but laugh. A little helplessly, unacceptingly still, feeling the earlier resistance still, the earlier bruising, the earlier guilt, but also the soothing.

"And now"—Harriet shook herself, and was at once briskly done with all colloquy, resettling the sailor, reaching for the dinner checks under her coffee cup, taking up handbag and gloves—"let's say I've blown you a big enough bubble. Bigger, I'll say this, than I intended blowing. You know, don't you, dolly, that if you do intend marrying you should avoid me like the seven plagues of Egypt? Mary Pickford, Beatrix Fairfax, pick them to consort with."

But when Christine rose she paused to add a word more, shaking Christine's arm in a solicitude half real, half mocking. "You know how people *do* marry, don't you, all self-respecting people? Not in reason, darling, not by looking at what looms. The least you marry with is dewy-eyed abnegation; you *rush* into marriage, dear. You know, the moth and the flame."

She stepped from the streetcar, and a shadow at once drew away from an elm on the parking. Carl.

"Christine, I couldn't sleep anyway," he said, for him, wretchedly. "I couldn't wait until tomorrow to see you. I know Harriet—what was it she wanted to say?"

Under her forearm his hand came cradlingly, but it twitched slightly; he was, she at once saw and knew, both tired and strained, his face darkened and bitten by weariness, his body taut with the strain. If she were absorbed by the questions confronting her, so was he, and he was more highly strung.

To ease him she made light of their common distraction. "You know Harriet; she couldn't say little."

"Anything against me?"

"Of course not. How could she? And would I have listened if she had?"

He walked, after that, just a trifle less jerkily, and feeling through her own body the partial relaxing of his, she heard herself again saying, "There are people, though——" and Harriet at once asking and answering, "Are there? Oh, maybe a few——"

So far she had thought of Carl as one with the flawless, the untouched, the secure; it took that "Anything against me?" and then the easing, to tell her how wrong she had been. "He too," she thought with understanding. "Nothing that shows, but he too." Perhaps she had been drawn slightly away from him; that talk with her mother, this just ended talk with Harriet, had been sobering and chilling, to say the least. Seeing him as he now was, however, so tired, glimpsing behind his defenses, she felt the pull back to him.

On their steps, quietly resting her hands in his, she rendered partial version of what Harriet said. "I don't think she thinks I'd be—bad for you; she thinks almost everyone has—faults. She thinks as a person you're very fine. She says she doesn't think she'd want to marry, herself, but then she's not in love. She thinks not marrying is lonesome, but that perhaps what you do when you marry is choose a—well, she said a major antagonist. In a world where you don't need antagonists, because just the way things are is enough. She got pretty serious, for Harriet."

She smiled as she said it, draining its force, but he didn't smile back.

"Nothing else?" he asked caustically. "Not even that I'd always want my own way?"

Forced admission. "She did sort of suggest that."

"I told you myself."

"I remember."

He didn't push it; he in fact stood quiet. "But even this," she thought with dismay, "is in its way a small battle, the two of us standing here, with nothing clear, actually, to say or do." But then after a while, just from time, he once more eased a little.

"I don't suppose," it was his turn to offer, "we need be so damn miserable. Isn't this what's supposed to be mainly all starshine? Finding a girl I want—come on, sit down. Do you think this is the usual latter-day preface to marriage, all this question and caution? Or did we just make a mistake? That's quite possible——"

His turn, too, to talk on. "I've told you I may not be suited to marriage; I've liked being alone, liked following my own way, liked not thinking of anyone else. I've had asthma, too, several attacks of it; that's what put me down in the army. When you think what might happen——"

To say the least, again, sobering. In marriage, as she began to see, you took on more than a partner, you took on all that partner's needs, his troubles. Haltingly at first, but then more fully, she brought out her uncertainties too. When she ended they sat silent. Perhaps she'd been right, yesterday, they'd been carried away. Perhaps he had used the right word, a mistake. They might owe it to themselves to stay apart awhile, examining their feelings with more detachment. Two weeks, three weeks, a month——

Resolution which she helped form, yet toward which she felt only an injuring ache, as of something tremendously lost. They stood up to clasp hands on it; he said, "And another thing, we'll get rest. We'll both of us shove it away and get sleep."

He already looked rested. He looked relieved. He bent almost gaily. "Besides, we can seal it." A kiss of mischievous lightness, but a kiss of no end. With an inarticulate, half-smothered protest, as soon as his lips touched hers, he snatched her in close to him, crushing her, burying his face in her neck, rolling flesh against flesh that before had known no flesh to meet it, her birthmark. He whispered, "I can't, Christine, I can't, I can't——"

Where was reason then? Where resolution? Stripped from her as it was stripped from him; falling away, sliding away, leaving her un-barriered, quivering—all those other barricades too, the long old barri-cades of her long old defensiveness, snatched away. Not anything her father said, not anything Harriet said, but this toppled those barri-cades: Carl loved her. No future disaster or hurts could destroy her, because this and this only had meaning; she had feared, but now knew without terror, he both loved and desired her. Beside the splendor of being desirable, the glory of being a woman, desirable, there was noth-ing to balance.

She sobbed to him, "Anything, anything. I shan't mind——" Dewy-eyed abnegation, and who said that? She knew now how deep abnegation could go; anything she had been, anything she might be, was so little to give up. She'd have other goals, Carl's, and a new one of her own. Other loves might not remain radiant, theirs must. What-ever the world might be, they would win over it.

It was a long time before Carl pulled away; exultance covered him too.

He said wryly, "It seems we do too decide on a physical basis."

4   Other loves might not remain radiant, theirs must——

Theirs for an engagement was brief; they were married the first Saturday of October, after no more than eight weeks. Long enough, though, to bring her against some of the forces she must sustain and cherish, because they were what maintained the illumination in which she and Carl now together were wrapped, as well as some of the forces she must resist and parry because they were what darkened or tar-nished it. Not important, always, perhaps not in detail important, but seeming important, seeming intensified in importance, because in this prelude every small incident, every phrase spoken, meant a measure to be later magnified.

On the side of the dream, to be hugged and remembered forever, were most of the hours she and Carl had together, the evening he slid down her fourth finger a high-set solitaire that had been his mother's, closing her hand tightly over the band, the late summer evenings they roller-skated again, or danced or walked, the Sunday afternoons—Carl's favorites—when they wandered from painting to painting in the Art Institute, or attended university concerts, picnics when he lay for hours quiet in the grass with his head in her lap, the September weeks when—wedding plans made—all their spare hours went for scrubbing and painting and furnishing the three rooms which were to be their home. The gaiety and the emotion-shot haziness and the rapt serious-ness which invested their working and talking and planning, the min-utes he held her again in his arms and she rested her head on his shoulder.

On the side of the dream, too, were comments such as Harriet's, coming into the Lake Room next day to shield her eyes resignedly, "No, don't tell me, all I had to do was step through the door to be blinded." From Harriet, or herself, the news spread infectiously, her waitresses sidling up to her beamingly, "Is that true, Miss Landa? Is that true, you're going to be married?" Even Mr. Hobart flashed his gold-filled teeth, unctuously hearty. "I hear I'll be losing a mighty fine girl."

Of what she had most feared, astoundingly little. It was almost as if, once she had come this far and been chosen, her disfigurement were to be forgiven her. Bob Gokey, admitting his knowledge, was boister-ously awkward. "Say, what's this I hear? You and Carl taking it hard?" One solitary waitress, one she had reprimanded, spat insolently with her eyes fixed to the birthmark, "Maybe they like coffee spilled in saucers; you never can tell about some people's tastes." For the rest, almost nothing. Harrison Salloway asked for her by name after a Policy Luncheon, and held out his hand, grinning widely. "That Reiss is a sharp-eyed young fellow; I hope I get asked to the wedding."

On the other side, to be contended against, endured or glossed over, as best they could, there was first of all telling her parents, a moment mutually supported because Carl of his own accord offered to be with her. "I'll have to face them sometime; we can just as well get through it together." But miserable just the same, she at first beside her father, because as usual she went to his study to fetch him—"Father, there's something I—we—want to tell you and Mother." And then in the living room, her father moving to stand patting her mother's back as she rose from the davenport, Christine herself moving to stand beside Carl. "We're—planning to be married." No other way to say it, not really. No way less bare.

Her mother answered stonily, "In spite of—your denials, Christine, I guess we—I guess we aren't surprised," but Christine convulsively lowered her face to her hands and her hands to the front of Carl's coat, where his arms came around her, and what she buried herself against was the bleak desolation—not reconciled, perhaps never to be entirely reconciled, but no longer contending—of her mother's eyes, and the equally desolate wetness of her father's.

After a while, after her father began his effort, "Now, now, this is a damp way, I must say, to greet such a joyous occasion," she pulled from Carl to brush tears first against her mother's shoulder, then her father's—"You won't be losing me; I'll never move far, like Douglas; we'll live right here in Chapaqua; probably you'll see me every week." But the words had a thumbed invalidity. This too so many girls and boys must have said through the ages, but it meant very little; she was breaking away from them; she no longer belonged with them but with Carl. If she had children she herself must someday meet the same heartbreak; they had brought the same grief to their parents, but that didn't lessen their present sorrow or her sharing of it, and perhaps —in the moment she felt it—they knew more of the future to which she went forward than she.

Then, too, against the hours when the two of them, she and Carl, were so joyously one with another, there were other hours when he drew into moods of revolt. "We can just as well know what we're doing, hopping along in the track, letting Mother Nature take over." One of his blackest moods followed a visit to his doctor. "Laughed, mostly. Asked if I was trying to shake you. But he had to admit asthma comes back, no one can say when or for how long. It's a magnificent prospect."

"Everyone's bound to be sick." By that time she repeated assurances sturdily. "I will be too. We can as well count on it." But he stayed angrily gloomy for days, chafing, she soon sensed, not only because of what this affliction might mean to their marriage but because of its threat to his future at Trurog's.

In most decisions—their choice of apartment, the picking of furniture, a hundred and one incidentals—compliance on her part was so easy it didn't exist as compliance. His interest in the home they were setting up was as detailed as her own, and his taste—this was a happy discovery of their courtship—proved much better than hers; time and again, taking his advice on paint or wallpaper, chairs or curtains, she came to delighted agreement.

Here and again, though, they met matters in which conformity wasn't so ready. Concerning their wedding date her mother, lips pitifully trembling, begged that they wait—"A year, Christine, until you're sure; you can't go into this unless you are." Her father too counseled delay. Carl was against any waiting at all. "This half state——" he impatiently gnashed. "Let's get it over and get on with our lives." She wouldn't have wanted him otherwise, but her parents' wish pulled at her too, and she herself would gladly have waited; the bliss in which she now lived, the planning, the buying, her very hesitances, were too sweet to let pass.

Carl's, here, was entirely the voice that decided. It was over the kind of wedding they should have that accord grew more difficult. "Weddings." Carl's grimace expressed his distaste. "You know yourself they're barbaric; they're vestigial, like an appendix. For heaven's sake let's plan something quiet, let's go to a judge or a justice."

"The *least* we can do"—this was her mother, pleading almost with horror—"Christine, the least you can do for us is a church wedding. All my friends, we've belonged so long at St. Augustine's—Christine, you can't *slink* into marriage."

Again, and to herself it was admitted, she was on the side of her parents. Once in a while, oh, not often, but once in a while, carefully telling herself it could never be possible, she had let herself dream of a wedding. St. Augustine's, always, dim orderly quiet and fern-banked spaces, music, ribbons, flowers, the pews filled with people come only for them, veiled shining white satin in which she would walk up the aisle with her father to stand at an altar—now when that vision had a right to be possible, now when she could see Carl awaiting her at that altar, the dream took on a stronger and more possessive force, holding something she deeply needed and wanted. Marrying in this way, it would be as if her parents gave her up proudly and perfectly, marrying in this way, it would be as if she walked to Carl proudly and perfectly too. She wouldn't use her mother's word, slinking, for the way Carl wanted to marry, but it wasn't acceptable either.

"You must have people you'd like to have see you get married," she entreated. "Your father, your aunt—why, I haven't even met them. We can't shunt them aside; they'll have a right to feel hurt all the rest of their lives. And Mr. Salloway." Here she felt herself almost adroit. "He told me he wanted to come to our wedding."

He answered tightly at once, "Whoever I have around, it won't be my father, it won't be any of my people. You can quit counting on that."

Once or twice before, haltingly suggesting a day trip to Elmwood, she had met this same tightness. In her own family there inevitably were frictions, but not serious cleavage; the contrary emotion in Carl confused and worried her. All she knew of his family, after these weeks, was little more than she'd learned the first evening. She tried probing——

"But why? They must think so much of you—an only child. And you can't be ashamed of them. Are you"—this must rear its head—"is it—are you ashamed of me?"

"Of course I'm not ashamed of you; how can you ask it? Nor of my father either. He's all right, as fathers go. I don't have to want him around. Just forget it."

She couldn't forget it, but confronted by his curtness, she had to abandon it, at least for the time being.

"That still leaves the others. Mr. Salloway——"

"Salloway doesn't belong to my private life."

They stood once again on their stairs, when he said it, she against the balustrade, he a step or two lower; abruptly, after flinging the last at her, he dropped contention to take her hands, lowering his cheek to hers, he in turn imploring.

"Christine, we don't want people mixed in this, do we? What we'll have is for the two of us alone. It won't affect anyone else."

"No," she wanted to answer. "Not true. Every marriage affects every other marriage, perhaps every marriage affects everyone else in the world." But she didn't say that because she didn't know how to defend it; it would have sounded no more than ridiculous. Responsively her arms rose, submissively her cheek met his. When he begged she wasn't able to reject. But this time she wasn't able to give in all the way, either.

Feeling a relinquishment like the spending of heart-strength from her body, she agreed, "We'll give up the church wedding; I'll persuade Mother somehow. But there'll have to be something."

Their compromise, finally, was on a wedding as small as a wedding could be, at her home. The two of them, her parents, the rector of St. Augustine's, Harriet for a bridesmaid, Bob Gokey for best man.

"And someone else for you," she insisted. "There has to be someone from your side."

"If there must be," this was his last unwilling concession, "then perhaps Mrs. Morrison, from where I room. But not that brat of hers——"

At times it was a substantial prospect enough; it was substantial enough, for instance, the late afternoon Harriet phoned to say Mr. Salloway wanted to see her, and she went up to find Carl there too, and Harriet's desk decked out with a wedding bell, frosted and decorated cakes, lemonade.

"Cheat us out of a wedding," Mr. Salloway grumbled, but the grin extended itself across most of his face. Critically taking her hands, he stood back to survey her, then kissed her resoundingly on both cheeks.

"There, that's bridal color," he pronounced with satisfaction. "Formula I'll recommend to you, Reiss." She was made to stand with Carl before the window in Salloway's office while people filed past them—"Good luck to you, Miss Landa." "Lucky dog, you are, Reiss; I'll trade shoes——" "You'll know what the world's about when you're a husband, Reiss." "It isn't so often we get a romance like this, both parties from Trurog's——" Not everyone in the store, naturally, but a good number from their departments, stock girls, buyers and merchandise men, Mr. Hobart shepherding a crew of waitresses, Mr. Bodali and Mr. Leverett, Mr. Ohman but not Barbara, Mr. Trurog sidling swiftly through the press at its thickest.

"You might let Carl know this—we're putting him on first. Gloves, handbags and jewelry. Little raise for him, too." Salloway whispered it to her privately, and then, much more publicly, produced a silver coffee service as a gift from the store.

"Oh, thank you," she said over and over. "It's lovely, I'll never forget." Definitely this glow was on the side of the dream; Carl too was taking it pleasantly; his answers wry and embarrassed, "Last position on earth I ever planned to be in—I guess when you're married you need luck—kitchen equipment I'm buying myself, all soft wood——" but they were good-humored and went well; with his shoulders and head back, high color in his face as there must be in hers, eyes more alight than ever, he looked handsome and vital and pleased and uplifted; emotion he shed toward her, touching her arm sometimes, glancing toward her, was controlled but, in some ways, as fiercely tender as in their closest moments.

Afterward, at their planned wedding, that day in Salloway's office was the balm which, part of the time anyway, she recalled; their planned wedding, when it so quickly came, inevitably mixed with its other qualities some of that insubstantiality she had feared it might have, and which by transference she had feared must be fought against for their marriage too.

Dressing alone in her room with its packed suitcases, she had no one to come in but her mother, who at once asked and answered, "Need help, Christine? I don't know why you should—it's a long time, isn't it, since I've helped you dress." Her mother, at eleven in the morning when the wedding was to be at one, was already fully dressed in the accordion-pleated crepe de chine which she and Christine had picked out together; her mother was abandoned entirely to an unnatural helplessness. One of the reasons for big weddings, Christine thought compassionately then, was to keep mothers too distraught for thinking; without commotion they felt only bereft.

Her own dress was of pale blue georgette with a gathered high neckline. "Too bad, just this once, you can't have it lower," the dressmaker said, but that was meant kindly. Pretty women, brides especially, were supposed to be filmy, doll-like, unearthly; the picture her mirror gave back to her—"You can't have anything but one of these new dropped waistlines," so the dressmaker also said, "and a short full skirt"—was merely rather childish—and marked. A veil would have covered her, people would have buoyed her; she wouldn't have had so much time for reminder and looking.

Harriet, when she came, was a temporary stopgap. "Christine, you're lovely." Harriet for the day was giving over philosophy, perhaps giving over intelligence, to be entirely kindly and warm. "I never before noticed—your hair where it springs from your head is much lighter. Not the least like a halo—halos roost on top, don't they? But very effective——" Harriet talked away time. It was when the moment came for the two of them, carrying their flowers, to start downstairs together, that things once more were so much too constricted. Carl and Bob Gokey facing the Reverend Mr. Pinckney under a chrysan-themum-covered wedding arch set against the dining-room folding doors, and beside them, in the everyday living-room chairs, only her father and mother, a strange middle-aged woman and a half-grown boy. Someone, probably the boy, said quite loudly, "Well, well, here's the bride." Her father, sitting fiercely erect, snapped "Quiet." After that, for a few minutes, moving forward against the hushed coolness to stand beside Carl, who half turned for a softly warm welcoming glance and then cupped a hand under her shaking right arm, feeling Harriet move up beside her supportingly, it was all right again, the dream and the wonder took her, the room with its few people faded backward. Only the two of them stood together when the black and gold book rose to the height of the Reverend Mr. Pinckney's chest, and his rumbling deep voice began, "Dearly beloved——"

But later, after those few, those incredibly few transported seconds —"Wilt thou," "I do," and the ring and Carl's kiss—there was so be-wilderingly little more. The Reverend Mr. Pinckney's handshake, her mother's kiss and her father's, Bob Gokey's and Harriet's, congratula-tions from the middle-aged woman and the boy, who were, of course, Mrs. Morrison and the son Carl hadn't wanted. That was all, or so nearly all; better indeed if it were all, and they hadn't had to go on to the flatness of the Reverend Mr. Pinckney so hurriedly leaving, "Sorry, yes, sorry, we ministers, you know, are busy people; another wedding in forty-five minutes."

"He can't leave yet," Christine's inner voices protested. "This can't be all there is to a marriage, not anything as important as a marriage; we need more than this to begin from." Her mother had hired a woman to put on a wedding breakfast, but there was a half hour of waiting, a half hour in which Harriet chattered and Bob Gokey joked and her father tried bravely, but in which remarks suitable to weddings seemed to die in an overgreat quiet. "Who'd ever believe that I'd cry, myself——" "Here you are, fella, a married man—ever think anything so painful would be done so fast?" "Simply lovely, everything is, my, that arch, streamered like that, and all white, don't tell me you made it yourselves." Things said at weddings needed press and din. Mrs. Morrison, it soon grew evident, was deciding Christine's parents had held to this small affair because they couldn't afford more—"I had a church wedding, myself, one of the things I said when Mr. Morrison went was I still was grateful I had a church wedding, but the way people look at things nowadays, I know it's all different; home weddings are nice too. So homey."

Her mother's stiff injury—"We'd have preferred a church wedding for Christine, this is entirely their choice"—introduced an oblique give-and-take which was almost unpleasant. As soon as his ring went on her finger Carl had clutched her hand tightly and kept it clutched, but once the interchange between her mother and Mrs. Morrison began he stood stiffly away from her, his mouth betraying his distaste and discomfort. He muttered, "I knew it was a mistake having that woman. And look at that son she had to drag along——"

The son, nothing better at hand, now sat plopped in a chair, leg over one arm, in a pose of superior boredom. "No," Christine protested again, "it can't be this way; this is starting us out wrong." Yet even if she too tried chattering, if she tried being feverish, she got nowhere. By the time the doors opened to the exquisite table, it too streamered and banked with chrysanthemums, the breakfast was only something to live through. Everyone tried again, a bright burst, "Mrs. Landa, I think you expected this, I think you knew you'd have company." "Nothing at all elaborate, since it's only a home wedding——" "Last fall, even this spring, we could have had a little something extra in this punch——"

It was Mrs. Morrison, though, now on a new tack, who got in the most wordage. "—can't tell you all how we'll miss him. It never was because of any practical reason we wanted Carl with us—Mr. Morrison left us very comfortably fixed, quite all we could ask for. But just for the company. Like another son to me, or more maybe a brother——"

At last a flurry, the flurry of rising from the table, of running upstairs to change, helped this time by both her mother and Harriet, of throwing her bouquet—caught by Mrs. Morrison—of stopping on the porch for last frantic embraces—"We'll write, Mother. Oh, Father, we'll send postcards every day"—while on the steps below Bob Gokey and the Morrison boy pounded Carl's back, pelting him with the ribaldry that also goes with weddings—"don't do anything I wouldn't do now, boy." "Remember, fella, remember all you been told." "Won't be long now, eh, Carl?"—and then that too was broken. She and Carl, together, escaping together, were running for Bob's car, once more loaned them; with Carl she was in the front seat; as Carl jerked the car into motion she was waving back at her mother and father and Harriet on the front porch. Bob Gokey and the Morrison boy, still throwing rice, clung to the running boards awhile but then they were gone too; nothing was left of the wedding but the white grains all around them, the suitcases tossed any which way in back, the streamers of white and green crepe paper with which they were decorated, the cans and old shoes jouncing from their rear bumper.

At their place on the lake stairs she smothered her face in his coat. "Oh, Carl," she moaned. "Oh, Carl, wasn't it awful?"

Carl, savagely, had wanted to stop at the first corner. "We're ripping that junk off right now." She was the one who urged him onward. "No, wait. Let's get to the lake." The scowl stayed on his face, past the horns that blared and the people on sidewalks who craned, but at the foot of the stairs, when the car stopped, he grinned at her crookedly before lifting his long legs over the car door. More sedately, on her side, she hurried to help; not until the last of the streamers and tin cans were well under water did they climb to their step.

"Wasn't it terrible?" she once more groaned. Tears bulged her throat; tears, then, seemed to have ached there through most of the day. All she wanted for their marriage, all Carl wanted for their marriage, and this for a beginning. If tears could rise to her eyes and then fall—instead, weakly, she giggled. "Carl, everyone tried so hard, we both tried so hard, we both made such mistakes—it would have been better to have a church wedding, better to have gone to the courthouse, anything would have been better than what we got. It has to be funny, it can't be anything else——" Clinging to him, she laughed helplessly, sobbing but laughing.

He said grimly, "Awful's no word," but then, if more reluctantly, he laughed too.

She gasped, "Seven casseroles, Carl, and four berry sets. My, that beautiful arch, Carl, don't tell me you made it yourselves—like another son to me, or more maybe a brother—Carl, I'll never *question* anything you want again; how could you ever have lived with that ridiculous woman?"

He admitted, "I never saw much of her, really; my room was at the back, upstairs. I kept out of her way——" Then, as she still gulped and giggled, "Christine, you're having hysterics."

Rubbing her forehead on his navy-blue bridegroom's lapel, she acquiesced. "I know, so should you have; we've got hysterics coming." But laughter was more relieving even than tears; slowly the ache was easing from her throat. After a while, feeling unburdened if shy, she held her head still.

"Carl, we mustn't let that wedding—affect us in any way. It's got to be a good wedding—maybe one made up of three pieces. That other afternoon, the one in Salloway's office. And a bit of today, those minutes under the arch. The rest from right now, here on our stairs, where we can laugh at the rest of it—Carl, that's enough, isn't it?"

Enough, she might hope, enough, she might plead, but, as she was shakily aware, not all of a wedding; there must be more, of beginning, to come. And that more must, above all else, be right. Carl, so sensitive. She needed no reminders of how Carl was sensitive. No more than—how long was it, actually?—eight weeks, two months, since she had given up everything else she had wanted to take on this new goal, the goal of good marriage, but already her want for it was swarming and desperate.

Carl. Only Carl counted. Only Carl. Only Carl——

For their wedding trip they planned at least seven days of driving— up through Wisconsin to Superior, over to Duluth, along the north shore of the great lake as far as they could get. They were, though, spending the first night at home, in their own new apartment. "We'll be tired," she'd said, "and besides——" She hadn't finished, hadn't thought she needed to finish; this had come up one evening while they worked on their rooms; they'd come into the habit of saying good night there, instead of on her porch. What she felt as she said it, almost violently, was that it was here, in the home they were making, that the closest part of their marriage must have its inception. "We probably will be tired," Carl agreed readily. "We couldn't go far in a few late afternoon hours anyway." Then he added his own incomplete "Besides——"

So it was to their own place they went after the pause on the stairs, Carl still a little constrained, she constrained too, but by then turned not to what lay behind them but to what she was so determined would be a sweet joyous building ahead. They went into a grocery, coming out laden—"We'll never eat all this," Carl protested over his burden, but she laughed at him gaily and practically.

"You'll see; we'll save money tomorrow; we'll take lunch. Cooking, remember, that's the one thing I know about. If there's time before dinner I might stir up a cake."

At the apartment, too, things went all right, even if with an expected awkwardness. Carl at the front door dropping his groceries against the wall, relieving her of hers, saying resignedly, "I can feel this is where I meet tradition," and then carrying her in, holding her tightly and burying his face in her bosom before putting her down. Constraint, after that, increased again; to ease it she whirled him around to the room.

"Carl, look at it; the first time we see it in marriage——"

The apartment was part of an old stucco fourplex, the back half of what had once been a seven-room flat; an apartment which when first seen was dingy, dark, narrow-windowed, but which now after their weeks of effort might indeed give them cause for content. "One thing I can't tolerate," Carl had said, "that's frippery. Let's not have silk sofa cushions, let's not have fringe dripping around, let's not have a hodgepodge of colors." At Midwestern she'd taken courses in Home Decoration, but furnishing schemes she knew most familiarly were those of faculty houses—oriental greens, blues, rusts and maroons, large areas of brown. This that Carl had evolved in the room now around her—cool soft gray in the walls, gray again in the light wicker furniture, green and blue with the gray of window hangings and seat covers, a few traces of salmon—was something entirely new to her, but something in which she exulted. Carl, though, even now, was no more than grudging.

"It'll do, I guess; we might have done better if we'd had more to go on."

"You and your need for perfection," she protested, the protest one of her love for him.

Still in his awkwardness, he said, "I might as well get at those jobs I have left—books to get into the bookcase, hooks to fix——" She let him go almost willingly—*never, oh, never, restrain him.* She had things to do too, stacking away their new groceries, taking down from their shelf their green bowl, scooping flour from their bin, cutting butter from a personally owned pound of it, setting their roast in a pan, each act so freshly and vernally new, and over it all the satisfaction which from now on would always be greatest: Carl near by, the two of them working to a common purpose, she living here, Carl belonging here too.

They ate late, at the gray gate-leg in the living room. "Quite often, probably," she said, because it was such fun thinking it, "we'll eat in the kitchen. We'll be old married people." She couldn't be near him without needing to touch him—the wonder of his arm, the hair at the back of his neck, curly even where it was no more than a sandy-brown stubble ruffled by his coat collar. He still was held well in restraint; sitting across from her at the small candlelit table, with the shades pulled and the draperies folded inward over the windows to let the candles show all of their glow, he spoke less than usual; they had sudden silences which, ridiculously, she rushed to break at the same time he did: "We've forgotten entirely about getting a newspaper; we don't even know what the weather will be tomorrow." "Did we look at the gas gauge, at all? First thing in the morning, we'll check that——"

I'm not doing too well, she admitted after a while, self-accusing, a little panicky. *For the time being, though, it's the best I can manage, I guess; for almost everyone this time right here must be difficult. I'll be all right tomorrow——*

He helped with the dishes, in the continuing constraint, and afterward, in the same constraint, because some activity must be kept up, she brought out a few letters he hadn't seen. From her brother Douglas, from her college adviser, Miss Yetstein, from friends. On the settee she hunched to sit doubled on her ankles, resting against him in his corner, reading first one of these congratulatory missives aloud, then another. "But these aren't important," she could have cried after a little, her heart thudding its expectancy. "We could stop reading these any time——"

Of what went on between men and women in marriage she knew something but too little—from her mother, oblique references and warnings, from school friends vaguely more; college hygiene had established the polysyllabic facts. But no factual knowledge, she knew now, had real meaning, not compared to experience; it was emotion, the frightening, chaotic, powering emotion, that made so much difference. During the last weeks, especially, when they'd worked on these rooms and their wedding plans were set, she'd begun being aware of deep vehement hungers, hungers which made her want to rip aside the remaining barriers between them, hungers which colored her dream with a vivid foreknowing of the hour when restraints would no longer be necessary.

This was that hour, come to them now; this was their hour of admittance to glory and power, more glorious and she more humble in it, because she had never thought to be freed to it. Any instant, now, Carl's arm at her back must tighten, his cheek lower to her hair. He'd say only, "Christine——"

Feeling the tremor that passed through his body whenever he moved, just as an answering tremor passed through hers, she knew understanding. "He's as frightened as I. For him too there's—fright." Yet she couldn't invite or reassure him, not openly; after the last letter she let her head rest more comfortably against his shoulder, she whispered, "Our own home——"

His cheek did come down to her hair, but his responding "That's right" held the unbroken stiffness. The arm stayed at her back, but it too was unyielding; after a moment, a moment in which her heart, with a different foreshadowing, began a bewildered freezing, he spoke again, jerkily.

"Christine, after a while, of course, after a few days, I suppose, we'll be like—other married people. I suppose that's what we'll come to; we'll be like other married people. Right now, though, tonight——"

He made a twisting movement, almost a wrenching movement, as if he tore himself from her. On his feet, while she stayed stricken, he stood turned from her, hunched, voice tormented as he continued the outburst. "Maybe it isn't understandable; if it isn't I can't help it. Maybe you think you've a right to expect what I guess every woman expects. It's only that—all my life, Christine, there are things about people I've hated. The meat market of carnality that people go in for, I've hated it. There today, at that wedding. 'Won't be long now, eh, Carl? Don't do anything I wouldn't do.' Can't you see, Christine? They're expecting us—everyone. Everyone there, everyone not there, even Salloway, my father—we're not alone here, they're all in here with us. We can't smear ourselves with their leering, their filth. We'll have to wait, Christine, wait till we can believe they're not thinking of us, wait till we're away from them, till we're really alone——"

She sat numbly. In part of what he was saying—"That wedding, that leering"—she was touched by recognition; she had felt that, disliked it, the too forward intrusion. For her, though, it had been something merely to cast aside. The rest of what he was saying served only to stun. "All my life, I've so hated——" Yes, she had recognized this quality in him, hadn't she? Carl, she'd said to herself, so fastidious; she'd been afraid, knowing the one thing must be right. But what enveloped her wasn't altered by any recognition, wasn't altered by anything she might think; what enveloped her was beyond either reason or recognition, primordial. She got someway erect, not reaching out for him, not trying to approach, clutching, if she clutched anything, only herself.

"Carl, I—I said I was never going to question you in anything again, Carl; I'm not going to question you; if you feel this way, then I'm sure that's your right. You've nothing to fear from me——"

He spoke again, with more control, but still turned from her. "I know that. I know I've nothing to fear from you, Christine. I know that. I suppose what I must want from you is—some kind of concurrence. If you'd seen of living what I've seen, if you'd been in the army, lived in a small town—most men's desires are so animal, untouched even by liking. You'll have to accept me as I am, Christine, accept what I'm trying to escape from for both of us. I don't want you apart from me; everything can be all right later; I do love you, I do want to keep you; just give us time to get away from their hands on us, just let us get by ourselves."

At last he was touching her, holding her wrists; his pleading carried true agony, for which, again, she had only her blundering lost reassurances——

"I'll understand, Carl, I'll understand——"

His arms wrapped her shoulders, then, fiercely and tensely; he said, "Christine——" but there was closeness in neither the embrace nor the name; he wasn't allowing himself closeness. "Things being as they are, I suppose it would be best if I—sleep somewhere else. I can't go to Morrison's, I can see that, but it's early enough yet; I can still get a room at the Y.M.C.A. I'll take just the one suitcase——"

She would never have recognized her voice now, its hoarse charged distortion. She cried, "No, you can't. No, you can't. That other, Carl, that's all right. That's as you will. But leaving me, Carl. You can't do that. You can't, Carl. You can't."

At another time—later—she might wonder why this one issue, of his leaving, burst outward to overshadow everything else; then she had no time, no faculty, no space for question; she knew only that this was one happening she couldn't survive.

He said, "You must see how things are, Christine; I can't stay here."

She answered only, "But you can't go. You can't go." She now the one who was pleading, pleading as if the whole of her life, the whole of her new goal, their marriage, all hope for the future, hinged on this one giving way.

He again twisted from her, part way. "You have to allow me to be what I am, Christine; don't ask me to stay." She ran after him, begging, throwing herself at him.

"Carl, stop and hold me. Was it wrong, then? All along? Don't you love me at all?" He did stop, he sternly held her, he sternly repeated, "I do love you, I do want to keep you, this tonight makes no difference. But we'll have to wait——"

It continued for hours. Nothing new said, nothing different from him, nothing different from her. Only repetition, repetition of his necessity, repetition of her terror. Once or twice, rising part way toward seeing herself, she thought with dazed horror, "This is someone else, this is never me, behaving thus with no dignity." But dignity in comparison held no importance. At one point, running to the bedroom, she brought back with her the white crepe de chine nightgown, blue-bound, shirred, inset with embroidery, which she'd bought with so many tremulous dreams. She held it out to him and then let it drift to the floor, she herself crumpling beside it.

"I thought—I thought you might have liked it."

He knelt too, clasping, supporting her. "I do, I do," he repeated. "I've told you I love you. But——"

Only when they were far beyond exhaustion did he accede, as far as he could accede.

"I guess you mean more to me—I'll stay. There's not much anyway left of the night. We've no chance for much sleep." His face by then was thinned, whitened, shining with weariness, his body trembling with stress. "You can give me a pillow and some blankets. I'll try sleeping in here, on the floor."

5

In the bed of their one bedroom she afterward lay while the waves of ungovernable emotion shook her like spasms.

This she had thought she was sure of, that he desired her; this was the glory to which she had risen, that he hungered for her as she had begun hungering for him. Desire had seemed to underlie even some of his earliest approaches, such as that afternoon when he came into the Lake Room to ask her to go skating the second time, desire had seemed to bloom around them like perfume the night after the play; he said of their engagement, "I guess we do too decide on a physical basis." He said now, "I do love you, I do want to keep you, I want only to wait," but no repetition of those phrases affected what she felt. She had married, accepted him, she was here for him, but he wouldn't have her.

"If I were prettier, if I weren't marked——" This was the thought which oftenest and most intensively bled.

She slept, after a while, not because she was done with her hurt, but simply because, after a while, the passages of her mind began responding inelastically to thoughts which from sameness were losing their meaning.

When she roused it was getting toward daylight; the oblong of a window before her was mistily gray. Dully, for long minutes, she stared at it, aware, at first waking, only of returning to injury, but quickly recalling its form. At fixed intervals the shivering still shook her, but now as little more than a muscular contraction. For the rest she was sodden and heavy.

"If he didn't want to—love me, then why did he marry me?" Rejection bled afresh, but without enlivening the dullness. And where did she now turn? Down the block from her father's there was a man who, soon after fifty, went to bed one night and stayed there; sometimes in the past she'd thought of him incredulously; how could anyone so retreat from his chances at living? Now, feeling how a bed held and supported her, feeling the inertia with which she lay stranded upon it, she thought of that man with a different comprehension. It might be easy, merely giving up. "It was wrong, I can understand that now; I love Carl, I want him, but to save myself I should leave him. Go back. To my father, my mother——"

Her father over a book at the breakfast table, her mother under the harsh ceiling light of a bedroom, raveling and replaiting the braids of her hair. The two of them swam in the murk of her mind, but not clearly. And if they were no true answer either, then what?

Emptily, when the oblong turned from gray to bright lemon, she thrust herself upright, found slippers and kimono, stood uncertain and dull in the center of the floor, not knowing even why she had risen, powered perhaps only by habit. Emptily, in the same way, she moved to the doorway. With its draperies still folded inward, the living room held a hushed dusk; in this dusk, on the floor between center table and settee, Carl lay on his side in a long blanket-wrapped cocoon, one arm flung over his face, only the top of his head showing against the pillow. More worn even than she, he slept soundlessly.

Standing so at his feet, looking down at him, looking down at his sleeping defenselessness, she once more was shaken, shaken anew by her injury, but also by something deeper. Carl, this was Carl here before her, and whatever he had done and was doing to her, however inexplicable he might seem to her, he still was the man she had come to love, who had plucked her from behind her barriers; the man with whom she had made this home, with whom she had spent the hours on the stairs, with whom she had stood in Salloway's office and under the arch—whatever was happening, she couldn't cut herself from him. Of marriage with him she might not have had much, but she still had had too much to leave.

The different submission, the different resolution which then came to her, stilled the trembling. Not once, but again and again she had told herself to acquiesce and give way. "I'll never criticize you again," she'd said only yesterday, but when clash came what did she do? Resist as always, deny, cry against him, wanting him to be the one who conformed, and to what? To her dream again, a dream built of no solids, because she knew so little of people, so little of men. *No* dream, her mother said, but she'd gone on anyway, insisting on dreaming. Maybe that was one of the first lessons of marriage, giving up your own dream. It was the marriage of which Carl dreamed that she must learn to see and help make. He said he did want her, asked only to wait. If she could quiescently follow him——

Nothing clear, really; nothing changed. But once more a path seen.

Nine and after when Carl finally stirred; from the kitchen she heard the soft slide of his waking, the equal quiet with which he got to his feet and retired to the bathroom for dressing. When he finally came out to where she poured coffee he did so with head averted, body rigid. "Expecting me to take up where I left off, expecting me to be sullen and furious——" Dropping the coffeepot to the stove, she fled to him, burying her face in his shirt front.

"Carl, I'm not angry—I'm grateful you stayed with me. Forgive me; you'll have to forgive me; I'm—ignorant; you can't expect me——"

Immediately his arms swept around her, his head bent; he was as ready to be remorseful as she.

"No, my fault; I know it was my fault; the fault of my—my insufferable touchiness. I'd much rather be different—if you can bear with me, Christine——"

She clung as he clung, the phrases she sobbed—"I'll do better, I'm sorry, no one can be such an idiot"—meaning nothing and everything; when they drew apart his mouth and eyes too were wet and tender.

Catching her breath, she was able to laugh shakily. "Practically, here, it's midmorning. Our trip waiting, our food getting cold——"

Nothing, not ever, could entirely heal her hurt; within her it softly bled. But it also was a marvel, it was hope for the future, to discover, after a rift so slashing, that a little of their radiance was restored. Glimmers from that radiance shot across their breakfast, they talked more easily, their eyes met without too much deliberate avoidance, their hands in passing touched. Abruptly they found they were ravenous, clearing away from the table fruit, bacon, eggs, toast; to complete the meal she opened her carefully packed lunch to get at what was left of the cake.

Later she remembered those first three days of their honeymoon as three days of abeyance, pushing on toward summation but not, for so long, reaching it. It was in this abeyance they began their traveling, lightly laughing, above their covered chasm, at the hurry with which, once they were started, they cleaned up the kitchen, laughing at the many things forgotten from the car, laughing when the car wouldn't start and she inexpertly jiggled the choke while he cranked.

"Not this way forever," she told herself, then. "We can't keep up this way forever. But for a little time—or until he decides he can't accept me, ever, and must give me up——"

Against what faced her if he came to this last alternative, she closed her eyes resolutely. He must feel different; sometime, for him too, the right hour must come. For the day's traveling they hadn't made hard and fast plans; Bob's Ford wasn't bad, a 1917 model, but it had met rough going on the gravel washboards around Chapaqua, its fenders rattled and its steering wheel shook. Once they were off the concrete beyond Baraboo they were glad to accept twenty miles an hour as the best they could make. Fall rains had recently fallen but their day itself was quite clear; bumping along over the ruts and stones, they looked out through thin October sunshine at hills and fields deepened in color to dun browns and ochers with long shadows of purple, while trees by the roadside flamed mellowly red, russet, mahogany, yellow.

"Every mile we go," she said once, "we're years deeper in country." Serenity was consoling, isolation must help. They stopped at the Delles, clambering about over the rocks like school children on holiday; they sat on the gray washed rocks, eyes toward the tumbled fast water below, while they lunched. At Eau Claire, that evening, she made the only possible suggestion.

"We've had almost no sleep for thirty-six hours and more; why don't we get two rooms adjoining?"

His eyes didn't meet hers, but his mouth was grateful; coming into her room later through their joint bathroom, he held her against his breast tightly before kissing her good night, saying awkwardly, "You're right about my needing sleep; I didn't know I could be so tired."

She too, by that time, was glad enough to settle for nothing but tumbling into a bed which, however strange, offered rest. She slept until a knock and Carl's careful "Awake, Christine?" woke her; she'd slept round the clock.

Carl too, that morning, was fresher; his kiss, when she was dressed and admitted him, had almost the eagerness of their engagement; he said cheerfully, "We really had pretty good driving, yesterday; if we start right away we might reach Superior tonight, even Duluth; it would be nice saying we'd got some way along the North Shore; almost no one in Chapaqua has, except sports like Bodali who go up for hunting."

"Our wedding, our honeymoon," she told herself once again that morning, struggling as before with incongruity, but holding to resolve. "You'd think all that counted was how far we could get." That second day, too, offered fine weather; beyond Eau Claire, though, the road rapidly worsened; in midmorning they bogged to the running boards in a mudhole from which Carl battled for hours to pull the car loose, sloshing it forward and back in a rutted small purchase, plunging into the yeasty sucking ground beside the road to dig out half-rotted branches and logs which the two of them shoved under the wheels, shoveling in stones with the spade from the back. Not until well past noon, both of them by that time mud-splattered, exhausted, did he give up to stump back along the road for a farmer to pull them out.

Sitting on the higher running board, panting, holding before her a mud-covered hand, half lifting it to a cheek on which more mud was felt drying and drawing, looking down at the skirt of her good blue serge suit and her gray kid next-to-best oxfords, she was brought to new wry wringing questions: what sardonic jokester, in the days when the patterns were being set, had thought up the idea of honeymoons? Who was so sadistic as to combine marriage with travel? As if there weren't enough else to contend with—or was this, like a crowd at a wedding, a one saving grace? Was it only by keeping their minds on this forward pushing that they kept themselves jerked from the other? On the stairs she and Carl together had laughed at their wedding. So someone somewhere might be laughing at this too. Not she, though. Not yet.

When Carl returned with a farmer and horses it was already past two, and even with horses it took another half hour for the car to be freed. No more mishaps such as that one delayed them, but still the best they made that night was Spooner; at the dingy small railroad hotel she didn't have to suggest separate rooms; Carl just asked for them. Once again they separated immediately after dinner, but it was earlier, barely six, when he waked her.

"I seem to be slept out, and I'd like to get started——" Yesterday's bad luck, obviously, only made even more dogged his determination to get where he was going. Once more, for her role, there was nothing but abeyance and hope.

That third morning wasn't encouraging; chilly, with a close gray fog drifting back and forth across a dank, tree-submerged landscape; even with lights on Carl had trouble seeing the road, which wasn't one to beckon, rocky on its low rises, black-oozing and jellylike in its depressions. Time and again, that third morning, the car stalled in mudholes; she came to sit silent, far in her corner, not daring even suggestion, while he fought his way out. In a way it was awing to see determination so fixed. "This much I should know now forever," she told herself, "never stand in his way." Yet with this, as before, went her love and her pity. "It's his own strength he uses to fight our way onward."

Stopping as they had on the first day, to ramble around looking at scenery, was by that time another suggestion she didn't dare; by herself, as they neared Superior and the road finally firmed, she looked about at a sandy and wood-smelling flatness; she by herself viewed the rocky high rim of the lake, the beating sharp waves, the high unsupported airiness of the bridge, the long gray ships visible far out on the water, the queer rocky steepness of approaching Duluth, with nothing but lake on one side, and, on the other, a perpendicular hill to which smoke-stained, cramped, yellow and brown workingmen's houses seemed to be attached by nothing but their back porches, while the fronts hung free over space. She saw the long lines of stubby small ore cars lined up like toys along the black elevated tracks running on stilts into the lake where freighters yawned for the ore loads; she saw the thick cement stacks of the grain elevators, the queer Finnish names—Haino's, Aakonen's—on stores they passed; Carl, she thought, saw only the road. To her comments and descriptions he replied almost nothing; almost the only unchanneled gesture he made was an occasional flexing of his hands on the wheel, the fingers starfishing outward, curling back, then once more clenching.

So in Duluth, so when the suburbs were past and the road reverted to form, bouncing them sometimes over rock and sand ledges so close to the lake that the loud slap of water against tumbled inshore rocks drowned her small efforts at chatter, sometimes veering abruptly inland among hillocks where trees, losing their yellow leaves, appeared dwarfed and contorted, and grass grew as meagerly as beard on an old man's chin. So on into territory where the only visible habitations were board fishing shacks far out on rocks.

"There's a town up here, somewhere. Two Harbors," he contributed. "It doesn't look too far on the map; we should get there. Tonight's about half of our time; tomorrow we'll have to turn back. If we can get to Two Harbors I'll be satisfied."

Why? She would have liked to ask, why this goal? But she was teaching herself not to ask questions, and in one way knew the answer: they must reach Two Harbors simply because it was picked. Good marriage and radiance, any held hope of happiness, these now seemed too far to consider; immediate hope was for nothing more than an end to the jouncing, to the ache in her back, the tension of her legs from pushing for support against the floor boards, to the hum in her head, the dryness of burned gasoline fumes in her throat.

At six she offered, "We could stop almost anywhere; some of these fishermen must take in summer people."

He answered, "It's still light; let's not stop yet."

At seven, so tired each jounce of the car throbbed along her spine like toothache, she begged, "Half an hour won't be important tomorrow. We can make Two Harbors then."

He answered grimly, "It's got to be along here soon. Got to be."

But in the end he was forced to give up without reaching it. Sometime after eight the car coughed, spluttered and stopped. To Christine even the coughing and spluttering, the more stuttering advance of the car, came as relief. Dazedly she looked out at surroundings which for the first time in hours had value—pushing into the lake, at some distance ahead, the long dark arm of what seemed a rocky spit, with yellow lights at the end of it. Loom of forest on the left, a suddenly thunderous slashing of water.

Carl said savagely, "Engine trouble. Now and out here, we would have engine trouble." Angrily he worked the choke and starter, more angrily got out to crank, all uselessly. After another twenty minutes, more furiously still, he admitted defeat.

"Nothing to do but walk on toward those lights, I guess, find what help we can get."

"No help." She offered a cross-hope, as silently she stumbled beside him along a margin of rocky road. "No help. At least none for to-night."

The long spit proved to be much farther ahead than she'd thought. With no sound except the sharp close crunch of their feet on the roadway and the unending smash of the waves on the rocks, they walked half a mile before reaching what, in the gray overcast night, was to be glimpsed as a faintly marked track leading off to the right. From there it was another quarter mile before they came to the houses, perched aridly separate on rock. One square building of two stories, and beyond that a smaller cabin.

The man who answered their knock at the larger house might in other circumstances have been frightening—hulking, black-bearded, shapelessly dressed, smelling of fish, holding a lamp to the right of his head as he stood in the doorway, but to Christine then no human being was frightening. Beyond the man, too, she caught sight of a woman, some children. Before Carl spoke, she did.

"We're stuck up the road; our car won't go. Do you—I don't suppose you could possibly put us up for the night?"

"What we really need," Carl said right after her, "is to find out what's wrong with our car. Two Harbors can't be much farther on, is it? If we get there——"

The man drawled pleasantly, answering Carl first, but her too, "Nope, 'tain't far, ten-twelve miles; we got a pretty good cabin here; people just went back to St. Paul two-three weeks ago. Dollar-fifty a night, if you want it."

Carl began, "If I could find out what's wrong with that car," but she cut across him.

"While you go back with a light I'll look at the cabin."

That was what happened. Carl and the man, carrying one winking lantern, disappeared down the track, while she and the woman and children, the woman bearing another lantern, slipped and slid over wet rock to the cabin.

" 'Tain't usually wet here," the woman offered. "We had some high wind today. Cabin's dry, though. A real nice cabin. We got regular people coming here summers."

The sting of the sharp air, the near wetness of spray, were reviving Christine a little; when the woman threw open a door and lifted the lantern to reveal the cabin's interior she might have echoed her. A nice cabin, and more. It had two beds. "I wonder what this woman would say," she thought, "if I said, 'We're on our honeymoon, and I see you have just what we need. Two beds, well apart.' "

Aloud, instead, she said, "We're lucky to get this; I'll pay now. When my husband comes back, you can tell him I'm here."

Alone, after a few minutes, she took the lamp the owner had lit, found matches and started a fire in the small round stove. On a rag rug, close to the fire, she huddled waiting. How far away, she thought then, were her parents; she had promised to write them, but until now hadn't even remembered the promise. They were as cut off from her as if she'd slipped back to a strange century of no landmarks and no maps, a queerly numb century where people felt at once too much and too little, a century where abeyance continued forever. Even on a matter so small as where they should spend the night, she was now prepared to make an issue; this was as far as she could go.

Carl, though, when he came in, raised no issue; he brought with him the man and their suitcases; the man carried a basket of groceries.

"Summers we keep supplies on hand. Now we ain't got so much." Setting the basket on a table, the man lumbered cheerfully to the stove, shook it—not by a grate handle but with one hand on each side of its lidded top—and then returned to the basket for a can of baked beans which he placed, just as it was, on the stove lid. "Your man says you can make out, though. Wood, blankets, everything's here. Want anything else just come on over to the house."

When he was gone Carl spoke drearily. "Sand in the gas, I guess. At least that's what this fellow thinks. Says cars along here often get sand in the gas tanks. He's got gas for his boat, but he doesn't want to tackle the change until morning."

He already had his suitcase open, was hanging up his suit coat and taking out a bathrobe; again, as she saw, he was more draggingly tired even than she, robbed of his tenacity. Mostly in silence they emptied the basket and, in a frying pan over the now roaring wood fire, cooked a simple supper and ate it. Still in silence and weariness they went then to their separate beds; she set up two chairs and a blanket as a screen behind which to undress. He extinguished the light, and behind her screen, in the quick, complete darkness, she heard his steps, not tonight coming over even to kiss her good night. Heard the creak as he lowered to the edge of the bed, the complaint of the springs as they accepted his weight.

More loudly than ever, too, when she lay on her own bed, she heard water hammering and lashing at the cabin's foundations; maybe in here—it was easy to feel it—she was cut off not only from her parents and their century, but from all other humanity beside. Maybe the fisherman, his wife and children were mirage, maybe she was as solitary as she felt. No sound at all came from the other bed. Could a marriage continue like this? Could it be custom to make your thoughts slow and drift, custom to force sleep——

Her thoughts did slow, did drift; she was nearly asleep, she perhaps did sleep. She didn't hear him cross the room, didn't hear his approach, knew only the waking press of his cheek against hers, of his arms, heard his cry, "Christine, I can't bear it. Can't bear being shut away from you——" His lips found her throat.

Afterward, as she lay long awake, she reassured herself flamingly. He did love her, did desire her, she hadn't been mistaken. They were whole now, their love could flow limpidly warm and unbarriered. But even while reassurance so flamed, it was qualified. He desired her, of that there was no doubt. But in his desire he took neither pride nor joy. It was something to which he yielded only because his own need grew too great for him.

If she were prettier, if she weren't marked—again inference was inescapable—he might love her exultantly, might glory in taking her; it must be because she was what she was that he gave way to his love for her with such reluctance.

He, for his part, now apparently felt no lack. In the morning he was tender and high-spirited, luminous and relaxed, waking before she did, lying beside her close and warm, running his chin lightly down the back of her neck so that she woke shivering from the scrape of his overnight whiskers, teasing her. "No reason why you should wear clothes today; then when the bouncing gets bad I can give you a back rub." She responded, the shine re-enveloped her too. But within her remained the subdual.

After breakfast, still in his high spirits, he disappeared toward the fisherman's house while she stripped beds, washed dishes and packed; when he came back it was with the car. "Bright guy, that fisherman, sand is what it was. I guess today we drive slower." As if the very weather joined in his mood, the day around them was almost incredibly bright, clear and sunny; the lake that yesterday was so dun a gray now sparkled bluely, ruffled with white along its nearer edges, showing glints of gold where the sun hit its farther waves; even the rocks on which they stood had color, threaded and speckled with purple, white, ocher, lichened with orange and green.

That morning Carl wanted her close to him, her hand tucked in his arm. Looking back at the cabin and the fisherman's house, as their car entered the narrow track, he said gently, "We'll never forget this place, will we? Perhaps we can come back every year."

Almost, in the warm brightness in which they spent all of that day, arriving early at Two Harbors, wandering hand in hand along the water front and the pier, looking out at the gulls and the ships, exploring the backwoods stores, finally buying and mailing postcards, walking a way up along the narrow-gauge railway that led down from the north with flat cars of logs, she might have believed herself wrong in the subdual she retained.

And through the next days, too, the rest of their honeymoon, as they returned to Chapaqua, there was nothing to indicate any division between them. Carl was entirely open to her, close to her, warm. They stuck in mud again, they worked furiously getting themselves out, they spent one night in a hotel where, well bitten before midnight, they stayed up the rest of the night with the lights on, going over themselves and their luggage to make sure they wouldn't take back any crawling souvenirs. Over all this they were merely hilarious. If she erred in accepting this illumination too entirely, though, if she came to believe too much in the warmth, if she let herself forget the subdual, she was soon to be reminded what the limits were.

They reached home in midafternoon of the Saturday which was exactly a week from their wedding day. Not too tired that day, having time and to spare for stopping again for supplies, able to congratulate themselves that Bob's car had suffered no major mishaps, that they'd kept to their honeymoon budget. Cool, sunny, so new but familiar, their apartment welcomed them, showing only a light filming of dust over its pristine surfaces. While Carl first unloaded the car and then washed it, she flew at unpacking and dusting; by the time he was finished she had dinner ready. For a second time—different, because they now were one and completed—they had dinner cozily in their own home.

It wasn't necessary, she agreed, to call her parents or take the car back this evening; they hadn't said when they'd be home. After dinner, with a whole day of leisure ahead, they were slow about washing dishes, they walked out together, disdaining the car; they'd had enough of cars and driving. Instinctively they found the shortest way to the lake, instinctively found their stairs. Together they stood in the old way, she against the balustrade, he a step or two lower so their heads were level; his lips met hers, and her throat. No one now came between them, no voice said they must go home soon; never again any evening must they separate; their togetherness was forever. After a while, saying little because so little was necessary, they strolled home. In the room which now was theirs to share, one on each side of the bed which was theirs to share too, they began undressing in the intimacy of which she must still be shy, but which also was rightfully theirs. From a drawer of the dresser she took the blue-ribboned nightgown which—no other course was possible—she had left behind her, and slipped it on, finishing her undressing beneath it. When she was ready she walked toward him, wearing it.

He met her, slipping his arms about her. He said, "It's lovely on you, Christine."

She wanted to offer herself to him; that was what she had wanted before. She had been mistaken then, but surely now after what had happened, after the day in Two Harbors, the other days since, and in spite of the reserve she felt, she should no longer hold back from him; perhaps she was wrong in that reserve. What she wanted for their marriage was freedom and openness, and if she wanted that from him she should be willing to yield the same from herself.

Lifting herself toward him, raising her arms to his neck, she whispered, "Carl, tonight——"

He couldn't mistake what she meant, or her proffer; under her arms she felt him grow rigid, felt his withdrawal; he stood an instant longer with his arms about her, but then as her own arms fell he pushed away.

He said coldly, "It's late by now; I suspect we're more tired than we think. I can't forget I've a new job coming up, Monday."

Walking around her, he reached to pull the light cord, then returned to slide into the bed, keeping himself well to one side, rolling a little to fold the sheet and blanket in along his back, which was toward the center of the bed.

Standing where he left her, she felt herself sway. All the freezing rejection, all the confusion of her wedding night, were over her once more, an inflowing flood. She was certain, she still was certain—but then on her wedding day she had been certain too—that the evening had moved toward a single end. Carl there on the stairs—no, she wasn't mistaken. Carl when he said, "It's lovely on you, Christine——" She wasn't mistaken. All she had done was let him know she wanted him as she believed he wanted her——

Stiffly and slowly, as if she were old, as if she perhaps had had a paralytic stroke such as the aged get, she moved around to her side of the bed and lay down upon it. Again the spasms shook her. When a half hour had gone by Carl spoke from his distance. "I'm having trouble sleeping. If you'd lie more quietly——" From then on she lay rigid, the shaking confined to her interior, staring out at a darkness no greater than the bewildered darkness within. If she were prettier, if she weren't marked——

Or was this what marriage was? Was this Carl's marriage, to which she was fitting herself? She tried thinking, tried getting away from herself, tried seeing her marriage as one among others. "Marriage," her mother had said, "can be very cruel——"

No, too early for that; she was incapable of thinking. All she knew was her returned misery which, once more alone and cast out, she must think of as continuing forever.

Yet Carl, next day, showed no sign of expecting it to continue forever; showed, in fact, no sign of expecting it to exist at all. There might, for him, have been almost no break from the union of the days before. At breakfast he was solicitous—"You don't look too well, Christine. Head doesn't ache, does it? I was afraid you were tired last night." As they washed dishes, afterward, when she remained silent, immersed in this latest hurt, he swung her about to him. "Christine, I hate seeing you distressed." He wanted her to go along when he took the car back, and was injured when she refused, he reminded her to call her parents, and that night in their bed he wrapped his arms softly about her, his mouth beginning a tentative seeking journey at the corner of her lips, moving up to her ear, along her throat to her bosom.

When she lay inert and unanswering he shook her a little, murmuring, "Christine, we've no lake here, we're in a city with people, but we're still alone——" And when she still didn't answer he rose on one elbow, crying against her stormily, "Have you no human feelings at all?"

6 He expected the adjustments of marriage to be difficult, but not to be as difficult as they were.

What he found hardest to bear was the invasion of privacy—no longer having any place outside a bathroom in which to be alone, not being able to retire to a thought or a mood without having Christine feel left out and hurt, having her always, no matter what he did, draw near with a touch or a smile or a word, having her rely always on his affection. The only previous time he had shared sleeping with anyone was in the army, a flinging together of moist exhaling fatigue-sodden animal bodies which he remembered with almost more abhorrence than other deadlier aspects of war. In Elmwood he'd at least had a room and a bed which his father had never invaded; at Morrison's he'd seldom asked anyone into his rented domain.

Now he was expected to yield up not only his room but his bed. Worse—Christine slept there first; in a way the room was her room, the bed her bed; he was the one allowed admission, from no rightfully held place of his own. Attempts to get rest, for the first weeks, were only distracted; he grew dizzy and lightheaded from lack of sleep. Instead of lessening, now that he had her, the almost terrible attraction she had for him, marriage seemed to increase it. During the last half week of their honeymoon, when in the car she sat sunnily close, when they laughed together at mudholes and bad meals and infested hotel rooms, there had been a sweetness so penetrating it was like a deep bruise. Most often he couldn't come near her without suffering a need to snatch her closely. Waking in the morning to feel her light warmth in the bed, having her cuddle drowsily lower, as she often did, brushing her forehead against his upper arm, having her spin around to him when they were up, whirling on her heel in a swirl of skirts to flash some comment at him, watching her move from stove to table with such sedate deftness, letting his eyes or his hands or his lips—this most necessitously of all—touch the rose-velvet rise of the mark that began at her ear and ran down to her shoulder—it was impossible not to be physically incited, not to be seized by an urge toward self-abandonment so immense it was frightening. He could have let himself go to spend himself with her exhaustedly; he could have yielded so completely there would have been nothing more to surrender.

Yet the need to fight these compulsions stayed equally great. He met them with detesting repugnance, opposing against them each ounce of strength, struggling to hold himself intact, to love her, when he did, with a decent reserve, to control and deflect her as well as himself. She for her part evidenced the blind ignorances he might have foreseen, and which he should forgive her because she was virgin and innocent, but which nevertheless he found hard to condone—expecting him on their wedding night to follow the beast-rule of a consummation so immediate the whole wedding party would have been in the bed, obviously waiting, obviously being hurt by his reticence, offering herself to him as if she were easy and careless. Not as bad as Barbara—a few weeks of marriage and he shuddered with thankfulness, thinking what he had escaped with Barbara. But still much too forward.

There were other ways though—and he reminded himself that physical accord was only a fractional part of a marriage—in which Christine was almost more satisfying than he had previously considered she might be. Coming home at night to have her fly from the kitchen at his first step, hearing her "Carl!" having her burrow her nose in his coat, her love for him at that hour purely affectionate, feeling the warmth she maintained for him, and which no matter how it was broken always returned, meeting her readiness to admit error with a sorrowing "It's been my fault"—in these he found the contentment and ease which were what a man's marriage should mean. No fault was to be found with the spotless order in which she kept the apartment, she worked with little muss, she was tirelessly eager to please him, and thrifty; once their kitchen was stocked, as he soon found, their meals cost less than his alone had cost, previously. The early evening hours at a daintily set, candlelit table were usually the most enjoyable of his day. She was an imaginative and exquisite cook, quickly finding out his likes, meeting them but not destroying them with monotony. For a while she had trouble with his clothes; going through his belongings on washday, he sometimes had trouble keeping comment unacid, while she stood flushed and downcast, hands locked behind her. "I can't seem to do better; all I get is burns from those—those execrable sadirons." But little by little she improved there too; by Christmas his collars were glossily smooth, and she even took over pressing his suits.

What was more important, her interest in his progress at Trurog's was as rapt as his own.

Return from his honeymoon meant that he moved, immediately, into the main-floor job which was part of his wedding gift, and which, as he had a little nervously apprehended, was a far cry from his former place. Gloves, handbags, and jewelry flanked the front doors, where traffic was thickest; for one inquiring customer upstairs he now met two hundred—"Where'll I find boys' knickerbockers?" "You couldn't say, could you, if you carry accordions?" Just the battering at his attention was staggering. So many more checks to scrutinize, so many more salesgirls to watch, so many more lunch hours to schedule, so many more complaints, so many more sly practiced breaches of discipline.

Salespeople in Housewares and China, many of them, were war imports, comfortable middle-aged women working not from necessity but because they were urged to it, and because their short-hour wages would buy Duofold living-room suites, reed lamps, Columbia Graphonolas. Salespeople on main were professional, groomed and dressed to give tone to the store. They couldn't be paid much more—a dollar of wages was a drop squeezed from John Trurog's thin veins—but much more was required of them. One of Salloway's innovations was "making your book," a system by which each salesperson was required to equal the sales of the person in that station the year before. Exceeding your book meant bonuses, failing it a lost job. On fourth, with its tempting new household contrivances, with kitchens yet unrecovered from war shortages, this system was child's play; on main the story was otherwise. No more than a few days in the new job were enough to bring him contaminatingly close to the invisible but nonetheless powerful snake pit of hatred which sucked and writhed close to the surface. "If I could come to work just one day, find this store burned into ashes——" "If those Big Boys had to stand on my feet, just one day——" "Mr. Reiss, that was my sale, I had it all sewed up. Turned aside just one second——" "Mr. Reiss, I'm through, that's all. I'm through here. Three mornings now I open this section alone, get off all the covers, dust all the stock—she comes twenty minutes late. It ain't enough she should get docked——" And perhaps, from the practical point of view, worst, "Rally, madame, you don't feel these are the right shade of sand color? Maybe you should try the basement."

He had no reason to hate Trurog's, he was no underpaid slave, he had prospects, but nevertheless sometimes it was hard to keep free of this. Then too, there on counters so near the door, lay the rings, breastpins and stickpins, the handbags and gloves, which more than anything else were temptations for sneak thieves. Again a problem which on fourth, with its heavier merchandise and its elevators to negotiate, wasn't pressing, but for which here he must be alerted constantly, his right hand forever half raised in a signal to close in a detective.

The first week of December, with his new job only six weeks along, a group of high school girls came in, giggling, scattering, pouncing, exclaiming, larking, to pick out, or so they said, a gift for a senior adviser. Settling at Jewelry, they chose finally and paid for a three-dollar cameo brooch. But with them when they left, apparently, went also three silver mesh bags at an unexchanged seven forty-nine, two lockets, a carnelian-set ring, three pairs of gray kid gloves, and—more impossible than anything else, as Salloway pointed out in a burst as sulphurous as any that ever rose from a steel foundry—a blue and pink gilded marble madonna, imported from Italy, weighing at least thirty pounds, valued at seventy-five dollars, loaned by China to Jewelry only for Christmas display.

Over the theft of the pink and blue marble madonna Christine insisted on giggling, sobering to admit it was terrible for him, Salloway had a right to be furious; incredible he should have let any such thing happen. But then going off in a new eruption, "But how could they have? It must be these new Japanese-lantern-shaped coats. Even then——"

For the rest, though, she was not only suitably serious; her comments sometimes were fruitful. "If Salloway had any sense," she indignantly threw at him, "he'd put in an information booth. Trurog's is big enough now to support one. One girl at ten dollars would save fifty dollars' worth of time for six floormen." Again, "Girls always have lunch errands, only system ever worked for me was posting a schedule and letting 'em sign up each day." Again, "Too bad you don't have a meeting for talk and complaints, you might siphon off some of that jealousy." "Maybe"—joking—"you should try some of your fourth-floor grandmothers on main; there must be shy people who come in for gloves, handbags and jewelry."

Not all his ensuing suggestions went over, but more than enough times to balance the loss of the marble madonna, that winter, Salloway had cause to tell him vigorously, "That's using your head, Reiss." By spring, in fact, he was thinking of his marriage as quite a fair bargain; for the first time in his life he was discovering the strength of not standing alone, of having a sympathy staunchly and unbreakably on his side. Christine, too, still made some mistakes, but their personal relationship was shaking down; she bothered him less and contented him more.

There were times when by nightfall he was so sickened by the press of people, who seemed to ricochet from him endlessly like balls against the side of a billiard table, that the thought of having nowhere to be alone returned in its original drag. Yet when he opened his door and Christine met him, face radiant, it was usually as if she weren't a separate person at all. Resting against her, he felt no buffeting, only the drain of his tensions. He thought, "I don't want loneliness, really, I want this."

Unhappily this state of affairs didn't go on indefinitely, either. One evening in late May he came home to a dinner especially fine—steak, new asparagus, fluffed and cheese-crusted potatoes, green salad, pineapple Bavarian cream. The day back of him was so upsetting he shrank from recalling it even for Christine, and the relaxation of the meal, of sitting to rest his chin on her hair in darkness later, closing his

eyes while she rattled on about a luncheon with Harriet, was something he sorely needed. Salloway, in midmorning, had come past with
a new young employee; Salloway was at his most pleasant, "Reiss, this
is Glen Shotwell; Glen, you want to take a look at Reiss, here; Reiss
is what you may be ten years from now if you're almost too good
to be true."

It was far from the first time Salloway had come around with such
young hopefuls; Chester Ohman might now handle employment, but
this was a prerogative Salloway kept. Each time he used it, Carl felt
the squeeze. He didn't expect to be Trurog's only young comer;
Trurog's needed too many men. But that didn't mean he didn't know
how small was the closed phalanx over him, how seldom there were
breaks in it, and how constant was this influx of youngsters, as alert,
as determined as he. This particular new young employee was especially ominous, too. Dark, tall, slender, slant-eyed, with a tough un-
concealed resiliency. "Don't worry," the glint in the slant eyes said
insolently, "when I'm your age I'll be where you are or better."

As if this weren't enough for one day, he also suffered a deeper
shock. Detached as he might mean to be, it was impossible not to
develop reactions of some kind toward people he directed. The one
for whom he came to have most liking was a Mrs. Willette, a widow
of perhaps forty-five, with pretty steel-blue-gray curls, a thin life-
bruised face, and a girl's slender figure. Against the writhing currents
of interstore hatred Mrs. Willette stood serenely aloof, charmingly
and harmlessly arch with Ohman and Salloway, both of whom knew
her and stopped for small gleefully flirtatious chats, co-operative,
deftly helpful and droll toward Carl, so that he'd formed a habit
of keeping his most constant station near her glove counter, where
he was refreshed by her quick but never personally intrusive quips,
where he enjoyed the apparently effortless skill of her salesmanship—
"That's the most devastating new bonnet; please let me see how this
gray goes with it." "Oh my, such small hands. You may be a trifle
hard to fit, but we'll do it." Her own hands, while she fitted, moved
as if she played a flute.

After Salloway left with his young satellite, Carl had left too, for
lunch. Coming back early, he threaded an inexpectant way through the
main-floor crowd, head lifted above it, already at a distance sending out
feelers for the things he must pick up. An entire counter of handbags

left unattended while Miss Harney, a blonde, lingered with another clerk. A man and three women waiting attendance in Jewelry. Mrs. Willette soon free for another customer, smilingly tendering a neat small packet in one hand while in the other she held her salesbook and, fluttering over it, two bills.

It was then, almost immediately, he was given the shock. Mrs. Willette's customer turned, so did Mrs. Willette. Toward the cash register, where she should turn. As she did so the bills vanished. Mrs. Willette was at the register, her fingers on the keys, but there was no ping. Did he—or didn't he—see an incredibly swift flick of those quick fingers, transferring the bills from the salesbook to the inside of her wrist-hugging, white-lace-frilled sleeve?

He drew back to the information booth he was passing with a movement like cringing. "Well, Mr. Reiss," the girl in the booth greeted him playfully. "Anything I can't do for you today? How about Indian clubs? How about a camisole, how about a dolman—wouldn't you be interested in any of those?" Sick and disoriented, he didn't answer. It would be easy, in a way it would be easy, to find out if he were right. In the nearest buyer's office a detective would rip open that sleeve. Money, though, was unmarked. "But that's my money," Mrs. Willette would say, incredulous and hurt, her long-lashed soft hazel eyes seeming to spread into the shadowed areas around them. "I was planning a small purchase this noon." No, the detective must be only alerted, told to watch if it happened again. The detective too would be unbelieving. "Now look here, Reiss, that's Mrs. Willette, she's been in this store pretty near twenty-one years; got the twenty-year ring last year same as I did." He himself knew Mrs. Willette's personal circumstances. Widowed soon after twenty, left with a son and a daughter, the girl now grown and married, the boy attending Midwestern. "How that woman does it I don't know," Salloway had once said admiringly. No one, no one in the whole store, would like to believe she did it by theft. If she were betrayed—betrayed wasn't the term to use, but it was the one that came to him—he would be far from the only one sickened.

After the instant by the information booth, hearing but not answering the girl's pouting "All right, Mr. Reiss, if we're not speaking today," he made himself move forward, pausing by Mrs. Willette. "Things in good shape?"

She smiled at him frankly, disingenuously, tranquilly, with the little lift of her outer eyelids that meant her recognition of his masculine attractiveness, but no effort to draw that attractiveness toward herself. "At least things should be, now you're back."

All the rest of the day he was ravaged and torn, unable to call the detective, equally unable to wrest his eyes from her. To the best of his knowledge she didn't repeat the act. "Of course," he must think, "if this is her practice she's forced herself not to overdo it; maybe two dollars, maybe one theft a day is all she lets herself make."

He'd felt no compunctions about the receiving-room ring, years before; what must it be, he'd thought then with loathing, to stand two people together, each thinking, "You're one thief, I'm another"? Why did he feel different about Mrs. Willette? Why, even if he caught her again, did he shrink from the thought of exposing her? Sitting with Christine, he formed phrases for his question, "Today I'm almost sure I saw——" but he couldn't give them voice. He did tell her of the new employee, Glen Shotwell; for that she laughed softly, warmly, instantly divining.

"Goose. Don't tell me you're alarmed. One thing I'll never worry over, not at all, your getting along in the store. How can I? Who else is as quick as you, who has so much presence? Who else among the floormen has your ideas, who does Salloway like as well?"

Confidence so impermeable, so whole and complete, that it should as usual have relieved him entirely. This night, though, with his other unrevealed problem to nag him, it didn't quite do so. He was, besides, halfway and annoyingly aware that for a day or two, lately, there had been a slight change in Christine. Almost as if, after their recent months of much more matter-of-fact and livable marriage, she were reimmersing herself in the cloudy dream of their courtship. While she was saying, "Who else among the floormen has your ideas," his impression was that she spoke by rote, her mind on something else; he was filled, somehow, with a feeling of imminence, and almost at once had that imminence confirmed.

Instead of going on to other reasons why his advance must be rapid, her voice faltered to a whisper. "I guess I can be especially glad, these days, that you're so—that you're so sure on your feet, Carl. I think—well, I'm almost sure—I don't believe we'll be only two of us forever."

In horror he jerked himself back from her. There'd been times, at least in the first weeks of marriage and before, when he faced the possibility a child might result from their union, but it was a possibility so opposed to everything he wanted that he had shut himself off from it tightly. Not a possibility to be decently mentioned; no one decently mentioned any such subject. But one he allowed himself to think he might leave to Christine. For all her virginity, she had been twenty-three when he married her. Girls among themselves knew things.

He stammered, "You can't—you're not sure of that. You——"

This time she certainly spoke from the dream. "No, not sure, yet. I've not been to a doctor. But I'm pretty sure, all by myself."

He forced himself to say, "Christine," and take her once more in his arms. She seemed content with no other response. For the better part of an hour, after that, until he admitted, "Ever since this morning, I guess, I've had a headache," they sat on so while she laughed at him and was foolishly tender, as if he were temporarily the child she expected. "Just think, Carl, if it's true——"

For all her practicality about most things, her vision was roseate; typical feminine imaginings of the child who would mirror them both. Lying awake later in his constricted half of their bed, while she slept beside him, her face this time pushed into his shoulder blade, his headache sprung to full throbbing strength, he looked at a more actual future. He knew, of course, how prospective fathers were supposed to take roseate parts in the roseate dream, filling with self-pride over the extensions of themselves about to be brought into the world. What filled his mind, instead, was the prospect of Christine retching. In the last years before her death his mother had had two miscarriages. It was his Aunt Stell, later, who told him they were miscarriages; all he knew at the time was that his mother was so violently, so pitiably ill, turning from him when he ran to her bed in the morning, moaning, "No, Carl, no, no, no." Strange women came, tending her, his resentment of his father, for some undiscerned reason, seemed to rise to sharp focus, the whole house smelled of vomit; coming in from play, he was halted as if hit in the stomach by that unhinging, shattering smell. Not for weeks, months actually, did his mother come back to him, and all too short a while after the last time she was forever gone.

This same thing needn't happen to Christine; within Christine's slenderness was the firmly solid core he so early had sensed. But the rest of it, the unshapeliness, the woebegone dragging heaviness, the ordeal of birth and what came after, housekeeping turned slattern, wet diapers hanging from lines in the kitchen, Christine's breasts exposed to a greedy small mouth——

Even this, though, wasn't worst. This might be worst later, but it wasn't worst now. What was worst now was that Christine's condition, if she were right, was such open avowal. No use saying their secret relations were common to marriage; no use saying a child was expected of marriage. As soon as he accepted a child as his own, he confessed.

Nor was this worst all. Cautiously rolling and twisting in a bed where he couldn't even turn unrestricted, he tried freeing himself from the financial trap. For the two of them, on the twenty-seven fifty he had reached with his wedding raise, their budget worked out not too badly. The two hundred he had taken from his savings to equip the apartment were almost returned. He could of course borrow for his Trurog stock when the day came; no borrowing base was sounder. That, though, wasn't what he wanted. What respect would there be for a man who, of a small sum like fifteen hundred dollars, must answer, "I'll see what I can scrape up"? No one need tell him how costly a child would be; he'd have to cut into his savings again.

From uneasy slumber and a nightmare of drowning he wakened to terror. At first, he thought as he fought it, terror continuing from a dream in which he was submerged and suffocating, but terror which grew more familiar, until finally he knew what it was.

Rolling to his elbow, he struggled to pull himself upward. That alone, for the time being, was vital; somehow he must pull himself upward. He labored to pull in breath, chest muscles responding sluggishly and reluctantly to the call of his will. Breath seeped in, but breath indrawn wasn't enough; he must express it again, and to this second call of his will there was no response. Within the expanded cavity of his chest all that air remained, bottled and choking; he lay gasping without any ability to gasp, only increasing the huge quantity of air already held.

As he threshed about, something moved against him protestingly, and with a wave of relief which, somehow, allowed his chest wall to collapse and then re-expand, he remembered he was married. Christine was beside him to help him. No sound would issue from his throat, but deliberately this time he rolled against her, eliciting a sleepy "You're squeezing me," and then, when he repeated the maneuver, "Carl, is anything——"

The space of an instant, and she was beside the bed with the light on. The immediate fright on her face, the anguish with which she leaped toward him, "Carl, what can I do for you?" told him how he must look. He managed a motion of his hand, and she pulled at him, dragging his shoulders up. Another flick of his hand—such tremendous effort, and the only response a hand that moved perhaps two inches—reminded her of the hypodermic which early in their marriage he had carefully shown her how to use. She ran to the dresser, she was shaking and clumsy, but she swabbed his arm and pressed the plunger; from the sting of the needle, first down his arm, then up over his shoulder and at last over the muscles of his throat and neck, spread enough relaxation so he could at least wheeze and gasp.

This time, too, he thought then, as she ran for the phone. This time too, probably, if she got the doctor quickly enough, if the hypo didn't wear off too soon, if he'd be able to cough, he would make it. This was the thing it was necessary to think, over and over. "It's all right, I'm making it, and that's all I have to do. Make it." If for a minute he let himself think anything else, then the constriction began again, the sweating, the oppression at his heart. Christine sat with him, holding his hand. "You look better, Carl; it can't be as bad as it was; he said he'll be here in a minute," until Dr. Daly came. After pilocarpine had followed the hypo he could begin coughing, freeing his throat and the top of his lungs, gasping still, but more easily. So that when Dr. Daly said breezily—dragged from his bed at midnight to a scene such as this, but he still was breezy—"Well, Reiss, you'll be getting a couple weeks' rest out of this; sounds like fun, I'd say; don't know what I'd give for a few days in bed," he wheezed savagely, "Me with a job to lose and a baby to pay for—I see myself staying in bed."

For that, as soon as he breathed at all, was the need that pulled at him, a need as strong as, and linked to, his urgent need for breath. This onslaught, too, must be pushed aside. Waiting for him was the

store and his necessity there, more than ever his necessity since he'd
be bearing more burdens.

Casting a single fleet glance toward Christine, Dr. Daly reinserted
the earpieces of his stethoscope.

"Well," he finished a second examination brusquely, "heart's
strong, but plenty of râles in that upper right chest. It's your life."

After he left, leaving his prescriptions, and while Christine wasn't
yet back from the door, he once again made the effort to draw himself
higher on his pillows, this time succeeding. For a while now, maybe
for weeks, this would be his only position for rest, propped this way
on pillows. He didn't care about that, didn't care about the oppressed
stumbling weariness which, just from the prospect, he felt overtaking
him. He had won over the doctor, he'd win over the illness. Against
the sheet of the bed, cooling, he stretched his flat palms.

At work the next morning Harriet stopped to flare at him, "Who
do you think you are, making us look like an outpatient dispensary?
Get away from here or I'll tell Salloway. It's Thursday—at least you
can stay home the rest of this week."

By then, after being in the store only two hours, he was willing
enough to accept this advice, even if Christine's hand was undoubtedly in it. Perspective was telling him that a day or two, actually,
didn't make any difference; anyone could have an occasional off day.
Averting his eyes from Mrs. Willette, he reported in as sick and made
his way home. It was incredibly relieving to sink into the bed he had
so recently left, incredibly relieving to have Christine take up min-
istering to him where she had left off.

Besides the restorative powers of rest and of nursing, as he was
soon to find, the four days in bed brought another advantage.
Plumped into his new job, he'd so far done little but battle against
being swamped, without any clear sense of direction ahead. Up to
now his road had lain fairly clearly, but where, exactly, would he go
from where he now was? When and how, for instance, would he move
on to being Ohman's assistant? It wasn't, he suspected, a move to be
made in one jump, not by him. Yet there wasn't, either, any well-
defined mid-jump. Salloway had preceded his leap into Personnel by
working in Maintenance. He too might go up in that way, and if so
it was time he began preparing.

This, at least, was a question to take up with Christine. For a good part of the three days, when she wasn't running about to cook or get something, she sat on the side of the bed while they talked of it. The best thing he could possibly do, they agreed, was go in for a frank talk with Salloway. Maybe in a way—this was a burst from Christine—illness right now was a much-needed way station.

He had to wait to see Salloway; on anything so important he couldn't, naturally, go up while his lips and his fingernails still were blue, or while he still sometimes panted and gasped to get breath. Time, in fact, was important, and he chose his carefully—an afternoon in late June, with the press of spring buying well past, and the big July sale prepared for but still ten days away.

Except for the sense of greater urgency which now drove him—Dr. Daly confirmed Christine's condition—he was, besides, returned by then to more normal condition, his breath flowed easily, he'd played tennis with Bob Gokey the last Sundays and gotten some color; he felt quick and firm. The question of Mrs. Willette and her thievery was still one he was shirking, but other than that, in the lazy June buying lull, his section was running well under control.

He'd made an appointment and had only a few minutes to wait, minutes he'd rather counted on spending with Harriet in their quickening familiar interchange, but from which he found himself shunted aside in fifth-wheel discomfort. Vic Bodali, when he came in, was leaning with both palms on Harriet's desk; Harriet, lounging back from her typewriter, wore the scattered, flutter-lidded smile of a woman enjoying a defensive dueling. Several times lately, it struck Carl, Bodali had been in Salloway's outer office with Harriet when he came up.

With a blithe, "Ah, our white-haired boy, well on time as usual," Harriet invited him to make it a trio. Bodali, too, greeted him. "More statistics? If it is, for God's sake let me in on 'em first." He answered shortly, "No, no statistics. I'm sorry," and turned his back to step with deliberate stiffness toward the store-progress graphs on the east wall.

Harriet mocked, "One of our Puritan forefathers; he's a little averse to mere people." Bodali's reply was for Harriet alone, "But you aren't?" and Carl shut his ears to their persiflage. If there was one woman in the store, he thought hotly, who shouldn't be open to Bodali's approach, it was Harriet, with her background, while Bodali for all his brilliance was slum growth, springing from God knew what immigrant hotbed, warmed and invigorated by God knew what suns and what fertilizer, a recognized rounder. And, besides all that, not as tall as Harriet by half a head.

When he was shortly admitted to Salloway's office he had difficulty not carrying over his distaste.

"It's seemed to me lately I'm not sure of what my next steps will be; I've thought I should talk over with you what I may move on to."

Salloway's welcome was warmly avuncular. "Well, Reiss, yourself again?" But it was no more than natural he should react to Carl's faint testiness. "Ambitious cuss, aren't you? I put in six years, myself, at managing sections. What've you done, a year and a half?"

"I don't want you to think"—reply must be quick, here—"that I'm hurrying you; I just find myself needing direction. If I should be preparing——"

Salloway growled, "You young sprouts," and even after that, after what was tantamount to a disclaimer on Carl's part, and acceptance on his, he didn't smooth to the easy good-fellowship which, ever since Carl's return from the service, he most often evinced. Behind a battered high roll-top—a relic from the first Trurog's—he sat with his swivel chair halfway back toward the window, both elbows planted on the chair arms, shoulders upthrust to the height of his ears, bald head jutting. Salloway in the last years was putting on weight; jowls, obvious if not yet pendulous, widened his face over his collar, the eyes so intrinsically icy had pitted a little in their firm surrounding cushions of ruddy flesh, the ridged dome above shone more pinkly. When he spoke again it was with a chilly deliberation belonging less to the genial patron than to the man who stood in the clearing, announcing, "There'll be no hiring today."

"You may be right, Reiss; this may be a time for stocktaking. It's not hard for a bright young man to get to be a salesclerk; salesclerks are a commodity we use by the hundred. Not too hard to get a section to manage; we may not need section managers by the hundred, but we do use them in numbers. Above that, above you, as you've seen for yourself, air gets rarefied. We use few assistants for our chief executives. Of me there's one, of Ohman one, of Bodali and Leverett, each one. Of Mr. Trurog, just one there, too."

Brutality had always been implicit in the eyes, the head, the wide hard mouth; a kind of brutality was evinced by them now, not so much, Carl recognized, a directed brutality against him, but one more diffusely directed against the world in general, the store, even the speaker himself.

He began carefully, "I have no intention, sir," but Salloway flung up a hand an intolerant two inches to shut him off, swinging about to the window, as suddenly back.

"Odd, in a way, you should bring this up right now. Just this past week we got together, the five of us"—grim humor entered here—"our happy top family, and decided that, for the good of the store, and excepting only Mr. Trurog, to whom the matter necessarily doesn't apply, all Trurog employees from now on, including executives, will retire at an automatic sixty-eight. This may not seem too germane to your problem, but it delineates it. Unfortunately for you, jobs ahead of you are held by rather young men. At forty-five I have twenty-three years to go. Leverett is three years older than I. Ohman about the same. Bodali's our foundling, still only thirty-seven, but at any rate you can't be thinking of replacing him; your talents aren't predominantly financial. Ohman, Leverett or I must be your target, and unless sudden death overtakes us, you're in for a pretty long haul."

In the chair he had automatically taken, the chair at the deskside to which, after all these years, it was so familiar to drop, Carl sat with beginning resentment replacing both his acerbity and the back-stepping humility to which he so quickly was forced. Salloway all along had nourished his ambitions; it was scarcely fair for him now to make this about-turn, excoriating the drives he had helped form. Yet he saw Salloway's position too. He now had climbed high enough for Salloway's job to come into focus as the one above him; Salloway naturally didn't enjoy that recognition. At the same time Salloway might as well come to grips with the fact that he wouldn't hold on forever; from somewhere, even if at a day as distant as one at the end of twenty-three years, Salloway must be replaced, and that replacement—himself—must be ready.

From this beginning resentment he replied staunchly and coolly, even if not quite forthrightly, "There's not necessarily any question of that; I'm not content, though, to settle into being a floorman forever; I'd never have stayed on in the store if the most I have to look forward to is a job at twenty-seven fifty. Living costs are too high, salaries outside too much better. You yourself——"

Again Salloway lifted the halting hand, again swung around to the window, speaking this time in mid-turn.

"Oh, I know that; I've liked your ambition. All right, let's look at your problem. I've no use for an assistant, I'm too fond of detail. Besides, I've got Harriet, and in some ways Harriet's better than a man. Ohman doesn't want that kind of help, not for a long time to come, if ever. Neither does Leverett. You may as well face it, we're a tough crew. Actually this isn't the first time I've considered this; if you want to go on from where you now are almost your only way up is through buying. We have twenty-nine buyers, as you know, counting those in the basement. Seven merchandisers, and they sometimes use assistants. Don't expect it early—frankly you're too useful where you are for me to push you, and you need the experience you're getting. You needn't expect to be stuck, though; I'll see to it you get your chances."

7

During his week of vacation that summer he applied for a job with Hoskins, Earlstetter and Bromfield, the recently established Chapaqua branch of a national advertising agency.

"Try writing us up a few samples," Bromfield told him at the first interview, and at the second, "Well, these aren't too bad—not too good, either. You have some idea ability, I'll say that; at least you have the selling approach, but you're no hand at writing. If you come in here it'll be at the bottom, an assistant, say, to one of our copywriters. You'll get about thirty a week to begin with, and raises if you make the grade. The sky's beginning to be the limit these days; just this summer we've taken in four new accounts at this branch, firms that would never have done our kind of advertising before the war. If this prosperity keeps up—we don't make promises, but you're a young man yet——"

The next week he was back at Trurog's, the approach to Hoskins, Earlstetter and Bromfield marking only the extent to which, after six weeks, his last talk with Salloway still rankled and shook him. After his final sentence that day Salloway had simply stood up, ending the colloquy; since then their meetings had been a little stiff on both sides.

"You aren't forced to stay on at Trurog's," Christine told him indignantly. "Jobs aren't the way they once were; you can get another one. Department stores have always been one of the most poorly paid places to work. You could do better for yourself——"

Even when, in his disturbance, he partially came to agree with her, he didn't actually think of himself as cut loose. Sitting at the living-room desk for two whole days of his vacation, blank paper before him and, it seemed, equally blank spaces in his mind, he found neither challenge nor satisfaction in his divergent effort. He knew nothing of advertising; what he turned out merely paraphrased ads that he read. Other people might think advertising had a silvery lure— Christine said she had talked to a young Midwestern student one day on a streetcar, and for him advertising was a fever, but Carl felt no heat. Research, Bromfield said, to begin with, after that the filling in of stray unimportant ad corners, such as the guarantees, finally perhaps an unpicturable state known as being an account executive, which seemed to consist mainly of kowtowing to manufacturers. Nothing there made his palms tingle; no unreal and forever subservient future such as this had force or pulling power, not against that other image slashed so deeply into his being—the ascent already half won, the one man in the clearing, the seat at the Policy Luncheon, the one swivel chair at the one roll-top desk, the one power ruling a whole moiling multitude.

When he went back, in fact, he did so with a hugged sense of escaping a dangerous disloyalty, a feeling which somehow was linked to his unresolved conflict about Mrs. Willette. In spite of his watching he never again caught her; he reinstituted a scrutiny which except for his lunch hour was seldom five minutes relaxed, a scrutiny which, blockingly, Mrs. Willette undoubtedly came to suspect—"Goodness, Mr. Reiss, I believe you're tied to my apron strings. Maybe I should offer you leeway." That situation remained at an impasse. The other, however, did not. Instead of wasting himself on more mutiny, he set his mind to work, and in late August was able to go to Salloway with another idea.

"These last weeks I'm being trampled by the high school and college crowd, in for its fall refurbishing. More and more it looks like nothing else human on earth. I've wondered if we mightn't perhaps have a separate department for school outfitting."

It was, he himself thought, perhaps the best idea he'd ever had; certainly it was the most far-reaching. Delivering it this way, like a peace offering, he quivered a little; Salloway couldn't mistake its import.

And Salloway didn't. After looking aside for a moment, his blunt fingers drumming the desk top, he swung around full face, only the basic coldness of his eyes not overlaid by responding if heavy warmth.

"Reiss, you continue to be quite a guy. I don't know, of course, how far we could go on a thought like this; it's pretty radical. We'd have to look into it——"

Tacitly, from then on, relations between them returned to what they had been earlier. In his next pay envelope he found an unasked increase, and a note in Salloway's hand, "Keep 'em flying."

"Two dollars and a half," he told Christine sardonically. "Bringing me right up to the beginning level at Hoskins, Earlstetter and Bromfield." But underneath he was pleased. Not only the money counted; what meant more was the gesture.

Apparently his suggestion about a school section was tabled; he heard nothing more of it. With a mind at last freer, though, he began considering the blunt answers Salloway had given him. Naturally he had previously considered buying and merchandising as possible fields for his action, but always to discard them. Salloway had put in time that way, but Ohman, Leverett and Bodali hadn't; his own interest lay not in getting goods into the store but in expediting their way outward, and in the governance of the store as a whole. Now he faced about to the different viewpoint, looking up—all too unrewardingly, especially at first—new evening courses he might take, going out of his way to form acquaintances among the buyers and their assistants, inviting them for dinner, reading the trade papers, during snatched half hours at noon exploring, just to get the feel of a market, Chapaqua's own small wholesale district, which served surrounding small towns but which for a big store like Trurog's, that could send its buyers to

New York, was too inconsiderable to patronize except in emergencies and for trifles.

Christine that January produced an eight-pound son, Craig, and, only thirteen months later, another son, Dustin; in some ways his marriage deteriorated as he had foreseen it deteriorating. To be sure, once embarrassment was over, there were instriking enjoyments in early fatherhood—his two sons were so plump and so healthy, so ridiculously like him, even in infancy, their delight in his smallest attention was so rapt, their small hands were so ready to curl over an extended finger. That still left the nights when they, and he, got little sleep, the tumult of suppertime, the diapers, preoccupations for Christine which left little leisure for him, the strain on his finances.

He thinned, in those many months, thinned until Christine worried endlessly, and until he himself, meeting his hallowed eyes once and again in a store mirror, looking down at his hands, seeing the blade-thin thrust of his shinbone against his trouser legs, sometimes was exasperated, knowing it wasn't only his family that frayed at his flesh, not the two milder attacks of asthma that followed the one in 1920, not the evenings he spent on his courses, not his job, not his hopes—what was eating him was his feeling of exigency, of having glimpsed a possibility of being no longer pushed by Salloway, of being at odds with him, of needing to hurry, of seeing his goal forever ahead of him while, struggle frantically as he might, he stayed on bound helplessly in the one spot.

As Salloway said, a long haul.　　　　　•

At that, a move came before he expected it.

In October of 1924, on the instant heels of store rumor, he once more bearded Salloway, this time more forthrightly. "It's being said around that Mrs. Williams is leaving; if she does, and Joe Eggen takes over—I've put in almost the six years of floor managing you seem to feel necessary. The job with Mrs. Pesek is still the one I'd like, but if there's a chance now in Hosiery I don't want to miss it."

Dourly leaning over his arms on the desk, Salloway growled, "Yeah, that ——" expletives blistered, "middle-aged flapper, she's leaving us for Stoke's in Cincinnati." He shrugged. "Joe's got thirteen years chalked up in Hosiery, selling and assisting; he'll probably get it." He swung about, then, brusquely. "Set on it, aren't you? I couldn't give you the place with Mrs. Pesek, but this, well"—again a pause, but grudgingly—"I suppose you try it."

From an already none too easy cradle beneath his belt, Carl's stomach jumped for his throat. He hadn't really thought, when he came up, that Salloway would give in; from pride if from nothing else Salloway would make him put in the full six years. Getting them skimped by even a few months was a victory.

"I think I'm making a damn mistake," Salloway still emitted his growl, but this time no scowl accompanied it, "sticking you in a back office. Even as a skeleton you're an ornament. You sure you should give up your ladies?"

Carl's upper lip lifted. "Forever."

Still not quite believing it, but with triumphant thanks spoken, he made for the under-stair cubbyhole shared by Hosiery, Neckwear and Handkerchiefs, to loose his news on Joe Eggen. Most of the springing jubilance within him must, he thought, sprout from the marvel of having his wait at last ended, more from this final compliance in Salloway, more from escaping the assaults of floor managing. Midway in the stretch behind him, at his own request, he'd been transferred from main to Women's Wear, on second; Women's Wear meant more area to patrol, meant more important unit sales, meant still more temperament in the saleswomen, but also meant a few less women thudding and swirling against him. Even at that there still were plenty; it would be all right with him if he never again heard "No clerk all this time?" Never again the bristling "That was my sale." All this in addition to being once more on his way, his feet on a new ledge of the mountainside——

In the paper- and box-littered, cramped small space under the stairway, Joe Eggen took his news temperately. Joe was near forty, the flat top of his head crisscrossed by strands of sparse auburn hair, his small pink-rimmed eyes blinking behind thick lenses. Fortunately he was one of the assistants with whom Carl had acquainted himself; Christine had invited him for dinner, but they never, actually, had come to be friendly; around the store Eggen was known as a stick. He also, however, was known as shrewd, and Carl was glad enough he was the first buyer with whom he'd work.

"Probably," Eggen advised him on Monday, "what you'd best start on is the paperwork. If you've not worked around buying you haven't any idea how much paperwork is involved. You'll keep busy——"

He was right. Plunging into the litter toward which he was waved, Carl thought at first he would never find anything in it but chaos. Both Joe and Mrs. Williams had previously kept records, but their main purpose apparently was to perplex each other; the indecipherable notations meant nothing or anything. He couldn't, besides, work in choked confusion; his first task, largely done overtime, was to clean out the office, weeding the effects of Hosiery from those of Neckwear and Handkerchiefs, discarding or finding space in the basement for files dating back to the 1800s, unearthing moth-eaten, dust-crusted samples and sample books from heaven knew when. By the time he was finished, Mrs. Lettice, the neckwear and handkerchief buyer, no longer spoke to him, but the office was such a model of order that Salloway, maliciously grinning, brought in other buyers to look at it.

Record-keeping, too, could be forced to a system. For the courses long ago taken in accounting, he had up to now had little use; it was pleasure now to rediscover the regimented precision with which figures worked. In the actual buying Eggen played his cards close to his chest, calling on Carl for opinions on samples, using him to collect information, depending on him for checking discounts, checking in merchandise, but making all agreements with manufacturers himself. Carl quickly grew intimate with the department's merchandise—the staple black and white lisles, the white and black silks, the zigzag snaky stripes, the diamond plaid wools being affected by college girls. Unlike most other departments, Hosiery did a fair part of its buying locally, at Chapaqua's Acme Mills. Over Acme purchases there was little argument, but with salesmen who came in from outside, setting up sample trunks in nearby hotels, or bringing samples into the office, there was, often, an almost endless haggling, the aspect of buying which, Carl soon realized, he liked least.

Never overtly hostile, Eggen nonetheless continued to keep Carl in his place. "Maybe you'd better get that from me," he would tell a copywriter down for an ad, "Mr. Reiss is pretty new here." "While I'm busy with Funkstein would be a good time for you to get up to the receiving room, Reiss." "You'll be in charge next week, Reiss, while I run over to Chicago," with never a hint of what the trip was for.

"What's he up to," Carl for a while wondered, "some kind of Mrs.

Willette?" But that was hard to believe too. Screens set up around him were more than provoking; for all the practice he was getting in buying, he sometimes thought furiously, he might as well have stayed on the floor. He had Eggen, a bachelor and hungry, again out for dinner; Christine took the boys to her mother's so the evening was entirely pleasurable. He treated Eggen to lunches downtown, he listened for tedious hours to descriptions of assembling a crystal set—Eggen, it seemed, was an enthusiast about a new fad called radio. All to no avail. Not until April, when he'd been in the department seven months, did insight come.

That week he had set up the new set of ledgers with his finally evolved system of bookkeeping; it was a shame, it was pure waste, to lay the completed production before Eggen, not Salloway. Eggen slowly turned first one page, then another, with nothing to contribute but a wooden appreciation.

"Very nice. Makes it all clear and quite simple, doesn't it?"

But his voice, then, abruptly slid up to a higher pitch. He continued, "In fact, you're quite the fellow, Reiss, aren't you? Quite clever. One of Salloway's pets. That's more than I've been, but I've got where I am now, and where I'm staying."

It came so unannounced that Carl merely blinked, but during the first taken-aback instant he dived beneath Eggen's skin. Unprepossessing, sprung from some malforming poverty, owning nothing alive of his own but coils of thin wire, old tin cans, and this department. For Eggen the height of ambition was to be the buyer, the ruler, of Hosiery, one of the store's most insignificant sections. There would never be a big turnover, never any radical departures, in Hosiery.

Slowly and carefully, against the fire flaming in Eggen's cheeks, he made clear his own position.

"I've no least desire to buy hosiery; I want to move on to assisting Mrs. Pesek. In the whole store you'd scarcely find anyone less anxious to fill your shoes than I am."

Spacing the three words of his answer at caustic deliberate intervals, Eggen replied, "Is—that—so." Before Carl could continue he scurried hotly from the cubbyhole. At their next encounter no reference was made to this interchange, but a day or two later, when occasion opened, he repeated Carl's statement before Salloway, giving it a flat, faintly sardonic inflection.

"Reiss here tells me his interest in hosiery doesn't amount to much; he wants to go on to women's wear. That being the case——"

Salloway allowed time for conclusion, but none came forth. After it was obvious there was no conclusion, Salloway glinted at Carl and then dryly drawled, "One thing to say for Reiss, all right, he sets his sights high." A comment slashing both ways—at Carl, again, but with contempt at Eggen, too, for wetting his pants over his small mediocrity.

After that, though, as if the statement undenied before Salloway must be binding, Eggen was somewhat less chary. "Off to see Steegal's in Kankakee," he told Carl before the next trip. "When their salesman was in here yesterday he offered a seven per cent discount—that smells to me like hot water."

The ensuing Steegall buy—eighteen gross, 2592 pairs, of the best mercerized lisle, twenty-four gross of silks, six of the latest-style novelties, all well under the market—was a coup of the season. In the following expansiveness Eggen imparted what he obviously felt to be a plum from his knowledge as buyer. "You've got to get so you smell hot water; that's when you can hit for price."

For this nugget Carl had only an intolerant disdain. Was this what buying amounted to? Knowing your merchandise, knowing your fashions, and then, other than that, slinking about like a ferret to find people in trouble, so you could beat them down on price? Far enough down, as with Steegal's, so the manufacturer consequently went bankrupt? His change to Women's Wear, where merchandise and fashion must mean more, price less, couldn't come soon enough.

In March of 1926, after seventeen months with Joe Eggen, he reached that apotheosis too.

"Whatever your pipe line is, it's certainly direct," Salloway this time told him resignedly. "I didn't know myself, until this morning, that we'd be taking Miss Bruce away from Mrs. Pesek to put her in the basement."

Into the new job he moved with an enthusiasm certainly more knowledgeable than that with which he had moved into Hosiery. Assisting in Hosiery, after a year, was something he handled with one hand.

As one of the first adjuncts of his later rise, he found on his new desk one morning a note in the copperplate hand of Mr. Trurog's secretary. "Mr. Trurog would like to have Mr. Reiss drop in at his office. Perhaps at three-fifteen on March twenty-seventh."

Standing there looking down at that note, even though it was expected, he had a sensation just under his breastbone as of wide wings unfolding to lift him strongly and soaringly upward. This royal summons was one accorded a Trurog employee only when he reached what was recognized as the upper levels.

Whatever contempt he might hold for Trurog as a person—and he was very aware, standing there, of the caustic comments he would make if Harriet stood beside him, or even Christine—that didn't alter what Trurog was as a symbol. Salloway controlled, but Trurog owned.

At three-fifteen on the afternoon named, with a heart thudding as thickly, for all its years of experience, as it had thudded on that day now so long lost in distance when he was picked by Salloway, he presented himself, in a flawlessly pressed new suit, at the desk held down by the middle-aged woman known in the store as St. Peter. That desk was quite accessible, contained within an anteroom to which the door during store hours was always open; in passing he often—in passing, in fact, he nearly always—looked over St. Peter's desk to the holy of holies beyond: a massive steel door like a safe door, bearing a massive bank lock, opening upon a dimness which to his distance exuded the odors of a sacrosanct luster and richness. He had got off the elevators at a split second of three-fifteen; after exactly two minutes St. Peter rose, her voice low.

"You may come now." Short of the inner door, stepping back to let Carl move past her, she murmured, "Mr. Reiss, Mr. Trurog," and faded away.

Once he was over the threshold, Carl paused. Mr. Trurog, his higher right shoulder more lifted than ever, was intently perusing a square white card which, except for his two hands, was the only object upon the long, dark-gleaming expanse of the table behind which he sat. Almost at once, however, the intense thin face lifted. "Reiss? Reiss? A kindness to take of your valuable time——"

Scrambling to his feet, the old man hobbled forward to meet Carl halfway, at Carl's respectful "The kindness is yours, Mr. Trurog," first halfway extending, then withdrawing, then more resolutely thrusting his right hand out all the way for Carl to shake.

"No, no," the owner of Trurog's insisted while this handshaking took place. "Yours, yours. You may not know it, my boy, but you've been much on our minds. Eighteen years, isn't it? You started here very young, only sixteen; two years more and you'll have your twenty-year ring, a badge of valued service; you've put in your time well, Mr. Reiss. I've learned—Mr. Salloway tells me—you're our new assistant in Ladies' Dresses; a key job, Mr. Reiss—perhaps you could spare me a few moments—please, this chair here—a key job, Mr. Reiss, of tremendous importance for you and the store."

While John Trurog was speaking, while in that hushed dimness the words fell, slurred slightly, rushed, tumbling, while Carl was patted toward a huge armchair in dark blue leather, his mind fled out to much more than was being said. The knowledge John Trurog was displaying came, he knew, from beautifully typed notes (Harriet's) on the card Mr. Trurog had been going over when he came in, but that didn't matter. Under his feet was the famous Bokhara, rose, blue, gray and gold, its enmeshing silkiness so soft it almost was slippery, which —or so rumor said—cost over twenty thousand before so much as the import duties were paid. Ahead, behind Trurog's desk, were the two lake-facing windows, entirely covered with blue-lined silk velvet of a gray so dark it was nearly oxford, and through which sifted the room's murky duskiness. To right and left of him, on two unbroken walls, they also apparently dark gray, hung the twelve old masters which, with no word to anyone, John Trurog had flitted away to buy in the New York galleries in July of 1914. The twelve old masters for which that same summer this office had been steel-cased, the paintings for which the window bars had been set and the vault door hung.

In the murky light, and within the embrasures of their heavy, carved, incurving, foot-deep gold frames, these canvases now appeared only as mistily dark vistas into which his glance was impelled to explore, but from which at the moment he must exclude himself. John Trurog had now scurried around to resume his original place behind the desk, still continuing his freshet of words.

"You can know little of me, Mr. Reiss; less, perhaps, than I know of you. There are great griefs in my life, Mr. Reiss, one of them that I have no sons. Daughters, yes, but no sons. I am a man left with no sons. If I had sons I would look to them to take up my burdens with me, since I have none I must—must get sons by—— Perhaps, Mr. Reiss, you may say I have sons by adoption."

For a second, at the "you can know little of me," Carl's lip corners jerked; longingly he thought, "If only Harriet were here." He, or Harriet, might not have affidavits on what was known of John Trurog, but no one could say it was little. The beseeching, ingratiating old man before him, or so the unsworn voice of legend ran, had been born of an Armenian mother and a here-today, gone-tomorrow French soldier; his earliest business experience had come with a maternal grandfather, touring the outlying farms of Maine and New Hampshire as a horse-and-buggy peddler, seldom, legend suggested, twice in the same area. He was still in his teens when, with a few inherited hundreds, he came west to Chapaqua in the early 1870s, starting a store in a dismal bystreet leading to an odorous, refuse-strewn water front. It was 1890 or later before the city grew aware of itself. When the way was opened by a huge colonnaded gray marble Greek post office, and other businesses looked to the lake front, it was found that John Trurog held options on half the property there.

It was on results of this enterprise that, shortly before 1900, the first real Trurog's rose, a Trurog's which in 1906 was enlarged and remodeled, and which twice since then had gone through the same process. He was said to have married, soon after he made the trek westward, a wife much older than he; sometime later that wife vanished, divorced, some said, for being childless. Soon after he married again, and issue of this marriage, as Carl knew by much more than hearsay, was two daughters near his own age; during his first years in the store they had been in and out often, insouciant marauders, bearing off the cream of each dress crop, as unlike their father as dragonflies are unlike ants. These girls now, he knew, were Mrs. Ilsley, of Long Island, and Mrs. Jones-Ferris, of San Francisco; every once in a while they still cut visiting swaths through the store, and their pictures, complete with small children, appeared in the Sunday society sections.

No sons—this was a fact of which John Trurog had no need to remind him, either; this was one of the mainstays behind his ambition. The two Trurog daughters would never enter the business, not they; they'd take dividends. Salloway's two sons had been born late, long after the Salloway daughter; they still were schoolboys of twelve and fourteen, who couldn't compete, not until it was too late. Ohman had only Barbara. Leverett had one son, a young doctor. Bodali, officially, was childless. He could scarcely have asked, and how often this thought was balm, for less competition by nepotism.

"I wish," John Trurog besought wistfully, "that you might begin thinking of yourself as one of my sons by adoption. You are important to this store, Mr. Reiss; it is my hope it will be important to you. There are so many ways, Mr. Reiss, in which simply by attitude—I've felt this so often, Mr. Reiss, simply by attitude—an employee of this store can make a sale or mar it. I remember a woman we had here once, a saleswoman in Ladies' Dresses. She was a trifle old when she came to us, past fifty; gone now, of course, we had to dismiss her; she got past the age for it. At her best, though, that woman was more than a saleswoman, she made selling an art. Just by the way she held a dress"—thin hands gestured tenderly—"that woman could make a customer look on almost any garment as rare and unusual. It's women like that we should all of us take to our hearts, Mr. Reiss. We must have merchandise, yes. The best we can find for our money; every penny you spend as a buyer, Mr. Reiss—never forget this—is a penny taken from the life of the store. But this other side, Mr. Reiss, the presentation of merchandise to the customer, this too has its art. As assistant buyer one of your duties will be the training of sales-people——"

Of Carl little was required beyond a sturdy "I already think of Trurog's as my family" and nods of affirmation. After the pointers on selling came other pointers on buying, and a wistful hope more, "I've suggested to Mr. Salloway that we might get more figures, we might get much more merchandise, into our display windows; to me they look often quite bare. When I think of sales we may be losing—a brilliant man, Salloway, very brilliant, you might see what you can do with it——" Again a scurry around the desk, this time for a dismissing handclasp.

"I feel we're well met, Mr. Reiss. Common interests."

The interview thus solemnly concluded, however, didn't quite end there. From a head so humbly tilted that the dark eyes, seen even in this gloom as gleaming with a fever heat, seemed to peer up from under Carl's chin, came a brisker question. One proffered, it might be, as treat or reward.

"You'd like to see my pictures?"

To that, Carl had no trouble making a convincing answer; he had heard too much, he had too many tastes that way, not to be consumed by desire to see the pictures.

Nodding, now, with pleased small jerks, brushing his hands with pleased small rubs, the old man trotted to the wall at the right. Extending darting long fingers under the first of the canvases, he clicked the switch of a blue bulb held in a cupping long shade.

From that bulb soft light bloomed upward, bringing into almost painfully acute existence a scene of coifed burly Renaissance peasants drinking and dancing in an Old World tavern. About the order in which the figures were placed, about the mingling of colors—reds, browns, ochers, oranges, off yellows—about some kind of affection which—despite the fat, drunken, riotous reality with which they were depicted—seemed to dwell in the people, there was an enjoying, tolerant sweetness which hit out at Carl like a blow. He blinked, his throat felt closed and tight, yet he could, he thought, have stood looking at that one picture for all of a day, his eyes following first one figure, then another, moving as the crowd for all its stillness seemed to move, aching at the lusty richness of color.

"Some people—I don't know what you'll think, Mr. Reiss—but some people think this is perhaps my best. Painted by a man named Pieter Breughel, a Fleming. Very common people, of course, but it's been much admired. Before buying my pictures I took the best advice I could find; it's a very uncertain matter, Mr. Reiss—one of those things which as a buyer you must always have in mind—the spending of money. It's always so easy, Mr. Reiss, to spend money and lose it; nothing can be a greater responsibility. Often as I lie awake at night— but you wouldn't think, would you, Mr. Reiss, that a picture like this would ever be worth less than I paid for it?"

Pleasure had ebbed now from the flurried purr; behind it was the torment of a man in a pit; out toward Carl reached the small nerveend patting and beseeching tentacles, begging reassurance. Something rose in Carl's craw; from a crushing hurt of his own he might have thrust stonily back, "You ask to have this and reassurance too?" Instead what he must proffer was a soothing, a reverent murmur, "Not much else in the world, Mr. Trurog, can be more solidly valuable than this."

From the little reaching feelers, stroked pleasure, though the inner torment didn't ease. "Mr. Reiss, thank you; I can hope you're right. And this next——"

Light died long before Carl was ready for it to die, snapping instantly away from the bulb, and in the picture over it a life more obscurely continued, though he must tear himself away from it.

"This next," old Trurog continued, as light once more rayed upward, "a Gainsborough. Not as fine, not as perfect an example of the master's work, they tell me, as that Breughel, but still quite good. It cost, of course, too, somewhat less. Not little, I may add—a purchase of this kind, as you can perhaps imagine, Mr. Reiss, is a truly terrifying decision. But still less. I can only hope——"

From the Gainsborough a court lady gazed out from arched eyes, serenely detached, her exquisite high powdered coiffure surmounted by side-falling plumes, her exquisite blue-green shoulder bearing a static gray curl, her exquisite small hands presenting a static small fan, her exquisite small waist compressed within the milky blue-green shimmering satin, her skirts billowing. From the Gainsborough they went on to a Reynolds—a small girl in white, her blowing hair blue-bound, her round dark eyes dreaming. From the Reynolds to a Fragonard—pink figures reveling under trees seen in the yellowing, deepening, last light of day. From that to a Turner, to a Peter Lely, to a Vermeer, to a Chardin.

At each the anguished question, "You wouldn't think now, Mr. Reiss, would you——" at each Carl's response, which somehow it grew more and more chokingly difficult to deliver.

"No question. A picture like this is beyond price."

Even after he was away, even after he was back downstairs, even after he passed one of the girls—"Back from hobnobbing with Our Father Who Art in Heaven, Mr. Reiss?"—and Mrs. Pesek—"Get to see the pictures? Well, that's always a good sign"—he felt he had been lashed with thin whips. Across his back, over his abdomen, down the backs of his legs, lay the smarting rise of the welts.

Why, just from those pictures, should he feel that way? Not the rug, not the room, not anything else. He had always—yes, his word was the right one—loathed Trurog. From report he more or less knew what Trurog would say; he knew the pictures were there. The only thing different was that now he had seen them.

Not right, not fair—this was the cry, the lash, that stung blood from his flesh. Not fair that one man such as John Trurog should own those twelve pictures to shut up with his insectlike self in a room like a bank vault. Other kinds of wealth, yes, but not that nourishing loveliness. Still, for his Sundays, he liked nothing better than an afternoon at the Art Institute; for himself he could produce nothing tolerable, not in a field where only perfection was acceptable. At Midwestern, early, he'd taken one art course, but from then on forced himself to the others, the practical ones. That, though, hadn't extinguished his instinctive response, his instinctive feeling for line, color and symmetry. Even the colors he'd used for his apartment came from a painting, and one of the reasons why, if he were to buy anything, he wanted to buy ladies' dresses, was that in them you looked for texture, you sought color and line. He had ideas about women's clothes, shoulder-shrugging distaste for the bloused, beaded, beflowered atrocities specialized in by Mrs. Pesek—Mrs. Pesek, Harriet said, bought clothes as if they were all to be worn by herself.

All this, though, was something aside. As he moved along the two rows of pictures, what had really flailed at him were other responses he wouldn't let rise to the surface, responses he didn't want to accept or recognize. Useless to decry the ownership, the exclusion of beauty; he was dedicated to ownership, or at least to its services.

Sharp and excoriating as was this reaction to his interview with Mr. Trurog, however, it was short-lived. For the rest of that day he found no peace anywhere, his evening with Christine and the boys was a snarling cry for escape. As early as the next day, though, it faded surprisingly, and from then on he seldom remembered it. He didn't, even, too often remember the paintings.

8 In addition to his belief that ladies' dresses were wares on which his tastes and abilities might rewardingly be spent, there were other and perhaps stronger reasons why they drew his attention. Stock boy for ladies' dresses had been one of his earliest jobs; the Mrs. Pesek of 1909 had been a fashionably buxom, high-colored, high-bosomed sport, harassed sometimes but on the whole good-naturedly genial. Casting out dull care, the Mrs. Pesek of that day said very often, with her rolling low laugh, was a thing she was good at. Time and the repeated casting away of care, in the years intervening, had levied penalties heavier than those of the new income taxes; the harassment that had been a temporary mantle became a permanent shroud. Fashions, in those years, changed faster and faster, not only in clothes but in people; by 1926 there still was a fair contingent of women who came to Trurog's for "Just the most perfect little yellow and coral print chiffon, you know, for my club afternoons," but there also were ominous rumblings from above, indicating that notice was beginning to be taken of the thriving trade enjoyed by the mushrooming small specialty shops, and even by rival emporiums.

In person, too, Mrs. Pesek had altered. Her silky black hair might not gray much, but layer after layer added itself to her flesh, broken blue-red veins crisscrossed her nose and her flushed winy cheeks; it came to be habit for her girls to lift significant brows over whispers when of mornings she waddled in—"Lordy, think she'll last the day?"

Not only all this, but Milo Geggenheim, too, Milo Geggenheim, the merchandiser whose heavy pinion extended over the entire Women's Wear section—dresses, suits, coats, millinery, skirts, furs, blouses —was nearing his latter days; the department was planning a party for his sixtieth birthday. Geggenheim's reputation was one of being a tartar, assistants given him averaged three months, but none of those assistants had been named Carl Reiss. Less than nine years to go for old Geggenheim—a little long, perhaps, but just about what he would have to count on for the jobs between. Assistant buyer at thirty-three, buyer at, say, thirty-five, merchandiser at forty-two—Salloway climbed to Personnel before he was thirty-five, but he wasn't necessarily out to beat Salloway's record. Merchandising at forty-two wouldn't be bad. When Salloway retired, Carl would be fifty, and that, as well, would be right.

Only a few weeks, besides, were all that were needed to prove how shrewd he was in his choosing, how much, for all his fretting, he'd learned with Joe Eggen. "For cripe's sake," was Mrs. Pesek's first wheezing request, "get me in shape the way you did Hosiery; sometimes I don't know where I am."

Actually any disorder in Dresses was nothing in comparison. Garments might hang thick from the six-by-six ladies' dress cubicle, but they were current garments, just down from Receiving, or bought and awaiting alteration; none were relics of thirty years back. Mrs. Pesek herself seldom touched pencil to paper; her records were mental. "What's this now? Oh, God, yes, I remember. It's a lot should have been here the fourteenth." Miss Bruce, though, had been fairly scrupulous, and a new file and ledger system took no time at all.

"What I ever did without you I don't know." Mrs. Pesek soon leaned on him as on a crutch. The routine of the receiving room and direction of the sales force fell to him as simply as apples fall from a tree; he began compressing his principles of salesmanship, not forgetting those imparted by John Trurog, into ten-minute once-weekly talks.

"I know what you're here for, a young man like you; I just don't see, though, how you can be sent to New York by yourself yet, and both of us going together—someone's got to be in the department." Even before he began any such worrying, Mrs. Pesek was doing that too; within Mrs. Pesek's swollen and unwieldy flesh existed a warm generosity which already had fallen on him once and again, which he counted on, and which she was more than ready to extend. In mid-May, when he'd been with her no more than two months, she engineered an arrangement beyond any hope he could yet have had. "Mrs. Henry and Brucie will both be home next week; I've fixed it for Brucie to come up from the basement."

At first, when she said it, he didn't comprehend. Only when she went on, "You better take this noon for getting tickets and wiring in reservations; you can stay at the New Yorker where I stay unless you prefer somewhere else," did he understand he was actually to have a buying trip, his first. His eyelids heated over his eyes, and his palms, too, quickly stung; while she was speaking he stood holding out toward her a dress being turned back because of dye streaks; she stood distraught as always, head tipped, brows pulled frowningly inward, one hand lifting the skirt to catch light; she spoke as if what she were doing for him was the most ordinary routine.

In a gesture half handclasp, half stroking affection, he reached out a hand to cup under her forearm. "Mrs. Pesek, of all good scouts anywhere you are probably the kindest." Not brilliant, but he wasn't interested, right then, in brilliance. Why, he could have asked at that juncture, must a way upward be over people? Other buyers might go on to other jobs. Mrs. Pesek wouldn't.

Through all of the three days ensuing—departures for New York were on Saturday evenings, to make the best use of working time—this pinch of bitterness misflavored his cup. Christine's pride was radiant, the boys danced to a tune of "Daddy's going away on a choo-choo," Salloway stopped for a shoulder clap—"Hear you're taking up traveling"—Bob Gokey shook out a rueful confession, "Guess you've got what I haven't." For the first time in his life he was traveling first class, with a lower, on the New York Central—none of it had the right flavor. Not until the Monday morning in New York when, sprucely fresh in the suit he had put on for John Trurog, he knocked at Mrs. Pesek's hotel door, did that acridity die from his tongue. Mrs. Pesek, rolling to the door, the cup of a slightly too youthful orchid hair-braid hat already concealing her hair, was not only once more entirely matter-of-fact but, it seemed, brisker and jauntier than at home.

"Well, boy, off to the races," she tossed to him, with a springing if slightly grim archness. "Relax now; a buying trip's always half holiday. Whatever we get ourselves into today, it won't be Geggenheim, Trurog or Salloway, blast that one's black soul."

Expressions of disaffection toward the store and the store higherups came his way so frequently that he believed himself immune. Speech such as this from Mrs. Pesek, though, shocked him a little; he hadn't thought such animosity extended to the buyers. He asked, "What've you got against Salloway?"

Lifting thick surah-covered shoulders in an elephantine shrug, Mrs. Pesek answered, "Salloway? Oh, nothing at all against Salloway. What could anyone have against Salloway?" This was followed by a short laugh still carrying the echo of a rolling contralto. Directing the prow of her bosom toward the door and the elevators, as soon as she had picked up gloves, handbag and silver foxes from the bed, Mrs. Pesek rechanneled the subject.

"Now, boy, we're started. And what you want to know first about our kind of buying——"

This was what he was here for, instruction. This was what his present and his future depended on, how well he picked up what she now taught him, how well he used what he learned, how he improved on it. He couldn't waste time on the old store-bound antipathies. As they traversed the long corridor, as they rode down in the elevator, as they emerged from the lobby into bright city sunshine and found a cab, he began to feel free from his repugnance again. This quick city life all around him held too much he must reach.

The first thing to know about their kind of buying, or so Mrs. Pesek said, was that a buyer from out of town, no matter how big his store might be, no matter how he kept up with his *Vogue* and his *Harper's Bazaar*, never went first to the markets. He shopped windows. Saks, Lord and Taylor, Stern's, Macy's.

"You could walk right into the departments. They don't know you yet. A fright, though, how quick they pick you up; sometimes I think we must smell, but I suppose it's a look we've got. I can do the same thing on comparison shoppers, back home. These New York stores don't keep much on display inside, and they don't bring you out much, not once they've spotted you. So it's windows—all right, here's where we start. Saks. Oh, blast, blast and double blast. Coats."

Other stores, fortunately, were more accommodating; Lord and Taylor, Stern's, each had a dress window, Macy's had two. While Mrs. Pesek passed and repassed, mumbling, he took notes of the mumbles. "Petal and ruffle skirts, those seem still good. Wing capes, crepe Elizabeth, tie collars and diamond beading—boleros, side pleats, godets and fringe——"

Cheerful once more, with this chore done, she made, via another cab, for the dress centers. Soon his head ached from the multiplicity of impressions he was trying too hard to take in too thoroughly. Most of the places they entered were warehouses of high ceilings, unvarnished and littered wood floors, fierce lights, aisle after seemingly endless aisle of dress racks; from beyond and above, incessantly, sounded a drumming thump and whir, feet trotted, voices jangled, cables whined. Only occasionally were the dress forests the areas actually penetrated; more usually they were ushered into partitioned-off showrooms, discreetly if a little dustily luxurious, carpeted, draped, furnished with lounges and smoking stands. "Mrs. Pesek! We couldn't imagine! How's the health these days? That bubble dot from last time, didn't that go like we said? You got now a new assistant——" Only after chirps of social greeting were overpassed was there a getting down to business. "Mrs. Pesek, this time we got for you such a number—one hundred dozen to Macy's, seventy dozen to Wanamaker——"

Mrs. Pesek, he came to know, bought charily and against outcry. "Only two dozen *this* number? Gone the first ten minutes. You——"

Mrs. Pesek's reply was a stock reply. "I can always reorder." Sometimes she was doubtful. "I may come back on this one tomorrow." Sometimes she chose by what seemed impulse and against advice. "That little girl walking over there toward that dressing room, what's she got on? I'll take that too. Orchid, canary and mint green, one each twelve to twenty."

"Those sons of bitches," she illuminated this particular transaction en route to the next house, "they've got a number going so well they're a little short. Do they bring it out? I should say not. They've got to keep in with you, so they don't usually show too bad stuff, but you've got to look out for 'em. They can unload, too."

Three days of it. Information necessary, pertinent, both like and unlike the expected. Usually, after five, Mrs. Pesek dismissed him. "I guess you can look after yourself now; I'm having dinner with that big hunk of kosher salami from Finkelstein's."

In spite of his headaches, the pressure of so many things learned, he was able, on his own, to get in a few things, breaking away early the second afternoon, when Mrs. Pesek admitted herself tired, for a visit to the Art Museum, taking top-deck bus rides, penetrating a few of the stores, many of them so astoundingly much smaller than Trurog's, but the richer ones carrying a gleam, in polished wood, in glass, in silver and gold, even in leather, which exceeded the Trurog gleam. One evening he heard Raquel Meller. His single previous experience of New York was of being herded through toward France; all his previous images were of the long approach by train through the tenements, of fat women in windows resting their elbows on bed pillows while they stared vacantly outward, of the wet shooting steam and the hot smell of the train sheds, of the cavernous foot-ringing vaults of Grand Central, the stink of water, the sheer black loom of the ship's side; he hadn't even seen the Statue of Liberty, since they'd moved out at night.

Now he drank in these other impressions: the daylong thunderous roar and the daylong riveting, the more muted drum roll of late nightfall, the night lights, the feeling of lusty upsurgence from the steel-girded skeleton skyscrapers in every midtown block, the hodgepodge of people. In Chapaqua people verged toward a median, the poor struggling toward a decent imitation of the well to do, the rich restraining themselves to a local good taste. Here there was no such conformity. In the same minute on the same sidewalk in the white cement-gleaming sunlight before the same building he heard polyglot tongues, saw men and women in thick shapeless queer earth-brown garments, who darted in and out like bent scurrying beetles—people in New York as a whole seemed so much swarthier than in Chapaqua —and at the same time startlingly resplendent women, some young, some old but as preciously groomed as the young, holding the fine leather leashes of silky small jewel-collared dogs, they themselves individual showpieces, hatted, furred, gloved in a way which, in Chapaqua, would have drawn crowds and immediate conclusion, "Must be some traveling burleyque queen," but which here drew no attention, and meant, apparently, only a well-off wife out getting some air.

It was the Wednesday evening, however, supposedly their last, which turned out to be momentous.

Just after four in the afternoon, lolling bouncingly against taxi cushions, Mrs. Pesek closed her eyes and kicked off her shoes, heaving a sigh so voluminous it eddied out over her billows like a ripple in water. She murmured, "Keep shut for a minute, boy, hm?" And then, after only the minute requested, "Yep, I guess that's the lot. There's a couple small houses where we could take a quick look-see in the morning. Come train time tomorrow afternoon, though, we'll be set. No hurry, either. What do you think—should we have ourselves a night?"

The immediate disinclination he felt wasn't in any way due to revulsion against a too wide invitation; there might be other men, older men, toward whom Mrs. Pesek was coy; toward him she was scrupulously straightforward. At the root of reluctance lay the other. He didn't want to get to know Mrs. Pesek better than he already knew her, or like her better than he already liked her.

Under the circumstances, though, he must produce the correct "That's kind of you, again; I don't really know much of New York."

"Well, Lord, I do." Mrs. Pesek was obtuse and comfortable. "Got my start at Best's, been back five or six times a year ever since. Let's see, now. Maybe that speak on Thirty-fourth Street. Italian. We could afterward stop at a scalper and see about tickets——"

By six-thirty they were afloat on this evening. First the speakeasy, which he found dingy and spurious, with its barred peephole door, checked and spotted red tablecloths, its general odor of hot oil and stale feathers, its raw redeye in cups. Then the scalper's and three hours in plush seats suffering (Mrs. Pesek's choice, naturally) through *Getting Gertie's Garter*. After that, again by Mrs. Pesek's choice— "You want to go home now?" "You're probably tired——" "Heck, no, me tired?"—they moved on to another speakeasy where, this time in tumblers, they had scotch described as right off a boat.

As a boy he'd been given blackberry brandy in spoonfuls for stomach-ache, in France he'd met crème de menthe and cognac, before prohibition he sometimes had a beer or two with Bob Gokey, but he wasn't accustomed to drinking, not as Mrs. Pesek and the other frequenters of the two speakeasies knew it. Uncomfortably, at tables in smoke-swirled semidarkness where his elbows were crowded by other tables at which shadowy figures seemed to sit forehead to forehead, he got down first the one cup of redeye and then the one glass of scotch and water which were what courtesy demanded. Mrs. Pesek, at each place, had three refills; reluctantly, at the second speak, when he repeated at least for a seventh time, "No, thanks, not tonight, I still have that slight headache," she rolled sighing to her feet.

"I guess then we'll have to get out of here. They don't like you just sitting around."

At her hotel, because she was slightly unsteady, he insisted on seeing her to her door. "All foolishness," she scolded. "Now you'll have to walk back to that elevator, over those lo-o-ong miles of carpet——"

Refusing to give him her key, she first lifted it to a sternly belligerent eye, then, backing slightly, bent at the waist to insert it, the tails of her foxes brushing the floor. It was while she was so bent, the key scratching at the lock plate, that she seemed to become transfixed. Over the cushions of her wide back ran a quiver, not of softness but rigidity; just as he was putting out his hand to her, beginning "Mrs. Pesek, what——" her face swung around to him, on it a grin which in the shaded light of the corridor seemed to be one of a mordant incredible humor, but which then almost instantly he knew as the risus of pain.

Again, horrified now, he said, "Mrs. Pesek!" and caught at her. Against his arms she hung heavily, struggling, all of her body contorted by motion. He looked about wildly; in the long hall with its rows of white enameled doors and door casings, its white-figured blue classical wallpaper, its white-figured blue classical carpet, its regularly spaced tall classical urns of white sand, he and Mrs. Pesek were alone. Around the corner were the elevators, but that was too far away; he might shout but it was after one; a weight of quiet seemed to press out from those other rooms in which people lay sleeping. Besides, as within half an instant he realized, he couldn't hold Mrs. Pesek until help got there; all he could do, exerting all the strength he had, was ease her collapse to the floor.

She still was conscious; when he turned her over she lay amid her furs, on her hat, staring agonizedly back at him, ripples of pain still jerking her body; her lips moved, but no sound came. Acting now without thinking, he stepped over her to snatch up her key from the floor.

Toward seven in the morning he stood in a different corridor.

Two doors below him was the room in which Mrs. Pesek now lay, a room into which doctors, nurses and wheeled cylinders had all night been vanishing, a room from which doctors and nurses, emerging, had for him little but a shrug. Now at seven, though, a doctor came who at Carl's quick "How is she?" let himself be halted.

"We don't really know yet." He glanced at a card he held, one for which Carl previously had supplied answers. "You this—assistant?"

"That's right."

"I see. Well, what she's suffered is a coronary thrombosis, a break in a heart artery, no doubt about that. May pull through, but more likely not. Her near relatives should certainly get here. If you can take care of that——"

Carl said dully, "I don't think she has any." Among stray bits of personal information scattered at him through the past few days was reply to a query put, on his part, simply because they'd come to a long lull in talking. "Heck, yes, had a husband once, don't even know where the old bum has been for the last ten, twelve years."

The doctor said smoothly, "We know you'll do what you can. I see you say you believe the patient able to care for expenses, but that temporarily your firm may underwrite them. You might stop off in the office——"

A few minutes later he was eased out, standing on a semicircular cement step, the light of another blinding and unseasonably warm day thudding against eyes and skin. Before him were trees, two barbered small segments of lawn; beyond them extended in patterned un-uniformity the light-reflecting sides and the shadowed sides of buildings; the day's roar was begun. He felt numb and insensate. His wrist watch said seven thirty-seven. What did he do now? Somewhere out beyond him was a hotel room, his until two-thirty. Sleep was what he needed, but the thought of sleep was guilt-touched. He'd been told he couldn't see Mrs. Pesek, heaven knew he didn't want to see Mrs. Pesek, but it couldn't be right to go off, leaving her alone.

A taxi pulled up and a flurried, half-dressed woman leaped out, drifting a bill like a leaf toward the driver, mumbling, "Oh, thank you, oh, thank you," running past Carl, her eyes distraught.

As she disappeared inward the driver more slowly followed, halting below Carl on the sidewalk, squeezing a cigarette from a packet, lighting it, shaking his head.

"Honest, things you see, sometimes——" Then, after two puffs, "How about you, buddy, you going anyplace?"

It was in the cab that, looking once more at his watch, he thought, with a rush, of Chapaqua. Seven forty-seven. That was six forty-seven, Chapaqua time. Christine and the boys would be waking. Salloway——

By ten o'clock, Eastern Time, he could call Salloway.

Thirty hours later, on the train, he repeated to himself that Mrs. Pesek's welfare was no longer his concern. The last wire from Salloway said: "Found niece arriving tomorrow you can return." Calls to the hospital elicited answers on the whole reassuring. "She seems to be holding her own." As instructed by Salloway, he'd signed orders for three private nurses, and from his own funds sent a flowering rosebush. Resting against Pullman plush, he tried fighting the burn of a later revolt. Why was this visited on him? Mrs. Pesek, actually, was nothing to him; the catastrophe befallen her was one to which she'd moved headlong by profligate living; if it had happened decently out of sight—if he'd come to work some morning, for instance, to have the girls meet him tiptoeing, "Mr. Reiss, have you heard——" he could have taken it with no more than the response it deserved: a pang of regret, a pang of thinking, "That's how people go, in the end."

Now what he must see was that grin she had turned to him; now what he must feel was a strengthened guilt, as if what came to her was in some way his fault, as if he'd wished it for her.

Nor was guilt all he had to bear, either. As the train sped toward Chapaqua he was visited by deepening depression. Dresses. What would Salloway do now about Dresses? Eleven weeks, exactly, he'd put in; eleven weeks wasn't possibly enough to let him take over. He'd miscalculated on Dresses, miscalculated on Mrs. Pesek. Salloway would get in someone else, someone young, someone hale. He might as well begin planning, right here, on a move to another department. But which one? Mrs. Bryant, in Coats, was very little past forty. Mr. Iccardi, in Millinery, not yet fifty. Not another buyer in the store was ripe for falling as Mrs. Pesek had been; only Mr. Geggenheim, of the merchandisers, had touched sixty.

Christine, meeting him with the boys, spent strength through her arms to assuage him. The girls of his department murmured, "That was a terrible thing for you to have to go through." Even Salloway was shortly sympathetic. "Couldn't have been a pleasant experience, I guess, Reiss." Depression, however, continued until something else came to replace it. No one said anything, but on the next Wednesday his pay envelope held seventy-five dollars.

It was in the dress cubicle, where he happened to be alone, that he opened the envelope; the pay tray came around just before noon. Already, from his breast pocket, he had taken his savings book; always, on payday, he slipped five dollars into the book for depositing at noon, even if he usually had to take it out again later. As a buyer's assistant he made thirty-five, but the boys saw to it the raise usually went.

With hot blood washing first up from his loins to his shoulders, then down again, leaving him chill, he stared at the bills. Seven tens and a five. "An error," his mind hollowly said, but then rejected that. Mistakes weren't made in pay envelopes.

The money meant only one thing. He was being left in as buyer. Salloway couldn't be leaving him in as dress buyer. Section managing had nothing whatever to do with buying. He knew nothing——

Coat fronts pulled back, thumbs in the armholes of his vest, Salloway with suspicious promptness walked in on him.

"Well, boy, and how do you like it?"

Mrs. Pesek was the one who called him *boy*, and Salloway knew it. He stammered, "So far I'm—I guess overwhelmed." Then, anger spurting, "You know I don't know enough. I shouldn't be——"

"Hell," Salloway broke that, "what've you been begging for, all these years? You're in it now, boy. Let's see what you do."

A buyer. He was a buyer, already. Christine was as stunned as he. Christine staunchly recovered. "You can handle it; you know you can handle it." The boys, awed, crowded his knees.

He felt no elation, only continuing resentment. All those years of crawling, of getting for so long nowhere, of not even inching forward, and now, so much too soon, being catapulted. As an act of some kind of propitiation he took around a list and sent Mrs. Pesek a radio. And through June it wasn't too bad; the ordinary routine of the department wasn't what worried him. The summer cottons and wash silks bought by Mrs. Pesek took care of June merchandise; he prepared for the mid-July sale by reorders and reductions. The week after the sale, though, another buying trip loomed, the one in which first fall styles must be chosen. No one need tell him that this trip was crucial; the first buys of any season, with manufacturers and designers themselves not sure what would emerge as a fashion, were always critical. No one, not Christine, not anyone else, could help him. Voraciously, at home and the store, he read *Women's Wear*, *Vogue*, and *Harper's Bazaar*; magazines could sponsor anything, the more outré the better, but Trurog's, as Geggenheim impressed on him, must be ninety per cent right or lose money.

All ten-day sales were a headache, but the one that summer—his first with a department to pilot—proved the worst in history. Two days before it a sweltering heat closed in; stone-built Trurog's was a little more livable than most places in town; hordes of people crowded in from the killing streets, not especially to buy, but to bump, sweat, swirl, and eddy. Stock that at sale's beginning hung at least reasonably crisp and unrumpled, by the end of the second day was a mangled and lipstick-smeared mess. Two saleswomen went boating on Sunday and came down with sunstroke. Three trained extras simply didn't show up. Loss from shoplifters jumped, and somewhere between his own checking pencil, a copyreader upstairs and a printer on the Chapaqua Courier, an ad came out offering a lot of dresses at $5.95 instead of $15.95, causing the department a straight money loss, even at wholesale, of nearly six hundred dollars.

Salloway was furious over the shoplifting; over the last, on which he might have been expected to take off Carl's skin inch by delicate inch, he merely said coolly, "A few more instances of that, and there won't be any Trurog's." As day followed day, each increasing his knowledge of pitfalls so readily awaiting his feet, as in fear of error he checked and rechecked each motion his hands made, he came to know why Mrs. Pesek was so often distraught. Anyone in a buyer's job must exist in distraction.

Between heat and the tight, repelling knot his nerves made of his stomach, he quit eating almost entirely; once a day, sometimes, he got down a pineapple malted. Christine scolded, the boys, shoved away from him, restrained by Christine, screamed rebellion. And to add to everything else, with the blooming of ragweed, he began feeling the congesting weight of his asthma. He fought it down, allowing himself such out-of-hours rest as he could, but most nights he spent no more than half drowsing, waking to gasp and cough, propped on pillows or in a chair. By the last Saturday of the sale, when at ten in the evening he boarded his train, the knot of his stomach was a small detached ball that tossed and pitched on a wide lake of panic. "Why?" Resistance repeated itself. "Why? For every other job, overtrained. For this one—why?"

Before anyone else, in New York, he saw Mrs. Pesek. Flat on her back on a pillowless bed, hands crossed over her collarbone, immobile except for her eyes and lips, her cheeks not so much thinned as blued, softened and hanging, Mrs. Pesek wheezed at him whisperingly, "Boy, I hear they did it to the both of us. You look like you been through a wringer. You can do it, though. Just remember what I said. The windows. Then Horowitz, maybe more than anyone you can trust Horowitz. Nobody needs tell me who got me that radio. I guess that's what keeps me going. I always did like it lively——"

He'd hurried to get there, but he could barely make himself stay the allotted ten minutes. From the flowers in the room, from the mound of her softened and decadent flesh, from the lingering whisper, came an emanation of mortal corrosion.

Early the next morning, after almost no sleep, he began on the path she had set for him. Windows and, in midmorning, Horowitz. He said plainly, "Mrs. Pesek's still buying; I want to take only what she'd take. Under the circumstances I'm depending on you——"

Mr. Horowitz, first calling in his associates for a concerted mourning—"Mr. Reiss, when we hear about Mrs. Pesek—every week flowers, every week someone visits"—wrung Carl's hands and assured him that if he, Horowitz, could manage, Carl would go back to Chapaqua without a dress that wouldn't fly from the racks like a bird. Obviously, too, he did a sweating best. "This bat silhouette—I guess not for you. Mrs. Pesek would take this red velvet with uneven hem. This fishtail back, maybe you try it. Not many, say three for the young girls, size twelve, size fourteen, size sixteen. You can always reorder. This eggplant——"

At other houses, too, he met kindness. At one place there was a too bland, too loud "We got the numbers you want to splurge on, Reiss——" He crossed that house from his list. By the second night, when he made another flying trip to the hospital, the constriction around his stomach was easing a little; he was actually hungry. It was raining that night, a straight, slashing, but cooling downpour; running from door to taxi his hat and shoulders got wet. But in spite of all this, that night, he slept twelve solid hours, lying down.

Altogether he bought only half as much as his files showed Mrs. Pesek had bought the preceding July, but he had almost as many styles. The last morning, daringly, he let his own taste operate a little; he bought a tubular satin, in raisin, much more severe than anything Mrs. Pesek ever went in for. Not until his buys began coming in, at home, did his stomach once more tighten and his appetite depart; he didn't seem to be living, sometimes, in a world he knew; he seemed shut off by glass walls.

As a whole, though, his purchases went well. The store's fashion writer told him comfortably, "What you sweating about? Trurog's is big enough to set styles; if we say this is the fashion, then that's that." She was particularly taken with the tubular satin, so much so she bought one herself and talked her department head into a good ad; the whole dozen and a half he had bought of that dress went out in a forenoon; he had to reorder by wire. After this small success his interior sometimes eased again; he began moving toward a dazed belief that perhaps he hadn't been too suddenly pitchforked. By late August, when his second solo buying trip came up, he took off with more mixed emotions. Again his first care was to visit Mrs. Pesek—still flat, but with flesh appreciably melted, and firmer.

"Get those windows, boy," she advised as before. "And you're lucky; the paper this morning said there'd be a Macy style show."

One of seven men in a room rocking with women, he got the Macy style show. This, he told himself over a seventy-one-cent lunch, tip included, was luck as Mrs. Pesek said, luck he hadn't counted on, luck maybe Salloway hadn't counted on, either. A tier-skirt crepe Elizabeth was paraded down the runway, then a panniered and scalloped taffeta. The costume with which he was taken, however, was a tight-skirted, tight-buttoned waistcoat dress of cinnamon suède cloth, with a white satin stock and vestee. On the model—stalking, tall, concave, inhabitant of another world, to which her chin haughtily lifted—it had a suave elegance.

Conferring upon him a slow individual revolution, the mannequin recited from her other world, "This is an Obermann original, exclusive here, one hundred twenty-five."

He murmured, "Thank you," but he was crushed. He should know elegance such as that wasn't for Chapaqua; Mrs. Ilsley might drop in for a costume at that price, or Mrs. Jones-Ferris, and of course there were the paper-mill wives, but as a whole Trurog's seldom went beyond eighty-nine fifty.

That afternoon and the next day, again beginning with Horowitz, he bought soberly, carefully. It was on the last morning, stopping at Rubens', one of the small houses down on Mrs. Pesek's list for a last-minute look-see, that a model once more stood before him in cinnamon suède cloth, waistcoat style, with a white satin stock and vestee.

He asked sharply, "What're you doing with this? I thought this was an Obermann."

At Rubens' it was Rubens himself who sold merchandise, a quick small dark man like a gadfly. Flicking the finger tips of his left hand with the palm of the right, in what seemed like a tic, Rubens laughed frankly.

"You're new, Mr. Reiss, or you'd know we're a copy house. Every fashion comes out, this is what happens, this is America. We got a price this Obermann exclusive so you can sell it thirty-nine fifty. You look now, Mr. Reiss, honestly you see much difference? Look the tailoring. Feel the suède cloth. Pinch once that satin. Look the buttons. Maybe not hand sewing, Mr. Reiss—we admit it. Cut by machine, Mr. Reiss, we admit that too. You got to look awhile, Mr. Reiss, before these days you tell the difference, machine cut and hand cut. On this dress, Mr. Reiss——"

Of the evening courses he had finally found at Midwestern, braving titters to be a sole male, one was in textiles. Using fingers and nose, now, he examined the suède cloth. Perhaps not as glossily supple as the other, but still a good suède cloth. The satin was good satin. The lines were as suave——

Nothing he had bought on the earlier trip had gone as well as the satin which was to his own taste. In an upsurge of mutinous confidence he bought the suède cloth. Four dozen, outright. Dark green, rust, the cinnamon, twelve to twenty.

When he stepped back into his department this time that upsurge was still with him. Why was he so slavish toward Pesek? Pesek hadn't been doing so well. That suède cloth vied with Peck and Peck; there were other dress wearers in Chapaqua than the size forty-fours.

Again, when the dresses came in, Miss Clements, the fashion writer, crooned over his favorite, and tried one on. She was a tall girl, quite slender but a little bony in the hips; the tightest portion of the waistcoat caught her in a wrong place. Regretfully she gave up one for herself, but outdid herself on the ad: "You're a Regency Dandy in Suède Cloth and Satin." Again in the morning he had the satisfaction of seeing women come early, their steps marked by purpose. "That Regency dress in the ad last night——" It wasn't until noon he noticed the stock-room racks of the suède cloth as almost undiminished.

He caught a salesgirl hanging one up. "What's the matter? Aren't they selling?"

She answered, "Well, everyone likes them, Mr. Reiss. Everyone thinks they're too smart for anything. But for all the customers I've had so far they're a little tight. The way they were on Miss Clements."

Spine turned icy, he checked. Total sales of the dress that morning were two, both to college girls supernaturally thin.

"You can see for yourself, Mr. Reiss," another salesgirl defensively told him, "how narrow that waistcoat is over the hips. In New York where there's all this new fad for dieting, it may fit people. It doesn't out here."

The tender young sprouts of his confidence shriveling as in a hot wind, he ordered the girls to proffer the suède cloth to every reasonably slender woman who came in, no matter what she asked for, then arranged another ad—"For the Fashionably Willowy." He wrote to Rubens, who wrote back, "This number we have no trouble selling here in the East." Desperation increasing, he went up to Miss Hazard in Corsets, who indulgently laughed.

"Oh sure, Mr. Reiss, didn't you know that? You always got to figure on plenty room around the hips, out here; women out here are too healthy."

Something Mrs. Pesek must have thought he knew. Or something she had forgotten to tell him. He couldn't believe, not of Mrs. Pesek, that oversight was deliberate. No use having thoughts such as this, though. Out of the forty-eight dresses, at the end of three weeks, he still had thirty-seven, tying up almost a thousand dollars. Discounts on remainders were a loss every department figured, but not in any such sum. News of the fiasco began seeping out, too; Geggenheim turned up one morning to pad soft-footed up and down the stock room. "Reiss, haven't we had these quite a while?" Almost imperceptibly there was a shift in Salloway, to what might be called satisfied malice. Harriet reported cheerfully, "Hear you laid a turkey egg."

He told himself frantically, "I can't let this thing floor me; I'll sell those dresses if it's the last thing on this earth I do." He solicited help from other departments, especially Corsets. "Any time you get a real beanpole——" He got the dress into a window and on a wax mannequin in the department, he had a woman from Alterations let out every possible seam. He pushed it, pushed too hard.

"Have you showed Mrs. Schilling our waistcoat dress?"

"Mrs. Schilling has tried that dress in three sizes, Mr. Reiss." It began to be a store joke. Bob Gokey roared at him, "Never see you any more; hear you're all wrapped up in waistcoats." Eggen stopped by to invite him to lunch, saying nothing, but with a sly pleasure lining his pink eyelids. Worst, though, was the fact that every time he stepped into the stock room there the garments hung, a solid phalanx. The day of reckoning, when he'd have to admit both to Salloway and Geggenheim that after all this effort he still had thirty-two dresses, each twenty-one fifty at wholesale, that would have to be practically given away, approached closer and closer. He thought desperately once, "I'll use up my own money; I'll get Christine—she can get friends of hers—to take them out." But that was no true answer, either; Salloway and Geggenheim already knew and were waiting. They knew about the six-hundred-dollar loss earlier——

In October, too, he'd be due to go to New York again. If they let him. This same thing couldn't happen, not this thing. But something would——

Not even pineapple malteds could be forced past the ladder in his throat. And yet in a way the glass walls still enclosed him, as if the day of disaster he so steadily headed toward couldn't actually reach him.

And it didn't. The last week of September his asthma struck at him instead.

9 All through the first year of their marriage Carl's continued avoidance of his aunt and his father hung over Christine as an undispelled shadow. It couldn't, she told herself, be possible that any real rift existed, or cause for a real rift; soon after their honeymoon a chest of flat silver arrived as a wedding gift, and the same day they had letters.

"Son," began the one from Carl's father, "We sure was surprised to hear you took the Big Step. Right away now you bring that little girl down here so we can get acquainted."

Reading the homely but friendly lines, she again had the thoughts she had dismissed: Carl couldn't be ashamed of his people, simply because they were a little unlettered. If he weren't a person to stand up for his choices, he'd never have married her.

"We could easily get to Elmwood and back in a Sunday," she once again hinted, and then, after May, "They'll have to know sometime, and it's a little awkward to put in a letter."

Not until late September, though, did Carl admit of his own accord that they should, perhaps, go. When they started out after work on a Saturday evening—Bob Gokey, this time in return for dinners eaten and evenings spent, was once more being generous with his car —she felt ruefully that again, because of an attitude of hers, Carl was doing something he'd have preferred avoiding. By the time they reached Elmwood it was shortly after nine, and coming on the small town from a low hill, its lights and its houses obscured by the darkness of trees, its meandering road-crossing river sending up autumn-sharp scents of leaf mold and wetness, its one downtown street alive with Saturday night cars and people, she felt a tugging nostalgia, as if it were to her past, not Carl's, that the place belonged.

"So many trees, and a river," she said. "I should think you'd want to come often; it's lovely."

He shrugged, from a rather long silence. "It's good enough as towns this size go."

He was, she sensed, both disturbed and restless. The house before which he drew up was on the outskirts on the farther side, a house which, from a gate in a staggering picket fence, was revealed as white, small, elled, its narrow front porch trimmed by wood lace and reached by a single low step, one door—the one Carl entered without knocking—leading into a square dining room, the other, its pane etched in white flowers, obviously giving on a parlor to the left.

His voice pleasant but entirely unanticipatory, Carl called, "Anyone home here? We've come."

Immediately he'd done so a big-boned, heavily fleshed woman of late middle age, her hair graying above a faintly rakish face, bustled in from the kitchen.

"Well now, well now," she greeted, "well, this couldn't be nicer. Carl, my own one boy——" Vigorously she hugged Carl before coming on to Christine. "All this time I thought I never would get my eyes set on you." Her voice had a quality of humming; she was energized and excited, holding Christine off to look at her both sharply and fondly before wrapping her in an embrace as deep as the one given Carl. After it she retained her hold of Christine's two arms. "All my life, seems like, I've been wanting a daughter; doesn't seem possible I've really got one. Now don't you two stand on ceremony; make yourselves home here. I was just putting the coffee on; any minute, now, I says to myself, they'll be coming along. Of course that dad of yours, Carl, he's still down with his farm machinery; can't leave that shop until closing time. Saturday night, you know how farmers are. But he'll be home ten sharp tonight, you can bet your bottom dollar on that. It sure was fine of you, dropping a postcard; never can tell what we'd of been up to if you hadn't——"

If Christine were there with any purpose beyond that of righting a family indifference, it was that she immediately be fond of Carl's people. Carl, while he now got along well with her father, had at the most forbearance for her mother; forbearance was the most her mother probably ever would manage for Carl. The least she could do, she had felt, was knit herself closely to this other group, so that on one side of the family there'd be solidarity; this was a duty she owed Carl, owed the child who in this house would be a first grandchild.

As Aunt Stell, however, rattled on from the rocker she presently overflowed, as Carl, like a restlessly home-coming cat, prowled the room's calendars and oleographs, she had a hard time not smiling at determinations which, somewhat abruptly, seemed silly and high-flown. Her pregnancy still didn't show too much, but as soon as Aunt Stell held her off she thought, "Goodness, I'll not have to *tell* her," and at the same time her left hand half rose toward her neck.

"This is the way people are," she reminded herself. "They look for personal things. Nothing to hold against her; she's being kindness it-self."

Just the same, when a little later Fred Reiss stumped in, a man of perhaps fifty-five, stocky and earthily vital, keeping one hand under the bib of blue and white striped overalls while the other came out for enveloping handshakes, she was a trifle less acceptive. He too, and no question, took in both her condition and the birthmark with the same celerity as Aunt Stell, and about his eyes and his overfull mouth was a look suggesting he saw her less as a new family member than as a woman.

The last thing she could do, so self-reminder ran at this point, was leap to snap antagonisms. She helped Aunt Stell bring in coffee and a lavish lunch, she and Carl sampled while the other two cut a heavy swath through sandwiches, pickles, cookies and three kinds of cake. Mostly Carl's father talked. "Remember Gus Wentzel? We got him out fishing here, too, three months back——" With ascending uproar-iousness the incident took Gus through fishing and sent him home with dried herring replacing the trout in his creel. "Poor Carl," Christine thought then. "He's crude, a little, that's all of his trouble. He makes Carl wince."

Before the next afternoon, when they left, she had two more perceptions to add to her store. The first of these came through a picture on the bureau in the room where she and Carl spent the night, a picture which, as soon as she glimpsed it, she eagerly took in her hands. Within the tarnished gilt filigree frame stood Carl as a child of perhaps four, round eyes wide, his characteristically high-templed forehead uncharacteristically serene, his hair in shoulder-long curls, he himself in a white-collared, tight-trousered black velvet Lord Fauntleroy suit, leaning against the arm and shoulder of a thin, serious-eyed young woman in a pompadour and an embroidered shirtwaist. A woman tremendously like not the child beside her but the Carl of today.

From behind her Carl said flatly, "If you don't mind I'll put that picture away while we're here." Taking it from her, he slid it into a top drawer of the dresser, face down. Both his voice and the closed-off intentness of his eyes warned against any intrusion, but also told their story—if love for his father was little, love for his dead mother was almost too much.

The other incident came the next noon. Carl, at midmorning, went off with his father to be shown the shop. Aunt Stell, while she and Christine prepared a gargantuan dinner, was garrulous, not only about everything else but about the affairs of the family. "Carl's mother, you know, came here a schoolteacher; what Fred saw in her I'll never know; she was pretty stuck-up. 'My boy won't work with his hands,' that's what she used to say, and I guess she was right there, but she didn't do too much for Fred. For Carl she was always ambitious, and Carl took it hard when she went; the times we had with that boy, I can tell you——" From it Christine began forming a comprehension of Carl deeper than any previously managed, and it was this comprehension which was to be rounded.

Toward the close of dinner, as they sat at table over coffee, Carl's father forking a third piece of pie which he obviously didn't want but which he was putting down simply because the sweet still had flavor for his tongue, he said expansively, "I suppose if you folks feel you've got to get that car back before suppertime there won't be no keeping you; seems like a shame, though; you don't get here often. We'd have plenty to feed you, I guess you can see that——"

Shaking with silent chuckles at the foot of the table, Aunt Stell cut in. "Don't you two believe him, he's got himself another widda, that's what's the matter with him. He knows what he'll be doing, soon as you're gone. He give her up last night, but if you stuck around you'd soon hear him making excuses——"

In answer Carl's father laughed loudly. "Before you decide anything about that, you'd ought to see that there widda. We've had a lot of widdas move into this town, but we never had one like this one. Redheaded——"

Teasing and tossed taunting reply. In sudden flaming discomfort Christine found herself unable to tear her glance from her plate, unable to look at Carl. In the room about her, with a heat which pressed close to her body, flooded an encompassing and somehow indecent sensuality, of which the essential unit was Carl's father and the unknown widow, but in which Aunt Stell too, liquorishly and in absentia, took part.

What was it Carl said on their wedding night, when he turned from her? "All my life, Christine, there are things about people I've hated —the meat market of carnality that people go in for, I've hated it. They're expecting us, probably even Salloway, my father—— She had been incapable of understanding, capable only of hurt. "My insufferable touchiness," Carl later said of himself, and she'd thought only that too; he was recoiling against living as he'd seen it in the army. Now she guessed to what that abhorrence was tied; it was his father's carnality he abhorred, that he in his childhood and probably in relation to his mother had begun abhorring. His back was turned to his father; his likeness to his mother was more than a physical likeness; she was the one he by choice was determined to mirror.

More than that, too. Yes, even more—in a flash, deeply plumbing, she knew it. Sometimes she had believed Carl lacking in desire; believed he lacked in desire for her. But that wasn't true either. Within Carl was a sensuousness as great as his father's; that was what he so rigidly governed; the thing against which he most deeply revolted was his father within him.

By accident, getting into the car, Carl touched her. Her arm. His hand flew from the contact as if she were contaminating. For the first homeward miles he drove furiously while, carefully withdrawn, she sat as far from him as possible. It would be awhile, she guessed, before he came anywhere near her again. Far behind her, by that time, were the long afternoons she had lain crying across their bed, trying to weep out her injuries, conning and reconning her early lessons of marriage —that she must never approach him, but that if he approached her she must be instantly and warmly responsive; if she wasn't, he was as hurt and bewildered by her rejection of him as she was hurt and bewildered by his rejections of her. Now she saw that differently too.

Just before they pulled into Chapaqua he asked one savage question, "I suppose after this you'll think we should drive down every week?"

She answered quietly, "No, I don't think so. We've—been there."

Twice after that, once in the spring of 1922 and again in the summer of 1924, Carl's father and Aunt Stell drove up on a Sunday. Both visits were brief and passed not too uncomfortably, though Carl was edgy both before and after. Each time Fred Reiss insisted on leaving twenty dollars for the boys, and Aunt Stell, too, brought gifts, much too lavish gifts. A real leather hobby horse, and an electric train. But both times Christine only amplified previous impressions.

For the whole situation she came to have a feeling of sorrow, pity for Carl, and also for his father and aunt. Carl and the boys should have meant pleasure to the two in the old house in Elmwood, Carl's father should have been a wonder to Craig and Dusty, just as her own father was. But gradually, also, she came to see it wasn't just one quality in the older couple that made good relations difficult. Carl's father and aunt liked to talk about Carl, liked to recall all they'd done for him—"Right up to the day he was married I got his clothes home to wash," Aunt Stell often said proudly. But true feeling, deep feeling, seemed to be absent; it was as if they observed in others the motions of devotion, and conscientiously put themselves through the same attitudes, as if they came up to see Craig and Dusty not from springing affection, but so they could return home to boast of their once-removed issue as other grandparents boasted.

"I guess you can see who's the daddy of those two," Aunt Stell crowed on arrival. "Look at those round little eyes they've got. Look at those curls. Just like Carl used to look."

After these first few minutes, even if they continued to dandle the children, their talk relievedly returned to themselves and the things that for them had reality, the things—it always came to this—they owned or experienced physically, their tremendous self-satisfactions. That year's new car, the money Fred Reiss made through his shop— as much, he hinted, as five and six thousand in a year. The practical jokes, sometimes backfiring, in which he endlessly embroiled himself, the card games they played with neighbors, the ducks, chickens, pork roasts, feathery cakes and pies that passed over their table, the succession of widows Fred Reiss added to his string.

So, when that racking September of 1926 fell upon them, one of the things that didn't surprise her—filled her with angry resentment, but didn't surprise her—was the way Carl's father and aunt took his illness.

It was an illness which, this time, didn't come on as suddenly as in 1920. There were, first, three days in which it seemed it might be one of the milder attacks, seventy-two hours when Carl fought furiously, sitting up at night, giving himself hypodermics, keeping his inhalers constantly in the palm of his hand, his chest walls sometimes appearing to solidify, but then, always in time, relaxing to move in and out as a bellows once more. Three days when he insisted, no matter what she said, on continuing at work. Three days when she walked about with the slapping pool of sharp worry constant in the pit of her stomach.

After the evening of the third day, however, no more of that. From the kitchen she heard the shaking thump and Craig's "Mama!" Running to the living room, she found Carl fallen just inside the door, contorted and helpless, eyes distended, cheeks purple, chest rigid. In the routine of evening Craig and Dusty had been lying in wait, ready to pounce for the games which so often were interdicted but for which they always hoped; they both screamed in panic. She herself was scarcely more sensible, running for hypodermic and pillows together, then for the telephone.

Nor did nightmare lessen. Dr. Daly, kneeling, was unbreezily grim.

"Man, what do you think you've been doing to yourself? What've you thought those red lumps along your waistline were—heat rash? This time you won't be out playing tricks. Get out of bed in six months, you'll be lucky. You'll be lucky you get out at all."

"Six months, be lucky. You'll be lucky you get out at all." Through all that followed—frantically getting Dusty and Craig to a neighbor, sitting beside Carl in an ambulance, sitting again numb and frightened beside his oxygen tent, watching through the small square window the blueness that didn't leave his face, the continuing distention of his eyes, the seemingly unbroken rigidity of his chest, seeing the convulsion of his efforts to cough, clutching, since there now was nothing else to clutch, the edge of the white hospital spread—these were the words that possessed her. "Six months, be lucky. You'll be lucky you get out at all." Carl couldn't—in sick terror she thrust the thought back—go under from asthma; he'd pulled through before; he was too young to go under from asthma; too strong. At bottom he was too strong to go under from asthma or shingles, either. Shingles couldn't be serious; they didn't sound serious. The refrain, though, stayed with her. "Six months—if at all."

In the slow-moving numbness which afterward seized her—"This is what it must be like," she thought once, "to be walking over an ocean floor, dragging the weight of a diver's suit against the tons of meeting and overhead water"—it was next afternoon before she so much as remembered there were people who must be told. Her own parents. His. Dr. Daly was there then, his third time that day. "He's sleeping right now, Mrs. Reiss; not very well, I'll admit, but sleeping. You can just as well go home; we'll phone if there's any least change."

Still in her diver's suit, she waded out to underwater light, underwater wind, an underwater illusion of reality. Wading home, she got Craig and Dusty from the neighbor. Wading into their living room—still the gray and blue living room of their wedding, but more battered now, and intruded upon by the brown leather Duofold Carl detested but which she had been glad enough to accept from her parents when they got their new mohair—she stood swaying, trying to rip off the diver's suit, trying to rise to the surface.

"Mama, I missed kindergarten, Mama; I didn't get to kindergarten at all; I got kept home the whole morning——" "Mama, why did you be gone so long, Mama——" Craig and Dusty hung on her, Dusty wanted to swing from her right arm as if he were a pendulum, Craig knocked and jerked at her, he too trying to get her to emerge. She dazedly brushed at them.

"Six months—if at all." All through the past year she'd been sick inside, often, at Carl's emaciation, his tension, his nervousness, his inability to eat; she'd been fear-stricken, often. This was what she had feared.

Telephoning wasn't anything she thought up to do; merely something that after a while she turned to do automatically. Her mother. "Christine, we'll be there at once." Aunt Stell, sharply, but at the same time with caution, "That so? Now, Christine, you know that boy's always had asthma; don't you worry your head none; he'll get over it. I've seen that boy so choked you'd think he had a stroke, but he always got over it. You keep on calling us every day, though, let us know——"

They came up on Sunday. Sunday, the day that was worst, when in despair and anguish she faced what a life without Carl would be, faced the indissolubility with which, after seven years, she was knit to him, facing that if Carl went she went too, not physically, perhaps, but in every way that counted. Nothing new, things that in earlier terrors, earlier anguish, she before had faced, but that now had a corrosive immediacy.

Carl's father and aunt came in soberly. "Boy still sick, is he? That's a shame, now, a shame you two have to go through anything like this." It was said with kindness, kindness which even in her terror impinged with incredulity, because it was so inadequate. Still soberly they went with her to the hospital, to smile, soberly, and wave through the window of the oxygen tent at Carl's unanswering convulsed rigidity within; Aunt Stell maternally patted his foot. Leaving, they were subdued, covered by that other overlay of caution and even truculence. In the car Aunt Stell said pointedly, "Before he got into a shape like that, seems to me somebody could of put a stop to it," and his father immediately added, "Somebody's been pretty hard on that boy, pretty hard."

Incredulity deepening, she got what they meant. They were blaming her. She had no need to be furnished with guilt; already she was crying to herself as so often before, "I should have made his life easier, stopped him somehow; somehow I should have kept him from coming to this." But no matter how deep her acceptance of responsibility might be, having it thrust upon her by these other people wasn't acceptable. Against them she wanted to lash, "And you, what have you done for him? Refusing the college he wanted, because that's what he's told me, saying you couldn't afford it, but boasting of your five and six thousand a year, always affording yourself a new car every year, affording food you swill yourself in, affording your widows."

Depth of vituperative anger to which she never before had sunk. She felt herself soiled by it, and at the same time ashamed. How could she think this, how be touched by it, when one thing and one thing only counted—Carl's continuing to live?

Before leaving that evening, reverting to the heavy, spurious kindness which had marked his arrival, Carl's father took twenty-five dollars from his billfold.

"I guess you better take this. You'll be finding all those doctor and hospital bills pretty steep."

Hospital. Oxygen. Three nurses. She answered stiffly, "Oh no, thanks, we'll manage."

"Don't take it that way, now, we want to help. Times a little hard, this season, farmers feeling the slump. Guess I'll be getting along with the old buggy another year, but you go on, now, take this."

The money remained on the desk, two tens and a five. Later it disappeared, her father or mother, here constantly in the crisis, must have seen how she felt and removed it. From her father and mother assistance and bolstering were flowing as effortlessly toward her as water flows; each morning now her mother came for the boys, each night her father slept on the Duofold so she'd have someone in the apartment, so she could leave if a call came from the hospital; when she stopped in at the hospital office to make a deposit she was told her father had paid the bill. In the midst of terror, in continuing anger at Carl's people, this was what she had on the other side—the almost swamping affection and gratitude she felt for her own parents.

But then, on the afternoon of the sixth day, change. Carl's nurse, opening the door, rustled more starchily, her smile was more firm. She said, "Well, Mrs. Reiss, we're quite pleased with ourselves today." Through the window she saw Carl as different—face still almost wine-blue, racked by coughing, but different. Coughing like this meant he was over the worst.

The nurse went on talking, "—weren't sure until a couple of hours ago, or we'd have called you—must've taken hold."

Carl smiled at her, a brief writhing of his lips before he returned to coughing; he lifted one hand. A smile and a lift of the hand she couldn't see for obscured eyes but that she must, she thought, remember forever. In sudden weariness she slipped to her knees. "This," she said to herself then. "Only this, nothing else. Nothing more to want, only this."

But there couldn't be only that, either. Not just the easing and gratitude which in their way were almost as breaking and racking as the anguish. Two more days got Carl out of the oxygen tent, three more put him on regular hospital care without private nurses, at the end of the second week he was allowed to come home. Still breathing stridently, the belt of his shingles still almost meeting at his back, still so nerve-bound he seemed to lie suspended over the bed rather than resting upon it, so emaciated now he looked like nothing but overlong bones bound together by sallow onionskin. But allowed to come home. It was in the next week that, tending him, she began turning to the rest of what faced them.

Salloway, when she called, said, "We're sorry to hear that. Anything we can do——" There were flowers, calls, visits, and a month's salary. Her father insisted on paying the rest of the hospital bill, but he had obligations of his own, annuity payments to keep up; she couldn't let him take over herself and her brood as a permanent burden. Letters from Carl's father—"You sure relieved our minds letting us know that big boy of ours is home—you tell him to get a hustle on now and get back on his feet"—were so grating she didn't even show them to Carl. Dr. Daly's bill came in. It didn't take long to prove how dizzyingly, without income, their bank balance must fall. If she could help it she mustn't sit back to see that balance shrink to nothing, not when for Carl it represented his share of Trurog's. If, added to all the other corrosives which now ate at him—the lost prominence so newly and hardily won, the break in his ambitions, all that yet remained ahead— he also must look forward to building up those savings from the beginning, or, worse, face debt, he might—she wouldn't acknowledge this in so many words, but in a locked cell of her mind the fear was a gnawing serpent—never get well at all.

In all the seven years of their marriage Carl's attitude toward her working hadn't changed; she hadn't wanted it to change. She didn't want to work now. But she began seeing there wasn't much alternative. Lying awake nights on the Duofold, listening, with the panicking adrenalin ready to pour into her arteries, for any break, any change in the rasping breath from the bedroom, listening under that for the light soft exhalations that meant Dusty asleep in his crib across the living room and Craig in his much too small companion crib in the kitchen, she thought out sharply just what job she must get. Not anything permanent, not any job for the job's sake. All that still counted with her was her marriage; she wouldn't be out for prestige or personal satisfaction, not this time; she couldn't take a job asking so much of her that she'd have too little left for Carl and the boys. Just a maintenance job to keep the four of them going.

Other people early saw what she must be about, too. Harriet, doing her friendly best, coming in on Sunday to sit with Carl while Christine got the boys to a park, motioned Christine to the hall.

"You know Trurog's will take you back; all you've got to do is see Hobart. If they don't, I'll go in for enough personal mayhem——"

Christine whispered her thanks, whispered that she'd have to see how things went. But she didn't go to see Hobart. She didn't have to see Hobart to know she didn't want to go back to Trurog's. Not alone because of the detestation she was forming for the place, with what it was doing to Carl. But because at six days a week and ten hours a day it would take too much of her time.

In a sotto voce kitchen conference almost identical to Harriet's, Bob Gokey relayed another tip. "Say, they got a new electric refrigerator plant going up north of town. Looks like quite a heap. Away out like that, they're almost bound to have a cafeteria——" On this one she did go to the plant, picking a way amid piles of lumber and brick to get in, skirting cement mixers and teetering planks, finally reaching a crisp, bright-eyed young man who was more than encouraging. "That's right, we'll not only want someone to run a cafeteria, but someone to equip and staff it. Of course we'll have other applicants, but you're a good age and your experience looks good——"

While he was talking, though, while they stood in a shored doorway looking down the vast empty wet cement space which was to be the cafeteria, she knew this wouldn't do. At a hundred-eighty a month, it was a plum for anyone else, but not for her. She couldn't give a job her best thought, her best energy; she couldn't spend an hour night and morning on a bus.

When, sitting on the edge of Carl's bed, holding his hand, she told

him what she was settling on, she knew he could hardly believe her.
"All I'll be is a cook. It's at Neesom's, that old college eating house
across from St. Augustine's. I noticed the sign saying 'Cook Wanted'
today in the window. It won't pay enough, either. Only twenty a
week. Mrs. Neesom was the one really ran it, but she died last spring;
it's terribly run down; I don't even know if it can afford the twenty.
But it's so near I can walk over, I'll work only from ten in the morning
to seven, I can take Dusty to Mother's on my way, and Craig can
learn to find his way past there from kindergarten——"

Twisting away the hand she held, twisting his face into the pillow,
Carl's reply was half suffocated. "I knew something like this had to
come up, but at least if you're going to work you might find something better than that. We can make out awhile yet——"

She managed to laugh at him brightly; only laughter made what
was going on bearable.

"Don't think I'm being pathetic; when I walked into that junk
heap—I hate to say this, but it sort of appealed to me. Imagine starting with a thing like that, imagine getting it back on its feet——"

What she wouldn't say, what he wouldn't say, though he knew,
was that it now was December, he breathed with little more than a
rasp, but other than that he showed almost no improvement. He spent
his days frayed and fretted, thinking over all he had lost and the unen-
durable new start he must make. He'd put on no weight, his eyes
looked at her from shadowed deep pits; his hand when he returned
it to her was sweatily damp and had no strength for clasping. Craig
and Dusty before their bedtime were in the apartment only two
hours, Dusty wanting to hang by his hands and locked ankles from
the footrail of the bed, pendantly swinging in 'possum style, shrilling.
"Look at me, Daddy, now, look at me." Craig had the bedroom rocker
upside down, jouncing it, calling, "No, Dad, look at me, look at my
bucking bronc." They didn't make more noise than boys of almost
six and almost five had to make, but for him it was intolerable.

This tiny apartment, the crowding—beyond illness and money to
live on loomed other problems she must be sensible enough to postpone. All she could do, immediately, was get Carl over this one
hurdle, this one hump. Other marriages might not remain radiant,
theirs must.

What she'd better concentrate on right now was survival.

10

"Don't think I'm being pathetic," she said, and laughed. "Imagine starting with a thing like that, imagine getting it back on its feet——"

Words, strung together to make Carl take what was happening more lightly. But in a way words with their own kind of truth.

She still didn't want to work. When the next Monday came, when she bundled Craig off to kindergarten at eight-thirty—"Remember, now, you're my biggest boy; remember you're a man in the family. When school lets out you walk straight down the street till you come to the streetcar tracks, the way I showed you yesterday, then you turn the way I showed you yesterday and keep on until you get to the house I showed you yesterday. I'll be in the kitchen and I'll take you to the corner to head you for Grandmother's"—Craig answered scornfully, "Mother, don't you think I know *anything?*" but there was tightness under his round, soft jaw, a tremble on his lips. Craig, too, was thinning and pulling himself in, feeling protection less absolute than it once was.

Standing on the front steps with Dusty to watch him move away from her, back stiff, her throat and her breast hurt. Craig was the one most like Carl. Dusty too, but Craig most. Both had Carl's curls—not as tight, light brown and not sandy, but still Carl's curls. Both had his high temples crossed by blue veins. But Craig was the one who would be tall and slender; Dusty would be shorter, a little more solid, like her.

Dusty beside her shrilled his daily rebellion, jerking to free himself. "Me too. I'm big too. I got to go to school too." Bracing to hold him was habit, but Dusty's fury, that morning, seemed more per-fervid than usual. Hurrying afterward, straightening the apartment, giving Carl his bath, changing his bed, arranging his lunch—cold lunch—on a tray, she thought for some minutes that she couldn't do it; anything—even borrowing until they were so deeply in debt they could never get out—wasn't as bad as this personal severance.

But once Dusty was at her mother's and, at ten, she had waded the unshoveled snow of Neesom's front walk to its front door, she began, almost in spite of herself, to be caught up by what met her there. Neesom's had stood on this corner when she was at Midwestern, a tall family house, gingerbread relic of the 1880s, once painted yellow but now badly faded, its high square front stoop and square bay sticking out from its otherwise flat face like twin lopsided pouts, its roof a collection of gables, its gutters sagging, a belt of vertical, two-foot lengths of siding—pointed at one end like pickets, but wider —girdling it twice, once just under the roof line, once between first and second stories; it sat high on its rough limestone foundation as if it sat on a pot. Never anything but a funny old house even if, at one time, it had been rather popular. As a senior she'd come to it for initiation to a Home Economics society. Chicken croquettes, shoe-string potatoes, thickly creamed peas, gelatine salad, Parker House rolls, biscuit shortcake—she still remembered the dinner. Mrs. Neesom mightn't have been imaginative, but she was a fairly good cook.

When she pushed open the front door the entrance hall, with its passageway to the right and its carpeted stairway rising steeply a few feet in from the vestibule, was quite deserted, just as it had been on the day when she'd answered the sign; its musty damp staleness hadn't altered either. Again, as on that other day, but more critically now, since in a way she belonged to it, she walked through the open double doors on the right into the long room which had been built for a living room but which for twenty years at least had been crowded by the straight chairs and small wood tables now filling it. That room, too, was empty, the hemmed squares of stiffened white bed sheeting covering its tables revealing neither glasses nor silver, but looking peppered by dust. Dust lay more lightly gray on the golden oak mantel over the chilly black grate and the mottled green tiles of the fireplace; lace curtains veiling the two square bays hung in folds so tired they might have been untouched for years. Not too bad a room, though. Rip those old curtains down, paint or repaper, clean thoroughly——

In the far wall of a second table-filled room, beyond, a swing door pushed open.

"Oh, you came, did you. Well. I—I wasn't quite sure. Quite sure if you'd bother, or not. Can't count much on people, not these days. People these days don't have the same gumption. I don't hardly know where you'll start in——"

Her new employer advancing, cautiously, nervously, first through the aperture of the door and then past tables toward her. Gaunt, tall, slightly stooped, gray everywhere except for the once white canvas butcher's apron—it too not far from gray—covering his front. Between his brow-ambushed eyes and his lips, the latter stretched over teeth much too big for them, played contrary emotions. Morose dejection and, it seemed, brightness. No break in his speech at all—"Maybe you just came to say you got something better. That wouldn't surprise me. I had that happen——"

"Heavens," she had thought when she first saw him, "not *this*. I couldn't work for or with *this*. The whole thing's too impossible." But then as she listened, "I guess I should have taken that card out," he had said drearily that initial time. "Had it there almost all summer. Not much an up-and-coming young woman like you would want to take on for herself. I been doing my best, keeping the place up; I got a sister in California—long ways off, California. 'You get that there place off your hands, Frank,' she writes to me, 'you come on out here to sunny California, man your age is a young man yet,' she writes to me. I don't know, if I could pick up a little change, maybe on the stock market, way some folks do——"

Garrulous. Worse than Aunt Stella. Probably senile, too. But as he stood drooling his speech, she was moved to some feeling for him. He was so old and inadequate, the dream he dreamed so pitifully small. Most employers were hard and sure, grasping. She had wanted to pick up this old man as if he were Craig or Dusty, to help him.

This morning she didn't feel that way; instead, a little recklessly, she felt able and ready; under her coat was a house dress. She said briskly, "Good morning, Mr. Neesom. No, I'm doing what I said I'd do, I'm here to start working. Perhaps if I go into the kitchen——"

Beyond the swinging doors, where she hadn't been previously—a mistake, but just as well—she wasn't exactly dismayed; in a way she expected what she saw.

"I tell you what, Mr. Neesom, today I'll serve meals from here as best I can. I smell you've a roast in the oven. The rest of this week, though, we'll close for house cleaning. Get a woman in——"

Wryly, afterward, she thought sometimes it wasn't pity for old Mr. Neesom that moved her. She knew, of course she knew, he was putty; from habit he expected some woman to run not only Neesom's but himself. Against her decisions he threw up a worried and dismal uncertainty—"I don't know about that, now, Mrs. Reiss; a whole week and almost no income—I don't know if I'll have enough to go on."

She answered, "Not much use my working here, if you don't make enough to pay me," to which he replied, "No, no, I guess not." After that, with weaker and weaker objections, he let her do almost as she pleased. He had, she found, worked out a menu he managed single-handed—pork roast, mashed potatoes, canned peas, coffee, bakery rolls and pie for a forty-five-cent lunch; beef roast, baked potatoes, canned corn, coffee, bakery rolls and pie for a sixty-five-cent dinner. Two of the college boys who rented the five upstairs bedrooms acted as waiters and bus boys, he himself washed dishes. That first day at noon they had eighteen customers, at dinner eleven.

Through all the rest of that week, too, as with a cleaning woman she first ripped down and then began refurbishing, most discoveries served only to reveal how precarious was the establishment. Bills thrust away in the pantry told of debts to grocers and butchers. Curtains fell apart like vapor when the rods were lifted down. Each morning Neesom spent at least two hours struggling with the rusty old furnace in a paper- and can-choked basement. On Thursday a plumber had to be called for the side-arm gas water heater; he came up shaking his head. "That clunk hold together another three months it'll beat my guess." Layered crusts of paper hung so loosely on the walls that a touch dislodged whole sheets. The cleaning woman, a Mrs. Pierson, asked incredulously, "You fixing to work here?" and Christine herself came to move about with a kind of litany on her lips.

"Out of my head, I guess. My brain must be softening. I don't know why I'm doing this." But at the same time she was relentless, knowing so easily what could be done and what couldn't. "Paper that comes off like this—we'll have to tear it all down, and paint. One thing, I've found plenty of tablecloths; we'll sew some together for draperies. That stair carpet—few people can want to eat, having looked at it. Trap for damage suits, too. Those'll have to be bare——"

But there were, also, discoveries for the other side. Basically the house wasn't too shaky. The kitchen gas ranges, while antiquated, were capacious, and worked. Mrs. Neesom must have had a weakness for pots, pans and dishes. The sink space was adequate, the kitchen big and well lit. By Thursday there was excitement in picking a path through the rubble-strewn, stacked tables and chairs, watching the two college boys slosh on paint—green paint, the darkest the hardware store man could be wheedled into mixing. Not her idea, Carl's. For the first time since his seizure, Carl looked alert but relaxed, sitting in bed, caught in spite of his distaste. "You'll have to be so cheap you can't be conservative. Dark green walls, if the tiles in the fireplace are green. Pale green or gray ceilings. Scarlet stairs, if you can put it over. You won't be losing anything——"

No, she thought, if anyone was losing anything it was the paint man —blandly she was indifferent to the paint man. There were other tradesmen, though, to whom she couldn't be so indifferent. On Friday, when she went to Vercelli's to put in a carefully planned grocery order, she was met by a pudgy little man who burst at her, "No more credit, no, no! Look, lady, look here, look here—bills, bills, all to Neesom's; for months five dollars here, five dollars there, such groceries I can't throw out for five dollars."

Paying the cleaning woman, as she knew by that time, would clean out Neesom's last pennies. She herself was waiting. To Vercelli she answered calmly, "Neesom's must owe you hundreds of dollars. Your only chance of any money at all, I'd guess, would be by adding a little more to those bills. Come over on—say Sunday. You may feel differently."

Vercelli's head continued to shake, but she left the order on the counter.

"A job that won't take too much of my time"—that also she had said. Harriet, when she heard, agreed shortly with the litany, "Christine, you must have taken leave of your senses." Her mother burst into tears. But on Sunday Craig and Dusty ran war-whooping about the back yard, half the college boys from upstairs, making a lark of it, carted refuse and scrubbed floors, her mother stitched tablecloths and Harriet hung them, Mr. Neesom wandered in and out, lost, galvanically once in a while attacking the fireplace or a tubful of shoveled-up wallpaper, she and the other college boys, in the kitchen, washed dishes. Into this bedlam at three o'clock stepped Vercelli, lifting his feet high, recoiling from the scarlet stairs, shaking his head slightly at the walls, staring at her mother and Harriet, jumping when Craig and Dusty right then zipped through from front door to back.

But the next morning, Monday, the meats and groceries she wanted stood neatly stacked on the kitchen tables when she got to work at ten.

Nothing at Neesom's went fast, nothing was easy; Neesom's was too far below bottom. That Monday they served nineteen lunches and thirty-three dinners, the additions mostly the boys from upstairs, eating out the time they had put in on Sunday. Tuesday it was twenty-two lunches, thirty-seven dinners. Wednesday they sank back to eighteen and twenty-nine; it was snowing. Only two weeks away, too, came Christmas vacation, when there'd be almost no business at all.

Just the same, as she began estimating on Thursday, Neesom's must have taken in over a hundred dollars, which should pay Vercelli for that week's groceries, pay her at least this week's twenty, leave a little over. Mr. Neesom, naturally, handled the money, keeping it in a tin tackle box on a shelf over the sink; Mr. Neesom, in fact, was proving a better help than she'd expected. He might not know much about cooking, but he was deft with vegetables, he had surprisingly doughty muscles for mixing and kneading; he moved, when the situation demanded, with a kind of flapping celerity. He still served the few breakfasts, he finished up after she left. Afternoons—certainly no more than his due—he vanished for two or three hours.

"You'll take care of Vercelli, I know, before anything else." Carefully she got this said.

"Yes, yes, certainly. The finances you can safely leave to me, Mrs. Reiss." He was nervous saying this, too. Perhaps—it struck her at the moment—he was even a little furtive; his glance stayed on the potatoes he was peeling. On Friday she found out why. Vercelli had been pleasant when she called in other orders; Friday he again was surly.

"I see I don't get paid nothing yet, Mrs. Reiss. Not too long I don't wait, now. You remember that."

The call took place during Mr. Neesom's postmeridian absence; going straight from the phone to the tackle box, she lifted the battered green lid. Three dollar bills, some silver.

As she realized while she let the lid fall, the situation was delicate as well as ominous. She could scarcely suggest that, owing to his furtiveness and a few other indications, she suspected Mr. Neesom of misapplying his own funds. Yet if she were to keep on here, something would have to be done.

"Vercelli this afternoon complained he hadn't been paid. I hope——" As soon as Mr. Neesom came home she approached the subject as forthrightly as possible.

Eyes once more averted, lips over the too big teeth writhing as with a tic, he took her up quickly.

"Now, now, don't you worry, Mrs. Reiss, I'll handle Vercelli. I've a few other irons in the fire beside this business, Mrs. Reiss; don't you worry about anything. You can see for yourself, Mrs. Reiss, I've got your money for this week right on me——"

Actually he pulled from his pocket a limp scuffed wallet, holding it out toward her gaping, so that she saw in it the four five-dollar bills. And nothing else.

Twenty dollars, and nothing else. Cold fingers touched her spine. Less than six in the cashbox, no bills paid—where was the rest of it? Again the hint of something evasive in Mr. Neesom's manner wasn't to be avoided. That "I've a few other irons" had a gambler's pompousness. Suddenly she remembered a phrase from the day she was hired, "If I could pick up a bit of change on the stock market——" Was that where he spent his afternoons, in some hole-in-the-corner broker's office, buying small lots of stock on margin? A good many people were doing that, lately; Harriet talked about steel common and Atwater Kent, Bob Gokey was rabid about Cities Service——

Money drained into the stock market the way water drained into a sink.

She said carefully, "I've had some experience keeping books, Mr. Neesom, in case you'd care to have me take over——"

He drew up loftily. "I could scarcely, Mrs. Reiss, withdraw from that aspect of the business. You need have no worry, Mrs. Reiss, I'll handle that part more than adequately. Just the cooking, Mrs. Reiss, just the cooking——" A loose hand gestured outward.

One thing it was no use to combat. "That aspect of my business," he said, but if that aspect was quicksand she'd best get out. Support for Carl, Craig and Dusty was what she was here for, and if that didn't exist she must find it elsewhere. She spoke quietly.

"In that case I'll finish my time here tomorrow."

He answered, "That will be as you wish."

All the rest of that day, the next morning, she worked against a drag, a sense of defeat. All the finding to do over, the hunting of a place which, whatever its better features, still would probably ask more of her.

Mr. Neesom also was newly downcast; after the lunch dishes were cleaned up on Saturday he lingered, humphing and clearing his throat. He went out, but came back in thirty minutes to sag against the door.

"You can see, Mrs. Reiss, surely you can see——"

Wearily, because she'd been up at five to wash clothes she'd iron in the evening, because she'd be job hunting again tomorrow, she answered, "I understand perfectly, Mr. Neesom."

Collapse came abruptly, completely. "If it would make any difference—nothing would relieve me more than to have you take over the books. Take over the cashbox. I'm not—I'm not a bookkeeper, Mrs. Reiss. I—I recognize, Mrs. Reiss, you're an excellent cook. Able in every way. There's twenty more in the cashbox——"

Rout so wild and inordinate she was sorry for him to the soles of her shoes. "Of course not, Mr. Neesom," she would have liked to tell him, "you keep on handling your money. Until you go bankrupt it's yours to gamble away as you wish." But that wouldn't take care of Mr. Neesom, any more than it would take care of Carl, Craig and Dusty. What she must say was "I think that will work better."

Keeping one twenty, she got around, that afternoon, to leave the other with Vercelli. Vercelli, also avoiding her eyes, rumbled angrily, "Not enough, Mrs. Reiss, you got to see that. You got to do better by me as this."

"Next week," she told him, "we go on a cash basis. You'll probably have to wait until after Christmas for payments on back bills, but from here on we buy only with cash." Rash, but that was the thing to do. Promise, so she couldn't back out.

Taking over the dog-eared, jumbled account books on Monday, she set out for rock bottom. Overdue food bills, as best she figured, came to almost five hundred, coal bills to over two hundred, 1926 taxes had never been paid, three years ago the house had been mortgaged for thirty-five hundred, on which both payments and interest were in arrears.

"My wife's illness, my wife's illness." Over the mortgage, Mr. Neesom again cleared his beleaguered throat. On the Wednesday, when she finally shoveled through to some kind of clarity, she sat forward over the rickety kitchen desk to thrust fingers into her hair. If she needed more evidence that Neesom's was a one-hoss shay in its last days, she definitely had it now. Any sense whatever would make her meet old Neesom on his return from this afternoon's wanderings with the cashbox in one hand and the ledger in the other. "Thank you for entrusting me with these, but after what I've found in them——"

What made her want to keep on, even now? Why, even as she sat at this desk, knowing what she knew, did one part of her mind coolly go about planning the next day's work? The answer was so far beyond her reach she couldn't even catch it to look at it. "What is it about people," she asked angrily, "what is it about me, that makes me cling to this forlorn hope?" Reply came—"I still know I can't find anything as convenient; if I'm tired it isn't because of work here but of what I must get done at home; I've worked for myself so long I don't want to be subservient. Here I don't work for Neesom, he works for me. He'd be ready to let me bully him, which I'm afraid is what he's used to." But even this, part of which she was admitting for the first time, wasn't the whole answer. Somewhere in the whole answer was the fact that, once started, she found it hard to give up.

Before going back to the cooking, she jerked the menu typewriter toward her.

"Oh yum," she wrote, not trying for anything fancy, just taking what came. "A new cook at Neesom's. Lunches 25c, 35c, 45c. Dinners 45c, 65c, 85c."

By the time Neesom was back she had thirty-three originals, sixty-six carbons. Reading over her shoulder, Neesom reared and startled like a stung horse.

"Those prices, Mrs. Reiss." Like a horse, too, he neighed in his fright. "We'll lose money. We'll be bankrupt, Mrs. Reiss. We——"

She finished it for him. "Having just gone over the books, Mr. Neesom, I'd say we are bankrupt. The quarter lunches will be a sandwich and coffee. Girls often don't want more. At thirty-five cents there'll be a vegetable plate, or macaroni or eggs."

The next day at noon, one of the boys having handed the slips around on the campus, they had thirty-three lunches, forty-three dinners. No more money than before, but more people. Besides Vercelli, that week, she paid gas and light bills, ten dollars on coal, the cleaning woman, replaced a broken window, took her twenty, handed over eighteen to Neesom. Neesom, folding his take in his grip, looked as startled as he'd been by the prices. When he gave over the cashbox, apparently, he thought he'd seen his last penny.

Christmas vacation, as she had foreseen, was a doldrum. To make the most of it she cut her time and wages to half, leaving the lunches to Neesom, shutting her eyes to the continued ebbing of Carl's bank balance, relishing the added time at home. But when school reopened after the holidays she returned to Neesom's with a determination she wouldn't have known she possessed, ransacking cookbooks for edibles never before seen in Chapaqua restaurants, checking plates as they came back, for what was cleaned up and what wasn't, establishing standards.

"We'll cut corners anywhere, but not on foodstuffs. No dried eggs, no dried milk, no margarine." Every day her slips went out. "Home-baked rolls, home-baked beans, home-baked pies. Where? Haven't you heard? Neesom's." "Neesom's, where no one leaves hungry." Maybe that didn't help, but something did, slightly. Her two college boys no longer dawdled at meal hours, each night found a few more dollars in the cashbox. One evening she was called out to meet a voluminous, dusky, booming woman in a cape. "Mrs. Reiss, I understand? I am Miss Bangs. Miss Valeria Bangs. I am planning a luncheon——"

Faculty. The luncheon, lamb chops and individual meringue pies, didn't exactly make a profit, but two weeks later it brought in two more luncheons.

No, not fast. But with its own slow progress, the way leaves come out on trees in the spring. One day in late February, struggling with an umbrella outside Vercelli's, she saw Vercelli almost knock another customer aside to open the door for her. So far she'd paid barely a tenth of his back bills, but he said "Mrs. Reiss" with a sustained tenderness. In March Bud Jessup every once in a while rushed in to report worriedly, "Mrs. Reiss, there's people waiting in the hall."

In a way she was split; she lived two lives. At home, in the evenings, she ironed or mended beside Carl's bed so they at least had these hours together; at home she shrugged. "Maybe we'll make it; sometimes we almost break even. Old Neesom's no ball of fire, and neither am I, I guess." All that was important, at home, was that finally, at the turn of the year, Carl began doing better. The days of quiet were what Carl needed. On a two-burner electric plate—Christmas gift from her parents—he was doing what he wryly called bedside cookery, and apparently liking it. The shingles broke out periodically, but she noticed it was week ends, when they all were home. He flew out at the boys, still, but there also were times when he kept them on his bed for hours, reading to them.

Better. Carl was better. She hugged herself with it. Not well yet, but out of the woods. And since Christmas they'd taken little of his bank money.

From ten to seven, the other life. No time, no occasion, if it came to that, for satisfaction or even relief. More customers didn't necessarily mean more profit. Neesom's was too much a sinkhole for profit. More customers, primarily, meant constant additions. A cashier at the door; it didn't work any longer for the waiters to pick up checks. Two more waiters. A boy for the kitchen. At least on a campus you got part-time help. Other things weren't as easily settled; mortgage payments, in April, came due again; for two days they had men from an insurance company, prodding walls, poking about in the basement, stalking upstairs to the attic, standing in kitchen corners while she was at her flying busiest. In the end, after long parleys, they decided not to foreclose, and drew up a bigger mortgage to cover back payments. The water heater at this same time finally and irrevocably burst; for three days all water was heated in the kitchen, and the new unit cost a hundred fifty.

"Why do I even try?" she asked again, but at week's end the figures arranged themselves in neat columns that were beginning to be standard. Income $189.77, cash reserve $6.28. Outgo—Vercelli $93.60, cleaning woman, $11, Mr. Neesom $20, Mrs. Reiss $20, mortgage $6.50, gas and light $5.00, laundry $4.00, telephone $2.00, coal $10, taxes $12.50, payment on water heater $5.00, cash to next week $6.45. Fortunate that the boys continued to take their pay in meals and room rent.

Maybe—Saturday afternoons while she worked on the books were the times she was most tempted to think so—they might actually, as she'd said to Carl, come out. Thirty-four weeks would pay off the water heater. A year and back taxes would be gone. Once the coal bills were caught up, too, and she'd squeezed a bit more for Vercelli——

In April she noticed that Mr. Neesom had taken on a new lease of furtiveness.

The cashbox was her first thought. After all, it was his business, his money. He might well think his twenty too little.

Checking, though, proved this suspicion unfounded. "I must be seeing things," she told herself. "Just more proof, if I need it, that I don't know what I'm up to," but her eyes only insisted. Over his vegetables Neesom had been chatty; now his speech was broken and forced. Returns after he had been out could be described only as slinking; during mealtimes he made surreptitious forays into the dining rooms.

"He can't"—this possibility also rose—"be suspecting me, can he? Or one of the boys? If it's the last he could say so——" She also told herself it was none of her business; if Mr. Neesom wanted to slink, slinking was his perfect right.

Not until May did she find out what he now had in mind. Called into the dining room, again by Miss Bangs, she stood discussing with that booming aristocrat the plans for a more ambitious party—a dinner, this time, at which Miss Bangs would entertain her department head. The small room under the stairs, she thought, with bridge to follow. Christine was aware that, in the room beyond, Mr. Neesom also was engaged in parley, with three people: one a tall man, nervous and elderly, who seemed to be doing the talking, one a large, solid, somehow grudging woman who stared about with pursed lips, one a bent, edgy little man who, for all a great difference in size and appearance, had something in common with Mr. Neesom.

After she was back in the kitchen Mr. Neesom also returned there, his manner now positively stealthy. Again she reminded herself that his business wasn't hers, but curiosity was too great. Casually she asked, "Another party?"

The false start given by Mr. Neesom was as much a giveaway as his stealth. He muttered, "Party? No, no—ah, those people with whom you saw me conversing—no, no, no party, merely friends of mine, Mrs. Reiss. Dropped in to see how I was doing."

It could only be let pass. From stealth, that afternoon, Mr. Neesom passed to downright guilt. He began dropping things, including the huge aluminum cauldron in which they mixed rolls; his foot was struck, and he limped for the rest of the day; whenever she moved near him he jumped. Again, that afternoon, he vanished; when he came back it was to stand against the door in much the same attitude he had stood when he surrendered the cashbox.

He began, "Mrs. Reiss——" choked, and began again. "Mrs. Reiss, there is something of which I—ah, should inform you. That deal today fell through, but——" The rest came in a rush. "No time can be like the present, Mrs. Reiss, for selling this business. We have customers. Anyone can see we have customers. Good will alone counts something. You'll never stay with me, Mrs. Reiss; when your husband is well and can work you'll be leaving. I'll be alone again. It's no use deceiving myself, Mrs. Reiss; I can't handle this business; I'd never find anyone like you again. I've got to sell now while I can get something over my debts and my mortgage. Mrs. Reiss, you must see——"

Sweat dripped from his gray face, his hands moved like lost children.

And she, standing silent, couldn't withhold understanding; every word he was saying was true. She'd rebuilt his trade, but she'd never stay on after Carl was well. Of course not. Summer was coming up, when there'd be only summer students. He'd be an idiot not to get out.

The trouble was all on her side. She wanted to leave sometime, yes, but not yet. New owners might keep her on, but if new owners were like that woman this noon, she wouldn't want to be kept on. She didn't—again recognition rushed forcibly upward—want to work for anyone but herself.

Aloud she said sympathetically, "Of course I see your point of view, Mr. Neesom. The best thing you can possibly do is sell now."

But the quiet to which she was stricken was entirely different from the loss which had touched her when she delivered the ultimatum about the books. Then she had realized—of course she did—that she might be pushing Mr. Neesom too far, but in her heart she had expected him to give way. About this there was no such likelihood; at seventy and more, the sooner Mr. Neesom got out to his sister and California, the better.

She went home that night in her quiet, to iron again by Carl's bed. At night now Carl slept flat, but during his waking hours he still lay propped by pillows, except for the thirty minutes of up-time Dr. Daly was recently allowing him. Each night Carl rendered a minute-by-minute account of that up-time, each night humorously and sardonically digested his day's reading—jokes from *Life* and *Judge*, comments on art magazines borrowed from the library, discussions of news. These evenings now were their marriage, the companionship which gave worth to her efforts. On this evening, though, even being with Carl didn't rouse her; after the ironing was finished and put away, after she'd straightened the bedroom and bedded Carl down for the night, she walked out to the living room to stand over Dusty in his crib. Dustin in the mild May night slept uncovered and sprawled in his faded outing-flannel sleeper, arms and legs spread-eagled, head turned only slightly to the side of his pillow; she couldn't touch him because he'd wake, but to her hand held just over him rose the soft curl of his hair, the soft moistness of his plump flesh. Dusty, five, in the last of his babyhood. This fall he'd reach his heart's wildest desire, he'd start kindergarten.

In the dark kitchen at the crib between icebox and table she stood again in the same way. Craig slept on his stomach, face pushed into the pillow so anyone must think he would suffocate, but the sound of his breathing came up lightly and easily. The six months since December had increased his length and leanness; he was getting to the tough-guy age. One leg was crooked under him, the other stuck out at least six inches from the side bars of the crib.

Another night when she wouldn't sleep much. On the Duofold, settling herself for at least physical rest, she folded her hands under her head and looked up at the amorphous light on the ceiling. She too, no less than Neesom, had realities to face. Months yet, no one knew how many—tacitly both she and Carl had quit estimating—before he'd be able to work. When he was, he'd go back to Trurog's. Beg as she would that he turn to almost anything else, that was one of the things about which he was adamant; he didn't answer, just tightened his lips. This time he wouldn't wear himself to shreds; next time he'd use sense. But Trurog's it would be. And there wouldn't, not for years, probably, be a job like the dress buying. While he waited, while he got his sea legs, it would be something minor. Perhaps the floor, again.

Dustin in the living room, Craig in the kitchen. "You can't live this way, Christine," her mother sometimes protested; against her mother she tightened her lips just as Carl tightened his about the store. She herself, though, knew they couldn't go on this way forever. Last summer before Carl got sick she'd taken Craig one day to a birthday party; she'd seen Craig standing in a bedroom doorway, contrasting what Denny Nelson had with what he had.

That next afternoon, while her employer was away, she methodically finished up in the kitchen and then, moving slowly, walked out first to the little room under the stairs, cool and clean in its white and deep green, its four tables crisp and orderly, the silver, the salt and pepper, the sugar, set on them for dinner, the two windows at the far end giving a view, over old-fashioned lilacs, of the west side lawn and St. Augustine's across the corner. In the main dining room she looked at that too—six tables, the most that could be jammed in. The long living room, eight tables. The hall—already the scarlet stairs were scuffed, but they looked clean, and they still had color. Upstairs——

Only once or twice had she been upstairs; the upstairs belonged to the college boys. Through doors carelessly left open, now, she looked into the five separate rooms. Old golden oak furniture, kicked, splintered and rickety. Ceilings spotted, wallpaper faded and broken, revealing large areas of glue-browned cracked plaster. Floors peeling dark brown paint, and littered with shoes, socks, jackets, shirts, books, wadded-up paper. At the door of the bathroom she looked in at a tattered diagonal blind, a rusty stool, a scrofulous tub. From the top of the attic stairs she glanced at the two gable windows, the open brown rafters from which necklaces of feathery grime hung in webbed festoons, the broken-down washstand and roughly covered cot which made up old Neesom's night home.

Dreary and depressing. Anyone must say it was. Dreary except for sun that beat in, the open yard visible on all sides, the yellow carriage house in the rear——

Last night in her bed she'd begun feeling chilly. All morning she'd been cold with a cold that was hard and impermeable, like ice. As she walked through the house, inspecting it, this chill increased in its weight and its density. When she pressed a fingernail against the inside of her forearm, producing a dent, she had no sensation of being dented. She wasn't to be dented, not that day; she was only to be chipped.

11

"Do you mind, Mr. Neesom, saying what you're asking for the place?"

"Well, I—it may seem a little steep, Mrs. Reiss; I'm asking ten thousand. Of course, Mrs. Reiss, that's the asking price, only. But if I'm to have a little to go on, a little to invest—if you should hear of anyone interested, you could say you believe I'd be reasonable——"

Her father. The fact, the sober arguments against, the sober arguments for. "A good corner. That's what I'd be buying. The corner. Three forty-foot lots, by a hundred and fifty—it may not be so often, after this, that property like that is available so near the university. The house would do for a while. It might be—that's the risk—throwing good money after bad, but it's the only way I can think, Father, of scraping up enough to pay you back all you gave us last fall——"

Then Carl. When she told him, he leadenly pulled on his bathrobe and got out of bed, to stand braced by both hands against the top of the bureau.

"I shan't like it. You can't expect me to like it. I suppose to you it must seem necessary. Here I am, lying around—for you I'd be better in jail. Craig sleeping in the kitchen—no one has to tell me. I haven't done well enough. I've never done well enough."

She cried, "But you did, Carl! You have and you will! You were buying, you'd made your way up; if you hadn't got sick, we'd have had everything. I don't mean this to be permanent; we'll sell again. This, too—it's only a stopgap. If we only had a little to go on—Father says he doesn't want any money back, but we still have to fill in your bank account——"

To that he didn't answer. Neither of them, in fact, said much more; still leadenly, after a few minutes, he returned to bed. Seeing the drag of his movements, she suffered what he suffered. This was no division such as shook their wedding night; he accepted as she accepted that under the circumstances she must do what she could. But that didn't mean his dislike was less. When he pulled the sheet across his shoulders and an arm over his eyes, shutting out the light, she ran to rub her forehead against his sheeted shoulder.

"No, I won't, Carl. It's too much to ask of you, that you live there. I can see it's too much. We'll find some other way——"

He answered quietly, "No, you've been right all along. You're usually right. It will be much better than this; I'll get used to it." When she stayed where she was, he lifted one hand after a while to brush it against her cheek, a movement of consolation and promised cohesion, but also of temporary sending away.

"—an offer, Mr. Neesom, from myself. Seventy-five hundred, I've thought, and I'll take over all business debts. I could give you seven hundred fifty in cash, the remainder above the mortgage at seventy-five dollars a month. The debts come to a thousand, so it's really an offer of eighty-five hundred. You may have much better chances——"

"I hadn't thought of accepting time payments." Mr. Neesom, considering the offer, was as bleak as she was in giving it. "I'd thought of a lump payment. Not a big lump payment, I've been aware of that, but still something to—ha, humph—turn over. I——"

"There'd be more safety, perhaps, in time payments. You'd have plenty to get to California; the rest would be like an annuity."

"Ha. Humph. Yes. Oh, decidedly. An annuity. More safety." Safety, perhaps, was what Mrs. Neesom had wanted, it might be something he recognized as a good, but it wasn't anything that had, for him, any gloss. Glumly, through the week following, he was seen as considering it, whistling tunelessly over his vegetables, but then, when she crossed his vision, recalled to dejection. Returning in late afternoon, from what probably were rounds of the real estate offices, more downcast than ever. Toward week end he fell on one happy fact——

"A good thing—I was absolutely sure of it—a good thing I didn't give exclusive listings; real estate people these days just like everyone else, don't have the gumption. Of course if I wait long enough they'll turn up somebody. Sell it myself, though, I save that commission——"

She answered carefully, "You want to take time, Mr. Neesom. The last thing I want to do is hurry you." But he was, and she knew it then, turning a corner; from then on, if she knew him, he would hunt reasons for completing the sale. The clincher, it seemed, came to him the following Monday. At his return on that afternoon he stepped jauntily, newspaper slapping his trouser leg, hat at an angle.

"Mrs. Reiss," he at once began chirkily, "you'll scarcely credit what I've been about, today. I visited a ticket agency. You'll scarcely credit this either, Mrs. Reiss—time and again I used to say to Mrs. Neesom, my late wife, 'What we ought to do in the summer,' I used to say to Mrs. Neesom, 'is take a trip out to California, see Blanche.' 'Hundreds of dollars,' Mrs. Neesom always used to say. 'A trip like that, we can always figure it would take hundreds of dollars.' Today I inquired about a one-way fare, Mrs. Reiss, and that's what you won't be able to credit. Fifty-nine fifty. Coach, of course, but fifty-nine fifty. That puts

—I must say that puts a very different complexion on things, Mrs. Reiss. You take fifty-nine fifty, take—oh, pretty close to two hundred for incidentals—that would still leave me five hundred to—ha—turn over. Of course five hundred isn't——"

"You'd have expenses in California," she reminded. "Your sister might not——"

He waved that aside energetically. "There's that seventy-five a month you'd be sending. My annuity. That's what you said, Mrs. Reiss. My annuity. One thing I know I can depend on with you, Mrs. Reiss. My payments would come in. Yessirree, that's one thing I'd bank on."

It appeared she'd made a purchase.

She was frightened; she was wretchedly regretful. Maybe from the first what she'd hoped for was obstruction so great she couldn't possibly overcome it; maybe in asking the price she'd hoped it would be so ridiculously high she couldn't consider it; maybe in going to her father she'd hoped he would refuse her; maybe in telling Carl she'd hoped he would restore her to reason. Maybe she yet should draw back.

At the same time she endured these tremors, however—so different from anxieties concerning Carl and the boys, but with their own shaking sharpness—she also experienced a defiant exultance. That very afternoon, snatching for it ten minutes that should have been spent on the dinner, she slipped out to walk sedately but possessively around the house. Three lots, all this grass—space for Craig and Dusty to run, space in the old carriage house for them to play. Five rooms upstairs—a living room and one each. No, she'd have to keep on some college boys, but at any rate a living room, one room for her and for Carl, another for the boys. Slapping the back of her hand against the limestone foundation, she felt the pleasure of abrading skin. Her own father said there was no foundation like limestone; an old house could be sound. That horrible attic, that more horrible bathroom, the battered upstairs, the rubbish-choked basement, the Byzantine furnace—necessarily these must give her pause, just as they doubtless frightened off other buyers. These, though, were things to repair.

Returning to the kitchen, she had a moment—this was on the other side, again—of seeing that, too, as repelling. The gas ranges blue-black, shaped like coal stoves, with cast legs, tall backs and warming ovens, the whole room a worn leaden battleship gray, cluttered and crowded, pots on the stove giving up steam, Mr. Neesom at the baking counter up to his forearms in biscuit dough, racks of too sweet-smelling rhubarb and chocolate pies stacked in the cart beside her. But then that, too, righted itself to its familiar disorderly order—not attractive, perhaps, but fit to its uses. Twelve hundred she was borrowing from her father. On a note, five per cent. Sixty a year for interest, almost astounding it would be so little. Seven hundred fifty to Neesom, four-fifty to go on until fall. Seventy-five a month to Neesom, about what he'd been getting. She'd be losing his help, though, she might remember that. Through the summer, perhaps, she'd manage, but by fall she'd need more help than the college boys——

At the station, to her surprise and also obviously to his, tears jumped to her eyes when she said good-by to old Neesom. Twice, after she had him settled, and stood outside his window waving and mouthing the added farewells people always mouth unheard outside train windows, he came jerking back to the vestibule.

"Mrs. Reiss, now you write to me; anything you need in the way of advice, now, just write to me—you've got the address, right on top of the cashbox. Scratched it myself with the paring knife. You can't lose it——"

Throwing up the steps, jumping up himself as the doors closed, the porter thrust old Neesom backward; the last she saw of him was his anxiety, colored, as usual, both by dolefulness and an opposite elated excitement over his trip. One thing at least she was grateful for, she thought, standing to wave as the train drew past her, was that she'd kept him so busy at the last he hadn't had a chance to get to a bucket shop with that five hundred. In a stock market going nowhere but up, other investors might make money. Mr. Neesom, she was convinced, never would.

That departure took place on the second of June. It was two weeks later, when the college boys also took off, that she moved her own family over. As expected, Carl's first view of the place only increased his distaste for it; when her father grasshoppered to a stop below the terraced steps, Carl asked, "*This* is it?" incredulously, and then walked without words into the house, through the downstairs, the upstairs.

He still had said nothing more when he began removing his clothes to get into the bed she had ready for him.

Yet he was the one who took over the job of improving their living quarters.

"Must say you're taking the move well." Dr. Daly, when he came in that week, was returned to his casual breeziness. "No reason at all now why you shouldn't increase your up periods. Plenty of little jobs to do around here, I'd guess. Don't push, but let's see you bestir yourself."

For a second time, then, Carl made a round of the rooms, and after that he abandoned his magazines. As she flew about downstairs she could be sweetly aware of him, so near at hand, studying lumber and plumbing pamphlets, just as she could feel warm about Craig and Dusty, released like spring colts to the yard and the carriage house.

She had thought of herself as putting in full days before this; not until Neesom was gone and they'd moved into the place did she find out how she could extend herself. Most of her preoccupations had been with the kitchen; she didn't realize, until the school year ended, how her patronage was reaching out to include stenographers and businessmen from the paper mills across the river, neighborhood families and dining-out couples. Instead of dropping as it had at Christmas, business fell only halfway, and, when summer school opened, pushed up again. Part-time help didn't begin to fill her needs; she missed Neesom as she'd have missed a left hand; frantically she reached out for assistance.

The first came rather simply. "You got that attic up there empty, now," Mrs. Pierson approached her one morning, and within minutes Mrs. Pierson was on full time, the addition covered by her living in. What she really needed help for, though, was the cooking, and nervously, in July, she wrote out an ad for the Sunday paper, and nervously, as the week end approached, she awaited replies. Spoil Neesom's with indifferent cooking, and she spoiled everything.

An elderly woman, late on Saturday afternoon, produced only a hasty addition to qualifications already in mind: whoever came must be quick of foot. No one else appeared until after eight, while she and Mrs. Pierson wearily cleared dishes. At a knock on the back door, then, she went out to find two pimpled thin youths of perhaps eighteen or nineteen, one ash-blond, one darker, leaning against the railing of the back porch, shirt collars open, cigarettes dangling from straight lips.

Both, when she appeared in the doorway, stood silent, occupied, it seemed, not in looking at her but in emitting smoke from their nostrils. There was, however, a flicker at the corners of their eyes, and she had an instant's disagreeable sensation, as if her clothes had been neatly zipped downward from neck to knees.

Hastily and defensively reassembling herself, she asked tartly, "You wished something? Usually only tradespeople come to this door."

In reply, after a moment, the darker boy asked, "You fill up that place yet?"

Only then did she connect them with her advertisement; what her mind had more immediately leaped toward was the cashbox.

In relief she laughed. "Goodness, I didn't think of a—of men answering. The ad ran—didn't it?—under female help wanted."

Inflectionlessly the dark boy cut across that. "We're cooks. We been working at Eihler's."

She began, "I'm sorry, I still think I——"

The darker boy silkily lifted himself from the rail. "You wouldn't care, would you, if we just looked around? We'd like to know what a little place works like."

Her first impulse was to deny them admission; they still looked to her sinister. Mrs. Pierson, though, was behind her, Carl upstairs, two tables hadn't finished dinner——

She began, "I hardly——" but when they advanced she fell back, letting them brush past.

Expressionlessly, in the kitchen, they stood in the center of the floor, here too not appearing to glance around much; certainly they didn't look at Mrs. Pierson. Lounging forward, they proceeded to the first of the dining rooms, and from there on to the hall where Bud Jessup, one of the college boys who stayed on with her, still sat at the cash table. Without speaking they turned about to return to the kitchen.

"How much you figure on paying?" Once more the speaker was the dark boy.

"It can't matter, since I want a girl or woman. But twenty a week."

"Thanks for showing us, anyway." Effortlessly they drifted on outward.

"Well!" Mrs. Pierson commented behind them. "I guess whoever you get, it won't be a couple of young thugs like that."

On Sunday no one turned up at all. Sunday was the free day—Mrs. Pierson went somewhere, the four college students ate out, she and Carl, Craig and Dusty, had the house to themselves. While they were at dinner—in state, downstairs—Carl brought out an absent "Few minutes before I came downstairs a woman was coming up the walk, but some man came across from St. Augustine's, stopped her. Someone must have thought you were open on Sunday."

Bending to wipe spilled cherries from Dusty's pie, she answered, "That's one thing we won't ever do. Open on Sunday."

The afternoon went on plans for upstairs—should they panel their living room in pine? And the bathroom—spang-dangle new fixtures, all three of them, only a hundred twenty. It was terrific temptation. If Carl did the installing, as he was sure he could——

A nuisance, that no one else answered the ad; that meant another week of sixteen-hour days. Besides paying for another ad. And nuisance, on Monday, was scarcely the word for it. From the drugstore where they went for breakfast, one of her college boys phoned to say he and his roommate had sore throats and were reporting in at the health service.

With only Mrs. Pierson, Bud Jessup, and one other boy, she knew grimly what the day would be. One thing to keep cool inside the bounds of possibility, another thing when you were outside those bounds. She was just making up her mind that at noon she would serve forty lunches exactly, the most four of them could handle, and then put out a sign saying closed until dinnertime, when a knock again sounded on the back door. Not lifting her head from the stirring of a white sauce, she called to Mrs. Pierson, "Would you answer?" She didn't know the two boys were in the kitchen until, turning, she saw them there, cigarettes as before drooping from mouth corners, thumbs hooked in the belts of low-slung trousers.

From his flatly inflectionless imperturbability, the dark boy said, "We could come on temporary if you happened to need anyone today."

She threw back sharply, "I thought you were working at Eihler's."

"That's right. Quit last week."

"I told you I want a woman. I——"

"You can get you a woman, lady. We just thought we might pick up a buck or two, maybe, today. Just a couple bucks apiece."

"I——" Breath came into her lungs and stayed there. "I don't so much as know your names. You've given no references. You——"

"I'm Joe. He's Norm. References wouldn't seem to be so necessary, one day."

"Oh, I——" Exasperation seized her; here she was talking, with no time for it. She began, "I can't——" but then a contrary emotion swept up. She wasn't accustomed to using strong language; she detested women who did. But she found herself answering, "All right, if you can work like two cats out of hell-fire, let's see you get at it. One of you take over this white sauce—you, Joe. Norm, you take over that roll dough. Cigarettes out, first. Hands washed——"

As directions shot at them there was, once more, that flicker from the corners of their eyelids, but they jumped to her bidding. For the rest of that morning she had time for little but issuing orders. They were, of course, ignorant of locations, the pantry, the icebox, they blundered a little, getting in her way, a whole troupe of stenographers came in at eleven instead of eleven-thirty, blithely announcing they'd got early lunch; she herself had to help wait tables. Not until toward one-thirty, when things began easing, did she admit to herself the boys weren't doing badly. They'd cooked before, they'd moved like the cats she'd said they'd have to move like. The kitchen had whipped into pace.

Over their late lunch she attempted an extraction which might have been easier if it had been their teeth she was after. Joe's last name, even this little yielded only after struggle, was Krazmarek. Norm's, as reluctantly, Butz. They'd had some courses at Occupational. They'd worked around. Eihler's last.

Both ate with a methodical, no-motion-lost concentration, bent over their plates, looking neither right nor left. Such answers as she got all proceeded from Joe, though Norm couldn't be speechless, since in working he emitted sparse syllables—"Eggs?" "Got a beater?" "Any marge?" No one, though, could say he was a talkative type. She gave them an off-hour, but they went no farther than the back porch, where they sat side by side, smoking, communicating, if at all, by some process of osmosis, while she grabbed the chance to do such checking as she could. Eihler's returned a noncommittal, "Who? Oh? Oh, Joe and Norm. Sure, that's right. Worked here. Ain't here today, though." Occupational was only slightly more informative. Yes, admitted a careful feminine voice, they had had a Joe Krazmarek and Norman Butz. Courses in cooking and baking, quite satisfactory. Mostly Bs. Mrs. Reiss, the voice hinted, was considering them for employment? That was fine. The voice hoped the arrangement would work out well on both sides.

Christine went on from there swiftly, "I'd like to know a bit more of their characters. They seem——"

"We've so many students." The voice was smooth on that too. "I'm afraid we can comment only on what they've done with us."

Far from conclusive. By starting ahead of time on dinner she allowed more time for observation. Joe returned one strong reaction when, mixing cake batter, he asked for the shortening. She pointed to the butter, he stared at her incredulously, held up a two-pound brick, glanced at her again, then dropped in the lump as if he expected it to sear him. No one said anything, but again there was the flicker.

"What are they deciding?" she asked herself. "That I'm so rich I can throw away butter? That I'll be an easy mark?" Or was she just exercising her imagination? Half the boys in Chapaqua, as she realized, were picturing themselves as George Raft; even Craig and Dusty swaggered around with clothespin guns, yelling, "Stick 'em up."

Accepting their day's pay that evening, Joe proffered another taciturnity. "We could fill in the rest of the week. Same pay."

That time her struggle was briefer. She answered, "We'll try that." And when Saturday noon came, she'd reached a decision. At lunch that day she announced crisply, "You're both really very good workers; I'll keep one of you on. You yourselves can decide which it will be."

Joe lifted his cobra head from its position over his plate.

"I stay, he stays."

"I'd like that—this week has been so much easier—I'm afraid, though, I can't afford it. You don't know, of course, but I've just bought this place. On a shoestring. I've debts enough to drown me."

"We'll take fourteen a week. Each. Until you can pay better."

"Even that I can't afford. It's eight dollars a week more than I've counted on. I'm afraid it's one of you or nothing; if you can't consider that I'll still have to find someone else."

"Mrs. Reiss, you ever think you've got that hall out there? A counter could go in there, easy. You could sell baked goods offen it."

Her mouth opened. She began, "But I——" and choked. From across the table, for the first time since he had come there, Joe's eyes met hers with a basilisk directness. Norm didn't look at her; he was carefully rolling ashes around his plate with the tip of his cigarette. But in both was an identical waiting intentness.

She said, "Why, I could, couldn't I?" and heard the astonishment of her own voice. One of them, she'd thought. If I break them up, one won't be as somehow ominous as both. A bakery counter. Not her idea. Theirs. When constriction had already closed on her. Eighteen tables in the three rooms, and she couldn't possibly crowd in more. No chance, ever, of serving upstairs; it was bad enough getting Carl's trays up the narrow stairs. No chance of serving in the basement, either. Not this basement. Every once in a while, asking favors, women sent messages out with the waiters. If Mrs. Reiss, just this once—two dozen of the butter rolls, on Saturday. Miss Bangs, just this once, was wondering if she could have one of the Lady Baltimore cakes, or a strawberry meringue pie——

The hall, too, was narrow. But a counter could be filled over and over.

Later, rather often, she was to remember that afternoon in the gray and black kitchen. Four of them at the scrubbed rectangular wood table. Mrs. Pierson with her special thick coffee cup which once was a shaving mug, held at chin height by both hands, on her face a disapproval as thick as the pink china of the mug. Joe and Norm, waiting. She so cautiously trying to hire one of them without the other, unsure even of that, and Joe saying "A counter could go in there, easy."

In so many ways, that was what did it. Neesom's was the ground she secured, the bakery counter was the seed that sprouted. No more rapidly than you would expect seed to sprout from Neesom's, but still thrusting upward. Without it she might never have managed, without it her margin was so small she might easily have been dragged under; it was the bakery counter that gave her leeway.

The bakery counter. Joe. Norm.

12

"Perhaps by this time you'll agree you have limits. It's a lesson most people accept, soon or late."

That, dryly, was Dr. Daly's dismissal; that sparked the worry behind Christine's eyes; that was the yielding to which he too came. No change in his purposes, but a change in the way he must reach them. A year and four months, he'd lost; it was January of 1928 before he worked again, and even after that, for a while, he had trouble reincorporating himself in the person he had once been.

Trurog's opened before him when he pulled at the door in the morning—long vistas, high gloom and low luster, a scurry of footsteps, a hum, a cool nose-assaulting prickle of fabric, new fabric, sweeping compound, metal, leather, fur dust, and stone. Jewelry to the right and left, handbags ahead, gloves beyond that, yellow and blue signs on high pillar brackets announcing a clearance, the scuffed oak of old counters replaced by walnut—intrinsically Trurog's was Trurog's; it was he who for a short while was alien, stepping more solidly—in passing mirrors, each time unexpectedly, he caught glimpses of the roundness which for the first time in his life concealed his bones. Within that roundness he was battened and held back. Christine had no real cause for worry. He knew now what happened when a blaze burned too furiously.

Salloway, not so much as rising from his chair, was both curt and deliberate. "Like old times, seeing you walk in here, Reiss. Must say you're looking well." Words fine enough, but a voice refrigerated and remote. No mention of the six-hundred-dollar loss on the $15.95 dresses, or the perhaps greater loss on the waistcoat models. "You left us in rather a spot, you may realize; we had to get in a woman from Fortune's—under the circumstances she naturally was extortionate. Of course we'll have a place for you, but I'm afraid the best we can do is the floor again. If you want that, at twenty-eight fifty——"

No urging, no promise, just the offer held out to take or reject as he chose. Accepting, his jaw jutted. "I foresaw that, of course; I don't expect anything better to be open. But I won't want to stick at it, not now any more than before."

"As always that's up to you."

Not what he previously had, but, as he told himself sturdily, all that he needed.

He was reassigned to second. Whether there was any reason behind that, any path deliberately left open, he couldn't say; certainly in Salloway's attitude there was no sign of favor. Nor was there much alleviation in his first weeks of work, either.

Predominantly in those first weeks his own approach was one of caution—within himself the new calm he mustn't disturb, and outside the changes to which he must also be oriented. Millinery billowing out to swallow Suits, Suits retired to a corner beside Furs, Dresses encroaching on Coats. A year away was revealing about turnover; among saleswomen it was the old faces that struck with surprise, not the new. Each person in his section knew his history, producing an initial strangeness; Mrs. Tost, the new dress buyer, delineated that strangeness as nailed down and permanent. "You once *bought* here? How queer things must seem to you!"

Inquiry about Mrs. Pesek brought reply so astonishing he at once took an elevator to verify it. Comfortably if humbly established as assistant buyer of basement dresses was indeed Mrs. Pesek. Not rising when he walked into her cubicle, her movements betraying a curious time lag, her hair at last graying, so thin she was but a minor fraction of her former self. But still Mrs. Pesek. "Well, boy, I guess they didn't get either of us for good, yet. This basement may be underground, but I still a hell of a lot prefer it to the other kind of underground."

On his way upstairs, moved by impulse, he paused to stand looking on at another old problem. Mrs. Willette, with well-remembered gestures, was smoothing black kid over a hand held rigidly before her. The blue-gray curls were as charmingly disarrayed as ever, the bruised eyes smiled as serenely, the sleeve of a black crepe Romaine extended as tightly over the narrow wrists. Mrs. Pesek, emerging a chrysalis self from corruption to inhabit the basement, Mrs. Willette maintaining her niche and—he had no doubt—her thievery—the two seemed to exemplify the something about Trurog's to which, in those first days, he had trouble accustoming himself.

In other ways, though, he could. Thoroughly. The routine was so known to him. Getting to his floor in the morning, checking in his salespeople, shifting where shifting was needed, posting his lunch schedules, taking up with old Geggenheim any question of increase or decrease in personnel, meeting the customers. "For evening? This way. Sorry, house dresses on third. Size sixteen? I'll have someone with you immediately." Asking himself what a next move might be didn't begin with his store return, but that return sharpened and focused the question.

"I'll have to buy again. Not dresses, they'll never let me in again on dresses. It'll have to be one of the smaller departments." While he still lay ill and exhausted, convulsed by his coughing, this had been one of his fever spots. Gloves, handbags, jewelry, neckwear, shoes, even china and housewares, men's furnishings, boys' wear—in imagination he considered them all, recalling overheard phrases—"Shoes, that's the bitchiest business you can ever get into." "Panties under those little short skirts, and that's every last stitch." "You'll never get a profit on kids' clothes; people won't put the money on kids the way they will on themselves." "This Japanese china—we might as well give up Bavarian, we'll maybe have to give up American——" He found clues to the hazards of each kind of merchandise. Just the thought of buying, in fact, crowded him with formless revulsion, and slowly he came to decision. No buying. The kind of astuteness, the practice you needed for buying, weren't to be formed in a half decade. To be a buyer you must begin in your teens, concentrating on one kind of merchandise only, like Eggen with hosiery. It was to the wide unchanneled area up over buying that he was headed; he must side-step and by-pass.

How he was to do so didn't, during his convalescence, appear. It was the glimpsed possibility, though, that made recovery possible, and once on the scene again he set himself to look about coolly, arming against the sensations of remoteness when they came. On the floor every day he saw Geggenheim; Geggenheim on the floor moved with a big old man's jauntiness, pads of flesh on his huge frame hanging loosely like pendant hot water bottles; when Geggenheim swung jerkily about, as he always swung, anyone near by shied warily; it was hard to escape the impression that those flesh pads might detach from their moorings to fly out as missiles. Geggenheim's reputation still fixed him as one of the worst men in the store to work for, but Geggenheim had, now, less than seven years to go.

In giving up the buying, Carl had also given up Geggenheim, but as winter waned and spring moved toward summer his determinations began reattaching. No use going to Geggenheim to ask for an assistanceship. Any wedge cut into Geggenheim must come as a sledge-hammer slash from above.

Ideas didn't come with the rapidity they'd once come; he was a machine slowly maneuvering toward an idea, rather than a magnet for them. In early September, though, he knew himself ready; by early September, in fact, he knew himself ready as he'd never been before. Walking across the dust-colored carpet between Salloway's door and the roll-top, sliding the typed sheets of his proposals and estimates in along the edge of the cut varnished oak desk shelf, taking the side chair, he felt a control almost as chill as the one raised to him.

And Salloway, he thought, quickly sensed that control and his certainty. The first glance cast toward him as he cleared the door rebounded from him crustily; the second, lifted after the moment it took the gray eyes to get through the first paragraphs, was still imperturable, but also slightly diffused.

"Not a new idea," Carl succinctly began as the gray eyes returned to the sheets again. "Not new for me or for anyone else, now. You may remember I came in years ago suggesting we install a college shop. We didn't. Now in almost any city newspaper—New York Sun, Philadelphia Record—you'll see ads over a college shop floor line. Last month when I asked three days off what I did was go to Chicago. Marshall Field's doesn't have its women's wear cut and dried into dresses, suits, coats, millinery; Marshall Field's is divided into intimate shops. Trurog's must be one of the few top-rank stores clinging to the old setup. High school and college girls don't like pawing through old-lady fashions. Why should they? Women size fifty-two don't like coming up against twelves. We're not holding our own in the women's wear business. We're mossbacks."

Salloway let the first pages fall on the last one. Picking up the small sheaf in his thick spatulate fingers, he curled it into a roll and then let it uncurl; the top sheet stayed dog-eared. Rising from the desk chair, he stumped to the window, keeping his back to Carl; when he came back it was to halt behind his chair, palms flattening along its back, head lowered between bull-hunched shoulders, face empty.

"If we go into any such readjustment," supposition came flatly, "you have something in mind you'd hope to get from it."

"Women's Wear assistant in charge of the change-over." Reply was as flat.

Lifting his hands from the chair, Salloway moved around to reseat himself, thrusting far back, lifting an ankle to cross it over a knee, staring at the hand with which he gripped the raised ankle. Eight years before, in much this same juxtaposition, Carl had seen the domed pink crown as higher, pinker and more ridged than when first seen, the jaw line of the heavy face heavier. Now again there was change to note—the hair line in back fallen lower, a dimpling under the chin foretelling the day when the jaw line would sag. Salloway was fifty-three, his time, too, shortening. Fifteen years, now, instead of the twenty-three he had boasted. Like Trurog's, though, Salloway, too, still was Salloway; his exterior might loosen, but his interior was constant.

"It can't surprise you"—the words were deliberate—"this isn't the first time I've considered such readjustments. Actually in executive committee we've been mulling over possibilities for several years. It also can't be news to you that there's opposition, first of all, I'll be frank enough to say, from Mr. Trurog. The day when Mr. Trurog accedes readily to heavy expenditure is over. Secondly, there's Geggenheim. The ramifications of Geggenheim's place in this firm I shan't go into, but you may as well take it for granted Geggenheim won't be counted out until he retires."

When Carl nodded, he didn't continue with that; instead his glance lifted to Carl.

"Peculiarly enough, in spite of opposition I know I'll meet on this, I believe that for a job of the kind you suggest, you would be adequate. That's always provided, of course, you don't take to your bed again. If we go into this, it won't be anything flimsy; what I have in my own mind is a solid rebuilding. Second's due for it. Major decisions, naturally, would be made in executive session, but for details—arrangement of temporary quarters, transfer of staff, transfer of inventory—there'll have to be someone, and Geggenheim's not up to it. You know, of course—Geggenheim would never accept you happily."

Against this, also, Carl was flat. "Working where I do, I could scarcely escape that."

When he left Salloway, no decision had been reached, but that, too, was expected conclusion; even Salloway didn't deal with such matters alone. Just the same, he walked out past Harriet confident; confidently a couple of weeks later he turned up at a board meeting to which he had been invited, almost imperturbably meeting a waspish sniping from Bodali and Leverett at details of his program which, it seemed, differed from previous plans—the establishment, for one thing, of what he had called a Maturity Shop, for gowns, suits, coats and lingerie in sizes forty-four to fifty-six, the inclusion of counters for lingerie and girdles with the outerwear of the Teen Agers' Shop. He heard, also, of proposals he hadn't considered, such as barber and beauty shops. Significant, at this meeting, was the absence of John Trurog. And Geggenheim.

The gathering broke in a general wrangling, but still he was confident, and no surprise touched him when, in the first week of November, still 1928, he was called in to hear that reorganization had been decided on. He had a new job.

More than Salloway and Leverett, Bodali and Ohman were present at this later meeting. In the board room Mr. Trurog crouched pale in his chair at the head of the table, his hands moving like bleached helpless butterflies come to the end of their summer. Beside him was Lefevriere, the store architect, and Milo Geggenheim. Usually Milo Geggenheim's visible coloring was an ocher-gray clay; this afternoon it was close to burgundy.

At Carl's entrance Lefevriere had the floor. "—believe I have incorporated all suggested changes. This section here, for instance, in back of your Young Girls' Shop, is now dedicated to your larger sizes. This section——"

In outline the shape of second, like that of all other floors, was a square U, with the stairways and elevators forming the central block. The long leg to the west, as also on most other floors, was taken up by storerooms, locker rooms, freight passages; what remained was roughly an L. Over the huge plans of a rearranged floor Carl bent himself studiously. It would have been pleasant—certainly he had this much coming—to feel over this wrested new victory some kind of exultance. He did feel something, his palms ached dryly, a little more intensely so than for the weeks past, but beyond that he was more than anything unsettled and disturbed. The cataclysm of his illness hadn't held him down; he was on his way again. In being once more on his way, however, there was loss as well as gain, loss of his calmness; he had learned how vulnerable he was in advancement.

This time there must be no fumbling. His hands against the floor plan must be quiet, his eyes sharp, his voice clear if deferent.

"Teen Agers open to the elevators—that's of course excellent. But if the Maturity Shop goes in behind there, that'll mean those heavier women will have to use Teen Agers as an aisle, rather impairing the purpose of having a Maturity Shop. It might be preferable——"

"Naturally"—stiffness from Lefevriere—"it would be preferable if all sections opened on the elevators. In that case you'd have a parallel series of Pullman cars. You can't——"

"Furs would be a perfectly good section for the heavier women to walk through. They like being tempted to white fox and leopardskin."

Choked contribution from Geggenheim. "Four new buyers. A woman to run this beauty shop. The other buyers cut down. It's appalling. I can promise you——"

"Gentlemen, gentlemen," from Trurog. "The expense, gentlemen. Consider the expenses of——"

Salloway, "Mr. Reiss is quite right, gentlemen; we can't make our fat women run a gantlet. That shop must go elsewhere."

A pattern which, in the next weeks, was to grow very familiar. Never any union of opinion, always resistance, objection, dissension, wrangling. And then, when plans finally were accepted and shown to the second-floor buyers, exactly the uproar Geggenheim promised.

So much satisfied malice sat Geggenheim's countenance, at this particular meeting, that the acid of it might have flowed down his front and then out to consume them all, both the people who on one side of the table sat adamant and those who on the other side stood to hammer and shrill. Yet nothing, by this time, really hindered the program; it now was the slow heavy piece of machinery, his part that of a mechanic springing forward to clear its path, to grind its valves, oil it, expedite and polish.

For his new duties he was given an office—not, as expected, a desk with Geggenheim, but a hastily cleared-out small storeroom opposite the time clocks, just beyond the No Admittance doors. Harriet, it happened, was at home with a cold when the news broke, but she was one of the first to see him in his new quarters.

"Of course I'm delighted." Her expression showed queer mixtures.

"This is late in the day—you must have heard about Geggenheim. He's not the bull moose he looks. He's an asp. People up against Geggenheim——"

"Usually go out on shutters?"

"Something like that."

"I'll look out."

And he did. Geggenheim during the early days of his incumbency came past to spray a thin sarcasm. "I enter your office, you see, not you mine. Doubtless you'll soon have a sign up—Head Women's Wear Office."

In return Carl good-naturedly laughed. Women's Wear Assistant was his new title, but he wasn't actually Geggenheim's assistant, as the position of his office proved. He was a separate executive, operating under Salloway and the board.

"Any harness race," he humored, "there's a driver and a horse, Mr. Geggenheim. We both know who's driver, who's horse."

"Ah," replied Geggenheim darkly, "I thought I might be the sulky."

This small interchange didn't worsen relations; a few days later the older man offered what sounded like armistice.

"I realize, Mr. Reiss, I'm not now as young as I once was. Your own age, Mr. Reiss, is—yes, thirty-five. Ah, I also recall a time I was thirty-five. I would never be where I am, Mr. Reiss, if I weren't able to accept the inevitable when it's forced upon me. I can't feel changes such as those ahead of us will be for the best, but the matter is out of my hands. I believe you'll find me co-operative."

It was a speech—so many of its overtones those of age and sadness—to move a hearer to pity. Even from Geggenheim it was moving. Fifty years at Trurog's, a man hired at eleven to run back and forth from store counters to Mr. Trurog on a balcony, taking up sales slips and money, bringing back change. Through all the store's growth he'd been integral; Women's Wear had been his for two decades. Now within a few years, a date being anticipated because he was past his age, the store would go on to flourish in the hands of younger men already waiting, while he vanished.

Compassion, though, as Carl realized, had best not temper caution. Scrupulously he confined his activities to forthcoming changes, avoiding as much as possible everything that might roil hatred.

But yet not avoiding it. In Geggenheim or in others.

For a while—this was part of the strangeness—he was insulated from those indigenous hatreds; now he was soon forced to meet them head on.

"But you'll still," he argued with Mr. Riccardi, "be buying all millinery; it's only that your more youthful numbers will be housed in the Teen Agers' section. If you——"

"Would you have any idea," Riccardi spat back, resentment forever stirred rather than soothed, "what it'll be like, keeping track of stock all over the store? Next thing you'll want hats next to shoes and handbags, for matching. Want hats in with coats. I'd rather quit now——"

"Anywhere you went, Mr. Riccardi, any big store, I'm afraid you'd find the same situation."

Riccardi, of course, didn't leave; neither did the others. They simply avoided him, or looked at him as if he were leprous. To the salespeople readjustments, in most cases, meant the simplest of changes—future transfer, it might be, from Ladies' Dresses to Sportswear, but they too regarded him spitefully. The remodeling plan, over the whole store, was spoken of as "That Reiss five-year stink plan." Mr. Trurog, too, of his own accord this time, called him in for a second interview; all over again he was forced to undergo the whine of the old man's fears; all over again he saw the pictures, and suffered the aftermath, the twisting and turning, the hours when the taste in his mouth was that of hot corroding metal.

It didn't stop him, though; nothing stopped him. Almost constantly, these days, there was heat in his hands; he formed a habit of stopping off in the washroom to hold them under cold water. He was finding out what being an executive meant—the control, the feeling of adequacy, the unguent pleasure of dealing directly with the board, of sitting with the board sometimes as if he were part of it, of being called on for decisions and judgments. Times when he said decisively, "With brown walnut paneling in the beauty shop it would, I think, be more interesting to use lavender. Perhaps lavender velvet." "With this gray we won't want a dark green, not in that gloomy corner; we'll want yellow green, chartreuse, an effect of interior sunlight."

Times when the powered wings once more strongly lifted.

In his personal life, too, at this time, there were pleasures and displeasures.

Dinner at the Piatt, and, after, Paul Keast as Villon in *The Vagabond King*—he and Christine, Bob Gokey and Harriet took an evening to celebrate; of all moments in his latest ascension, these perhaps were the most limpid and unalloyed. Christine, for the evening, bought a *robe de style*, he himself merely wore his best suit—the tailor-made, his first, wasn't yet finished—but in spirit it was the tailor-made he had on. Bob Gokey and Harriet were entirely festive and larking, Harriet stropping her tongue over almost everyone of any consequence in the store, but scrupulously excluding old Geggenheim and the second-floor buyers.

Later, though, when he and Christine were undressed and in bed, still too stirred up for sleeping, she pushed her nose against his shoulder, in the gesture as old as their marriage, and from that smothered vantage point murmured warmly and happily—warmly and happily at least on the surface—"This is the day, I guess. We can start saying good-by to Neesom's."

Moved to twist away from her, but forcing himself to lie quietly, he answered, "That should lie ahead somewhere, though I suppose there's no hurry. Anything can happen yet."

That he detested her working—even if, nowadays since she'd taken on those two hoodlums of hers, *working* was scarcely the name for it; *occupying* herself with Neesom's came closer—was a matter of such course he didn't have to look to know what his reactions were. Their living room now had its pine paneling, their bathroom its pristine fittings, people like Bob and Harriet couldn't be done exclaiming over what he'd managed with the place, but for him it was public. Coming home at night, he came to a door by which anyone might enter. Anyone, by paying, ate at his table. Christine was scrupulous with Craig and Dusty, giving them most of her time both before school and after; she was scrupulous, too, with him. Her interest in him was forever intense, he knew that; when the boys were in bed it was Trurog's they talked about. Just the same, he was forced to feel that interest as less complete than it once was; even if she didn't obtrude it, she held this other absorption, this divergent activity.

In any flat proposal of casting off Neesom's, however, he had to feel the uncertainties. Fifty a week in his new job, twenty-six hundred a year, not bad by department store standards. But never enough when it came to expenditure. At twenty-eight fifty there'd been nothing at all for his bank account, still dangerously under a thousand; Salloway hadn't yet mentioned a chance at stock, but surely now the day couldn't be far. Holding the job he now held meant clothes, more appearances in the Lake Room, lunching often with Lefevriere and men from Carpets and Draperies, sometimes even with Salloway. Craig and Dusty each year grew more costly—at eight Dusty must have braces for his crooked incisors, Craig wanted a bicycle. With Neesom's, distasteful as it was, there was support of a kind. At least they lived inexpensively, ate inexpensively——

A few weeks later, in January, Christine brought up the subject once more.

"I hate to—oh, I know it's not important, but if we're to sell this place we shouldn't delay. The middle of the season's the best time to unload. And if we're to buy a house—spring's the best time for that. There should be at least something over, enough for a down payment——"

The day behind him had been a hard one; all his days were hard. In planning he'd thought a beginning should be made at the end of the second-floor L, either in furs or, opposite, in lingerie. Salloway was hot to get in the beauty shop. Salloway, of course, was the one not to be talked down, and the beauty shop, right in the middle, at the angle, was being done first, which meant tearing out parts of both Coats and Dresses, as well as relocating old Geggenheim. He exploded, "For God's sake, Christine! I can't waste myself on that question! If you spent your time downtown, if you had Tost and Riccardi on your neck——"

She answered, subdued, that subdual which was so easy for her to take on, but with her terrible inflexibility, too, her glance toward her ankles, stretched far in front of her as she sat on a footstool, "I don't want you to think of it. Just tell me. Just tell me what you want. I can't do anything as serious as that—can I?—without knowing what you want. Sometimes it seems to me——"

Sharply, before she added to that, he burst again, "What you mean is that you're not willingly giving up Neesom's, not really. So you're pushing the decision on me. Then if things go wrong, later, you can think 'If we'd only kept Neesom's.' All right, keep it. Keep it just as it is."

She too was vehement in reply to that; she cried, "But if I keep it, it won't stay as it is! It's getting away from me, Carl, right now! The bakery counter—we can't supply it, not with the ovens in this kitchen. We can hardly bake enough to keep up with the tables, any more. I don't know—I haven't brought this up—a Mr. Binns came to see me. Mr. Binns from the big grocery downtown. He wants to take on our bread and our rolls. He's suggested—all by themselves Joe and Norm have hunted up an old firehouse down by the river, an empty one. They say we can rent it for thirty a month, with an option to buy at six thousand. It's brick and as solid as a rock, Joe and Norm say, just too small for the newer style engines. I don't know, Carl—I'd have to borrow for ovens and mixers, but then Joe and Norm—they're not satisfied as things are, they keep seeing chances to do better——"

He said furiously, "You've had all this in your mind, but to me you're pretending you want to get out of it? Can you ever be reasonable? Spread out, if you want to, let Joe and Norm spread you out, spread out till you cover Chapaqua; to me it won't make any difference."

A quarrel, one of their worst, with not all the unreasonableness, as he knew even while he continued it, confined to Christine; he was too nettled to be reasonable; the position in which he was caught was too insufferable.

After their stored resentments were spent they both calmed again, Christine bringing out her repeated, "But it *doesn't* mean anything to me, Carl, not compared to the things that do." He as stiffly reiterating, "That's useless, your saying that; I can't think of depriving you."

For days afterward she remained uncertain and troubled, but she didn't again force an issue; later in the spring he was aware the old firehouse was taken up, aware, though he tried to keep clear, of her perturbations over ovens and mixers.

In all conscience, that spring, he was having enough of his own to perturb him.

13 Back in 1921,
for a short time, the country had suffered what was known as deflation, farm prices splintered, Trurog's since then had had to get along with much less buying from the small-town and farm wives who came in on trips to finger the goods in the basement. Fortunately there were other customers; after the temporary upset city activities zoomed, building was incessant—of houses, of office buildings, of huge industrial plants; the wages of plumbers and carpenters, of toolmakers and diemakers, of men who stood at machines making refrigerators and radios, overstuffed parlor suites and auto parts, electric irons and toasters, sterling silver and hair clippers, poured through Chapaqua in a flood; installment buying meant you could acquire an ego-swelling new possession today and not make much of any payment until tomorrow.

On the whole, like most of his fellows, he was indifferent to overall situations. Sometimes, true, he went in for discussions with Bob Gokey and Glen Shotwell who, no longer a newcomer, advanced to take over Carl's discarded post on second. "Banking's the basic business," he said. "Everything else in the country depends on good banking." Or again, with disdain, "There's nothing in this country more loathsome than politics. Politicians who aren't skunks to begin with soon get that way in office." Glen Shotwell was given to sounding off, Glen Shotwell said a good deal more than this, but on anything verging toward interference Carl disagreed. Business, he felt, was best left to itself.

As early as 1927, though, at home and in bed, forced to spend too much time with books and magazines, he began to be troubled by events outside himself. The Florida land boom and its collapse were to be viewed with contempt; anyone fool enough to toss money into a sinkhole deserved what he got. What followed, however, was more disconcerting. It now was the stock market into which people threw themselves. All the tried ways of advancement—producing food, manufacturing merchandise, buying it, selling it—were cast aside as for stumble bums; the new way to wealth was through gambling. Any time he saw a newspaper on a buyer's desk it was folded to the small print of stock market quotations. In the Lake Room he heard "Twenty-six thousand in four days, and she's a beauty operator, that's every bit she is." "I said to George yesterday, if everyone else gets all that money for nothing, I don't see why we can't." Lefevriere was a plunger in American Can, Bob Gokey was borrowing to buy Cities Service on margin, Glen Shotwell's specialty was Union Carbide and Carbon.

"You going on as a dumb cluck forever?" From a profit margin of seven thousand, in that spring of 1929, it was Bob Gokey's turn to be indulgently superior. "Say, give me a couple more months like this and I'll be saying good-by to old Trurog's forever. Time's soon coming when *nobody's* going to work, boy. You must be about the only guy in Chapaqua, for gosh sakes, still bumping along with a *savings* account. What you getting there—two per cent? I figure I'm making about eight hundred. *Per cent*, that is. That's *per cent*."

The disbeliefs and aversions he felt toward gambling—remainders of his courses in Economics and Business Law—stayed as before, but he also was touched by the fever. "If I'd taken my twelve hundred, if I'd gone into Union Carbide when Shotwell did, I'd have a clear profit of nine thousand." A thought not only stunning, but also indecent; money wasn't to be made that way, money must come hard, be worth striving for. He went as far as to ask Christine if he should try it, and when her reply was negative, his disbeliefs returned in full force. Just the same, temptation wore at him as it wore at everyone, even, he came to know, at the hierarchy over him. Bodali, he learned, played heavily with Trurog funds in the summer of 1927 and again in the summer and fall of 1928; the very funds set aside for remodeling were from this enterprise. Bodali now, though, was pulling in his horns. "Not any more with store money. Not even with any more of my own, except what I'm willing to lose for the fun of it. All right, I'm a bear on America. All right, I'm a traitor to business. What I'm doing for Trurog's right now—myself too—is retrench and liquefy. I'm telling you——"

Bodali sat with head lowered and weaving. Carl never, before, had seen much power in Bodali, too compactly graceful, too swart, too smiling, too deliberately and suavely shy, but he saw it that day. Salloway stood with Bodali. That was the line-up of the board, that was Trurog's cunning hold of his own power: Salloway and Bodali against

Ohman and Leverett. Ohman and Leverett were the ones who wanted to keep on playing Trurog money, and who, from the incredible fortunes they themselves were amassing, looked now at Bodali and Salloway, even at Trurog's, with the amused commiseration Bob Gokey and Glen Shotwell were according Carl.

Through spring and summer of 1929, through early fall, this was what went on, this bursting reversal of everything normal, this hectic vision of chances forever coming up, forever passing, forever lost. General Electric today at 320, from which it could go nowhere but down, as Bodali said, though last week it had been 304, and he'd said it couldn't stay at that, either. Westinghouse at 268½, going higher. In addition to the pressures of his second-floor activities, where even the carpenters collected in corners to talk Kennecott Copper and American Gypsum, and had to be kept at their work by main vigor, there was always and forever this other pressure, the pressure of retaining perspective in a world in which Trurog's and everything in it was miniscule in comparison to what was going on outside.

And then in October he too, of course, he as well as everyone else —even if in a way, since he had ventured none of his own funds, he in the beginning was little more than a bystander—came to Armageddon.

Scarifying, just to be present and look on at the slaughter. Bob Gokey and Shotwell, together in his office, clay-pale, sweating, hoarse. "Carl, now look. Look. There's this little readjustment. You know those old bastards. Trying to shake out us little guys. You've got that twelve hundred—we wouldn't need more than that. These things— you know yourself, boy, we've had these little shakedowns before. This minute, boy, it's on its way up again. Mitchell. That's what my broker told me. Charles E. Mitchell. You've got to've heard of Charles E. Mitchell, boy——"

Bob Gokey and Glen Shotwell four days later agreeing dully, apathetically, "It wouldn't of made any difference," but dully and apathetically joining the others who hated him. Chester Ohman, in a week, losing the substance from out his firm flesh, shrinking inside until his skin hung in elephant folds, walking the store as if he walked in sleep. Leverett thinning to whipsaw brittleness. Riccardi, the hat buyer, staying on in his office one evening and then, when the building was empty of everyone but the night workers, throwing himself from a Lake Room window. A woman in the wrapping room, a widow, killing herself and her small son with gas.

Fever like no other fever, the apex of illness. Hysterical believing-against-anything hope. And then the terrible bleakness, the apathy, the misery which was the misery of a separate people mourning not for anyone else but themselves, their own desire-ridden dream of a Babylonian hanging-garden lushness with no support, no nourishment but air, fairer for being unsupported and unnourished, as hard to give up as it once was hard to give up hoping toward heaven. This was a world in which for years now, ever since the war ended, they had cynically given up most of their old beliefs—that there would be a surcease of struggling, or much intrinsic goodness in mankind, or any humanity of nations toward each other, or any high God-compassion. But in which they still believed one thing—that there could be free-flung un-attached unproduced irresponsible wealth.

Now they were giving up this too. And it seemed like the last that they had.

In the midst of the holocaust Salloway, who lost little or nothing, stumped about losing the dimples of age from under his chin, growing harder, more compact, who already was hard and compact, muscles bunching like those of a fighter going into a first round. Bodali coiling to serpentine readiness. Both of them flexing for what came next. "The nation's wealth reserves are now so shrunken——" Not food resources, not man resources, not oil, coal or forests, but credit. Sixty billion in a fall and winter. Unemployment figures to be watched with a sickened absorption—three million, six million, eight million. Banks that were the base of all, failing. Industries shutting down, laying off.

"Hell," Salloway popped coldly at one board meeting, "we've never been in as good a position as we are right now. We've never been as set for profits. We'll be offering prices that haven't been seen for two decades. Don't tell me we can't pack 'em in."

Maybe they didn't pack them in. But when the first of the distress purchases got to the counters—rayon pants at nineteen cents, silk hose at fifty-nine cents, men's suits at nineteen-fifty, people came in to buy, all right; people bought as if chances to buy, too, must be grabbed while the grabbing was good. Merchandise on hand at the time of the crash had to be discounted, but on the whole it was the producers who took the big jounce, not Trurog's. No later than the spring of 1930, Trurog's was selling for less but also buying for less, preserving a comfortable margin of profit between.

Just the same, what grew cancerously at Trurog's as elsewhere was continuing and panic terror. Not of what had happened, but of what might happen, of a slide with no bottom. To Carl, too, no longer a bystander, fear must be close and immediate. By September of 1929 he and Lefevriere had finished the Charm Room; on October first, three weeks before the crash, the Charm Room had its grand opening —exquisite waxed walnut panels, mirrors and lavender velvet for the huge reception room, rows and rows of businesslike compartments back of that, with the gleaming latest in shampoo basins, croquinole machines, dryers, sterilizers, cabinets, water softeners; women crowded in to stand hushed and awed as in a cathedral; until the crash the place was thronged, and even afterward didn't do badly—one's looks, as Harriet said, would be a last thing to go. A start had been made, too, on the new millinery section, which was to flank the Charm Room on one side as dresses were to flank it on the other; few women —this was Salloway's psychology—could get a new hairdo without wanting a hat and a dress to go with it. It was here, with a good fifth of second, behind its flimsy temporary barriers, no more than a naked and clattering lumber room of bare joists and worn floor, that paralysis struck. Carpenters moving with such lethargy they affixed perhaps ten boards in eight hours, Lefevriere not so much as appearing, old Trurog at board meetings breaking into dreary tears—"No more, gentlemen, no more, no more. Even a penny, gentlemen—each cent may be precious." Ohman seconding him grayly. "We've learned, perhaps, about overexpansion." Leverett, "Mr. Trurog is right, we can only retrench." Bodali growling, "Retrench? You blasted idiots, I did retrench. What're you howling about? We've got our capital, we've got——" Salloway, more sober but belligerent, "We perhaps can't decide on a long-term basis, but that millinery section will have to be finished."

That much reprieve, then. A job to last until the millinery section was done.

To Carl, it was a life foreshortened. In the world·where only a short while ago he had been having so much trouble in keeping perspective, Trurog's shrinking while the world expanded, there now was an opposite violence. Trurog's bursting outward to be the only solidity in a world softened and insubstantial. No more need for stopping off in the washroom to hold his hands under water; his hands were forever cold. A job lost meant no other job anywhere, a job lost meant not only the loss of ambition, of life, but going out to be drowned in the eight million, nine million, ten million others. It meant that even if Christine—shrinking horror in itself—were able to feed and clothe him, he would become one in spirit with men who sat day in and day out in library reading rooms, drugging themselves with crime novels or Westerns, men who stalked in small groups through chain groceries filling their bags, and then at the counter roughly thrusting a way out without paying, men glimpsed at ravaging hotel garbage cans, men of no hope, no present, no future. As he took up the work on the millinery section, he found himself frantically wanting to prolong it, jealously eying each workman, hungering to go to Salloway with plans for a cutback.

"Easily," he might tell Salloway, "we can do this job with five men instead of our fifteen, working them harder, working them longer, cutting their wages——" He had no belief, not actually, in Salloway's showing him mercy when his time came, but what seemed to stop him, as he realized with a shame striking all the way into his spirit, wasn't fellow feeling for his men, but simply that if he forged merci- lessness as a weapon it increased the savagery of a fate which eventu- ally must turn against him.

If he'd ever prayed, "Lord, let me live long," as he sometimes wryly thought, he was getting an answer. He too, like everyone else, in these days lived lengthily, dragging his body through leaden uncer- tain motions, soul quickened to anticipant anguish, expecting each week to be his last of self-respect and hope. When the resplendent new maize and gray millinery section was finished in April of 1930, he came to another caesura, to more stormy board sessions, more tears from Trurog, but again reprieve. "We may lose money, gentlemen"— conclusion by Salloway—"but we're not losing it yet. You see what's happening in Millinery—women like walking into what at least looks like prosperity; we may not sell much, but we're getting what business there is. I vote we go on to the dress section."

"I can't go on this way." After the second postponement Carl's pendulum swung toward revolt. "Having this minute only, being as unsure as this, foreseeing no future." The years of his undeflected drive toward his high goal now appeared as mirage; he still had his consuming necessity, but all he could do in the present was cling to his ledge. That was the month when Mrs. Tost, on a Saturday which saw a quarter of her sales force dismissed, the rest accepting deep pay cuts, said benignly before such staff as was left, "I suppose I should be grateful I'll be the last in the department to go; I'm the only one can both sell and buy."

Yet all the while the depression continued, life kept up its more individual snares too.

Called to Salloway's office early in the summer of 1930 while the work on the dress section was in mid-course, Carl found Salloway frowning above the tattoo of his fingers on the desk.

"Sit down, Reiss." Then, when Carl obeyed, abruptly, "Barbara Lucas—you may remember her, Chet Ohman's daughter—was in here this morning; she's asking for Teen Agers. I rather doubt if she'll get it; she hasn't experience to handle anything that big. But she may get the Sports Shop. What I've called you in for is to see if you can't get up a little more speed. You're doing all right; do it faster. Teen Agers and the Sports Shop should be next. Both at once."

Reprieve again, this time not even fought over in board session. But, with the haste Salloway was now advocating, lessening rather than lengthening the time ahead of him. As for Barbara——

If he had any emotion to feel for her by this time, beyond indifference, it must only be pity. She too had married, the same fall he had; in fact, a month earlier; he remembered the relief with which he'd heard it. Married and gone to New York to live, her husband the scowling young man who had come up so often that night at the Piatt. Now lately he'd heard she was home again, widowed by the same act as Riccardi's, only it was from a hotel window that her husband jumped. When the news broke in the store, he thought with illness how evasion was forming itself to this pattern, as if each fugitive must in his own person repeat the parabola of the stock market graphs—height, fall, and a splattering meet with a final solidity.

If he believed, though, that pity, disinterest, would cover his meetings with Barbara, he was soon to find otherwise. That next week she came into the store as an added saleswoman for dresses, and one morning appeared in his office.

"Mr. Reiss." Not question, but a quiet approach. "Mr. Salloway says you have the plans for the Sports Shop—could I see them? You've perhaps forgotten me. Barbara Lucas."

He replied at once, twisting himself from his chair to his feet, answering only the last, "No, no, of course not. Good Lord, it must be all of ten years——"

Pity didn't operate; she was quite composed. Disinterest didn't operate, either; in his memory she might have faded to the shadowy half-transparent sepias of an old daguerreotype, but the woman before him bore no tones of shadowy sepia. Her person, if anything, was more opulent than in her twenties, more slender at waist and ankles, more swellingly full at breast and hips, her hair was as glossily dusky, her dark eyes as lazily low-lidded, her skin as disquieting in its silky delicacy, as they had been in her first youth. Yet if in her person she was more appealing than ever, she had also acquired control; the glance emerging from under the negligent lids was in no sense provoking; she extended no aura. Hers, now, might be the disinterest, the disinclination, the concentration on a subject outside them both.

Awkwardly, not knowing what his reference should be, he went on, "I've been terribly sorry——"

She answered as composedly as before, so composedly that, in fact, he wondered if her widowhood were indeed a tragedy, "Almost everyone now seems to be having catastrophe either behind or ahead of them; I suppose I should be relieved mine seems behind me. If those plans——"

With nothing else to answer, he replied hastily, "Oh, right here," and took down the blue scroll from the shelf over his desk.

Over it she bent as studiously as he many times had bent to it, hooking back over her ears as she did so the tortoise earpieces of heavy spectacles. He had never before seen her in glasses, never thought of her—not with those houri eyes—as ever possibly needing them; seeing her in them again disturbed him. In a way—the thought came at a tangent—her position now wasn't too unlike his own. She too, now, must impress Salloway and the board, must show her ability; she'd be buying.

Pencil in hand, he traced along the white lines. "Here's the part already completed; you can easily place it. Charm Room at the angle, Millinery this side, Dresses that. Teen Agers will open in here, next to Dresses, your Sports Shop will be behind it. Good juxtaposition, we think. After all, it's mostly——"

She nodded. "Samples yet? Walls, carpets, upholstery?"

He took down the ticketed bundle. "I've fallen for the walnut panels in gray, and trying to keep them throughout, except where they're already brown, as in the Charm Room. For upholstery in Teen Agers I found this off pink. Carpets, too, will be gray. Not dull gray, but this one. Quite light, shading toward both pink and blue. The same thing for carpets and walls in your shop. For hangings there, though, I've picked this heavy block linen. Repeating the pink and the gray, you see, but against this other color. Not cinnamon, not sepia; it's too alive for that. It reminds me——"

Again she nodded, and her tone was quicker. "Mr. Trurog's Breughel."

She unhooked the spectacles, straightening, looking across at him with another glance that should have been at variance with her eyes, a glance shrewd and estimating, but it too quickened, as if for her also, in the years between, an interest had faded, but she now were being haunted by its nearer memory. She said, "Frankly, I came in to find fault and throw weight. But I shan't quarrel with that gray or that print; they're unusual separately and gorgeous together. The other shops, too, the ones you've finished. They're all good."

Straightforward and generous. It couldn't be anything but warming, and he was warmed. Although in acceptance he was also ill at ease. "That's very kind; praise around here doesn't usually come in straight doses."

"I don't suppose it does anywhere." When she went, a little later, taking snipped corners from his samples, she still went quietly, but there was also, he sensed, that small quickening in her, and somehow he couldn't be aware of it without a responding quickening in himself.

Of all people he'd known, he thought uncomfortably that afternoon, Barbara was the one in whom he'd have least expected growth. In her, such growth was unsettling. Her recognition, for instance, of the relation between that print and the Breughel. Christine, even if she'd seen the picture recently, would never have seen the relationship. Christine liked good color, and was comfortable with it, but she wasn't sensitive.

For a man in a store there was always temptation from women; since his marriage, though, he'd been insulated. Meeting Barbara haphazardly, he never could tell when, in an elevator—"Your dress section's really coming along"—in his office, "About those fitting rooms" —with Harriet outside Salloway's office—"Go on in, don't bother us. We're gossiping"—he was subjected to a disturbance which, he told himself, was based on nothing but a single careless compliment. He couldn't again mean anything to Barbara; she meant nothing to him. Store affairs, like the one between Bodali and Harriet—once notorious, but now sunk to the commonplaceness of marriage—weren't too unusual, either, but he always had found them despicable.

As he had once before discovered, however, not principle, not judgment, not decision, not any force he mustered, quite governed him. When in August the dress section was finished and work on the next two departments begun, his meetings with Barbara were even more frequent, her interest grew supervisory and proprietary. "I'd like my office at this end rather than the other; I'll need light more than the fitting rooms do." "Could I have ceiling cornices instead of window cornices? That print's so tremendous I want all I can get." One day a girl of about eight was with her, stepping carefully across a floor still littered with sawdust and remnants of molding. "My daughter, my own one production. You probably haven't known I had one."

Quiet, again, but—by this time he was almost sure—entire deliberation. Showing him her daughter made another link. He heard himself telling the child, "I have two boys your age."

Anything more came only on the heels of overturn—his. Returning to his office one afternoon in the first week of 1931, he walked in such blindness he didn't so much as see Barbara waiting. Yet he must have accepted her presence.

"That's the last. Yours. They just told me. Salloway. They're postponing the rest of it."

The person against whom he spoke answered sharply, "Postponing? The rest of the remodeling? That's purely ridiculous. They've got funds enough——"

"They can't hold out longer against what's going on." His chair came up under him.

Still sharply, "That doesn't mean, does it—you're not out?"

"I guess not." This part, too, could only be dull. "They're—that's what I understand—returning me to the floor again."

"Oh." From wherever she had been, she moved to stand behind him; after a while he felt her hand on his shoulder. "I can—I know what this is like for you. But it's not too bad, not really; if they're keeping you on, then they must intend going on with the work sometime. They know they can't get anyone better for the job. They're like Father—stripped to a whopping big salary, but you'd think we were surviving on crusts. Trurog's isn't shaky. They've got hundreds of thousands in government bonds——"

He wasn't worried about Trurog's; it was his own position within Trurog's that was being cut down. Nevertheless, as she talked, strength began returning to his body, sharper hearing to his ears, sharper sight to his eyes, some feeling to his hands. He sat immobile, but when she stopped he was able to answer.

"It could be worse, I know. Just don't ask me to be happy immediately."

At that she laughed. Amused, tolerant, on his side. "You know, Carl, you don't give yourself leeway. Mother and I were hearing that new pianist, Iturbi, at the Auditorium tonight; Mother's in bed today. Flu. If you feel like it, I'd be glad to have you go with me. It's not, I've found, too much fun, being a widow."

The first time she'd in any way referred to the harshness of this stretch in her own life. Coming as it did, it swung him around to her.

He stammered, "I—I'd not planned on anything like that. I don't ——"

The eyes offered a different amusement. "It can't be very—threatening. A concert. My car's in the parking lot. We might have dinner, perhaps. You might drive me——"

So easy. Not even having to call for her at Ohman's. Tickets for Iturbi were running from $2.85 to $6.00; he'd noticed the price schedule the previous Sunday, angry because the time wasn't yet come when he could afford concerts. Behind him was a practice of the most rigid propriety, a propriety he himself recognized as outmoded, but to which he held by preference; he didn't now, any more than before, want a serious involvement. The sudden geyser within him, however, said nothing but go. For the hurt he was suffering Barbara's offer was in some way an unguent; it was healing to have a woman still so desirable almost wistfully beg for his company. Offering it, too, on his own terms. A dinner, a concert. No more.

Dinner, a concert, no more. But, of course, there was more. If nothing else, then his discovery that doing something so outside his usual courses gave him escape.

Calling Christine, he heard his voice firm and buoyant, as if nothing whatever had happened that day to destroy him. He remembered to ask about Craig, who was threatening whooping cough. Sitting across a table from Barbara, he felt around him the release and the lightly sad, well-controlled adventurousness which she took on.

"Runaways." She made it explicit. "That's what we are, both of us. It's lifesaving, once in a while, just to run away."

By herself she suggested the Blue Door, whose dinners nowadays were down to sixty-five cents; in her car, a Cadillac, she relaxed easily in her share of the front seat, extending no tendrils. Most people protected car seats with covers, or at least Indian blankets; to Barbara the silky plush of the upholstery was there to use and enjoy. Stepping into her car, driving it, was like stepping into her home as it once was, freely rich, an atmosphere to which he responded with a nostalgic ache.

The concert, too, its semidarkness and hush, the rows of well-dressed people rustling their programs and their conversations, Iturbi's entry on the brilliant stage, the applause, the complacent acceptance in the midst of which he sat—"Life can't be too bad; here's this Iturbi, now, struggling all his life not only to develop this really surpassing music, but all that personal charm he sheds, too, just so we who pay can enjoy it"—within it he was able to forget his demotion, forget the yet mounting millions toward whom he'd that day drawn another step nearer, forget the responsibilities of marriage and fatherhood.

A return had to be made, at no later than eleven-thirty that evening, when he drove Barbara's car into her garage and, on the walk below her front steps, handed over her keys. From there he must get home by streetcar—galling that at his age he hadn't so much as attained to a car of his own, freshly galling under these circumstances. That next week, too, after no more than a few days of cleaning up and storing away, there was his actual demotion, not, since Glen Shotwell had that, to second, but to jewelry, handbags and gloves again, that worst of all stations, with Mrs. Willette one of his people. Reversal almost too intolerable to be borne. And telling Christine—that, too, was intolerable. Although she made a point of not bringing them up with him, Christine, he well realized, was having her own depression troubles; her assumption of the fire-station bakery couldn't have been made at a worse time, her prices, too, had cascaded; sometimes at night she looked dreary and pinched. He in fact put off telling her too long. "Carl! Today I called Harriet—Carl, surely you couldn't have thought——" She took his concealment as hurting, bewildering. No quarrel, but perhaps something worse, unresolved injury on her side, unformulated resistance on his.

From the small guilt of this separateness, from whooping cough which all spring racked both boys, from the lacerations of his setback, from condolences such as Bob Gokey's, "Maybe I should welcome you back to us little shots," it was overwhelmingly tempting to repeat the escape he had once found. After an especially nerveracking day he suggested a movie; it came to be habit that he stay downtown with Barbara once a week. Always her acceptances were forthright and grateful—"Don't think I'll say no."

Sometimes on these dates she was a shrugging sophisticate. "I hear your wife's working. Not many kept wives any longer, I guess; good thing all around." Sometimes she was restlessly bitter. "Men are a lot less available, I must say, to a widow than they are to a wife." Sometimes she mocked. "At least with you I needn't keep up defenses." Provocative as these might sound, she in herself wasn't provocative; when in the summer he began a light love-making, playing with her hands, drawing his thumb down her cheek, kissing her good night, it wasn't because she awaited it or responded but simply because, having found so much surcease, he began wanting more. It was exciting to go out with Barbara, exciting to think of her as available. Exciting and, in a way, retaliatory, as if by what he now did, against everything he before had done, he was attaining some kind of revenge. But then excitement and retaliation both began to fade behind other impulses. Friendship with a woman like Barbara didn't run on in midcourse forever.

14

Frowning, un-
certain, impatient, intolerant with the intolerance that wasn't foi
anyone but himself, he told Christine on a Sunday in October, "A
group of store people are putting on a picnic today. I don't know—I
didn't plan much on going——"

Lifting her head from her scribbling—not anything to do with Neesom affairs, since those weren't allowed to intrude on Sunday, but
for some of her PTA business, she at once answered, "Oh, go, Carl;
I'll think up something for the boys. You need to get away."

Almost surely, he thought, she knew what was going on; from
somewhere there'd be someone to tell her. If she resisted more, he
thought with resentment, it would be fairer, give him much more
to go on.

They were at breakfast when he began on his opening; on his side
of the table egg-sticky, bacon-traced plates and the litter of newspapers, on hers, other plates and the notes on which she worked.
Across the small space her face, too, was close to his. He loved her,
of course he loved her, and people nowadays seemed to think she
was handsomer than she used to be, but without make-up, this early
in the morning, she almost was pallid, except for the one unhappy
respect. It wasn't too often, any more, that the birthmark obtruded
itself, but it did this morning, unpleasantly distinct against her pale
neck, above the ice-blue satin of the lounging pajamas she wore. All
day, if he stayed home, they would keep harking back to Craig, long
recovered from whooping cough, thank heaven, but now taken to
running food out of the kitchens—three boys in his schoolroom,
Craig said, were getting nothing whatever to eat at home. Or Dusty.
Or Trurog's. Or Christine would bring up her indignation because
some man named Verek—that heel Verek, she called him—was such
a corrupt superintendent of schools. More and more, lately, Christine
was concerned in matters outside herself. PTA—that was the sort of
thing to which some women naturally gravitated.

When Barbara in midweek had stopped by for a careless suggestion,
"This Indian summer keeps up, it could be tempting to go for a long
ride this Sunday," he had answered immediately, "For me I'm afraid

that's impossible," though even then his bursting need was to get away again, anywhere, anyhow. Never in previous years had store hours been confining; eight-thirty to six, Monday through Saturday, this was the period of his major embattlement, his major progress, his major living. Only now, after his demotion, did they begin to press, restrain and stifle. He overstayed lunch hours, dallied in the locker rooms, ran up to the employees' cafeteria for coffee and cigarettes, dreamed of flight, vagabond and on foot, if need be, anything to get away from that assaulting floor.

Now Christine too, Neesom's, the table in the room under the stairs, the other Sunday-empty tables ranged beyond, the boys hammering and yelling over the shack they were building beside the barn, the gumminess on his hand from a section of newspaper trailed over the egg on Dusty's plate—all were outrages he couldn't stay to endure. Taking a Sunday for Barbara was something he hadn't yet done, but later that morning, walking toward her car from a drugstore where he phoned, very little guilt touched him; all he felt was elated release. Stepping into Barbara's Cadillac was no longer a matter of stepping into another way of living; it was stepping into another skin.

For a change Barbara didn't give him the driver's seat. With an indifferent smoothness, which set the car lounging along the street like a ranging and satisfied leopard, she kept the wheel herself, leaving him nothing to do but relax beside her, in a breeze-threaded sunshine which, through the open windows, began seeping into his body like wine. Acrid carbons from chimney stacks gave place, as soon as they were outside the city, to wood smoke; he occasionally pointed out brilliant maples or oaks, a bank with purple underlying the dun of its grass, but Barbara asked nothing of him, answered mostly in murmurs, giving herself to the indolence of their progress, her flight from her own problems.

At the Delles, still unhurried, they paused for late dinner; not a fortunate choice, since he and Christine had been there on their honeymoon, but coincidence toward which he was indifferent even when, after eating, they lazily clambered around for a while on the rocks, admiring the views and the river. His honeymoon wasn't anything he often recalled; it had been, on the whole, not too satisfying. Back in the car, they once again drove unhurriedly through an afternoon slowly chilling, but only increasing its tang. Regretfully, but not too regretfully, after a while, they turned homeward.

"The good old Ohman summer cottage isn't far from here," she told him. "On Lake Constance. Closed now, of course, but it's not a bad spot. Like to see it?"

Warning shot through him. Something like this had occurred once before. What was it she'd said then? "With a lake in the middle of town——"

He returned coolly, "I don't especially care for lake cottages. Infested by spiders, usually, aren't they?"

She laughed. "If you say so. Then let's stop somewhere else, for Cokes and a sandwich."

While they were having the Cokes and a sandwich, though, a little wariness stayed with him; he wasn't surprised when, after another twenty minutes of riding, the car turned into a side road.

He asked distastefully, "You mean I meet up with the web spinners anyway?" In spite of wariness, however, in spite of his certainty that again, under apparent indifference, she was acting with deliberation, a kind of lethargy held him, a lethargy under which his pulses began drumming.

If revolt could go so far, if need for escape could go so far, and be so satisfying when he had it, then there wasn't, perhaps, any real reason why it shouldn't go farther. "Carl, one of our puritan fore-fathers——" Harriet wasn't the only one who jeered at him; even Christine, he sometimes thought, wished he had more capacity for looseness. Perhaps, he considered, with a grim excitement spreading, this might be a time to give his jeerers the lie. If he were mistaken, and abandonment was the source of final comfort and surcease, he might find those too.

As the car rolled under trees along a rutted sandy track, until it emerged on the lawn of a clearing, he found it possible, over a tightening anticipation, to look about with sardonic amusement. "Expected brown cottage, check. Expected blue lake, check. Do I get by with this cursory view?"

Barbara spun for him her mock indignation. "Can you honestly be so uninquisitive? Don't you know there are people—I quote—who would give up their eyeteeth to visit here? Come along, shake the legs, flex the body, make with the feet." She still made no least gesture toward him; in fact, slipping from the car, she turned her back on him to walk across the lawn and out on a plank pier. At the end of this pier, hands thrust so deeply into the pockets of her white coat that its front jutted forward, she stood looking out over the water, silver-shadowed in the late light, her face smoothing as she did so.

"Now's the time to come, now when everyone else is gone. Cottages all along under those trees. Too many. I remember when there weren't, but that's long ago." After another moment of quiet she added surprisingly, flicking a glance at him, "Space and peace, the great soulmakers. Maybe you should come here more often." Then, in immediate retroactive flipness, "For gosh sakes, let's see if Father forgot any bottles."

What she said about space and peace set him back. He replied, "I don't drink much," but when she walked matter-of-factly back along the planks there wasn't much for him to do but follow.

Inside the screened porch of the cottage she looked about at bare boards. "Well, we'll leave time some footprints." Then, at the inner door, "Probably now I'll not have the key—yes, I do too. Mr. Reiss, my friend, enter."

The rooms beyond the door smelled as he had known they must smell—dry, chill, fleshless; he never had liked uninhabited and untended dwellings. When he stepped after her, he did so with the distaste he had expected to experience. The long living room held, at one end, a clutter of tightly stacked rustic tables and chairs, obviously brought in from the porch; the other end was more orderly, with an Indian rug on the floor before a stone fireplace, a maple table and chairs, two peel cane chaise longues covered in chintz. As Barbara moved on, he stood accustoming himself to the room and the dim light; she called back, "Electricity's off, naturally, but you might start up that fire——"

Going past the maple table, he drew a finger along its edge. Dust. Leaning against the waxed solid maple plank of the mantel, after he had touched a match to the paper and birch logs in the fireplace, he stood watching the flames sprout and crackle. Well dissipated, now, was the impulse toward abandonment that had come over him in the car; if what the woman clinking bottles and glasses in the kitchen intended for this next hour was a big seduction scene, he thought harshly, she had picked the wrong place for it, just as she had picked the wrong man. Deliberation and planning in love-making he had never been able to tolerate, not now any more than before. When she came toward him with the filled glasses, smiling—"Ginger ale and whiskey, yes; ice, no. Would you rather have water?"—he was able to turn toward her, to accept one of the highballs, with much the same detachment he had for the room.

Good-looking, yes. He couldn't deny her that. Duskily luxuriant. In another ten years she might be overplump like her mother, but now she walked on her tiny feet as if she were weightless. A woman who, in the blue-yellow, flickering light from the fire, extended not the old-time aura, but a downy lush bloom.

She said lightly, "We might relax while we drink these," and dropped to stretch in one of the long chairs.

He felt luxurious and powerful. "It's a good game," he thought, "and I'm willing to play. But you'll never get me to fall." In the second chair he too stretched; he said, "The perfections of living. A fire, and being let alone." But it was because he saw flaws in the perfection that he said it, and it was from her divination of his attitude that she answered, "At least better than Trurog's. Lord, keep me forgetting."

Again she wasn't disposed to talk; she might have been as indifferent, as antagonistic as he, accepting his company only as a means of avoiding other companionships grown tiresome and unrelieving. When he was pushed to speak—"You still have a cricket" and "Not many more days like this; we can soon count on frosts"—she replied unrewardingly, "I hear him," and "Let's not begin winter before we get to it." When the glasses were empty, she rose to refill them, but in moving her face was as closed as when she had looked over the lake, and taking his glass from his fingers, she managed not to touch him. That was nettling; he felt antagonistic still, but in a different way. If he were wrong as to her intentions——

When she came back with the drinks, holding one out to him without speaking, he caught at her wrist.

"You're being entirely too indifferent." His voice—satisfyingly—carried his harshness. Moving to make space for her beside him, he was conscious of the other and more masterful side of arrogance—dominance. This might be a time he set the pattern and made her conform.

She answered, "For you I thought perfection was being let alone." She settled beside him, but with little yielding in the motion, and her voice, too, was derisive.

"I like to be let alone, yes. But should I let you alone?"

Warmth from the fire, warmth from his one drink, coursed pleasantly now through his body. Setting his glass carefully on the floor, he took her free hand in his, keeping an arm at her back, bringing the two linked hands up to turn her face toward him. Behind the movement of his lips against hers was again that remembered love-making after the Piatt; somehow now that remembered evening intensified this one. The mouth under his still meant little to him, when he murmured savagely and pulled her body around to his that meant little too; that was what gave sudden point and desire to this moment. She wasn't asking anything of him; there wouldn't be any aftermath, not of duty or anything else. He needn't so much as say he liked or admired her.

She laughed a little, breathlessly, pushing against him. "Carl—you're forgetting yourself. You're not going too far. Not you, Carl."

"No?" What she said, her resistance, only increased the determinations toward which he was veering, the determinations which had half formed in the car, then ebbed, and now sprang wildly strong. He pulled away, staring across the three inches which then separated her face from his, feeling within his body the ferocity with which a powering concentration formed. In shadow her lids lay at half mast, her small mouth moved a little, as if it were bruised and sought comfort. His left hand reached until it lay on her hip. Under those fingers was the same silky smoothness his other hand met at her cheek.

Transfixed at a last moment, he felt himself swinging, knew what he would be giving up if, once more, he bent to her; all that enclosed him now was a last giving way of his will. If she made, again, some least gesture of resistance, he would, he knew, be gone. Instead, as he awaited it, the low lids lifted from the dark gleam of her eyes; when they redescended there remained, at the eye corners, a slight sly lift, the look of a woman who knows a moment of sensual fulfillment as captured and coming.

Change, he thought. He'd believed her changed. Perhaps she was, in some ways, but underneath change was the exact Barbara of ten years before. The major difference to which she'd attained was only one of a little more subtlety.

As soon as he descried this, the blood ebbed from his loins, dwindling as desire dwindled; once more almost at once detached, he continued to look at her, seeing now the ridiculous swelling, the facial fulsomeness, of a woman in heat, revolting against it, losing strength from the arms that held her. But then again—another old pattern repeating itself—he bent once more to kiss her, fully master of himself, playing with her, experiencing the upsurge greater if different than the one that subsided, because it was in this superiority that real mastery lay.

Still another pattern repeating, he had no need to ask resistance. Her eyes were closed, she was too rapt to sense alteration in him when it came. But as soon as his mouth touched hers she knew of it. Tigerishly twisting away, she struck at him while he easily laughed.

"Isn't this the station," he asked, "where we got off once before?"

The words she used for him were blistering. But getting to his feet, forgetting his glass, so that he kicked it over, stooping to pick it from its puddle, he felt entirely his own man.

This time she didn't let it leave her unaltered. On the way home she admitted coldly, "I guess I asked for it," which—he didn't quite remember—might have been what she'd said before too. But the next day at Trurog's, passing him at the corner of the elevator banks, just in front of the curved portals of the Charm Room, she nodded curtly, as if he were someone she'd met perhaps once or twice.

He greeted cheerfully, "Morning, Barbara, another nice day." But he knew any cohesion between them was ended. She was too handsome, she'd have too many other chances, not to take twice for an answer.

Toward the incident of the day before, though, toward the whole sequence of his meetings with Barbara, in fact, he found himself feeling exhilarated. However unfulfilling the afternoon before might have been for Barbara, it in some unscrutinized way had been most fulfilling for him. Returning home on the Sunday evening, he had walked buoyantly, thinking fondly of Christine and the boys, looking forward to a few minutes with them before bedtime; he walked buoyantly from his streetcar toward Trurog's in the morning.

All the eight—or was it nine?—months since his demotion, he'd been held by frustration; now it was as if that mood were finished, and he could return to longer and stronger stratagems. Depression, it was true, continued, depression was deeper and more swamping than at the first of the year, business failures and layoffs kept mounting, wages again dropped, but just the same, if he stood off to look at himself, what he saw was that his ledge had at least some solidity; it was bearing his weight.

That afternoon he stopped Salloway to mention—not pressing it, just taking it for granted—the time when the change-overs would resume. "God help us for what we're doing to our shoppers on second; it must be hard taking those modern sections and that faded baroque side by side."

Salloway, then, merely grunted. Between that day and the later one when, warmed, revivified, Salloway paused at his station for a back-slap which almost took him from his feet—"You can haul out that slide rule, Reiss"—over a year and a half extended, a year and a half in which, together with Trurog's and the rest of the world, he too endured 1932 and '33, shot-out bonus marchers and milk-spilling farmers' blockades, the turmoil of an election with the dangerous Democrats upsurgent, worthless scrip offered as money, a holiday for banks, and barter schemes which in their inception—the best horse-hair mattresses turned out by the unemployed in their scrappy old warehouses, at prices that made Trurog prices look malign—threatened to overturn such economic cohesion as was left, but in which he managed never to let his purposes fall so far from him again. At the clap on his shoulder he was ready to go.

Nor was the year then ensuing much less fulfilling than he had planned it should be. Suits, Coats, Furs, the Maturity Shop, Skirts and Blouses, a swank French Room, Beachwear—slowly but certainly, with a ritualistic growth, each took form and grew graceful, luxurious, complete; his touch with color and fabric more sure in each one. At the final grand opening, late in 1934, when the last niche, a Bride's Shop, was completed, he walked solidly from end to end of second, surrounded by nothing that wasn't to his taste—the soft patina of his waxed walnut panels, the unbroken foot-welcome of his beautiful carpets, the extending gleam of his mirrors, the symphony of his lavender, pink, silver, beige-cinnamon, chartreuse, satiny white, all open, all blended, all spacious, with merchandise laid out on glass or cased be. hind sliding panels, each article housed or displayed as precious, with no clutter anywhere, no detestable department store racks. Achievement, that year, was his workright.

Achievement. But with it, of course, the inevitable rankle. It wasn't certain, not absolutely, what he'd go on to next.

Remodeling might be an activity in which he found satisfaction, but no one need tell him that it might, also, dangerously, be a dead end. Geggenheim's job still was the one he must get; no one could move into Salloway's shoes without knowledge of merchandising.

For a while in 1933, for two months, especially, after Harriet in passing had dropped idle comment, "Merritt's shucking the skin of Princeton this spring; I see us with a bright-eyed little garter snake wriggling its way upward," he spent his time in cold sweats. Unbeliev- able that Salloway's older son, a child who, as late as 1926, was dis- missible as a school child of fourteen, had now come along to be com- petition. In another of the cold sweats, he stopped at St. Peter's desk. Oh yes, St. Peter informed him benignly, Mr. Trurog's grandsons were quite big boys now; one of them was—let's see, was it a junior or senior, at Groton? And of course the Jones-Ferris boy had been at Yale for two years.

What was it he'd thought about nepotism, how casually had he dismissed it? If those boys came in, he was as good as done. Ten years only until Salloway was due to retire, but Salloway might think ten years enough, for a son of his own. Everything would be different, for a son of Salloway or a grandson of Trurog.

In June of that same year, though, Salloway himself had lightened that terror. "Guess"—proudly—"Salloway blood still runs. The kid's got himself his own job. Worst depression we ever had, only seven- teen per cent of his class getting work, but he gets it. Wanamaker's, Philadelphia. No hanging on the old man's coattails for Merritt, no bush-league stuff. He's hooking himself to the big time."

The ensuing relief, softening his leg and abdominal muscles until they would hardly hold up and hold in his interior, was almost as racking as the terror. After it, too, there remained thoughts of the younger Salloway son, the Jones-Ferris boy. Six years' experience would be very little; those two couldn't possibly, he tried to reassure himself, be in line for anything immediate, but on the threshold of his consciousness they stayed hooded and ominous.

Geggenheim, by the time Carl returned to remodeling, had shown himself more than ever senile and fuming. "All this uproar again? I can't understand it. Things going along well enough as things were." After saying this he flung about so violently that his flesh pads shifted by visible inches. Once more, though, after days of fretting and recalcitrance, he came to terms, returning such inventory and personnel files as Carl needed, consenting to a second moving of his office and effects. Unobtrusively, this time, Carl moved farther into the actual working of the second-floor office; Geggenheim, after all, was past his sixty-sixth birthday.

Carefully, at a moment when Salloway was caught in good mood, he made the exactly right statement. "You know, of course, I'm hoping to be considered for second-floor merchandising when Mr. Geggenheim leaves us. In with remodeling I'm already taking over as many details as I can; it's a floor and an activity with which I'm thoroughly familiar."

Salloway in answer produced one of his sidelong tight glances and a throat sound just above a murmur and under a grunt. "Geggenheim's successor is something we haven't yet come to; we'll let you know when we do." After that, though, he almost certainly knew it when, quietly, Carl substituted his clearer ledger and file systems, when floormen gathered in his office, not Geggenheim's, for after-hours shop talk, when he reinstituted his ten-minute, once-weekly talks on selling, covering, now, the entire floor.

In all this it was only the rebuilding that seemed to annoy Geggenheim. If he noticed other activities, he did so acceptingly. "That's all right, my boy, that accounting system of yours; thought of making it common practice myself, but didn't get around to it. Always something more important." As he inferred, the vital affairs of the floor did remain in his wavering hands. Saleswomen and floormen might consult Carl, but the buyers conferred with Geggenheim; it was Geggenheim who, with other merchandisers and the board, decided on special promotions, Geggenheim who was the arbiter of second-floor prices, advertising expenditures, markups, amounts of stock to buy and carry, times of purchase.

As the end of his remodeling neared, therefore, Carl knew he had reason, beneath his satisfactions, to be on tenterhooks. Salloway called him in the day after the opening, but it was merely to discuss odds and ends of clearing up, such as what should be done about extra bolts of material Carl kept on hand for repairs. When Salloway said, "That's that, then," and turned, expecting Carl to leave, Carl was forced to bring out his query bluntly.

"One more batch of fabric to be disposed of, Mr. Salloway. Me. Do I keep on with Geggenheim?"

Salloway frowned. "I'd rather have another day or two on that. For the moment, though, I'd say yes."

Not what Carl wanted, but, he told himself as he walked out past Harriet, not what he didn't want, either. Harriet cocked at him a sardonic eyebrow. "Who gets the next satin-padded walls—me?" He answered, "For your office I'd go to monkey island for my inspirations," but his mind wasn't on the jibing, it was on the steps by which he would dismantle his office and move in with Geggenheim. Geggenheim, at this date of latest reckoning, had exactly ten months to go.

Ten months for Geggenheim, nine years for Salloway. Sometimes, taking pause to consider how life was foreshortening, he had lung-crowding sensations of fright. Nothing was wrong about ten months for Geggenheim; for years now, each sight a long one, he had looked forward to the day Geggenheim would move on. Nine years for Salloway, though. Thinking of Trurog's without Salloway, he sometimes saw his whole vision as shattering, like a Christmas tree ball too tightly grasped; he stood with nothing in his hand but jagged bright splinters. He himself, on his last birthday, had been forty-one, and that was where real incredulity entered; that his twenties, his thirties, his best years for climbing, should be spent. The depression, his illness, in no way was he responsible for those. And forty-one of course wasn't old; merely it was old enough so that from here on he must make no slips and take no chances.

Geggenheim, against the newer invasion, offered again only the twittering resistance of the old. "Your desk will now be in here, Mr. Reiss? Dear me. It's rather a small office you've made me, but I suppose we'll make do."

At the nearer quarters it was easier not only to pick up such routine as he hadn't previously taken over, but to enter into other affairs of the office as well. Vogue and Harper's Bazaar kept him abreast of fashions, just as they'd helped enlighten him on décor. Salloway left him where he was. In December, tumult for the other floors but always a lull on second, he asked to be included in planning sessions for the big after-Christmas clearances and promotions.

Sometimes when Geggenheim bleated uncertainly, "Well—well— we've got Mr. Reiss here—young fellow, young enterprising fellow— might be a good idea to get his opinion," he again was touched by pity, just as he'd been touched by pity for Geggenheim before, just as he'd been touched by pity for Mrs. Pesek, who had served out her post-coronary years in the basement and then, late in this last sum-mer, died. Mrs. Pesek was quite a woman in her day, Mr. Geggen-heim might have been quite a man in his, but with his time rapidly shrinking Geggenheim now faced an inevitability which rendered him harmless. It had been a long time—when was that, 1928?—since Har-riet stopped by to warn him.

"Young hands," Geggenheim said it himself, one day. "Young hands—there'll be a time when Trurog's may have to get along with-out mine."

Never a sign, anywhere, of what Geggenheim intended.

15 Direction of second-floor inventory, just after the new year, fell to Carl naturally. A single day, Trurog's allowed for its twice-yearly totting up; originally a Sunday, but public opinion, for the last twenty years or so, frowned on that. Now it was always a Monday, the week's quietest. Odds and ends, storage lots, cleaned up beforehand, and then the offensive. Counting, measuring, ticketing, stacking. Before the day Carl girded himself as for football with Craig and Dusty; during the straight seventeen hours it lasted he was only a few minutes off his feet, moving from department to department, dividing the job into equi-table sections, looking out for lost unreceived customers, checking, catching glaring inaccuracies, later watching for hands that trembled and eyes grown glazed. "Mrs. Morney, take ten minutes." "Mrs. Tost, you're ahead of schedule. You might get more girls on the floor."

Of the people who caused him most trouble, as he irately told himself he should have foreseen, one was a young stock girl in millinery, Bette Jones. Sometime before Christmas the child had come in for a job. "Really pathetic situation," the new millinery buyer confided to Carl. "Seems to be of good family—father was a small-town banker. Came up for mishandling of funds. Now he's all shot to pieces, and so is the mother. Drink, I guess. There's a younger child——"

Hearing it, Carl shrugged, though he was slightly moved. Not too unfamiliar a story, not these days. With the recruit he was patient, though she didn't make much return to patience. An amorphous, overfleshed child, with mournful brown eyes and long loose hair, slow and given to bungling.

At the height of his pleasure in the finished remodeling, the past fall, he and Christine together had at last splurged on their first car, secondhand but a chariot of triumph, a 1932 Buick. "That charity case of ours," again it was the new millinery buyer who approached him, "lives on your way home; if you'd be kind enough—even carfare, in a family like that, must be a consideration." Feeling cool and unwilling, Carl yet was forced to nod. His own car, driving it himself, being beholden to no one, was even more of a release than riding with Barbara.

After that he all too often noticed the child, painfully anxious and waiting, standing on the sidewalk when he came up out of the garage ramp. Sometimes he stopped for her; sometimes, when being alone meant too much, he didn't. She lived, he found, only five blocks below him, in an old house converted into light housekeeping apartments. Any timid word she uttered during these rides was so inept, so gauche, so puerile that he endured her only with exasperated pity, and sighed with relief when he slammed the door after her.

What she managed during inventory, on the other hand, was almost distinguished. "Oh, my God." He came up as Miss Yelland, in charge of millinery stocktaking, moaned it despairingly. "What have you been up to, girl?"

Bette, it seemed, had been haphazardly shoving listed hat trimmings in among those not yet docketed.

The hour when this travesty of competence was discovered was late afternoon; eight weary saleswomen would have to repeat at least four hours' work. Bette, as he later remembered, was pink-eyed before a collective bitterness broke over her; at the first syllables of recrimination tears arched from her eyes like popped hailstones.

She gulped, "I can't, I can't. Everything's too hard for me. I can't, I can't," and from then on sobbed convulsively, even after Miss Yelland dismissed her to other and less disastrous tasks. Toward one in the morning, when the day at last neared its fumbling exhausted conclusion, no less a person than Geggenheim interceded for her.

"That Jones child—I hear she's had a bad day. I don't suppose we should send her on her way at this hour alone. I understand you've been good enough——"

Carl wanted nothing less, but the answer, "Drive her yourself if you're so damn worried," was scarcely to be uttered; Geggenheim lived in a diametrically opposite direction and was, beside, old.

He managed an ungracious, "I suppose I'll have to," and shortly was to rue even that. Bette, walking with him from the department to the garage, was vacantly dry-eyed enough, the ovals of flesh around her eyes no more than puffed and pink. No sooner was the car on the street, however, than she bent at the waist until her face met her hands at her knees.

She wailed, "Mr. Reiss, you don't know what's happening to me, Mr. Reiss. I can't stand it, Mr. Reiss; if we don't get two thousand dollars my daddy will be going in jail. We've got to get two thousand dollars; you don't understand, Mr. Reiss——"

The paroxysms gripping her—real terror, real frenzy—were so patent, they pushed out from her in such waves, that he wasn't able, this time, to keep from being affected. A day like this one, he thought, and to top it off—!

"Now, Bette," he tried consoling her, "that's no problem for a youngster; your parents must handle it. All you need do is get on with your own life." And when in return to this she wailed more loudly, "There isn't anyone but me, though, my daddy's all different, there's nobody but me," he again tried calming her as he stopped the car before her house, moved finally so much as to offer, "Look, child, if it's as bad as that, other people will help; I'll talk to my wife. We can't give you two thousand dollars, that's—well, these days that's money. But we'll see what we can do."

She remained distracted; when she burst from the car to run for her front door she still sobbed hysterically.

If it were earlier, he thought angrily and tiredly, he'd stamp in after her. No adult should burden an infant with any such problems. What that father of hers needed—her mother too, probably—was a kick in the teeth.

But then as he sat there, too disturbed to go on immediately, he got, as if it were an emanation from the house, or as if it were something Bette released through the door she opened, an intimation of what it was to be her parents. They, too, like Bette, only a little older, their experience the handed-out experience—"Here, take this, draw what conclusions you will from it"—of their living, narrow as all living is narrow, cased now inside circumstances which, like their experience, weren't actually of their making, or to which they had added only their foolish expansive bits. "Second mortgage for that farm of yours, Herb? Well, I don't know now; sure, you're a good friend of mine——" A million instances of that, a million other imbecile weaknesses, and the result took over. You got children like Bette crying, "But I'm the only one, Mr. Reiss. I'm the only one."

For this particular child he and Christine, he supposed, would have to see what might be done. That new millinery buyer, too, might take a hand; he seemed interested. Or Geggenheim. He'd see Geggenheim in the morning.

Only it wasn't he who saw Geggenheim in the morning. It was Geggenheim who saw him.

On his way in from the locker rooms, that particular morning, Mrs. Bryant, the coat buyer, halted him. "I hardly dare show you this, Mr. Reiss. Yesterday while we were so busy—some damn fool customer——"

The damn fool customer, all too obviously, had left a long brown cigarette burn in the chartreuse silk of one of the lounges. That was where he was, examining the damage, waiting for a woman from Upholstery, when Geggenheim approached.

Approach from Geggenheim wasn't anything to be noticed especially; only the edges of his eyes and ears caught the loose gray moose figure, and the flap. He broke what he was saying to interpolate courteously, "Morning, Mr. Geggenheim," and then continued as before. When Geggenheim halted abruptly before him, bringing to rest first his inner person and then his flesh pads, he thought at first that

Geggenheim must have been informed of the cigarette damage earlier and stopped to see how it was being handled. He turned from Mrs. Bryant to add crossly, "What we can expect, I suppose. Fortunately I kept over enough of this fabric——"

It was only when Geggenheim cut icily across this—"You did come down to the store this morning, Mr. Reiss. I own I'm a little surprised. Perhaps, Mr. Reiss, it might be better if we gave up this matter of the lounge to retire to my office"—that he goggled around to stare at Geggenheim more particularly, and to get, then, the peculiar grenadier-guard portentousness of Geggenheim's manner, the spaced, deliberate portentousness of his words.

Entirely at sea, he asked, "What's wrong? Something in inventory?" Only error, horrendous error of some kind, could explain the attitude Geggenheim was evincing; there was only inventory in which any such error might have occurred.

Iciness undiminished, portentousness untouched, Geggenheim answered this. "Oh no, not inventory, Mr. Reiss. I rather believe you know to what I'm referring. Perhaps now if you come with me——"

With a swift glance at Mrs. Bryant, as taken aback and alerted as he, and also at three saleswomen who hung on the fringe of this colloquy, Carl said rigidly, "I don't know what the mistake can be, but of course I'll come with you to iron it out." Turning to follow the older man, he tossed over his shoulder to Mrs. Bryant, with a shrug to hint at vagaries of age, "You can see that woman when she gets here; I'll want to know whether she patches, or re-covers the whole arm. Be back later."

Among the possibilities to which his mind now sped was some kind of theft; stocktaking days were great days for shoplifters. That was why, year to year, inventory shifted a week or two. Geggenheim could never—not even Geggenheim—have fallen so below his wits he'd believe Carl had a hand in anything of that kind, no matter how stupendous the haul might have been.

Catching up to the other man, he asked, "What's afoot?" Instead of answering, Geggenheim sped up his elephant's waddle until he was again a pace or two in front; he snapped back, "You'll see, Mr. Reiss," which was all he would vouchsafe until he turned in at his office. In that office, as Carl saw with increasing mystification, sat only the girl, Bette Jones, squeezed into the chair at his own desk, not crying when he rounded the door, possessed, instead, by what looked like abject terror. No more than his entrance, indeed, was needed to send her into another paroxysm—the doubled, face-in-hands crouch of the car.

"I can't help it, Mr. Reiss. I can't, I can't——"

"And now"—Geggenheim paused at the door, letting Carl step past him—"I believe it may be better if we close ourselves in. This could be a very unsavory matter. Very unsavory to get out among customers."

As the door closed, Carl swung around.

Instead of the icy portentousness in which Geggenheim walked surrounded on the floor, what seemed to hold him now was a virulent triumph. He added, "Perhaps now, Mr. Reiss, you see your position."

Carl snapped, "No, I don't. If you mean——"

But the words weren't entirely truthful. Something about the picture, something about the girl wailing, something about Geggenheim made a horrid possibility come flooding.

"Tut, Mr. Reiss," Geggenheim chided derisively, virulence increasing. "Tut. You, a man who would take into your car an innocent child, and attack her. A child who as you will notice, Mr. Reiss, is well under the age of consent. Bette couldn't have done better, Mr. Reiss, than to come to me with her story, as she did. She knew I would see justice done."

Against the Medusalike slime-tangle then held in front of him, Carl was able to do nothing but stare forward stupidly. His body, at first, stopped existing entirely; all that had form in the room was the snare the old man had constructed. Not appearing in it himself, not at all, until just at the end, when he had to be sure. A snare in which Carl— his mind fled to the corners—might be frantically helpless. Not just once he'd taken Bette home, several times. Last night he'd walked out with her openly.

Sternly he turned to the girl, who remained in her corner, rocking herself back and forth, emitting from her covered face squeezed squeals like those of a rabbit in torment.

"Bette, you know there's no truth in this; I suppose you're doing it for the money you told me you needed. I suppose that's what you meant last night. But you can't commit an outrage like this, don't you see? You'd be ruining my life. This is serious. Rather than have you take money from Geggenheim for a thing like this, my wife and I will help get it; I'll promise you, Bette. You can't——"

She continued squealing, but toward the last of his appeal returned to words again. "You don't understand, Mr. Reiss. I can't help it, Mr. Reiss. I've got to, I've got to——"

He turned to Geggenheim, the body that had been absent rushing back to him, filling with fighting anger.

"You can't put this over. I haven't touched that girl——"

"Oh yes, Mr. Reiss," reply came softly. "Any doctor will find that the child has been—touched."

Conjecture too loathsome to face. If Geggenheim, Geggenheim himself——

As steadily as might be, against the horror that wasn't to be glimpsed, he said, "It wouldn't stand up. That child's no hardened liar. Any lawyer could——"

Soft answer again, "Oh, I don't know, Mr. Reiss. Bette might do quite well. Bette, after all, would have to do very little more than she's doing right now. Cry. Have you thought yet, Mr. Reiss, what it would mean to a man in your position just to have such a charge brought? No matter what a judge or jury might decide, Mr. Reiss, there would always be question. I doubt, Mr. Reiss, if you'd keep on at Trurog's. Or in Chapaqua. Or in a department store of any size in the United States. Department stores, Mr. Reiss, are a very cohesive little universe."

Just to have such a charge brought. No need to say more than that. Trurog's. Christine, even if she were the one person who'd never believe. Craig and Dusty, his sons. His father, Bob Gokey, Harriet, the world. "Of course, he was cleared of it. His lawyer proved——"

Sickly, he stared forward at the old man. The old man past being an asp. The old man standing with his senility about him still, just as it had been about him these last several years. But capable yet of this. A huge man, loose-membered, gray hair a thick outthrust bush at the back. Cheeks pendulous, eyes as colorless as water but glittering, flattened to points at each end.

He said, "All this, just to ruin me."

"Ruin you, Mr. Reiss?" Virulence now grew jocular, almost affectionate. "I wouldn't think of such a thing, Mr. Reiss. You're too valuable a man, Mr. Reiss. I enjoy having you in the organization, Mr. Reiss."

Against Carl's renewed wild confusion—where now was this leading?—he paused tantalizingly, emphasizingly, and when he next spoke it was with the force of small separate explosions. "But I do not enjoy having you edge me out, Mr. Reiss. Can that be understandable? Anywhere else, Mr. Reiss, but not in here with me. In my job, Mr. Reiss, I take no interference. Until the remodeling was completed, Mr. Reiss, yes. That remodeling I didn't approve and wouldn't be bothered by. That now, though, is done. You can't really have thought, Mr. Reiss, that I haven't seen what you've been up to since."

Shaken to new incredulity, Carl heard himself blurting, "But no one's edging you out, Mr. Geggenheim. You retire this year. Someone must fill in——"

Over the old man standing close by the door, the old man who in a few minutes had traveled so much triumph, so much vindictiveness, so much venom, something else fell like a mantle. Something under which he straightened majestically, gazing at Carl with a condescending, elevated faith.

He asked, "And have you believed, Mr. Reiss, that for me the store won't make an exception? That when the day comes for my retirement—ridiculous, I'm as able as I ever was—the board won't beg me to keep on? Other men may retire from Trurog's, Mr. Reiss. I assure you, not I."

He believed it. Believed in his difference from other men, believed Trurog's could get along without Trurog, get along without Salloway, get along without any other employee, but not without Geggenheim. Believed perhaps that he alone of all men would never soften or die. Aberration so complete, so sublime, it brooked no contradiction. For all his revulsion, his horror, his illness, Carl knew it useless to argue.

Instead, bitterly but much more quietly, he said, "I see. What you want is a bargain. What am I supposed to do, resign from the store?"

"No, no." From his elevation, ignoring all that had worked up to this, the old man was immediately affable. "I've said you are valuable. All you need do is go to Salloway, ask for a transfer. Transfer to any department in the store whatsoever, just so it isn't one of mine. No written agreements; I know none will be necessary. Bette can always be brought forward later; you needn't worry; I'll know what goes on. Any other department, I say; I shan't care in the least. We'll give you this entire forenoon to decide."

Turning, Carl looked once more at Bette. When attention switched

from her she'd lifted her face and quit audibly crying; lifted her face
about a foot and a half. From that half crouch, from her tear-sodden
face, her dull eyes, her opened mouth, what wits she yet had seemed
to be directed, with a kind of wondering blankness, toward what was
going on between the two men. As soon as Carl once more faced her,
though, her head again plummeted and the wailing began afresh.

"I can't help it, Mr. Reiss. I can't help it——"

Thrusting Geggenheim from his way, Carl pushed out of the office.

A trap. Trapped. He'd fight out of it. Of course he'd fight out of it.
Salloway would never believe, Christine would never believe, no one
knowing anything of him would believe him guilty of any such crimi-
nal violence.

By the time he'd traversed Furs and then the Maturity Shop, the
whole affair was so melodramatic, so impossible—a frame, that was the
name for a thing like this. Things like this happened on theater stages
and in movies, they happened perhaps in the lives of gangsters and
gamblers. Not in department stores. Not to sane, normal, well-controlled, principled lives like his own. He'd go to Salloway——

"Mr. Salloway," he'd say forthrightly, "what's happening is so ridiculous—Geggenheim. The man's out of his reason. He not only
thinks he'll be kept on here forever, but he's trumped up a story I
violated——"

At the elevators, at the fountain, just to have something to do, he
bent above an arched jet, drinking thirstily. "Mr. Salloway," he'd say.
"Mr. Salloway——"

It was what came next that froze him to such paralysis. What would
Salloway do? Call Geggenheim into his office? Call in the girl? "Look
here, Geggenheim," Salloway would say coldly, "I've known about the
tricks you play; you've a reputation here. I'll never believe that
Reiss——"

Although he quit drinking, he stayed bent over the fountain, seemed
to be held there. A single name thrust itself at him. Barbara. Bette he
hadn't violated. But Barbara——

He hadn't violated Barbara either, not in any way people called
violation. Just the opposite. But there'd been last fall, last summer,
last spring. There must have been rumors, and Salloway could never

have missed hearing those rumors. Salloway wouldn't miss knowing the association had ceased. Salloway might think——

Numbly, held by horror, he got away from the fountain. Somewhere must be a place he could go, be alone. A woman jostled him, and over him, shudderingly, came a dislike of women, all women; *a store was no place for a man; there were too many women*. He saw a face that was like a seal's; yes, that was it; it was a seal, an animal, that jostled him. Wet black fur, murky paperweight eyes, snout and flippers, a smell of musk—— He murmured, "Excuse me," and pushed past. A little later he caromed into the door of "Employees Only," a little later he stood along the carton-piled hand trucks occupying the spot where his temporary remodeling office had stood.

"This forenoon to decide."

At the time they were spoken, those particular words hadn't hit with more impact than those preceding them, but now they emerged as the climax of all. This forenoon. Only this forenoon in which to act. If he didn't go to Salloway before noon, Bette would be taken to a lawyer. Or there might already be a lawyer, briefed and waiting. Sooner or later a uniformed arm would reach to him. "You Carl Reiss?"

Unbelievable. Unbelievable, unbelievable, unbelievable. He, who all his life had been so upright, who so seldom—almost never, you might say—did any straying. Only Barbara, and that came to nothing. Only Estelle, all those years ago in Paris. Not a quarter, not a tenth of what other men had in their lives, not a twentieth of what other men openly boasted. He, Carl Reiss——

His father——

Reaching his hand to a joist, a rough joist, the separate wiry tendrils of whose unsmoothed surface prickled against his palm like an insect's legs, he bent his head to his arm. He, Carl Reiss. A lunacy commission, that was what Geggenheim was due for. Only no one knew that yet. He hadn't known it yet. Except for the one aberration——

"Any doctor," Geggenheim said. "Any doctor will find the child has been—touched."

Somewhere around twenty minutes after one, it must have been, when they left the store last night. Four minutes, perhaps, getting out of the garage. She must have been with her parents inside twenty minutes. Her parents——

Her parents might be in this too. "I've got to get two thousand dollars, Mr. Reiss, or my daddy will be going in jail." They couldn't be in on it; the evil of that idea was too sodden to contemplate. But at a word they would be in on it, believing their child, vociferous and malign in a fury they thought righteous.

Until noon.

Moving his wrists, he looked at the watch on it. Moving his palm, he took it down from the joist; against the dryness, the lifelessness, of that palm he drew the other, equally lifeless, equally dry. Quite a while now, quite a while, since he'd been bothered by heat in his hands; why was that? Nothing there to feel, not today, but the dryness. It was nine forty-two. Since leaving Geggenheim's office his minutes had sped. He shouldn't be standing here, where people saw him in passing; he himself should be going to the police. "Sometime after noon today an old man and a girl may come in here——"

Or he should get Bette by herself alone, away from Geggenheim.

For the first time, at that last thought, some semblance of possible order returned to his universe. Quietly, feeling the slowness with which he moved, the enveloping dryness, he moved. Geggenheim might keep Bette all morning in his office, or immured somewhere else. That, though—so sure, apparently, was Geggenheim—wasn't what was going on at all. At the door of the millinery stock room he met Miss Yelland, so stormy she didn't notice any trouble in him. "For cripe's sake, Mr. Reiss, can't something be done about that stooge? All she's done all morning is weep. If I'm to put up with this——"

"That stooge"—name to be fiercely seized. Of course it must be understood Bette was no more than that; somehow the line would be traced back to Geggenheim. More strongly, glancing swiftly about to make certain Miss Yelland was gone and no one else present, he walked down an aisle of hat-hung posts to the table at the back where Bette bent over her work. When he came up she was no more than sniffling, but as she saw him her head jerked aside. Surely, he thought, there must be some level at which her reason functioned, she must in some way be reachable.

He began, "Bette, to you I'm—just a man in this store. You don't think of me as a person, a person as you are. But I am, Bette, exactly that same kind of person. I have a wife and two boys. I feel about them exactly—exactly as you feel toward your parents, your brother or sister. Mr. Geggenheim's an old man, Bette; whatever he says to you, he won't be here after his sixty-eighth birthday; it's not my fault he'll have to leave here while someone else replaces him. My wife and I will come to see your parents tonight; I meant what I said in the office; we'll get you your money. You're a good girl, Bette, and I've tried to be kind to you. You can't do what Geggenheim asks of you; it wouldn't only ruin my life; it would ruin yours too. You'd have to go in front of people, you'd have to sit by a judge in an open court-room with your hand on a Bible, swearing I'd offered you violence when all I'd done was be good to you——"

No more than sullen and overcome, that droop of her head. In his gathering, desperate tensity he took her arm, and not roughly but urgently, as if by contact alone he must impel her toward compliance, he shook her a little. Her head stayed averted, until at the word *Bible* it shot downward as it had in the car and the office. The tears and the wailing respurted, "You don't understand, Mr. Reiss. You don't understand, you don't understand——"

"*This* time I'll call on high heaven," said Miss Yelland, behind him. "What *is* going on here? Mr. Reiss, are you the one making this child cry?" Miss Yelland was one of his better friends, but as he swung about what he saw on her face, if not suspicion, was the beginning of distrust. This too, he thought wrathfully and despairingly. Geggenheim had no need to worry about letting his cat's-paw loose. The more Carl tried to see her, to argue with her, the more witnesses there would be against him, the more people who later might begin remembering, "Say, you know now I think of it——"

He answered stonily, "Miss Jones is having trouble at home. Mr. Geggenheim and I are trying to help her as much as we can."

Miss Yelland's face smoothed; she said more maternally, "Poor kid, these days it's a crime what some of 'em live through." But that didn't mean the other idea mightn't at any moment reassert itself.

Out and away from Millinery he walked wearily. No use going back there. Whatever he said to Bette would get him nowhere. Ordinarily right now he should be checking inventory sheets; thinking of it, just thinking of it, served to move him back to his desk; it was as if there must be another Carl Reiss in the Women's Wear office, pencil in hand, head absorbedly bent. He was some other dispossessed wanderer.

Shortly after his wrist watch told him it was ten o'clock, he went up to the employees' cafeteria where, at this hour, Bob Gokey was certain to be sitting over coffee with Glen Shotwell, perhaps other floormen.

Bob, as expected, was. "Whose funeral you attending today?" he asked as Carl approached. "What'd you do—squire some babe home last night?"

By then he was enough under control so that Bob's jibe was discernible as what it was, not a home hit; by then he was enough under control so that what was happening to him showed only as nervousness. Coffee spilled from his cup when he lifted it; coffee slipped again when he lowered the cup toward the saucer; coffee ran over his hand. Bob could be counted on for lingering, and as soon as the others were gone he jerkily brought out what needed to be brought out.

"I'm a little—upset. Friend of mine—Morrison boy, remember him at my wedding?" That Morrison boy, of some service at last. "Came around to see me this—morning. Married now, has a kid. Some girl's claiming he—I suppose you'd call it rape. Morrison says he never touched her. But he had been alone with her, quite—quite late at night. In a car. What does a guy do, case like that?"

Over Bob Gokey's face, even Bob Gokey's, moved the peculiar fixity he had foreseen moving over all faces; Bob looked aside at his cigarette, rolling it in its ash.

"Say how old the girl was?"

"He said sixteen. Someone's putting her up to it. A shakedown."

Bob's cigarette continued to roll, his glance remained toward the table, but the eyes behind the glance were chill. His lips pursed for a low whistle; he shrugged.

"He can jump out a window. He can run out of the state. Or he can let himself get shaken."

The voice, too, was cool. Since the crash, since the business about the loan, he and Bob had got back to a place where they were amicable. Shotwell too. But not as they once were.

At twenty minutes after eleven, having found support nowhere, he was walking toward Salloway's office.

16

At the inner vestibule door of Neesom's, late that next May, the Reverend Mr. Pinckney paused for one of his orotund and self-conscious farewells.

"Must hurry along, I'm afraid; as you're well aware, Mrs. Reiss, I'm playing hooky—yes, playing hooky, that's the term—from Friday night Youth Center. I wish our errand here might have been—well, more fruitful——"

"I know," murmured Christine, "if it were the other Friday, I'd be at Youth Center too. And of course Craig and Dusty are. I'm most terribly sorry——"

So much shorter, so much smaller beside Horace Pinckney's robust height, Tom Binns stood with hands dropped, flipping his hat by its brim. He was, she knew, displeased with her; guiltily she felt his reasons for being so. It would have been easy, three years ago in 1932, when the going was perhaps at its roughest, for Tom Binns to have shaken his head as so many others shook theirs. "I'm afraid, Mrs. Reiss, even Binns's can't hope to keep on with luxuries such as Neesom's homemade bread and rolls, Neesom's cakes, not in these times." Binns, though, never did. Even today it was the Binns account——

"You've said no, Mrs. Reiss," he told her formally, now. "Have you ever considered that family walls no longer close outside a husband and two sons?"

Nothing they'd said before, no argument they'd brought up, really touched her. Chapaqua's school board was supposed to be made up of public-spirited citizens who served without recompense; no one had to tell her the present board was corrupt; Chub Hagenheit, one of its members, lived near by; Mrs. Hagenheit had given a luncheon, just this past month, in one of the big new rooms Norm had talked her into adding at the side and back. "Now you be sure, girls," she herself had heard Mrs. Hagenheit laughing, "you be sure you vote for Chub this fall; we need that money." Keeping in Verek as school superintendent was openly scandalous. All this past spring, at Schaeffer Junior High, a building almost new, put up under Verek, Craig and Dusty with the other boys had had to use the girls' toilets, hour on, hour off, because the boys' toilets were flooded and couldn't seem to be repaired. Junior high youngsters were a wrong age for that. Contractors, the maintenance staff, even teachers, were flagrantly subject to kickbacks.

Just the same, that didn't mean that this coming fall she should run for election to the school board with Horace Pinckney and Tom Binns. Not she, Christine Reiss. "A woman," they said. "We need a woman to get at the woman's vote." That didn't mean much; heaven knew, as she pointed out, one commodity always in oversupply was women.

"Family walls no longer close outside a husband and two sons."

As soon as he'd said it, Tom knew he had reached her; for just a perceptible instant the little flare of success went up behind his eyes. He added smoothly, "I don't believe we'll take your no for an answer, Mrs. Reiss. There's still no immediate hurry; we'll see you again."

After Horace Pinckney, who already was past the vestibule, he too stepped, closing doors softly, catching Pinckney up on the porch outside—not anything she heard, not anything she saw, but something of which she was certain—to conclude in good cheer, "I'm not despairing of Mrs. Reiss; I believe Mrs. Reiss will come round."

Pushing a suddenly impatient hand up over her neck and her face, she turned to climb the stairs. Her neck. In so-called community service, she thought wryly, she was definitely meeting an activity in which birthmarks seemed to be no deterrent. How had they worked up, all these pressures? Neesom's. The PTA——

"Good Lord," she would once have laughed, just as Carl still laughed, just as Harriet laughed. "One of those women active in PTAs? Honestly——"

Only there'd been Craig and Dusty. Standing side by side in the togetherness they seemed to clutch as a major security. At the end of the long kitchen work counter, at noon, back in the days when she'd been almost too harried to look at them. Small, their round eyes barely clearing the counter top, undefended and desperate. "But, Mother, the rooms with the most mothers get a prize, Mother." That was how she'd started in PTA. Then once she was in——

Children in school weren't their parents' children; they were the school's children. "Have you ever considered, Mrs. Reiss——" Six hours a day, at least, the core of their waking hours, Craig and Dusty

spent in schoolrooms and schoolyards. When you saw those schoolrooms and schoolyards, found out what they needed, found out what
your son's playmates needed——

"I know how relieved we all are to hear Mrs. Reiss has been per-
suaded to lead our group another year." How often she'd heard that
said. "I don't know how we'll manage, but when children start coming
to school without breakfasts——" How often she'd said things like that
herself. "Family walls no longer close outside a husband and two
sons." First Neesom's. And then her family walls had ballooned out
to include what sometimes seemed like all Montcalm Place School.
Two years ago, when Craig went to Schaeffer, Schaeffer crowded in
too. St. Augustine's—"Since you've children of your own in the or-
ganizations, Mrs. Reiss, we wonder——" The League of Women
Voters—"You can't be indifferent to our purposes, Mrs. Reiss; we
wonder——" The Community Chest—"We never have enough able
speakers, Mrs. Reiss. We wonder——"

Late, when Binns and Pinckney called. After nine. When she got
back upstairs to the paneled living room which, now they no longer
had college boys living in, extended across the whole front of the
house, Carl was moving about shoving chairs into place, emptying ash
trays, picking up newspapers. "Oh, Carl," she thought then, her heart
moving with love and some other wringing emotions she couldn't
define, "the same now as forever; he can't sleep in one room if another is the least disordered."

At her entry he half turned, flipping a cigar butt left by Horace
Pinckney from the smoking stand to a wastebasket. One eyebrow a
little caustically lifted, he smiled.

"Repented yet? Madame School Board Member—it must be a title
rather hard to forgo."

Love, something like pity, and then, after it, her recent uncertainties. Other loves might not remain radiant, theirs must—during sixteen years other needs, other necessities, had sometimes seemed to
mushroom, but the one good above any good still was her marriage.
Even during those worst years of fright and Carl's illness, her hold of
her purposes had stayed firm and certain; at least it seemed that way
now, looking back. It was only lately, this last half year, especially,
since he'd so abruptly given up the place with Geggenheim, that he'd
seemed to be moving away from her, that the light they both grasped

had been wavering. What had gone wrong in there? If she could get nearer him——

Bending to pick up a magazine, she began cautious answer. "That's what's easy to forgo." And then that part of this evening and what was behind it—Binns and Pinckney in the soft May night outside, probably pausing for a last leave-taking at the church across the street, with the stamp and crackle of young feet and young music splattering from all St. Augustine's yellowed basement windows, while up here she and Carl, equally formal, were tidying the living room before going to bed—the whole thing had an artificiality she must break.

Whirling, she held her hands out to him.

"You know I'm not anyone to be on a school board; if anyone in this family should take on a job like that—you're the one, Carl. Not me. You'd get something out of it, Carl, you'd enjoy it, if you had other interests than Trurog's; no one can close himself in like that, no one stay in a channel so narrow——"

In response his hands half rose, then dropped. It was the sleeves of his coat her hands met.

Head a little turned from her, he answered, shrugging, "Isn't this getting familiar? I'm satisfied with my aims; perfectly willing these other—interests should fall to you."

Here again, more of the quiet which, ever since January, seemed to invest him. When she looked up, his face was lifted. Thin, rapt, stern. In a way, an almost astounding way, so much what it was when he married her. Within herself, only occasionally to be thrown off, were so many weights of change, and when she looked in a glass she saw change there too. She was so much less soft, so much more formed. Carl, though, had been thin to begin with; he'd lost the little fat of his enforced bed rest and returned to his origins; his sandy tight curls hadn't noticeably faded, his temples had always been high, veins always had crossed them; his eyes were as furiously blue, his shoulders as flat and lifted, his body against hers was as rigid, as when he'd courted her. Perhaps the lines at eye and mouth corners were a little more incut and permanent, his cheeks a little more hollowed; otherwise she saw no difference for the sixteen years. While he was at home and in bed, Dr. Daly had tested his allergies; ragweed, wheat germ and rose pollen were the substances to which he'd reacted; with shots, since then, he'd had no more serious illnesses. It wasn't his physical health, now, that so worried her——

Moving closer, brushing her cheek lightly against the front of his jacket, she tried again.

"But I don't want them to fall to me, Carl. Not alone. I still haven't wanted to be anything for myself. Only your wife. And Craig's mother. And Dusty's. I keep feeling that for you I'm—not being of use, as I once was. I can't——"

Area to be entered sensitively, but in which even this careful approach touched him too harshly. As soon as she said, "I'm not being of use," he twisted farther away, jamming hands into his pockets.

He said stiffly, "You had the Salloways and Leveretts here for dinner only two weeks ago. It doesn't seem you should do much more, unless you wheel me to work in a buggy, and stand by me holding my hand."

There again, the chill against which it was hard not to oppose more chill. "I haven't—taken part in your work. I've been troubled because lately—you've closed me away from it. You can't think I've lost interest; I'm as——"

"I'm aware you're alert for the smallest detail."

Need, it seemed, to hurt. She was forced to a quiet of her own, "At least you're assured I get no such details." Then, with an effort to return to the warmth and impetuousness with which she'd started, "There's been no need for explaining; I can easily see why you'd give up merchandising to stay with remodeling; it's in building, in making things, in creating interiors, that your talents are coming out. Your path from here on lies just as surely——"

He cut across it. "Would you mind, Christine, not going into this?" And then, after effort toward control, "I'm tired. If you'll allow it, I'll go to bed."

Already lifting his hands to unloop his necktie, he moved away from her, striding out of the room and down the hall toward their bedroom.

Sighing, she stood where he left her, reaching out after a moment for the switch of the floor lamp, remaining for a last instant in light, transferred to darkness.

Whenever she tried reaching him, lately, this was the way he ended it, seeming, each time, to fold himself more and more tightly into his remoteness. She might follow and force him, insisting—on what? That he renew their closeness? Behind his withdrawal lay something. What? Remnants of that affair with Barbara, which she had been so sure would come to nothing? Or only his working life, of which she knew progressively less and less? Or faults and wrong turnings in her? Perhaps one trouble was that she no longer seemed to know her own positions.

If not Carl on whom to try out uncertainty, then someone else; her thoughts in her mind were a millrace, repetitive. And thoughts you kept to yourself, as she well knew, developed a spurious overintensity, in which it was impossible to sift out the ridiculous from the true.

Only one day a week any longer when, except for emergencies, she still did much cooking. She asked Harriet for dinner that Sunday. Afterward, when Carl not too unwillingly started off with the boys for a ball game, she stood at the west window until the three of them turned up on the lawn, crossing toward the car in the carriage house. Carl in the middle, moving a little jerkily, lean and long in his most worn brown tweeds, Craig on his right, Dusty on his left. Formation into which they almost always fell. Craig at fourteen only a half head shorter than Carl, Dusty at thirteen coming up to his shoulder. Both boys in careless jeans and striped polo shirts, but with the intrinsic neatness they had from Carl, and that somehow stayed with them even when they themselves slid in thick mud for home plate. Two heads darker, rounder, sleekly combed into waves, two bodies shimmering youngness, quick with a skyrocket eagerness——

From a tolerant and amused affection, as practiced as the ease with which she sat the davenport, Harriet rolled out dry commentary.

"The most enthralling backs in the world, I don't doubt. Do you see them turned toward you, though, with anything but thanks to God? Whew. My contacts with males of that age have been limited—is it common for them never to walk around furniture, always to vault over? I don't recall that in my day my own peers had such—zoom. How you survive all this——"

Christine stayed at the window. "Yes, it's quite usual—we'll have to move out of here; they're getting cramped." Carriage-house doors splitting open—Dusty. The car emerging, Dusty leaping the near door as it came abreast, lifting his feet both together. Carl had done that once, too, swinging his longer legs over a car door to strip off boots and tin cans.

Over the wheel, as the car came on past the house—that was Craig. One more problem, but one shared with parents of all fourteen-year-olds.

Feeling the ebb in her cheek muscles as the smile she had been maintaining faded, she turned.

"Harriet——" It might as well be abrupt; with Harriet you often did best, being abrupt. "You're so familiar with my—perturbations. What does a woman do, would you think, when her husband's life, it seems to her, is too thin and too meager, while her own bursts out in all directions?" Not—perhaps nothing could be—an adequate expression of her uneasiness, but at least an approach.

In a corner of the davenport, cigarette in its clear green holder held up and away from her mouth, Harriet flattened her shoulders against the cushions, and her head, too, drew back.

"While I was eating that dinner I dimly suspected—filets, for heaven's sake—that I might expect guns to go off. 'What does a woman do, would I think'—and not, as you infer, a discussion in abstractions, either. Just after I've gorged, couldn't you bring up a diversion a little less tasking?"

The tone, naturally, was rallying, but the eyes narrowed almost at once, and what followed, when Christine didn't at once proceed, was more cautiously exploratory. "It might be possible to question, it seems to me, whether the life of the man in question is so damn thin. Isn't it well enough, compared to most men's? You and the boys, if it comes to that. What he's worked into at Trurog's——"

"I'm not minimizing what he's worked into at Trurog's." Already resnared by her millrace, Christine had stayed near the window, but automatically, now, she moved inward to the big chair, dropping into it, head seekingly forward, thumbs under her lower lip. "One trouble, of course—he's not satisfied with what he's worked into. He wants to go on from there. He will. I'm as confident of that as I've ever been. But lately——"

Caution still overlay Harriet, the little look of not being willing, entirely, to disclose an attitude. She said, "I know what you mean there," and then, tall and elegant in her frilled rust bouclé, she stood up to walk across the room, extinguishing her cigarette not in the small ash tray beside her, but in the big smoking stand at Christine's elbow. Urbanity, her own crisp, disengaged urbanity, had sat naturally on Harriet at twenty-nine; at forty-five it was most of her quality, or what people sensed as her quality. Harriet at twenty-nine had been brittle, retaining the edges of awkwardness, conscious of herself as too tall; Harriet at forty-five, fingers of gray lighting her brown hair at the temples, was handsome with a sharp settled certainty. There'd been times—years ago, now, but times—when stubborn friendship for Harriet turned Carl furious. "How can you, Christine, when you know——" But that was well past. "I can't stay all afternoon," Harriet often said equably, "I'll be meeting Vic." Or "You think you know highhanded men; you should know Vic!" Vic Bodali was Catholic, perhaps averse to divorce, but excuses weren't made. Harriet seemed to prefer not marrying; glimpses she dropped of an entirely different way of living exposed its sharper excitements, but also its penalties. Whatever these were, though, they didn't alter Harriet, a fact Carl, like most other people, had come to accept.

Rolling her holder to free the dead stub, Harriet asked flatly, "You haven't any idea why he gave up with Geggenheim?"

"No." Reply must be as flat. "He hasn't wanted to discuss it."

"Mmm." No admission from Harriet of what that must mean. "Whatever went on there, you may as well suspect it wasn't pleasant. I know Geggenheim. It can't be anything, though, to dent Carl permanently; he knows about competition in the store; he was warned." The next came more sharply. "It's hardly a wife's province, at any rate, to smooth out her husband's business rivalries; isn't that a field in which he does his own operating?"

Christine's turn to be restless; during the last of this she too rose, moving across to the davenport, speaking with her back to the room. "It's a field where I want him to do his own operating." Lowering herself to the center of the davenport, pulling her legs up, she stretched one hand over her ankles and looked at the hand. "I'm not getting this out well—what I'm feeling, I suppose, is comparison. Carl so unsatisfied, seeming to me so constricted——"

She paused so long that Harriet, taking over the chair she'd left, picked it up, voice again sharpening. "You aren't by any means referring to this school board business, are you, Christine? You heard Carl on that at dinner; he doesn't think it's a thing in the world but funny. Look." Behind sharpness, then, the comfortable, returning amusement. "Suppose you do run. You'll very likely, you know, not make it. Verek's dug himself deep. Though I admit you'd certainly sound well. Interschool president—that's it, isn't it?—of the PTA. Secretary of the League of Women Voters. Patroness of St. Augustine's. On the women's committee of the Community Chest." She was entirely grinning, now. "To say nothing of Neesom's. Could anything sound more wholesome? Home-baked bread——"

Glance still on the hand at her ankles, Christine had no smile for it. She said evenly, "You're coming to part of it." And then, because it must be arrived at somehow, blurted, "Neesom's has been making money. All these years, such a knife edge, but now all of a sudden, I seem to be paid up. Not Mr. Neesom or the mortgages, those I expect to carry. But the rest."

"Well." The eyes over the green holder were immediately alert, speculative. "I can see why you'd be astounded. Well. Of course, I guessed you were easier—the car last fall, those new rooms you've put on——" With her clear low laugh, Harriet twisted upward, swinging across to the davenport, pushing with her hand against Christine's shoulder. "Idiot," she said fondly, "what's wrong with you? Confessing a profit as if it were crime? D'you think anyone's going to resent your coming out on top? That's wonderful, Christine. Think what this can mean to Carl, if it comes to that——"

Christine's gaze still wouldn't lift. "It might be resented if it's almost too much."

"What's that mean?" Delight ebbed for a returning caution, tempered with a little asperity. "If you're trying to hint you make more than Carl—well." The last was an expletive of thought and altered contemplation. "Suppose you do make more, a little. Carl's not going to be bowled over by it. Not by anything Neesom's can turn in. Have you told him?"

A headshake. "No. I——"

"Mmm." Decisiveness, in Harriet, made swift descents. "That's where your trouble lies, if you ask me. You know how you are, Christine; you've a tendency to feel guilts and impute faults to yourself. But Carl might very well resent your expecting him to be envious."

"Not envious. I'd never expect his envy." A headshake wouldn't suffice for this, and within her, too, was all the rest of what she must get out. She began afresh, this also with abruptness, "I don't know how I'm to get at what I'm feeling. But you may remember, a couple of weeks ago we had the Salloways and the Leveretts for dinner. At the table—I don't even know how it came up—I said to Mr. Salloway, 'Trurog's has never had any women in its top executive positions, has it?' He answered, 'Oh, women get as high at Trurog's as they're capable of getting, I guess: we use them for buyers.' He said it as if he'd been patted, and I noticed Carl's face and Mr. Leverett's. No disagreement at all. A minute or two later, out of something entirely different, Salloway added that statement I remember hearing in so many forms from so many men; he said, 'Curious, isn't it, when you come to think of it? All the great names in painting, in sculpture, in music, invention and industry, statesmanship and finance—never a woman.' It's always been a statement hard for me to take; I said, 'Of course there've been Cleopatra and Queen Elizabeth and Sarah Bernhardt and Jenny Lind——' He answered, 'Oh, queens and singers and actresses, of course; I'm talking about the real work of the world.' And after he'd said it Mrs. Salloway laughed, with exactly the kind of smug complacency he was showing. She said, so indulgently, 'Well, Harrison, what do you expect, dear?' And again it was so apparent that for everyone but me the inferences were acceptable."

Harriet broke in, with her smile, "Is there any other——" but Christine wasn't done.

"No, wait. I've got to get this out, now I've really begun; please bear with me. I'd already begun wondering, before that. I remember how I used to feel about Mother. I used to be bothered because women seemed to have so much belligerence and antagonism against men. It's come to be accepted by so many people, men and women both, that they should in most ways be equals. Suppose, though, they're not that. Suppose they can't ever be. And I don't mean just superficially—suppose there is just one tenable relationship between men and women, only one in which men can function and be successful. A relationship in which toward their own women they can be as amused and tolerant and condescending as Harrison Salloway is."

Low and troubled, hard to say, harder even than the other, but at last emerging in words, in a spending whose force she felt in her throat, in her hands, in the pit of her stomach. "A relationship," she went on, because this wasn't all, either, "in which women will be submissive and respectful and adoring—only perhaps submissive isn't quite the right word, perhaps a better word is submerged. Women have an instinct toward submergence; I feel it in myself. Put me in circumstances where I have to start working, though, and I turn out to be not so much woman as human; I work to succeed; I can't seem to function any other way. Maybe it's the way I was brought up, the way we've most of us been brought up lately. But down at the bottom I still have that other instinct; I could give myself up to just Carl's successes, just Craig's life, and Dusty's. I like men who are arrogant and swaggering, a little. That's what makes them attractive. The last thing I want is for Carl to be in any way submerged by me."

Harriet said, "Whew. That, friend, is about as much talking as I've heard you do, in one piece." It wasn't often that Harriet's aplomb was in any way shaken, but she was looking unsettled right then. She went on doubtfully, "You aren't, are you, holding up Wilma Salloway as an example of what women should be? Wilma's never had an attitude —at least none I've met—that isn't a cliché. She's the clucking 'Harrison says' type. Her own husband sneers at her. You can't take Wilma Salloway as——"

"Why not? Her husband has strength and arrogance. Plenty."

"Shades of a woman named Pankhurst, Christine, what are you advocating? That we go back to a Germanic *Kirche, Kuchen* and *Kinder?*"

"I'm not advocating anything. I just know what I—seem to discern." More trouble, but also, again, more to be spent. "I keep thinking—maybe it's only when a civilization is very young, so young all its work is rough work, best done by men's muscles, that a people are actually healthy. Maybe as soon as it's so refined that women can compete on anything like an even basis, it's already sickening. I'm no isolated instance of what's going on; women working, women being successful, aren't a rarity any more; the system used to be rigged so they worked only subordinately, but now that's partly falling apart. How many families do you know, actually, where both husband and wife are succeeding?"

"There aren't many cases like that. Why should there be?"

"You've seen men like Mr. Neesom. His wife was competent. Perhaps—I keep on feeling it—that's a mistake I've made. Being competent." Still more to be said. "I got in a situation where the mores of my time said I should get out and work. I felt I had to come to the financial rescue of my family group. But it might have been better if I'd been Victorian. Better if I'd sponged on my father or begged of Carl's father or gone on relief. Carl might have——"

"Yes," lightening for this, after an increasing restlessness. "Or Carl might have gone under completely. Look, chum, you can't draw conclusions—what you're saying is against everything—one of the end results of our bill of rights is that women should have a fair chance with men, when it comes to achievement. You can't throw out——"

"Women before us have known things too." This came more steadily. "Suppose that one reason they've never worked for distinction in arts or in music, in invention, or trade—not too hard, not most of them, the normal ones—is that they've recognized that if they did so they paid a terrible price, the destruction of their men. Women have always been allowably alluring and provocative and queenly and adroit, just as they're allowably patient and resigned, good cooks and good nurses—anything that falls within a pattern of men being the ones ministered to, women the ministers. Queens and singers and Hollywood movie stars—if a few of their consorts are decadent, it doesn't mean much. But if the bulk of women begin working and achieving, gaining equal stature with men, if the bulk of men are affected—men may begin to feel themselves destroyed, without knowing why; women may be frightened at seeing their men destroyed, they too not knowing why."

"Christine." Harriet was floundering. "I've known men too. They're not fragile. Vic isn't. Harrison Salloway isn't. They're yeggs. Yeggs in gentlemen's clothing. No——"

"Are you sure of that, all the way down to the bottom? And they're not the usual run. They belong to a very tough few. Maybe there'd always be some men like that, men almost nothing can dent. We can hope so. But can you say it's not the submergence of the women around them—their mothers, wives, sisters, you, Harriet, not even asking Vic to marry you—that gives them their toughness? Most men are more like Carl. Just people. Not too secure in themselves to begin with. The world's getting no easier; men's drives are as strong as they ever were, maybe stronger, because of their very insecurities; the competitions they meet from other driving men are more severe. If then, on top of that, they have to compete with their own close-at-hand attached women, what then?"

Harriet stood up. She said again, "Christine——" and twisted herself away. It was her turn to speak with difficulty. "Do you mind my saying I don't like where this gets us?" She walked to a window, not the one from which Christine had stood watching, but the farther of the two at Christine's back, looking toward the street.

With a first sense of being partially emptied, some of the tightness in her forehead eased, some of the worked-up strength of her feverish thinking drained away, Christine sat on, on the davenport. But at the window, after a while, Harriet took up where she'd left off, the troubled searching intensity now transferred to her.

"It's been one of my prides—as much of an illusion, maybe, as the prides most people live by, but still one of my prides—that I'm able to look at the truth about myself and my fellow humans without too much flinching. I've faced and accepted that physically we maintain ourselves on dead flesh—that we act from emotional compulsions in which our minds seldom operate—that our interests move with such force around the centrifugal cores of our own persons that we only occasionally shoot off a small particle toward anyone else. This that you've been saying now, though, Christine—if there's only one tenable relationship between men and women, one in which men are forever superior, women forever submerged—do you see what you get, if you go on to the end of that? You're saying men aren't just physically carnivorous, they're spiritually carnivorous as well. That they maintain dominance only when they can eat the spirits of those around them, especially their women. I don't like that——"

Harriet stood at the window, fallen—the last was no more than a harsh whisper—into silence. On the davenport, Christine sat silent too. The ultimate forced out by Harriet was one to which in her own thinking she had been unable or unwilling to reach; hearing it, she shrank as Harriet shrank; shrank perhaps more. "No," she thought, even while Harriet was speaking, rejecting it, rejecting behind it all the tortuous perception and thinking that had filled her mind. If this was the end to which perception and thinking came, she'd have none of it.

And as she drew away, so did Harriet. Allowing herself a shudder, at the window, Harriet asked, "How did we get into this? This beats any bubble I ever blew for you." Returning to the davenport, she fitted a new cigarette to the holder and spoke carefully of other things —the heat, under which Carl and the boys at the game must be sweltering, the cooling system whose installation Carl was supervising at the store. Not until later, just before leaving, did she go back, tangentially, to their discussion.

"All that philosophizing—I suppose you had in mind some concrete action?"

"Nothing new. I've been unsure of that too." Still spent, Christine had the reply to that, but its delivery must be almost emotionless. "It should be possible again, now, for me to get out of Neesom's. And the school board election—that's not anything I need go into, either."

"Make Carl's life rich, you mean, by seeing to it yours is meager." Sarcasm, for this, was entire. "I must say, when you come to the practical, the whole thing falls apart. Carl may not like Neesom's, but I haven't heard him suggesting the situation be changed, not once since you got into it. Those two boys are getting to college age. There must be support, for a man, in a wife pulling her weight. You've said yourself that's no rarity nowadays; this is 1935, dear. No one's ever yet turned back a clock."

Vigorously, when Christine put in her troubled "I know," she stood up.

"I wouldn't give up anything without finding, first, if I'd merely be considered incredible, and a wreaker of wide family havoc. Neesom's, my sweet, may mean much more to you than you think."

17 Sitting next morning at the desk now built into the small office between kitchen and new east dining room, she took in—so practiced by this time she covered a page at a stroke—the entries on the bookkeeping sheets which Joe, from the chair at her left, slid before her.

"Taking on that Jessup guy for a salesman, that was a square hunch, Mrs. Reiss. That guy shouldn't ever of gone away from us when he graduated. He's got us the Piatt. You give me a little more time with that Jessup——"

Grinning around the smoke which, since he was out of the kitchen, naturally drooped from a lip corner, Norman, on her right, rocked slightly, enjoyingly, over the flat hands between himself and the desk top on which he was seated.

"Make with the ante, pal," he suggested. "You're drawing it out."

Stung from his step-by-step gloating analysis, Joe shot up a defiant head. "One hundred twenty-eight fifty-seven net, pal," he rejoined in triumph, "and how you like that?"

"One hundred thirty-two sixty-three, pal. How you like that?"

"You moldy hunk of old limburger, you left out some overhead."

"Not me, pal. She already checked me." The wave was to Christine, and toward Joe's vibrating unbelief she was forced to nod.

Joe's head took on the cobra jut.

"You mean—Mrs. Reiss, we got something to talk about. Serious. Right now. I got too many things holding me down. Wages we got to pay, sure, but some of those babes and guys I got over there could take anyway a little cut. One hundred per cent fresh eggs, not even ten per cent dried—you take the swellest hotels, Mrs. Reiss, they don't stick to rules like that. And preservatives. There's the worst of my troubles, Mrs. Reiss. I can't have enough territory. Only Chapaqua, everything has got to be so fresh. You take any other bakery——"

She leaned back to smile. "Joe, I believe you fork over."

"Monkey's uncle."

So smooth that by this time there must be question of its being legal tender, dug up with baffled scowling resignation on one side, accepted with a clench of victorious overhead hands on the other, the old silver dollar changed holders.

"You wait till next week, you——"

Sell Neesom's, and this would be a thing to go, her place in the working triumvirate eight years had made of herself, Joe and Norman. Joe's the bakery, Norm's the restaurant, hers the place of an adjudicator, deferred to, her favor vied for—next to her love for Carl, next to her absorption in Craig and Dusty, almost, there by now was her fondness, half maternal, half very much not so, for the two solid-stepping if still somewhat tough young men of twenty-five and twenty-six who were today's Joe Krazmarek and Norman Butz. When had she quit being afraid of them? So far back in the eight years she scarcely remembered. Perhaps late in their first summer when, coming into the kitchen during a midafternoon break, she one day stopped deliberately to eavesdrop on one of their word-stingy, smoke-dispersed colloquies.

"—better legs than Juney." Contemplatively, that was Joe.

"Uh."

"More shape in the back."

"Uh."

"That's where you got to look at legs from. Standing up. In the back."

"Uh."

"Waist. Cuts in neat."

"Uh."

"Chesty, boy. Not too much, not too little."

"You said it on that one."

"For awhile there I thought that mark on her might give me the heebies. Now I got so it sort of belongs."

"Yeah. Must be funny to feel it."

Choking, she'd fled. Choking again, in the front hall, she'd stood before a mirror to consider a person that, for the preceding several years, she'd not taken much time to look over. Legs, Joe said—— Kids, that was all they were. With the discursive objectivity of the interested young male, ruminating on women. Nothing but kids. Bright kids, as she should know from the bakery counter——

That was what she'd moved on from, yielding first small trusts, then big ones. Between that day of eavesdropping and the one of deliberate and fuller revelation, just before Hallowe'en in 1933, more than six years intervened.

"We'd like it, both me and Norm would be very much pleased, Mrs. Reiss, if you'd come around to our places for supper. Say a week from this Sunday." Over Joe, saying it, was a restraint by then wholly unnatural, and he wasn't in shirt sleeves; he had on a suit coat.

"Why, I'd of course be delighted. Is it—just me you want, or Mr. Reiss too? I'm sure he'd——" She herself was taken off balance, the occasion was so uncommon. In the spring before, as she'd been made aware, both boys had become family men. "We thought maybe you'd ought to know," Joe announced that as abruptly, "we both got married last Saturday night." She'd immediately produced the proper amazement, congratulations and gifts; "I'd like to meet your wives,"

228 THE STRANGER BESIDE ME CHAPTER SEVENTEEN

she'd also invited. "Would you come for a small party, after work Saturday?" At the time, though, that was slid over—"We—well, we got a little something else planned this week end." About their wives, she'd inferred, they were going to be as hedged as they were in the rest of their personal lives.

"Just you, Mrs. Reiss, I guess. We—well, I guess we didn't think about Mr. Reiss. We—I—I guess you might sort of call it business." Apparently unprepared for the idea Carl might be expected to accompany her, Joe floundered worse even than she did.

So it was alone that, anticipant, wondering what in the nature of business Joe meant, she made her way by streetcar on the Sunday named, to the address given her. The neighborhood, as she found when she neared it, was one of new bungalows; along the new sidewalk the new small square houses sat at even neat intervals, each fronted by two squares of sidewalk-bisected new lawn and one fledgling birch, each pristinely shining in white paint, each providing, as signs before the vacant ones proclaimed, five rooms and bath, each presenting a variation to hold monotony at bay—a projecting vestibule, an arch at the side, a gable. Her destination was at the middle of one of these blocks, a bungalow whose variation was a bit more pretentious: a gray fieldstone front.

At the door she was met by Joe, spruce in a suit so new its creases weren't dented, once more unnaturally constrained; he ushered her into a living room where the three others stood in her honor.

"This here is my wife, Velma," Joe introduced, and, after him, Norman. "This here's mine, Mrs. Reiss. Marge." Both girls—the blonde, naturally, Joe's wife, the brunette, Norman's—were thin, very young, almost wordlessly shy, small watermelon bumps at their waistlines announcing them as approximately, and equally, five months pregnant.

"Maybe you'd want to try this chair here, Mrs. Reiss. Everything around here's pretty new, I guess. We just moved in, few weeks back. Just bought. Just got settled. Aren't quite used to it ourselves." Courtesy tendered her was so intent, so hovering—"You sure you're comfortable there, Mrs. Reiss? Light comes down a little hard from that lamp"—that she took refuge in blanket admiration—for the house, the street, the room itself, in which the textured green and white rug was so virgin it might have been unrolled that morning, the margin of hardwood around it so shining its varnish might have been equally recent; the living-room suite, it also green, in cut velvet, showed never a depression in its stiffly arched cushions, a magazine rack held two careful magazines. Only afterward, when under this admiration the initial stiffness began slightly to thaw, after Joe, throttling any least note of pride, answered, shrugging, "Oh, nothing special, but it don't look to us like too bad a deal; you get a lot of up-and-coming young folks out this way, kids——" did she get her bearings. This, just this admiration, was of course what she'd been asked for; this, this nestling bungalow, this vernal furniture, this wife, were Joe's accomplishment, a height he'd reached, a background in which, casting off all other backgrounds, he was willing she should place him. Perhaps what he was doing included some tribute to her, because in a way it was through her he'd become what he was.

From then on the course of the visit, or so she'd thought, fell into a preordained channel. Velma's shy invitation, "Maybe you'd like to see the rest of it?" with an ensuing pilgrimage through the dining room, its table already lace-covered and set for five with silver and crystal that could never possibly before have been used, a bedroom with a new walnut suite and one chair, a peach-tiled bathroom, a kitchen smelling hotly of rich baking food, but with never anywhere a dust particle, a smear, or a scratch on its new stove, new refrigerator, tiled counter, new sink, frilled organdy curtains. Following that, Marge's turn. "We're right next door, Mrs. Reiss. We'd admire to have you see our place too." Only the girls went along for this second inspection, stepping back always to let her go first, heads bent slightly, murmuring, "We think it's pretty too" or "Not such a big living room, but I guess it will do for us."

Joe and Norm, when they got back to the first house, had supper ready for serving. Lobster Newburg in puff-paste shells, a green salad, coffee and rolls, pears baked in wine, and small exquisite cakes. As she sat eating, maintaining a flow of chatter with only their unaccustomed responses for support, a kind of aching filled her. This sophisticated, too sophisticated, food, these naïve small houses, the department store suites, the absence of almost all imprints of living, the unevinced pride, were too touching almost to bear.

Yet her so-far-held explanation of her presence was to prove incomplete too. After the supper, again in the living room—"Heck, no, we don't do these dishes; there'll be plenty of us here to do dishes"—it grew evident that Joe, with emerging purpose, was steering the conversation.

"Seems like quite a while, don't it, since Norm and I turned up on your back porch, Mrs. Reiss?" He should have smiled over the remark, expansively; in the past year or two that's what he'd have done. Instead, he was poker-faced, one of the flickers belonging to long ago passed between the two men, and Velma, in her corner of the davenport, ducked her head, certainly in more than shyness, to rub the fingers of one hand in abstraction up and down the opposite inside elbow.

A little warily, asking herself, "And now what?" Christine did the smiling. "A good long time. When I think how near I came——" There was more to say, more being drawn from her. "You never knew, probably—I guess now you can laugh at it—what I thought when you turned up. I thought you were thugs."

Brightly she looked from one face to the other, expecting the laughter. There was none. Out of silence beginning to be overlong, Joe answered evenly, "That was about right, Mrs. Reiss. Norm and I both done some time back there. Swiping cars. Training school. We thought maybe you'd ought to know, Mrs. Reiss. After we saw you that first night we hung around next day, over by the church. We shook off anybody else came answering that ad. We got a couple of your boys Monday morning and told 'em we'd cut out their livers if they turned up for work."

She sat caught, remembering. What was it? Carl saying something about a woman coming up the walk. She'd thought she'd have to advertise again. That Monday she'd been frantic——

Again, the four in the room about her, the girls side by side on the davenport, their shining hair half covering their turned-aside faces; Joe and Norm in the old immobility, waiting—for what? They were giving her their confidence, but not all the way, since they waited. Her reception of the full fact, that must be what, from some invincible, arrived-at need, they must have.

But then something else hit her more strongly; air pulled into her lungs came as a smother. She said, smiling, "Imagine a compliment like that one—imagine having someone see you just once, and decide then you were who they wanted to work for."

They'd chosen her, taking on as they did so obligations of behavior on which they'd never gone back. And she on her side, by allowing their association to ramify, had taken on obligations toward them.

On this Monday, which was a year and a half after that visit to their homes, Joe—now the father of a daughter—cocked toward her an impudent challenging grin as he picked up his balance sheets.

"You know, Mrs. Reiss, you ever stop trusting us and we'll be stealing you blind."

The Christine Reiss of downstairs had differences from the Christine Reiss of upstairs; the clouds of clogging emotion that seemed to block the thinking of the woman abovestairs didn't obtain down here. To Joe she was cool in her answer. "Who had an idea of any such situation as that coming up?"

At the door, waiting for Norm—now the father of a son—to fall in step, Joe tossed back another grin before leaving.

Still smiling, she sat on. Joe and Norm, deft and forever ingenious. The Christine Reiss of Neesom's might have a clarity that the woman upstairs sometimes found failing her, but right now the problems of both were identical. Herself, Joe and Norm. No other owner, coming in, would maintain the balance. If she sold, only one sale was possible, the restaurant to Norman, the bakery to Joe. They were the ones who handled most of the work; if she was making money it was largely due to them. Yet it was as lieutenants they functioned; what would happen if she cut them loose? At the prod of nothing more than a worn customary rivalry, Joe urged, "Some of those babes and guys could take anyway a little cut. One hundred per cent fresh eggs—no preservatives—I don't have enough territory." Her insistence on standards was one they recurrently admired, but one which, left to themselves, they'd never maintain. If they were free from her, she could think of them only as adrift before temptations arising more than anywhere else from themselves.

"Imagine starting with a thing like that," she'd said to Carl, long ago. "Imagine getting it back on its feet again." If Neesom's was anything, it was she who'd made it. Meals served in the old and new rooms, bread emerging in brown fragrant loaves from Joe's oversize ovens, the egg- and butter-filled rolls, the rich cakes—all were made by her recipes, unadulterated, uncommercialized, as good as those made in home kitchens by spendthrifty cooks. She too was human; in what she'd made she felt pride and completion.

Perhaps—she let thinking run free—it was somewhere in this fact she'd found her first sense of opposing resentments. There was the time—also in 1933, but warm summer—when she'd come running toward commotion in the hall to find counter girl and cashier struggling to restrain a stranger who was hurling cakes, rolls and cookies from the counter to the floor.

"You can't be in business for business like decent folks——" Fury shaped the man's tirade. "You got to go sloppin' in your eggs, you got to go sloppin' in your butter, takin' food outa decent folks' mouths. It ain't fair I got to have skunks like you comin' in breakin' up my business; you go on, get outa here; I'll make you get outa here, I don't hafta have you un-Americans runnin' no bakery, you'll see what your fancy stuff gets you——"

Before the patrol car got there she knew who the vandal was. The owner of a small commercial bakery, a man who for thirty years had served the housewives of the neighborhood from a shop three blocks down. That instance for a while was isolated, but just this past month she'd taken part in a panel directed toward the year's high school graduates. Together with three other persons, all men, owners of Chapaqua's big bread houses, she'd sat at a table before a microphone.

"You're the only baker here, apparently, Mrs. Reiss," the moderator said chummily into his end microphone, "who seems to have started from scratch. Did you have any *ideas* in mind, Mrs. Reiss, that you feel perhaps shaped your success?"

She'd answered, "I probably can't be called successful, exactly, not compared to these other people. I'm not a commercial baker, simply a home baker on a larger scale. Ideas I've had aren't out of the ordinary, simply what everyone knows, that you can't make good food without good materials. There's a difference in cost, naturally, but it's one I've found people willing to pay."

She didn't mean it to flick anyone. But against what came into the faces of the three men at the table the moderator cut quickly, hunching closer to the microphone. "Ah, and now that's a woman's view. As a man, Mr. Flinch, what would you say was the good business attitude for the young man or woman looking to your profession?"

"We can't all," replied the owner of Flinch's, with acid emphasis, "be women like Mrs. Reiss; we can't all, unfortunately, cater to a luxury trade and charge the prices Mrs. Reiss charges. If we did, most people, I'm afraid, would go without bread. Some of us find it better to look on the practical side. My advice to the ambitious young man or woman——"

Mr. Flinch's advice was to get into a big commercial bakery at the bottom, learn up-to-date production methods, keep abreast of developments——

Inferring, Christine thought hotly, that the idea behind Neesom's was not only inconsiderably feminine, but also subversive, underhanded, and, as that other man also had said, un-American. She'd have felt worse, she wickedly had an impulse to bend forward into her microphone to say, if Mr. Flinch weren't a maid's-night-out diner at Neesom's, whose wife, through Binns, supplied her own table with Neesom bread, cake and rolls.

Incidents such as these, though, might bear on her position in business, on her position as a woman; they didn't bear on whether or not she should sell Neesom's. For that, on the one side, what she had were the anomalous thoughts and perceptions she had tried to pour out to Harriet yesterday, balanced against the things which, here at her desk, were so close to her.

Once there had been only her father and mother, her brother, for whom she'd dared let personal feeling be strong; against everyone else, in fear of inacceptance, she'd kept herself timidly closed. Because Carl loved her, she'd dared open herself not only to him, to Craig and to Dusty, but also—because if she'd do for him, who was so hard to please, then she must do for these others too—to Harriet and to Joe and Norm, to old Mrs. Pierson, still stoutly cleaning, to the two new second cooks and Florence at the counter, to the college boys who as before, only in such increased numbers, came in to wait on her tables, to Bud Jessup, beaten so terribly in the depression but back in the fold again, to the whole staff at the bakery, to Herbie the truck driver. If she gave up Neesom's, she gave up all these people; she wouldn't be closing herself off entirely because there'd still be the women she knew in PTA, in the League, at St. Augustine's. But still a foreshortening. "Trying to enrich Carl's life," Harriet said, "by making your own more meager."

Besides, there was money. Money, as she'd lately found, might be a disturbance, but it also had warmth and strong comfort. Lifting out the Neesom checkbook, the Neesom ledgers from a desk drawer, she opened the first to look down at the balance she hadn't been able to put into figures for Harriet or anyone else. Five thousand, six hundred and forty-two dollars, ninety-three cents. Most of it accumulated over no more than seven months. Astonishing, incredible, but there.

Pushing aside the checkbook, after she had tasted that astonishment, that incredulity, once more, she took up the ledgers. Year by year, accumulations and changes. Nothing that stood out at the time, but now when she considered them, they too must be startling. Each month for the eight years a credit to old Mr. Neesom, raised now to a modest hundred instead of the seventy-five; slipped in at one page was a snapshot: Mr. Neesom almost dapper in a palm beach suit, standing in strong sunshine on a lawn before a dazzling small stucco house, what looked like a poinsettia in his buttonhole; beside him a complacent stout woman in flowered chiffon and a younger woman with a judo hold on a straining and rubbery infant. "Easter, 1934," ran the legend on the back, in Mr. Neesom's ornate scrolled script, "with sister Blanche, niece and grandnephew."

Unmentioned on his side, as on hers, the fact that payments on her debt to him were now completed. "An annuity," she'd told Mr. Neesom, and that was what she'd long ago determined those payments must be. Sell Neesom's, and even if she in turn got her payments, could she always make sure of his? And the support of Montcalm Place School lunches—it hadn't meant too much to Neesom's when she took those over. Her mother's maid—only nine years ago it was her parents who had helped her. Now her father was retired; last winter her mother had fractured a hip. So abruptly, her father grown tenuously fragile, her mother's quick brightness dimmed. Not the way things were. Not the way, with every year bringing her further from belonging to the younger generation, closer to belonging to the old. Craig and Dusty, each year, wanting more, needing more, ambitiously planning, this summer, to establish a good fund of spending money by putting in half days at the bakery. Right for them, cementing their work habits, spurring their early-teen spurt toward independence.

Only if there were any truth at all in the things she'd tried to tell Harriet, then Neesom's, no matter what it meant to her, couldn't count too much.

One more talk with Carl, then, one for which she must wait her right time. Not the evenings he came home distraught and bone-tired, wanting nothing, able to bear nothing, but dinner and being left alone with the radio and the professional decorator's journals which now made up most of his reading. Not the Sunday his father and aunt drove up from Elmwood, a trip which, these last years, they'd worked into making more often.

"Quite a layout you got here," they said each time, cautiously, stepping from end to end of the Sunday-empty new dining galleries, their eyes shrewd and estimating, looking out the long plate-glass windows at St. Augustine's and the landscaped back yard, brushing their hands along stoves and counter tops in the made-over kitchen. "Yes sirree. Quite a layout. Suppose next you'll tear out these old rooms, get better space all around." They also aging, the skin of their faces wrinkling and creeping. But in essence unchanged.

No minute in the week of Dusty's eighth-grade graduation. But then in the last week of June, an evening when, as she met Carl at the vestibule door, it seemed to her that his jaw and his eye corners were perceptibly less tight than they'd been for months. With a sensation of arrival, but also of sudden and choppy drifting, she realized the time for the talk might be coming.

"Boys upstairs?" he asked strongly. "Good. Then let's get in to dinner. I'm starving." Glances he accorded other diners, as they filed in to their table, were no more than excluding. "What're you two up to tonight, anything?" he asked Craig and Dusty while he unfolded his napkin, and when they chorused, "It's Friday, Dad. Youth Center," he turned to Christine with a grimace of no more than normal disappointment.

"I noticed a Western. I don't suppose——"

In the family she was famous for not liking Westerns. Exaggerating the wrinkling of her nose, trying to cast off the sensation of sinking, she answered, "This once I see that I bear it."

At the movie, too, aware of the pulls toward, the pulls against, she rechecked impression. Yes, no doubt. By the dim frontal light from the screen, his face showed as absorbed, almost content; the forearm against hers lay in quiet, relaxed. Happily misreading her abstraction, when the picture was ended and they inched up the aisle side by side, he squeezed her arm lightly. "Don't tell me you suffered."

So much, with Carl, depended on how a thing was put; with care and suspension she tried formulating what she must say. She answered, "No, not too much," and then, when they were on the walk outside, emerging from the brightly lit rectangle of the marquee, let impulse make a suggestion.

"It's a lovely night. Let's not go straight home; let's walk."

"Walk? Old crocks like us?" Marking the extent of the good spirits which for some reason had seized him, he was no more than affectionately derisive. "Okay then, let's walk."

As they passed the hamburger shop, the tavern and the corner drugstore, as they crossed the street and turned into the first of the leaf-arched residence avenues, his buoyancy maintained its level. He said ramblingly, amiably, "We might stop in for a hamburger, or I'll buy you a soda. Not that I especially want any. One thing you consistently manage is feeding me well; it's not odd you get customers——"

More open, more close, than he'd been for so long. About the way they walked, in fact, about the starlit, moonlit, warmly earth-moist June night, about the appearance of other strolling and hand-holding couples, there was something which washed her with memory. This, so much like, so much unlike this, was the way they'd walked their first June.

Sliding her hand into his, interlocking the fingers, she let herself re-create the unfolding sweet dedication, the benumbed gratitude, the dream of that earlier summer. And in a minute or two, as if brought about by her willing it, he too seemed to be moved; he walked a few paces more swiftly, tightening, but then once more slowed and relaxed, his fingers gripping hers. When he spoke he was recognizably the husband who had sat with her on the settee, her head against his shoulder, while he poured out his efforts and plans.

"I guess I haven't told you." In inception it was halting and apologetic, but it didn't stop. "That cooling system—the installations are nearly done. Not much of a job, just detail, moving out, moving back. On the side, though, I've been working on plans for the Lake Room, and it looks now as if they'll go through. The biggest thing I've tackled, bigger even than the Charm Room. Much bigger. I'll be getting a good raise in salary, one of the first they've put through for years. Sixty a week. There's been—you might call it a delayed reaction.

Salloway and Bodali have had to hear a lot of comments, I guess, before they've realized how good some of my work was, on second. To tell the truth, I've been surprised myself, how well those shops wear. After all, it was my first—but at a board meeting today they were—pleasant. Especially over the Lake Room ideas. Lord, when I think how wonderful I used to think that Lake Room was, those stingy bays—now I'll rip out the whole lake wall, for glass. You'll be able to see the lake from anywhere in the room; I'm slanting the floor slightly, too. Downward. When you walk in I hope it's going to be like walking in toward water. I've found a color like nothing you ever saw, a pale terra cotta. I'll be having rugs dyed, the best silky wool velvet. There's a man in New York who's been working in ceiling lights. He's designed us some chandeliers in tiered circles—when I brought out the price I thought Trurog would faint, but they'll take them. A color I've always liked is that blue-green; I'm keeping that, mostly for draperies and in shades much paler; there's a house or two working on nub silks——"

Gradual easing, against which she posed only soft comments. "Carl, and you've not told me! Carl, sixty a week, that's——! Salloway and Bodali, haven't they eyes of their own? Carl, those colors, when I think of them together——"

So almost entirely what they before had been. They didn't watch where they were going, but as if this too were natural impulse their feet found an old way; she felt stone at her back, stone under her hands, and, looking around, knew where they were. Carl stood on steps; above and beyond were the trees of the lake front, below the steel-gray crisp wrinkles, the lights and shades of water; far out glimmered the white sails of boats.

When he'd told her the whole he stood silent, hands under her elbows. She bent forward, brushing his shirt front with her cheek, hating to venture any intrusion on their accord, but also knowing it might be long before she'd have any time as good.

She too, initially, must be awkward and halting. "Carl, if you can know how wonderful this is, talking this way, after so long—I can see that's my fault too; I've—held myself from you. With the income you'll now have there's no reason at all why we shouldn't live in a regular house. Why we shouldn't buy one. I know you may dislike my bringing this up again, but it seems to me—Neesom's has served out our purpose. I can——"

The way he dropped her arms, the reserve immediately coming into his face, were a recall to their later lives, yet he too obviously held to what they'd re-created, struggled to retain his patience.

He said moderately, "Of course I can't like being linked with Neesom's, not now any more than before. If you feel we're now in a position to move, that move can't come soon enough. Whether you should sell Neesom's, though——"

When he paused she began, "We wouldn't be giving it away, you know; we'd get enough from it——"

"Whatever it's worth to a buyer it's also worth to you, as a going concern. I realize you've made a good thing of it. I've also—well, in the years since we married I've come to realize I may be mistaken about women working. Someone told me a while ago that very few wives, any longer, were kept wives. I've seen the advantage of that; independence must be good for everyone."

She denied, "But I don't want independence! I want—interdependence! I can't——"

"It's not a world in which you especially get what you want." This was shorter.

"I know that. But I still—I can't say I don't know what I want, because I do. I want you to reach your goals. Our marriage. I——"

"I can't say Neesom's has interfered with our marriage, exactly; you've managed very well, much better than I'd have expected, to keep it unobtrusive, in spite of our living there. It may be a very good thing—you can't believe I haven't perceived this—to have a family business for Dusty and Craig to work into; whatever I get to at Trurog's won't be anything I can hand down. I can't say I'm enjoying having to make this explicit; it seems to me we might have left things as they were. I've indicated before that I recognized your satisfactions in Neesom's, and your right to those satisfactions; I can't like it, that's too much to ask of me. But I can see how unwise you'd be to give it up."

So clear, so cool, so filled with common sense. Against this, what were those graspings she'd brought out for Harriet? Could she tell him, could any woman tell her husband, that by being too helpful, too competent, she suspected herself of undermining his dominance?

The Carl who stood before her tonight wasn't showing many signs of having his dominance undermined; he was as set, as directed, as determined in his purposes as when she first knew him.

As she had hoped it might be, the whole of her recent thinking must be delusionary, a chimera, fear-born because of her fear of their severance. It wasn't from her, or from any facet of their relationship, that his quiet must have risen, but simply, as Harriet guessed, from a reverse in his work, from which he now was emerging. He'd gone through such reverses before. Re-exposed to his rich and full interest in what he was doing, could she keep on thinking of his life as meager? Of course it wasn't, no more than her life with Neesom's was meager.

The shaking sweep of restoration—for then, if this were true, she could keep Neesom's—was almost overwhelming; she bent forward again, this time leaving tears on his shirt front; she thought—this marriage did to you—"It's a good thing I chose evening for this, or he'd have had to change shirts."

She said, "I've thought myself such a fountain of good sense, but I guess you're the one. Heavens, with two of us—you can't tell. A house this year, maybe next year a Chrysler. You've deserved so much more than you've had, Carl, worked for so much more than you've had——"

He laughed lightly. "Hold up, there. I'm not in Salloway's office yet. We might remember I may never get there."

But he didn't mean it; his head lowered to her hair and his arms came up, wrapping her; not as tightly—marriage did this to you too—as of old, but at least tightly enough so that, against his shoulder, she was held in warmth and union, the warmth and union that were deeper and more penetrating, more comforting, than any other warmth and union to be found on earth.

Within the warmth and union she was conscious of fissuring sadnesses not to be healed over. She'd wanted to tell him fully of Neesom's, but no more than with Harriet had she achieved that; she couldn't flatten him by letting him know that if he were to make sixty a week, that was only a quarter of what Neesom's made. She might desire to share in his business life, but he had no desire to share in hers; it was almost as if Neesom's were a clandestine affair he allowed her, but which he asked her never to obtrude upon him.

Years ago she had learned that what she hoped of their physical union could never be possible; perhaps what she asked of their emotional union—free and full openness on both sides—was also impossible; this they'd reached tonight might be the alternate she must finally accept. Like everyone else, he now said, he too accepted that few wives, any longer, were kept wives.

Put that way, there was only one answei.

18 After that January morning in Geggenheim's office there could be no quick returning to what he had been. The blow, the kind of blow, slashed in too deeply. Heaviness, rigidity in his chest walls, shortness of breath—a day or two later he was visited by the familiar, the almost welcome sensations, but out of duty he went around to Daly.

"Don't see how it can be rose pollen," Daly reasoned with his offensive levity, "don't see how it can be ragweed. Not in January. You must be quarreling with what you put butter on."

A course of shots, a change of diet, two days at home. After that, shadowing its usual routine, his body rose in the morning and took him to work, it went up in elevators, down in elevators, it sat at desks, made arrangements, accepted directions, saw solutions, issued orders. Except that it was an automaton, almost nothing was wrong with his physical self, almost nothing at all.

Robbed of illness, however, some other part of his person was stricken and stayed stricken, passed through fever and strain to a contained delirium (No one can make me accept a living in which this is what happens) and then, from that, to the weak lingering emergence which was convalescence. The part of him that was ill protested exhaustedly through this convalescence, "Don't ask me to recovei, don't ask me to begin again, don't ask me to go on to still one more overthrow." Yet while his spirit was saying this, his body continued its labors.

"Do I understand——" Not Geggenheim saying this, but Salloway. "Do I understand you're giving up your interest in second-floor meichandising?"

"That's correct, Mr. Salloway." His own voice came as an echo from an empty cavern. "I've decided I'd rather go back to remodeling." Not reasonable, not understandable; nothing he said could make it either reasonable or understandable. "I've—had enough contact now with Geggenheim's office to realize it's not my field. I seem to have a repugnance for women's wear."

"I see." Salloway's stare fell toward papers on his desk top. "We'll be perfectly willing to have you take such a step, naturally; you've done very well at remodeling. We'll scarcely force a merchandising job on a man who doesn't want it."

Salloway's voice suggested that dryness might underlie it for some time; he scarcely cared. Scarcely cared when, dragging himself back to his desk because nowhere else in the store was there retreat either, he met a taunting solicitude. "Inventory a little much for you, Reiss? You're looking—I hope you won't mind this—the least trifle seedy." Geggenheim had said he would know, and he knew; Geggenheim carried through the rest of his play with an affable unction.

"You'll be setting up your office again, and on fourth this time? That's our loss, Mr. Reiss, our great loss. We'll miss you." Bette Jones, after a week or two, disappeared from the store. "What became of that pet of yours," he dared ask Miss Yelland, "the one who cried all the time?" She shrugged. "Just didn't turn up one morning; I must say it's an improvement." Occasionally, very occasionally, the child thrust herself into his thoughts. Into what moral miasma, he wondered, shuddering, had she vanished? For the most part, however, he shoved her out of existence, and on Geggenheim, for any length of time, he didn't let thought center, either; the corruptions he saw when he did so remained too loathsome to contemplate.

There was, though, one future occurrence to which, with a virulence equal to Geggenheim's own, he looked forward—the day in October when Geggenheim would meet the answer to his aberration. Somehow, as he knew now, he should have protected himself, have prevented what happened, but even after the fact he never saw how. If Geggenheim hadn't got him in one way, he'd have substituted another.

Fortunately, as he also came to realize, the first job to which he was put was one that went with automatism; little imagination was needed on the store side of installing a cooling system. By April he began on the pains of renascence, looking out once more at himself and his whereabouts. Shut into an alley, a dead end. Now he was in this alley, however, his penetrations, no matter how drearily they rose, must quicken; it was one thing to accept an alley as bricked off before you were into it, another to accept escape as impossible from inside. Merchandising was the activity that naturally fed into managing; before his years in Personnel, before his months as a Maintenance assistant, Salloway had put in one year as a salesclerk, six on the floor, one at buying, four at merchandising. Fast, but then Salloway was sprung from a retailing cradle, Salloway Brothers, Detroit. "A couple of skirmishes with those Brothers," Salloway once agreed, grinning, "and I got out where all of the knee-kicks weren't straight for the kidneys."

Unlike Salloway, though, he, Carl Reiss, had already side-stepped. Successfully. He'd got out of buying. Was it possible—could it by any means be possible—to by-pass the other job too? Not solid enough, answer immediately came; foundations under managing must be rock-firm. His knowledge of merchandising was too little. Could he scrape by with that little?

Still dragging, these questions, these answers, but with determination little by little reforging. When no more than one way out existed, that was the way to be forced. If remodeling took on stature, became a major job in itself——

If, through Mrs. Pesek, he hadn't already found with what suddenness change could come, he was, that summer, to have such discovery underscored. With a pyrotechnic bitterness, in June, Glen Shotwell threw up his job and left for Chicago. Only being mesmerized into idiocy, Glen Shotwell told everyone, including, it was said, Ohman and Salloway, had kept him around this long; Trurog's never intended him to be anything but subordinate. It might be too late, Shotwell said, for much to come of his working life, but from now on a good deal more was going to go on outside it. Within a few weeks of each other, in the heat of late July, early August, first John Trurog and then Chester Ohman had strokes, Ohman after two days succumbing to his, Trurog rallying, partly paralyzed, but refusing a final relinquishment.

"Couldn't it of been the other way round?" Carl heard a salesgirl in an elevator voicing an indignant protest. "Years I been waiting for the old stinker to shove off so I'd get an extra half day. They'll never give any half day for Ohman."

"Mr. Trurog die?" Harriet in turn was quoted as saying. "Certainly not. Not until God rescinds that one about not taking it with you."

For the first time in Carl's memory, on the Monday before the Lake Room was closed for dismantling, a gap, a double gap, marked the group at the Policy Luncheon. Purposely to look on at it, he too lunched there. Only Bodali, Leverett, Salloway, huddled with their backs to the room, reduced and minimized, their mortality for the moment exposed. No one could much miss John Trurog, no more than anyone would miss the gold prickings of the Lake Room pillar tops and ceilings, after he'd torn them down. But Chester Ohman, out so quickly, ahead of time—in addition to the inevitable somberness, there was also a spurt of chemicals into his blood stream and, for the first time in months, a heating of his palms.

In the break after the clash with Geggenheim, he'd been released from the pressures of time, but now those, too, pinched close once more. Four years, little more, until Leverett was due out; eight years for Salloway. Later that same week, Salloway came along to stand beside him in the bare clattering space from which, in so short a time, he'd stripped tables, chairs, carpets, draperies.

"Coming right along, I see." Salloway's glance was to the men hoisted on runways, detaching and lowering the huge prismed chandelier of the dome. Some curtness, in Salloway, had persisted ever since January, but so, on the surface, had a smooth accepting amiability, and lately this amiability had been tempered by the new admiring agreement with the Lake Room plans he and Lefevriere had worked out together. "Thought you might like to know," Salloway went on now, "we've gotten a fellow for Ohman's place. Chap named Kressling, from Minneapolis. Good man, one I've had my eye on."

"Me. I'm the one you should have had ready for that job." One part of Carl's mind proffered the injury not to be spoken, while the other released the adrenalin that powered him. He'd been open about Pesek's job, open about Geggenheim's. Openness had brought him misfortune; this time he'd be as offhand as Salloway.

"Good news." He nodded detached satisfaction. "We need a full board again. I've noticed in this last job—I've been a little—islanded. I suppose major reconstruction like this should really come under

Maintenance. I don't know that a closer alignment would make much difference, but it might make Mr. Leverett feel happier about my use of his men."

"Natural-born organizer, aren't you, Reiss? Naturally a tidier." It wasn't said unpleasantly; it was, in fact, spoken with an accustomed tolerance. In the glint of the gray eyes, however, was immediate perception of the wall which, if this were accepted, might be breached. Remodeling to maintenance to general managing. Setbacks he'd had, Carl thought fiercely in the pause following, but no one could say he hadn't plowed out of them. In spite of all and everything, when you summed it, the way ahead was now as short as that. Simply next maintenance, then managing.

After the pause, perception fading to heaviness, Salloway said, "I'll speak to Leverett; he may rather approve. Leverett—his work's weighing harder than it once did."

The last was even more heavy. Nothing more was said, then, about the wedge driven, nothing more was said, either, during the eight months ensuing. Work on the Lake Room, during those eight months, was enough to absorb him entirely, but on the side he managed also to begin exploring the job ahead of him. Supervision of routine upkeep, supervision of heating and lighting, supervision of interior and window display, supervision of freight handling, supervision of delivery.

With routine upkeep and maintenance, he told himself, he'd never have trouble; it was child's play to what he was doing. Engineers and electricians were a little more districted, but the cooling system was a break for him there; he'd come to know at least something of the runs and warrens under the store, the pipe-funneled furnace rooms, the grimy overalled men who dwelt in them. Men in window display were approachable for shop talk on colors and lighting, freight handlers were to be neared only tangentially, their chaotic, crate-huddled, box-piled, gas-choked thundering underground limbos re-explored with sharper eyes, a few contacts made. "Stanley? I'll be getting more crates of that sheet glass; call me up when they're in and I'll send down my own men to handle them."

Confidence, his rebolstered, revivified confidence, underlay most of this; he told himself his vision was as clear, his control of his purposes as strong, as at any time of the past. There were, though, other moments when the effort, the continual spreading of himself, the amassing, seemed too much. A store, all of Trurog's, was what he'd set out to master, only he hadn't, at the beginning, had any conception of what such mastery covered. Leverett had as many workers under him, in servicing, as Salloway had under him in buying and selling. He himself looked back to so many labors. At night when he slept, or by day when he struggled with problems, he found himself now and again starting to awareness, sweating and borne down, feeling throughout his body a fractional disparate scurrying, as if he were split into constituent selves, and in the separate persons carried through all these functions alone.

Up to now Leverett had been simply one of the hierarchy; tall, silver-thatched, more than spare, shaken by his losses in 1929 to a close-curled retirement, but able just the same, capable of steel-blade snap and flash. Salloway must have spoken to Leverett as promised; when Carl made his first tentative approaches, Leverett was tentatively more approachable, displaying a mind more volatile than Salloway's, less harsh, more intuitive, more cynical, less given to crunching forward onslaughts, more to lightning side strokes.

"Freeze 'em out, starve 'em out," Salloway had snarled when, late in 1935, all truck drivers struck.

"No, no, I don't believe that should be necessary," Leverett had put forth dispassionately. "My experience has been that a few small personal benefits to the organizers cost very little, and that these are what count. If that doesn't work, we can always infiltrate."

No one, for Carl, could take precedence over Salloway, but then he didn't want Leverett to take precedence; simply he must attach himself because, in four years, he would take over Leverett's shoes.

In the midst of campaigning for the school board, that fall, Christine found a house and bought it; they moved; he drew up color plans for the new residence, suggested some changes. His Aunt Stell died in her sleep and he had to go down with Christine to Elmwood (so much more mortal, flesh, than it was in the past), meeting and supporting his father's bewildered injury. "Younger than I was, son. Don't see how she could do a thing like that." Craig, when they got back, was found in a hospital, arm and collarbone broken from a night accident in a friend's car, and there was a question of who had been driving. Harassment piling on harassment, crowding in over him, all to be endured and fretted through, assaulting, fatiguing, yet occurring in a way only on the periphery, because at the core, as he found with another upsurge of power, he was by then growing reabsorbed, concentrating on the effort which, he well knew, must be a penultimate, telling one.

As a measure of how swiftly, once it was started, this reconvergence took place, there was the unpreparedness with which, in October, he met a passing quip from Harriet.

"What, you're not in on Geggenheim's farewell? You, of all people —I don't see how you can miss it."

Almost entirely, he found then, he'd lost the brooding virulence with which, only a few months before, he'd waited for this day. With no more than a sense of taunting and enjoying cruelty, after hesitating —should he allow himself such an indulgence?—he pushed work aside and took an elevator to the employees' cafeteria where, as Harriet had added, the party was being held. In a continuation of no more than that lightly enjoying cruelty, he stood at the side lines, watching what, he thought, must be a refinement of sadism such as only a Christian civilization could produce—a wake at which a man suffering his death blow must stand smiling to acknowledge the congratulations of his survivors.

If he held any remnants of need for vengeance, then surely the unguent was spread for him here. Back to an arch of violently artificial, violently green leaves and pink roses—relics of some long past window or departmental display—stood a Geggenheim whose eyes were ghost-struck, whose lips murmured blurred syllables, whose right arm reached forward, drew back, with the mechanical unawareness and precision of a driving rod. To the people perfunctorily lining up, filing past—"Trurog's just won't ever be the same after this," "Don't forget now, come around after you've had that Florida trip"—he was already gone and forgotten, dismissed. He stood flanked by Salloway, Leverett and the new man, Kressling; near by were the other merchandisers and the whole corps of second-floor buyers, but these people too, by the time Carl got there, were falling back, forming in caught-aside groups, straying for refreshments. Geggenheim, it was patent, had held out to the end, believing—perhaps until this very afternoon believing—that the store would never let him go. He was making efforts to maintain himself in honor; within the pendulous pads of flesh he stood rigidly, but it was the rigidity of a tent with its side walls all loosened, its canvases collapsed, only its center pole still infirmly fixed.

Willingly Carl would have turned back. In case it might be a debt he owed himself, however, he made himself go forward, he in turn clasping the flabby undirected hand. The lips mumbled, "Very kind, very kind," the eyes, meeting his, focused to a pinpoint of re-evoked venom, but then helplessly rediffused.

Carl drew past quickly, nodding to Leverett and Salloway, pausing to meet Kressling.

"Don't just glance at Reiss, here," Salloway told Kressling. "He's a favorite son." But he wasn't interested, right then, in making an impression on Kressling, not too interested in the sizing up he must do of the neat, whip-thin, whip-small, bulging-browed man of more or less his own age who smiled at him when Salloway spoke. Not stopping for cake or for coffee, he got back to his work.

Each detail of the emerging Lake Room, as usual, was a matter of endless arbitration, but also, by and large, a matter of sustenant contentment.

"Good Lord, man, you can't slant a floor, not for an eating room. Liquids wouldn't stay level." Lefevriere took care of practical aspects. In compromise they worked out a raised-dais entrance, semicircular, generous, from the top of which, pausing, any entrant—any entrant not blind, numb, entirely insensate—must get the effect Carl wanted, an effect of being lifted, poised, above the tremendous waiting water-openness, the dreamrapt wooing color into which one swam downward.

Pushing in through the anteroom crowd on the day of the opening in April of 1936, Salloway and Lefevriere just ahead of him, meeting the deference with which, for the three of them, the rope was unhooked and free passage left open, emerging upon the flower-banked elevation with the orchestra playing softly on the companion elevation to the right, he momently had a sensation as if, with no more than a slight moving of his arms, he might have taken off to wing easily, lightly, over the humming crowd of the impressed lunchers below, on out through the color, on over the Policy table, on out through that immense clearness of plate glass to the freedom beyond.

In great regret, in real anguish, he'd given up his faded terra cotta; with the blue-green it was much too vigorous. It was the blue-green that stayed. Not the thick dull blue-green of the old room, but tones silkier, lighter—deep underfoot, pale on the walls, coolly glowing in the hangings, barely reflected at all in the ceilings, curved and arched like the flights of heaven over the cloud-frosted planes of his chandeliers.

"I'll hand it to you fellows." Salloway, today, was being regally handsome. "I thought maybe this time you'd come part of a cropper. To me it's been looking naked and cold. What I see now is that you counted on people. They finish your scheme out——"

Walking into the Lake Room with Salloway, toward the Policy table—it was so much a part of his visioning. "Who's that, now? A new one? Permanent?" As he walked he felt all the ebbs and the flows in the hum, felt the tendriled eyes. "No, not permanent," his feet beat out answer, "not now. Not yet. Wait, though——"

"You still keeping a yen to go on as assistant in Maintenance?" Salloway had asked, just before they came down. "Well, I guess you can. Leverett says he's no more objection. I might add that this noon's little occasion is in the nature of a celebration for you, Reiss; we're damn pleased. So damn pleased we're lifting you to forty-two hundred a year. How's that for a shocker? I hope you know where that puts you—right up with the buyers."

For all the beneficent grin, there was something held back in Salloway, something once more slightly heavy, but that again was only his manner, these days. Forty-two hundred, rank as a buyer, a major executive—that wasn't bad.

Nor was the celebration bad, either, even though, in a way, it must be embarrassing. Leverett, Bodali and Kressling standing up as they approached the big table; Bodali, with his assumed smiling shyness, stepping forward to tender first Lefevriere, then Carl, small plaster models of Trurog's. At the same time the distant orchestra swung into "Hail, the Conquering Hero Comes," and Salloway, moving to stand with the rest of the board, began clapping. From that small node, in the contagion with which applause spreads, people at nearby tables took up the clapping; in a light burst of smiles and understanding it spread across the room; from off to the right a photographer's bulb flashed.

For an instant, stunned—"the nature of a small celebration," Salloway had said, but certainly not hinting anything like this—he stood with Lefevriere in a white concentration, receiving the waves of a good-natured tribute. In spite of embarrassment he must be exultant, must think, *"This, more than I looked forward to!"* The clapping, naturally, subsided quickly, but even after it was over, after Lefevriere protested, "Scare a guy out of his last thirty years," and they all laughed, taking places, the emotions roused by that clapping remained. Where now was Geggenheim? Where the overwhelmed shrinking— here he could admit it—with which he'd neared the yarn-tangled radials of Leverett's office?

Afterward, though, after all the excitement of the opening was past, there was an upswing of lassitude. In all that applause, that tribute, that camaraderie offered him, wasn't there something too easy? Something perhaps condescending, paternally indulgent? Quickly, as these questions woke, he lulled them; what ailed him of course was the return to pedestrianism, the first slow approaches to a new effort, this time Men's Wear, on third. Results for Men's Wear couldn't be as spectacular as the Lake Room; what was wanted for men was substantiality and conservatism. He began studying woods. If he didn't feel as vehement about Leverett as he had about Geggenheim, that was because, when Leverett too handed over minor details but retained major governing, he expected it. Time would take care of Leverett too.

And if in his home life he also was subject to the same lack of sharpness, that was simply because that pattern was as familiar. Clash, effort and urgency. Christine, Binns and Pinckney, to the jolted astonishment of a good many, won their school board election; Verek swiftly resigned. Christine's activities of course sometimes were vexing. "Oh, Carl, I'm sorry, sorry," she'd groan remorsefully when he came home to find her snatching a bite in the kitchen. "The College Women's Club—their speaker for this evening was caught in a blizzard in Utah." "You any relation to that Mrs. Reiss on the school board?" men he met sometimes asked. "Say, that's quite a little woman you got there, quite a little woman." Still these didn't have the bite they would once have had. Most evenings and week ends Christine was quite unattached. At least she didn't insist on discussing again whether she should or shouldn't give up Neesom's.

Harriet must have called about the Lake Room splurge: when he got home that night it was to find all three of them, Christine, Craig, Dusty, waiting to burst at him, embracing him, hanging over him to beam while he repeated—far beyond any desire of his own to do so— each minute incident; Christine brought out, of all things, champagne. Enduring their raptures—he was already, then, into the lassitude—he fought off the feeling of dryness which, again, was most sensible in the palms of his hands. They were forcing from him, insisting on sharing, something he might rightfully have saved for himself alone.

For the first time in his life, though, he was discovering the expansions of money. Any time now, any day, must come that invitation from Salloway—"By the way, Reiss, if you're interested in a small voting block of Trurog stock"—but his bank account, by this time, easily covered anything he might be offered. That summer he bought the joked-about Chrysler, he and Christine had two weeks in New York and Maine, they bought the vacant lot next door for a tennis court, and built a game room in the basement.

More and more, in time he and Christine had together, it was on subjects such as these they talked. Whether the game room should have its own kitchen, whether they'd get good use of a sleeping porch upstairs. Craig and Dusty, of course, kept on being individual fountains of problems: Dusty at sixteen fell in love, not with a nice girl from the neighborhood, but with a divorcee at the bakery. Recovering from this, after two months, he blandly announced he was done with high school; he thought he'd go out to a ranch. Craig that summer insisted on staying in Elmwood, with his grandfather. For them too, though, Carl found, not effort but time was the solvent; wait a few weeks and they trotted back to break out in different directions.

All in all, he would have said, as good a family life as most men had in their forties. All in all, as good a business progress as he could ask. Quicksands beneath both, naturally; now and again he felt the slipperiness. The time in 1937 when a workman fell from a scaffolding, and, going home to the usual scurry, the boys off for a basketball game, Christine awaiting a messenger bringing agenda of some kind from the new school superintendent, he knew for an instant what a retching relief it would be to pull Christine's face to his shoulder and describe that one hoarse shout of terror, that snapping impact. He needed her reassurance. "But that couldn't in any way be your fault, Carl. If the scaffolding stayed standing, if it's strong, then not your fault. The misstep was the man's own."

There was the spring of 1938 when Bill Jones-Ferris, one of old Trurog's grandsons, after three years with Neiman-Marcus in Dallas, was quietly brought in as assistant to the basement buyer of ladies' coats. Quicksand, though, underlay everything. Quicksand was what you came to expect.

19

Solid enough. That was the term with which, by 1939, he would have described his position. Salloway never came out to say, not in so many words, that when Leverett retired in March of 1940, the next man in Maintenance would be named Carl Reiss. Salloway never indicated, not in so many words, who was the leading aspirant to general managing. Between himself and Salloway, though, between himself and Leverett, Bodali and Kressling, there by this time existed links of matter-of-fact interpersonal acceptance. No new catastrophes, such as those in the buying and with Geggenheim, marked these later years; from 1939 he looked back to untempered successes: not only the Lake Room but the Men's Store, the new tearooms in the basement, all of main, the entire reorganization of freight handling. In front lay an area as ordered: plans for two added floors, already in process of step-by-step scrutiny.

If Salloway, Leverett, Bodali, Kressling and Lefevriere, in moments of wrangling, felt free to swear angrily, he was as free to swear back. John Trurog clawed back enough strength to be wheeled to the store three mornings a week; board meetings, at his insistence, took place on these mornings. From the shriveled lopsided figure, lifted like a child's to the head chair at the table, issued—sometimes in suddenly collected acuteness, sometimes in lapses of almost all understanding or meaning—the mosquito shrill of old pleading. "Two more floors? No need, gentlemen, surely no need. We can crowd up more, gentlemen, customers can't object to a little crowding. Too much money spent, gentlemen. Too much, too much." In the close-held, ignoring endurance maintained by the board toward the owner of Trurog's, Carl was entirely one.

When the truth was dashed over him, it came with the force of an ice-hastened avalanche.

He wasn't expecting anything to break on the afternoon in mid-October of 1939 when he went into Salloway's office. Or maybe he was just faintly more taut than usual. October eleventh, and Leverett due to go out at the end of next March. This day might not be climactic, but someday soon must be; Salloway not too long from now must make some remark, and the thing would be settled.

The matter with which he went to Salloway, however, was entirely routine—a lighting study for the offices which were to be housed on the new floors. "Hm," Salloway grunted as he went through Carl's notes. "I can see I'll have to go into this; I was rather in favor of ordinary ceiling lights, but if these findings can be taken at face——" Thoughtfully he leafed back to a table, reread it, then shoved the notes aside.

"Good job as usual, Reiss. Damn good. Well digested, well ordered, even the typing perfection. It can still be a pleasure to have you work for me."

Said deliberately, said, in fact, with a determined deliberation. Not the easier, more detached commendation of his later and public recognitions, but the older personal praise which had helped bind Carl to him at the beginning.

Feeling the immediate rush of hot blood to his forehead and hands, impelled by something palpably present in the room, Carl at once answered, "I've never met more than one man for whom it means as much to me to turn out a good job." A statement it would have been impossible—too impossible, at his age—for him to make under most circumstances, but which a momentary attitude in Salloway made not only permissible but even imperative.

When it was out Salloway nodded. "I'm glad you said that, Reiss. Glad for one special reason. I think it's truer than you perhaps know."

At this point dismissal should have ensued, or at least a quick return to the casual. "Tell Lefevriere to hurry along those changes on the cafeteria wing, will you?" Or "Next time you come down you might bring in those samples of wall tints; I'd like a second look." Instead, hunched over his desk as he was, Salloway flipped the lower left corners of the report with his thumb against his middle finger, while his eyes and mouth settled to an inner abstraction.

Waiting, Carl at once recognized, and with recognition came the surge of inflooding concentration. Opening and waiting must have a single purpose.

He couldn't draw breath. His hands, reaching forward, stung so intolerably he laid them flat to the desk side. One thing to work and look forward, one thing to have hopes, another thing to arrive finally at the moment when that work and those hopes must be realized. He sat, feeling not only the throbbing of heat in his hands but the abeyance—the push forward and the equal push back, the ebbing, the flowing away of confidence. Yet his mind, or the part of his mind that was potent and thrusting, knew this was the chance that might never come again. Salloway, the Salloway in such complete contrast to an appreciative Salloway, could lash at him cruelly, "Leverett's job? You wanted Leverett's job? It's hardly an apple to throw to just anyone, why didn't you come out and say so?" He must, once more, emerge into the open, the dangerous, too exposed open, and with the less hesitation the better.

He said, "You know, of course, I'm hoping to be considered for Leverett's place; with the experience I've now had I believe I could handle it ably."

The words fell with an effect of colorlessness, as words must that are too pruned, too peeled, too often thumbed. And Salloway answered as colorlessly, as if the answer, too, were an old one, considered.

"I've been expecting that, Reiss; impossible for me to say I haven't known it was coming."

He pushed his chair back, standing up. Involuntarily, as he did so, Carl stood, too, freeing his hands from the desk side. The thick compact figure—sixty-five, but flesh would never hang from Salloway as it hung from Geggenheim; flesh, on Salloway, hugged tight to the solid bones—moved away across the rug toward the window, paused there only to turn and walk back, shoving the swivel chair from its way, coming to rocklike rest in the spot where the chair had been, feet a little wide, hands jammed in coat pockets, head—that massive head with the ridged polished dome, the incut gray eyes, the jowls not even yet pendulous—thrust slightly forward, in a stance that might have been a pantomimic rendering of everything Salloway had been and always would be, fortified, buttressed.

Against him, against the perceptible calling in of forces, Carl drew up his own reserves, hands clenching. It wasn't a good sign, Salloway's not plunging more directly; this wasn't the Salloway of bestowal. Just the same, the end result must be as he desired it; anything else was unthinkable. In one instant, flashingly, he relived each of his ascensions, including the earliest. The job secured over others turned away, the hunting out of the receiving-room thieves, selling, coming back from war—no letup, really, not anywhere.

Too long a wait, but Salloway at last was speaking.

"You can't have mistaken my sympathies, Reiss; you've most often had them. Losing them sometimes, but always winning them back. I think that by now, though, we'll have to put cards on the table. You're a good man, Reiss, one of the best we've developed in the store. I hope you'll continue to stay here through all of your working life. There's one thing I believe you must face, though. You're working right now at top level. I very much doubt if you'll go on much higher."

Only one way statements such as those statements could hit. Under the thunder and ensuing roar, under an obscuring, explosive dust, under impact, Carl snatched out for anything, anywhere. What he reached was perhaps a corner of the desk top, but under his searing palms it had the jagged harsh surface of an ungraspable boulder.

He blurted, "But I've understood——"

Within the dust Salloway nodded. "The sky's the limit. I suppose I did say that when I took you on. It's what I usually say to young men coming in. You can't have believed, though—I must also have said it depended on you. As a matter of fact, you've done infinitely better than I ever expected. 'Two perfect floormen, two in one haul'— I can remember thinking that, the day I hired you. You and Bob Gokey. 'The redhead for men's wear,' I thought, 'the other one for women.' You've so exactly the kind of looks, overscrupulous and high-principled, to be a showpiece for the store. I groomed you along into floor managing like a favorite colt—you must remember that. I was nettled when you wouldn't stay there. I let you try yourself out, though; I gave you your head. You didn't do too well at buying, but well enough to surprise me. As a matter of fact, you've astonished me, Reiss; you've displayed an amount of drive, you've overcome handicaps, you've been ingenious and resourceful, you've developed abilities and talents——"

He halted there, and Carl struggled to speak. He felt cold, very cold everywhere but in his hands. Cold and thinned, substance pelted and broken, but from somewhere, within or without him, must come the things to be said. "You've led me, encouraged me——" Any phrase his mind offered was but the bleeding bleat of the fallen.

When nothing was brought forth, Salloway again spoke.

"You've—troubled me, now and again, Reiss; I'll admit this too. It may be I've handled you badly; I perhaps should have indicated how limited I believed your possibilities to be. If I had, though, I'd have been wrong; you must see that yourself. You'd probably never have got where you are. Because you don't go on to the board doesn't mean you should consider yourself a failure, for heaven's sake, man; the advances you've made are tremendous. What you've done with this store, what we expect you to do with it—none of us have skimped occasion to honor you; you're one of us; we want you to stay that way. If I could have avoided this talk today, believe me I'd have avoided it; the last thing we want is for you to feel injury. You're already getting a salary that puts you in the top ten per cent for the country; I've proposed another increase for you, and don't doubt it'll go through; if times improve and your good work continues you can count on many more increases."

The obscuring dust was now fallen a little: Carl found he stood steadily, clutch fallen from the desk edge.

"But not Leverett's job."

The movement of the bull-heavy head was from left to right.

"That's why I provoked this talk. You'd have to know in a week or two, anyway. I'm pulling in my boy Merritt for that job. He's been an assistant in Maintenance at Wanamaker's now for two years. Merritt is a ball of young fire, I guess; that's what I hear, anyway."

Under geniality, under chill, under his warmest affections, there had always existed in Salloway this same brutality, and that was what stood naked now. Not you, Reiss, that was what Salloway was saying. A good man, one of the best in the store, we need your work, Reiss, we don't want to lose you. But my boy Merritt, he's the one gets the job.

No crushing then, no more weight, no more obscuring. Instead, the hot white intensity, spreading inward from his hands. Nepotism. What were those blind idle assurances he'd given himself? Salloway's boys, nothing but children, and going off, anyway, to other stores. Trurog grandsons——

He managed, if with difficulty, "I see. That Jones-Ferris boy in the basement. Your second son, Harker. Somewhere at farm you'll have the Ilsley boy too. Perhaps others. A tight, locked corporation. There's never been the least possibility——"

"Hold up there." Brutality opposed grew harsher. "Aren't you leaving out a little something? How about Kressling? Would we have hunted out Kressling, if we'd had anyone ready inside? Do you think my son Harker, or Bill Jones-Ferris, or the Ilsley boy, or even Merritt, will get on the board if they can't prove out? Employed by the store, yes. Drawing money from the store, yes. But control, Reiss; that's something else again. The store—perhaps in all your experience here, Reiss, you haven't quite formed the right concepts about the store. This store has a life of its own, Reiss, corporately the life of each one of us, but corporately surviving us all, and in its way delicate; it can't and won't suffer much. Men controlling a business like this are a particular kind of men, Reiss. Not just able. They've got to have unhallowed guts."

Down now to basic substrata, or to what Salloway saw as substrata. Nostrils in the broad face took on an arched white flare, the eyes almost vanished, the voice dug undeflectedly.

"There's the thing you haven't got, Reiss. I shouldn't have to tell you. Fall into a jam in your buying, and what do you do? Get sick. Come up against Geggenheim—I don't know how he did it, I don't care how he did it. What counts is your backing down. D'you think he'd have backed me down? Could you have done what I did when banks closed in '33—decide we'd take checks? Could you have waded into that truck strike, the way you saw Leverett wade, old as he was? Or would you have backed down there too? You don't want to go on to the board, Reiss. Not really. It isn't the inside of the board you want, only the outside. The Policy Luncheon, that's how you think of the board, not the infighting. You're a man for surfaces, Reiss; that's what you should stick to. Be glad you can have your successes there, be glad you've got men to support you. Come on now, Reiss, face up to what's really your interest. Let's shake and go on from here."

Forced driving conclusion, maintained as conclusion. After it the full halt. But then, when Carl still proffered nothing, the about-face, the drawing on of a robustly cajoling heartiness. The hand came forward, under its matter-of-factness a ruthless insistence.

Nothing whatever to do. Nothing whatever, but to suffer a hand of his own to be taken and clasped. Nothing but to turn and withdraw.

Nothing wrong with you, Reiss. Nothing lacking but—strength. You're an excellent man, Reiss; we've said so, and not just this once. Good at detail. Adequate at handling people. An ornament to the store, Reiss. We hate to hide you away in a back office. Look, here's the store, Reiss; we'll open it for you. It's your ripe watermelon. The store itself, Reiss, is much what you've made and are making it—second, the Charm Room, the Lake Room, Men's, main, two whole new floors. You're a man for surfaces, though, Reiss, with no true concept of what a store is. When it comes to control, not you, but Kressling. Merritt Salloway. Bill Jones-Ferris and some youngster named Ilsley. Not because of blood descent, but because——

Phrases that lost meaning, but that continued to fall like shocking rain. The Lake Room, remade, was the scene of an entrance he had been allowed once. A crowd parting, a rope let fall, a pause on a dais, swimming descent, a break in the humming, applause. Bright, generous, but so emptily dying. Not ahead, but behind him, the big day of his life. Money at the bank, money bled in driblets from a salesclerk's wage, money bled in driblets from war, money bled in driblets from Christine, Craig and Dusty, money bled from himself. Lying now, rotting now to no purpose in the bank that housed it, never to be reclaimed, never to be metamorphosed to his share of living flesh. Other money offered him carelessly. "I've proposed another increase for you, Reiss." Anything. You can have almost anything. Money. Not too much money, naturally, not money as it's made by the few of us on the inside. But enough. Enough for you. Recognition and prestige. Haven't we lavished both on you, generously? Enough for you. Don't try to push further, though——

This time he at least had an office, a place of retreat. He went into it, locking his door; he stood at his desk, leaning against its near edge, resting on both palms. Unsticking those palms from the desk top, letting them once more glue fast. No ointment, anywhere, would heal those palms. People knocked on his door—no, he was too given to surfaces. He heard knocks; presumably they were made by people. He didn't inquire. His phone rang. Nothing wrong with you, Reiss, nothing lacking but——

After a while something seemed to be missing—the recurrent knocking, the ringing. A wrist was turned and the watch on it brought into focus. A Patek Philippe watch with a gold link bracelet, given him by his family just this last Christmas. Seven-ten. Ten minutes, that was, after seven. Time had slipped from him, perhaps consciousness had slipped too. In another twenty minutes it would be two hours after closing time.

Supported still by his palms, he remained where he was, occasionally turning the wrist, until the watch said seven-thirty. Moving then quietly, once more carefully drawing the sucking palms from the desk edge, he straightened, tidied the desk, unlocked the door and went out. "In all your experience here, Mr. Reiss, you haven't perhaps formed the right concept about the store." At the store's heart, in the corridors along the banks of elevators, lights. Here and there otherwise, too, as if marking the locations of more important organs, other lights. Lights, no doubt—or was that a black area?—in Salloway's office. Everywhere else, darkness. A long L of lights, encompassing the blood circulation of the elevators, but beyond that, in the far-flung limbs, an extending darkness, lightly rising, lightly falling, in the pulsations of breath. "This store has a life of its own, Reiss, corporately the life of each one of us, but delicate, it can't and won't suffer much."

One thing it suffered, though. Death strife and hatred. Death striving such as had leaped at him today and before today, hatred such as existed within it forever. Hatred that writhed in the corporate members, swollenly venomous against the store, against its governors, against the competitors who by choice or necessity worked there. Hatred, coagulated, was what condensed in the store into dust; fallen hatred was what the night force of cleaning women mopped into their buckets.

In the garage he found his car, his Chrysler; for all their new injury his hands knew how to drive. A little later on, halting the car's course, he had an instant's illusion—that he wasn't stopping before the square substantial stucco he and Christine so lately had bought, but before that other square stucco, the apartment house of their first residence. A few steps would take him to the vestibule; he'd walk up the echoing stairs; before his key was in the lock Christine would fling the door open, running from the kitchen where she was tossing a salad, or from the bedroom where, listening for him, she was combing her hair. Ahead of him then there'd be dinner, the two of them in the gray and green kitchen, or if she thought this a special occasion—was it in any way special?—then at the gate-leg in the living room, with shades drawn and candles. Dishes to do, and then the settee, her hair for his cheek to smooth. He'd tell her, then. All of it. All of it, all of it. Freeing himself, expressing the quick-gathered pus of his wounds. Cooling his hands——

Illusion, though, that held briefly. On the pillar-supported, capacious porch of the house before which he was sitting, a screen door thrust outward, and two young men came forward, running like antelopes on crepe-soled feet, jumping the steps, making for the black and orange jalopy—a concession of last year—parked just before him.

"Hi, Pop," one boy called carelessly. "Hi, where you been?" Without waiting for answer, he leaped to a seat in the vehicle which, in the hands of his brother, was already in spluttering motion.

Candles faded, the settee fell back. He mounted steps, entered a hall. From that hall he looked into a living room done in the gray, the dull blue-green, the terra cotta which were his favorite colors. At card tables in this living room six girls clattered at typewriters; Christine, bent over one of them, looked up long enough to say, "Darling! I'm so relieved——" before the girl protested, "I'll never get in that whole letter if I leave that wide a margin, Mrs. Reiss," and Christine bent to her again. In the dining room a woman rushed up to him as he passed through; the dining table was surrounded by more women, folding, stuffing, stamping. "Everything possible is being done, Mr. Reiss," the woman assured him. "Believe me, everything possible."

He might have remembered. This invasion wasn't new. Christine was up for her first re-election; another week would decide whether Verek and Hagenheit got back their gravy train. Everything possible, naturally, was being done.

He went on to the kitchen. Swedish, the latest and gayest in kitchens, where Mrs. Pierson, too old now for Neesom's but fine for the house, might have kept him some leftover dinner.

Go on from there. But to what, with his goal taken? On the next Monday he went up to the Lake Room, entering again through the crowd and the rope. No trouble, now, about filling the Lake Room. "Where'll I meet you? Oh, let's make it the Lake Room." From teen-agers whose hand-size zip pocketbooks held perhaps two dollars, to paper-mill matrons whose antelope carryalls held that sum a hundred times over, he'd made the answer standard. On the dais he once more paused, recalling, even if he wasn't again to be moved by it, the sensation of being enticed to the beauty before him. He stepped carefully down to his undersea color, he was met by a hostess who, recognizing him, granted exactly the deference due him, and found him the table he wanted. Far enough away from the Policy table so he wouldn't be noticed, not so far he himself couldn't see.

In along the lane, after a while, came Bodali and Kressling, followed quickly by Leverett. Not often, any more, that John Trurog made his appearances public, but for some reason he was doing so that day; when Salloway entered it was beside the old man in his nurse-pro-pelled wheel chair. The flutter along the lane was intensified, the twisted dark face above the shrunken figure gazed out with its plead-ing. "See me now, fallen to this. Surely now you will pity me, buy from me, buy as you've never bought; surely now you'll begrudge me nothing."

Ceremony in which Carl Reiss never again—or only on occasion, as a treat—would form a part.

From his office on fourth, that same afternoon, he went down the stairways to second, pushing open another of the doors that on the varnished side said "Employees Only," moving on through Teen Agers, arriving at Sportswear. At the desk in her office, entirely un-aware of his footfall on his soft gray carpets, Barbara Lucas sat turned toward a stack of boxes piled in a chair to her right, one forefinger following down notations on the boxes, gaze alternating between these and other notations on a long sheet of paper. Over her ears extended the flat tortoise lines of her spectacles; by this time she should have put on the weight he expected, but she hadn't; she'd thinned, rather. The soft lines of her back were more pliantly lissome than he re-membered.

The most detached of passing courtesies—since the episode in the summer cottage, their relationship had been confined entirely to these. Yet he was almost sure, standing beside her, that if he said "Barbara" now with the right intonation, if he stepped closer and let his thumb draw slowly along the line of her neck, if he said, "I've a car too, Barbara; I've thought we might ride in it," she would turn lingeringly, easily, the low-lidded strike of her eyes would rise as far as his mouth but no farther, she might answer, "Don't think I'll say no."

In the savagery, the abandon to which he now could unleash himself, not even Barbara should find much left to ask for. Yet when, starting, she turned around to him—"Mr. Reiss! Why didn't you say something? I hadn't the slightest—is there anything special?"—he answered only, "No, I go through every once in a while, seeing how things hold up. I notice your draperies have sun-faded, a little; we'll have to replace."

He'd had earlier lassitudes. But now he had something deeper, going back to the illness, the long holding illness after his brush with Geggenheim, the more physical illness after the buying. Only, in a way, deeper than these, too. Then at least his goal had been there, constant; the wavering was in himself. Stopped at one point, he had forced other ways open. Now there was no way.

A phrase he repeated. No way. Alternately it had too much meaning, or none. Lefevriere was beginning work on the two new floors, conferences took place almost daily, but he who had been so fertile in suggestion and resources had little to say. When figures were asked of him, he produced figures. If facts were needed, he hunted facts out. From old color charts he listlessly selected combinations that passed muster; he had no desire to conceive the startling or new. "What's the matter with you, man?" Lefevriere upbraided him testily one day. "You're sleepwalking." Leverett, who must know, dropped a kindlier hand on his shoulder. Salloway almost ignored him. "Go ahead, have your sulks," Salloway's manner said. "Just don't make them too lengthy."

Salloway, that while, was less heavy than for years, bouncing about almost jauntily. "Wire from the kid this morning," he announced, beaming. "Be here the twenty-ninth."

Work. Only it was never the work, not any of the jobs he'd done, not even this last, which really held him. What held him was always his destination, his steady surge forward. From work without purpose he turned as revolted as he turned from food without purpose, when he was satiate.

A time came—within how many days he scarcely knew—when he

began to be aware of a few things he did want, a few he didn't. Among the things he did want, not fiercely but dully, because he wanted nothing now with intensity, one was to get away. He found himself thinking, with a nostalgic longing, of the long rides, the movies, the dinners with Barbara. He found himself thinking, with the same nostalgia, of the long days in bed when he was ill, the freedom of no responsibility, of being nursed, of having Christine take over, of confining himself to a single activity only, a primitive struggling for breath. For some reason, though, this time, he didn't get sick. Didn't feel even the beginning exhaustion, the beginning weight. What, something within him asked, was the use? He'd merely stop in to see Daly, get shots, change diets——

In his bed he slept little, staring out unblinking at darkness. Away from that bed, he was more and more aware of it as refuge. Of the things he didn't want, this, too, dully, but with its own vehemence, first of all was to greet Merritt Salloway. He was able to look forward to such a meeting, to see the youthful Salloway—owning fewer years, surely, than his father, perhaps thinner than his father, possessing more hair than his father, but undiminished in his holding of the Salloway force. He saw, very clearly, the outstretched hearty hand, heard the words, "Mr. Reiss? You'll let me admire your work here, I hope; Dad admits you're quite the guy." Yes, he was able to see Merritt Salloway. It was Carl Reiss who, in this visioning, faded. The hearty hand stretched forward to encounter a shadow.

Get away. Not as with Barbara, but differently. A wish to be repudiated—I can't run. That too I've tried. I came back from Hoskins, Earlstetter and Bromfield. There's nowhere to go. But to Leverett one morning he said, "*Women's Wear* ran an article last week—I've thought I should maybe run over to Chicago again, see what's doing in the big stores. Wouldn't take long; I could be back by Wednesday." To Christine, much the same. "Oh, but, darling," Christine protested, "then you can't vote!"

It was, though, very easy. That was where he'd got to. A major executive, a man in the top ten per cent of American incomes, who, if he maintained his usual surfaces, might go as he chose.

20 Somewhere a
way forward. That, perhaps, was what the vestigial desperate flicker
insisted. If not at Trurog's, then, once more, elsewhere. He sat in an
employment office in Chicago, beside a young woman who—pleasant,
impressed, faintly frowning—glanced from him to his card.

"Really, Mr. Reiss, I scarcely know—Mr. Huebsch, our employment manager, is out of town this week. I don't very often get men
with your kind of experience. I should think your best approach
would be through a vice-president. You'd almost need contacts—do
you know anyone in our Maintenance? I'd be glad to go round with
you——"

He went with the young woman to Maintenance. "Reiss? Reiss
from Trurog's? Can't say I place the name, but I know the store, of
course. Heard of the work there. One of our vice-presidents has a
sister in Chapaqua. He spoke to me about some—what is it, Boat
Room? Lake Room, that's right. I recall, now. Sounds like quite a
production."

The man from Maintenance—able, his own age—was quick, alert,
elder-brotherly. "Like to look at a couple of our jobs? I'm working
right now on China—half a dozen jobs on hand at the same time
around here, of course—we're pretty well up to quota, I suspect, but a
good experienced man—I tell you, hang around till he gets here—he's
a late-lunching lout—and I'll take you in to a hunk of top brass."

He hung around, he met a vice-president. Pleasant, like the others,
but more chary, more probing. "We're pretty well up to quota, as I
expect you've been told, Mr. Reiss, but you're not a man to overlook.
I have your name and address, and if anything opens——"

No brush-off. A way. A way out of which, possibly, some quiet man
who knew Salloway might appear at Trurog's, might cross main, might
stop off in the men's section, meander through second, pause to ask
questions, take lunch in the Lake Room. A way through which eventually he might be made an offer, just as he'd been made an offer by
Hoskins, Earlstetter and Bromfield.

"Coming in from the outside to a larger department, Mr. Reiss,
we naturally can't place you in a position quite equal to the one you

presently hold, but the future ahead of you here—we take it for granted we're touching on your reason for approaching us, since you'd scarcely do so otherwise—is practically limitless."

Practically limitless. Only he couldn't start over. Not at forty-six. He knew it with the young woman, knew it with the man from Maintenance, knew it with the vice-president. It was Trurog's to which he was bound, not this larger leviathan; Trurog's he'd set out to hold and govern. Walking the avenues of these wider aisles, looking up to the heights of these ceilings, meeting the almost endless vistas that opened at their farther reaches to vistas yet longer, he felt no extending of himself, no attaching. This was another store. Too great, not his. Within it he might indeed have a limitless future, but sooner or later—*the one thing wrong with you, Reiss*—

Shortly before closing time he was on his way out, but on a moment's thought, pausing, as if his experience here yet lacked something and must be completed, he went back to Employment, where the young woman, her face warming as he approached, waited receptively. "The visiting fireman," he thought with cynicism but no sharpness, "and she's gone out of her way. The least I can do, as she knows, is invite her to dinner."

Instead he said what he'd returned to say. "I'm sure this is an added imposition, but there's a possibility a friend of mine may be working here. Shotwell. Glen Shotwell. If it's not too much trouble——"

"No trouble. Glen Shotwell?" Pleasantness merely increasing as expectation lessened, she swung about to a long card file, pulled open a drawer, thumbed halfway.

"Yes, we do. Glen Shotwell. Section manager in Lingerie, fourth."

He thanked her and left. Why had he thought of Glen Shotwell? What was it Glen Shotwell might do for him? Overtly the question didn't rise; he wasn't asking himself, not these days, why he did things. On fourth he walked over gray carpets. Not his gray, much darker. At a counter corner he looked beyond at glass cases, at occasional art figures displaying slips and nightgowns, at garments disposed on chromium rods. Space. If John Trurog thought stores might do with crowding, he should come to see this immensity.

Beside him a practiced voice murmured, "Was there something——?" and he turned to Glen Shotwell's grin, his two welcoming hands. For a friend from out of town, Shotwell's manner said, all bygones were handsomely bygone. "Reiss, you old horse thief, what brings you up here to the big time? Out borrowing ideas?"

Since leaving Chapaqua Glen Shotwell had put on weight, slightly; hammocks hung under his eyes. Shotwell long ago had quit being the slender vibrant sprout of his induction at Trurog's to turn raffish, not marrying but given to what he called one-night stands; now he was too smooth, too suave, smelled a little too redolently of shaving lotion, showed traces of powdering. Just the same he was Shotwell, familiar in this place which, like all other stores, joined the familiar to the strange. Pliantly but with insulations intact, he followed Shotwell in a country-cousin viewing of sights not yet seen—displays of imports, a picture collection, and, finally, the scenes behind scenes—freightways and locker rooms, an employee exit. Pliantly, when Shotwell suggested a few drinks and dinner, he went along then too.

"You're not too chipper," Shotwell hazarded exploratively and carefully over the second drink. "Anything up?"

Heretofore unasked, heretofore unanswered, but a question which, since he also by that time was on his second drink, pricked an almost terrifying necessity. Necessity, however, to which he wouldn't yield.

He answered pallidly, neutrally, "Nothing especially. I'm not satisfied but not doing badly. I'm told I can't complain."

"Just fed up in general? Man, you're in the right company. I been there too." Upending his glass, Shotwell licked his lips lightly and took on a look of profundity. "I've worked out some answers, some answers that suit me, but good. Like to know why stores are such a bloodsucking business? I'll tell you. Because they're uneconomic, that's why. Ever figure out what happens to a customer's ten bucks when she buys, say, a cotton dress? Five bucks, altogether, to the farmer who grows up the cotton, the guys who pick and handle it, the spinner who spins it, the weavers who weave it, the dyers who dye it, the designer who works out the fabric pattern, the cutters who cut it, another designer who draws up the dress style, the seamstresses who sew it, the dress house that handles that deal. Five bucks really spread around. What about the other five? All to one outfit, the store that does nothing but sell the dress. Store making too much? Trurog's, yes. But not usually. It's just a bad, too costly distributing system, that's all. Someday someone will think up a better one."

Jerking his head sideward, Shotwell held up a finger for another round. And when Carl didn't immediately answer, he laughed, leaning forward.

"That takes care of stores. You got to develop a philosophy, Reiss. That's what I found out. You got to develop a philosophy, or you can't take it. Now about the world in general. Know what's the worst thing wrong there? I'll tell you. It's women, Reiss. Women. They're tougher than us, Reiss; they hold on longer. They keep on living while we men die off. They're drowning us out, Reiss, they're pushing us. Women ought to be hard-working, good-looking, quick-dying and few, so we could keep on having the fun of courting and marrying 'em, fighting for 'em like prizes, the way it used to be. That way they mean something. This way they don't. Medical science, that's what's doing us out, Reiss, upsetting the equilibrium; not enough women are dying where Nature figured they would die, in childbed. About the only place we can go to get away from women, now, Reiss, is a war; maybe that's why we just had one and for sure are getting another. I tell you what, Reiss, after dinner I'll take you up to North Dearborn. You'll see something will cure you of everything you ever suffered from. I know you, Reiss. What I've got to show you will cure you, but good."

Back in Chapaqua, and to Bob Gokey, Glen Shotwell ever since the depression had been in the habit of sounding off; in Chapaqua what Glen Shotwell said never had been more than maundering, not to his ears. What was being tossed at him now, though, sounded different. That first part, about stores, in particular. Within his mind went up red flags of danger. Once in a while, tentatively and long ago, hadn't he had ideas which might have verged in some such direction too, if he'd let them take form? The dregs in his mind after his visits in John Trurog's office, his vacillations about Mrs. Willette, his reactions when, during the depression, he watched pregnant women wistfully lingering near a counter of baby blankets——

He'd closed off such ideas quickly. Somewhere along there was the something he couldn't think. Any pondering of your purposes was to be avoided. The time for choosing, for questioning, came before your goal was adopted, not afterward. Afterward you were left with a single activity, the relentless drive forward.

An alley. A blocked-off, blind alley. After Geggenheim, too, he'd thought himself so enclosed. Now after this final catastrophe there was no question: he was bricked in. While Shotwell was speaking, however, what occurred inside him was a shifting transference. Not outside him any longer, that blind alley, but inside. Somewhere within his person, now, was that foreshortened corridor, lined with doors, all of them closed. A corridor in which he existed as no more than a pinpoint of consciousness, exhausted and fugitive, springing from one door to the next.

Not noticing, or noticing only with his exterior person, he ate dinner, and again went where Shotwell went. "Something will cure you," Shotwell had said. Nothing Shotwell knew could cure him; nothing could cure what wasn't to be healed, but he went where Shotwell went. A taxi sped them to squalor and neon signs; the particular neon beneath which they descended bore red and violet letters: Hell's Alley.

The dive into which they then entered was just that, a dive; he had known, or been told, such places existed; he had never wanted to be in one; he didn't want to be in one now. Darkness at the door where he stood, darkness to the right, not too much light along the bar down the middle. Or at least it seemed that way; so much light, thrusting light, beat upon the stage set above and behind the bartenders, where, against a backdrop of faded brown velvet, a three-piece black orchestra slapped out jangling rhythms, a baggy man blatted and swung over a microphone, a tall brunette, naked except for a fringed triangle, stepped twisting and bumping from one end of the stage to the other.

"Come on," Shotwell ordered. "Couple places down here farther along the bar. What'll you have? One thing you don't have to worry about in these joints is getting drunk; they hardly have to pay any liquor licenses, they use so little alcohol. You don't come here for alcohol."

Shotwell moved, Shotwell swung a leg up and over a stool; Carl moved with him. Shotwell in speaking sounded loud and abrasive, even over the blare of the orchestra, the stillness of the room was so deadly. But no one seemed bothered by them; a man, thick, squat, with the general build of a plug-ugly, was standing beside the door as they came in; he might be some kind of manager, but he did no welcoming; like the other men ranged in semiobscurity along the bar, his entire silent attention was fixed on the tall brunette. In the whole room the only eyes that moved toward Carl and Shotwell, fleetingly, were those of two pompadoured girls—they also at the bar—and the man who unspeakingly brought them their drinks.

"Look at that shape, boys," the uninflected voice at the microphone invited raspingly, "the famous Miss Mimi, that's who you're looking at now, boys; generous gal, boys, you're getting all of her; throw a snowball at me, somebody, it's getting hot up here. Miss Mimi, sweetest sugar in Chicago, boys. Hold on now, Mimi, hold on, hold on."

He couldn't look. Not as these other men looked. They were the ones of whom he must be most aware, the other men. Entities like himself, they too in their corridors, but hunched into somber intentness. *Don't recognize me*, he would have begged in that initial shrinking. *I'm no person to come here. I was brought.*

"Sweetest sugar in Chicago," murmured Shotwell beside him. "Ask me, though, and I'd say she'd dropped a couple of pups."

What was it Shotwell had said earlier? *Cure!* A place such as this. Comments such as the one just made. Disgust, repugnance—he must be feeling them. They too, though, no longer had sharpness; if they touched him, it was not as reactions immediate and activating, but as echoes of tired responses gone by. Shotwell leaned forward, pressing his face to the forward light; light glanced flatly along Shotwell's front surfaces, from which suavity and cynicism alike faded, from which suavity and cynicism both might have been said to smooth away for something hungrier.

Nowhere in the room, then, any remaining awareness of Carl Reiss. He sat on his stool in an entire solitude. And he too, then, as he felt that solitude, began looking forward, still recoiling slightly but holding himself more hardily, seeing more fully the light and the weaving bare girl. Young, perhaps. Her set, turned-aside face, on which no smile showed, no interest broke, might be that of youth, but her body lines betrayed the first blurrings of fat, her brown-aureoled breasts hung limply, her stomach was flaccid.

How could he look on at this? Again disgust rose, but barely. Long before this, he thought, concentrations of nausea should have risen, to send him away; that nausea existed, but didn't power him. At a climactic burst from the orchestra, the brunette wove to the right of the stage for a stylized pause, her wrist flicked, the fringed black velvet triangle was snatched off and flourished, leaving only a narrower banding of net; instantly she was gone behind the curtain. Along the bar some applause ran lightly, initiated by the man at the microphone, but it was disinterested, hard-given, and after no more than a second's break the man at the microphone pressed toward another attraction.

"Now, boys, the hit of our evening, the hit of this or any other evening, brand new in Chicago, Miss Sue Rose from Memphis. Come on, Memphis, let's go!"

Miss Sue Rose from Memphis, shorter and blond, emerged in a clinging black evening gown. Soon discarded, the gown yielded to black filmy brassière and pants, these to another fringed triangle, this one blue satin. A pattern, Carl found, to be followed unbroken. One girl, then another, with scarcely a break between climax and fanfare, scarcely a halt in the monologue at the microphone, scarcely a variation in step, a wriggling of the posterior, a writhing of the arms in what might have been meant to be dancing, yet which made little attempt to reach any such height.

Scene—he thought this—of raw sin, raw seduction. Girls along the bar, as he realized later, were girls off-turn from the stage; after each performance the performer moved down the bar, by that time back in her evening dress. At his shoulder or at other shoulders each girl murmured, "Anyone dying to buy me a drink?" He answered, "No, thank you," the common answer around him was "Not me, sister." Once in a while some girl, such as the more firmly fleshed redhead, stopped somewhere; mostly they just vanished again at the end of the bar. Sin and seduction, he repeated. Sin and seduction, though, of a peculiar sobriety.

He looked up at a later performer, a woman certainly into her thirties, face and body too thin and too strained, motions too jerky, flesh blue-pocketed by the harsh lights, yet receiving an attention as rapt as the others. And then with a burst of motion, as if one of the closed doors along his interior corridor blew open before a sweeping wind, he recognized something. Not seduction, not desire—to neither of those did this place minister. These women who walked this stage didn't appear for a possible acceptance, they appeared for rejection. With the outsides of their minds they might pathetically believe they were there to be admired and taken, but inside they knew better; it was rejection they were steeled against; that was why they asked at his shoulder "Anyone dying to buy me a drink?" with no expectation whatever.

Rejection. It was in rejection, not in acceptance, that a man's final and irrevocable pleasure in women lay. He knew it like a flower blooming, knew at last openly and clearly why with Christine an unease always lingered, while with Barbara——

There was where he'd had satisfaction. Of all women he'd known, Barbara, by offering herself too confidently, had allowed him the most exquisite savoring. Denial.

It was ten the next night when his train got in. Chapaqua—no particular reason why he should return to Chapaqua, but then there was nowhere else he should especially go, either. No reason especially why he should go home, but he went there too.

His house, as he saw from the corner, was brightly lit. Porch, first story, second story, even the basement. Of course, he remembered then. This was election day. "But, darling," Christine had said to him, "If you go then you won't be able to vote."

On his porch groups of people stood laughing and talking exultantly; in his hall other people, most of them furnished with drinks, circled and beamed at each other; from the archway he looked down the living room to a spot just before the fireplace where, with Tom Binns on one side of her, Horace Pinckney on the other, Christine stood flushed and alight—as aflame, he saw, as the house—shaking first one proffered hand, then another.

"That's terribly kind of you," she was saying. "I just hope it's as sure as it seems to be; it doesn't seem safe to think it's all over, already——"

Teeth white, Craig pushed up to him, offering a wide tray of drinks. "Welcome home, dad. How's it look? How's it look? Great days in the old homestead, I guess. Hey, you over there——"

Craig was gone with his drinks and his tray, only to give way to Norm and Joe, they also with trays. "Quite a day around here, Mr. Reiss——"

"You a voter, this district?" some other man asked him, a man balancing a little precariously, glass in hand. "Can't say I recall—wha'd you say the name was? Reiss? Reiss? I guess I don't—say, not

Mr. Christine Reiss? What do you know! You ought to be a pretty proud man, Mr. Reiss, you got the greatest little—oh, 'scuse." The beeline was for Joe's tray of drinks.

Celebration. Survival. Like Geggenheim's farewell—no, not like Geggenheim's farewell. More like his day, his one day in the Lake Room. Salloway stepping back to clap his hands lightly, and the lunchers at all the tables taking up the applause. That, not this, was what should occur and reoccur. Why was Christine to be honored and lauded? She was wearing gray wool. Gray wool covered her arms and rose high at her throat. Gray wool didn't cover the birthmark; when her head turned it flashed at him luridly. When her head turned, her glance, also, turned, not reaching to him at the archway, but pausing halfway at the amiable drunk, who, having already disposed of the drink from Joe's tray, was now reaching for another from Norm's. From halfway across the room her glance tangled with Norman's, and almost imperceptibly her head shook.

Norm nodded and grinned, and then with a fondling hand under the drunk's elbow, he piloted him smoothly out. "We got a bar set up in back, chum. You come with me——"

A drunk might have been an unpleasant little spot of trouble. Christine didn't wait for trouble; Christine took care of trouble beforehand. Her head gestured toward a door, trouble went. It was as simple as that. Christine stood at a table beside a cringing old man, Christine said, "Frances——"

Someone else stood in a clearing, someone said, "That'll be enough of that; there'll be no hiring today." Was that Christine too? No, that was Salloway. Or his father. It somehow was hard to remember. Christine, Salloway, his father, the three flowed forward and back, interchangeably. His father said, "Frances——" Salloway said, "I'm just teaching him man's work; he'll have to learn sometime," Christine said, "There's one thing you may as well face, Reiss; you're working right now at top level."

Not anything he thought, merely something he heard, merely something his hands remembered. Wind swept at him once more, the wind of another door opening, a blast. *Strength*, that was what Salloway said he didn't have. *Strength*—that was what he'd denied in his father, that was what had bound him to Salloway. Quiet, competent strength—that was what, long ago in the Lake Room, he'd fallen in love with, when Christine said, "Frances."

Only, again, who and what had been which? Which one was it he'd denied, which been bound to, which one loved? The three images stayed blurred for the moments he fumbled, but then cleared again, leaving Christine before him, a woman covered almost entirely in gray, a woman standing to be judged for work and service, for standards, for competence and ability, when everyone knew those were men's qualities in which no woman dared clothe herself; women should stand to be stripped naked; women by right should be judged for their physical selves and no more than that. Women by right should be jeered at and rejected for what they were in their physical selves; no woman by right kept herself covered.

"Man's work," someone said once, and "Not with his hands." He moved forward, moved a long way, moved until someone cried out to him. He found the gray covering, stripping it downward. But when he touched the red flesh of the birthmark he knew that that, actually, was what must be ripped away.

His hands reached to their work. But the other hands—as always—now moved forward against him. Resisting, impeding, obstructing, denying.